THE KILL LOCK

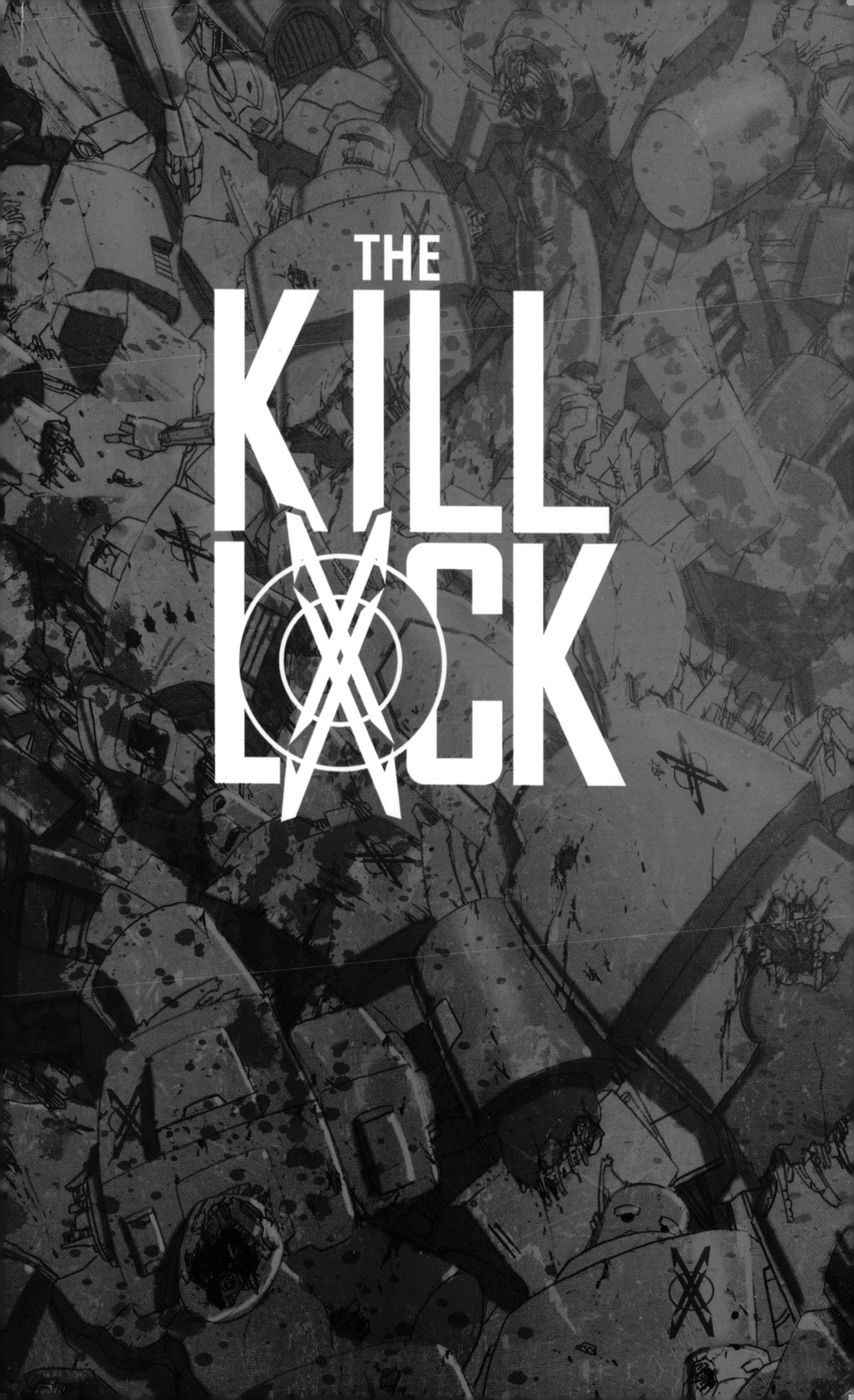

Facebook: **facebook.com/idwpublishing**
Twitter: **@idwpublishing**
YouTube: **youtube.com/idwpublishing**
Tumblr: **tumblr.idwpublishing.com**
Instagram: **instagram.com/idwpublishing**

ISBN: 978-1-68405-719-1   23 22 21 20   1 2 3 4

Cover Art
Livio Ramondelli

Series Editor
David Mariotte

Collection Editors
Alonzo Simon and
Zac Boone

Collection Design
Jeff Powell

Jerry Bennington, President
Cara Morrison, Chief Financial Officer
Matthew Ruzicka, Chief Accounting Officer
Rebekah Cahalin, EVP of Operations
John Barber, Editor-in-Chief
Justin Eisinger, Editorial Director, Graphic Novels and Collections
Scott Dunbier, Director, Special Projects

Blake Kobashigawa, VP of Sales
Lorelei Bunjes, VP of Technology & Information Services
Anna Morrow, Sr Marketing Director
Tara McCrillis, Director of Design & Production
Mike Ford, Director of Operations
Shauna Monteforte, Manufacturing Operations Director

Ted Adams and Robbie Robbins, IDW Founders

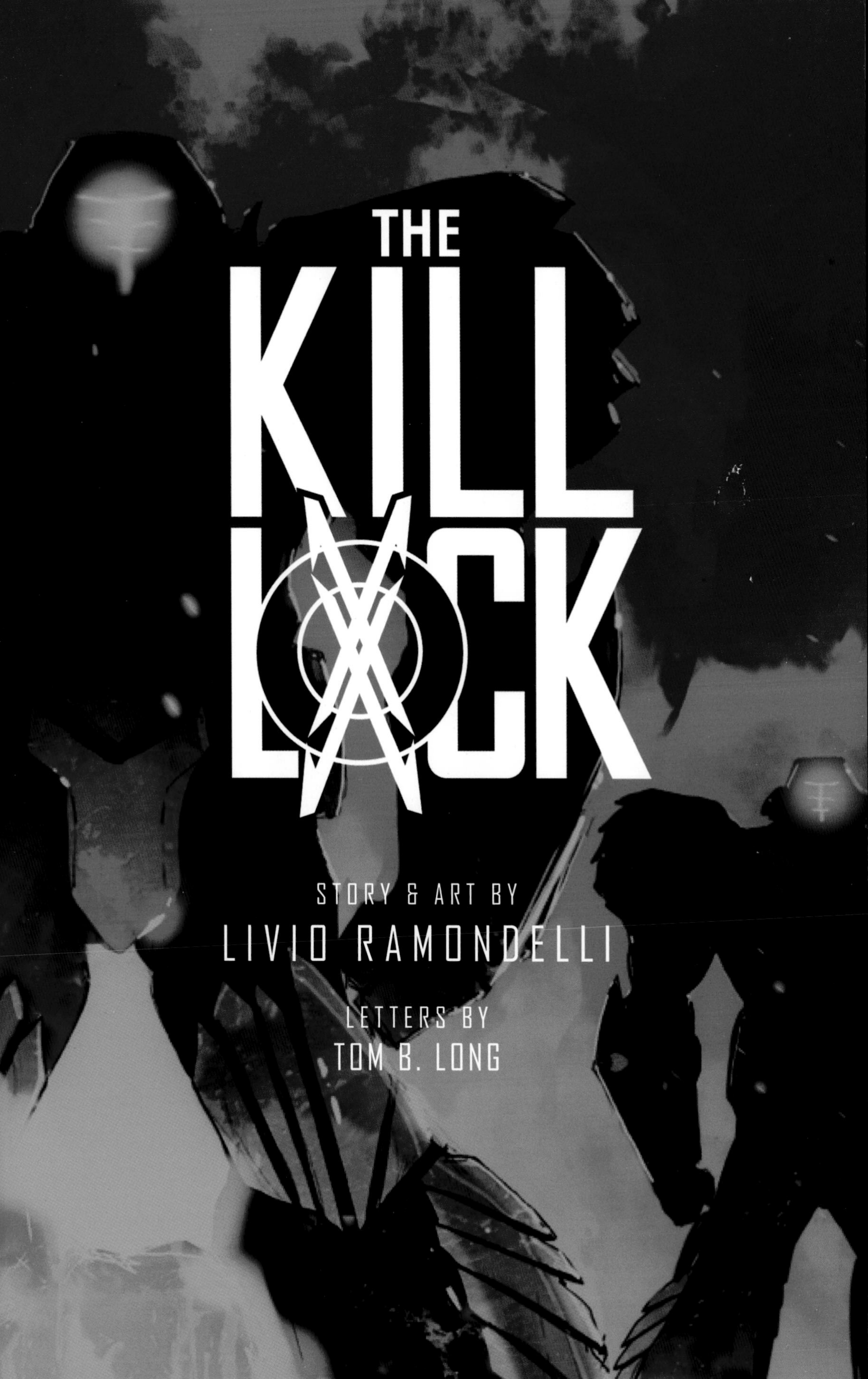

THE KILL LOCK

STORY & ART BY

LIVIO RAMONDELLI

LETTERS BY

TOM B. LONG

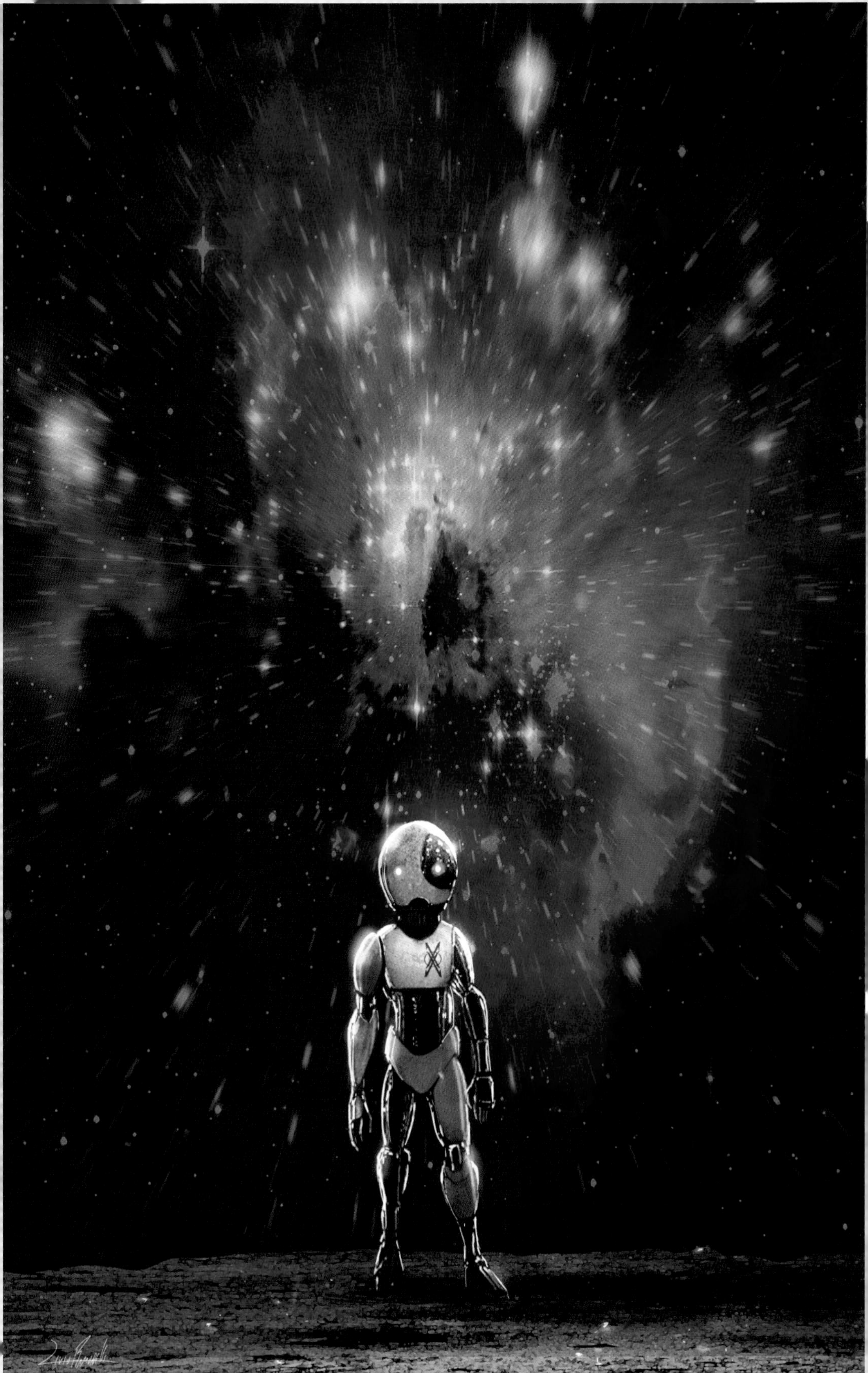

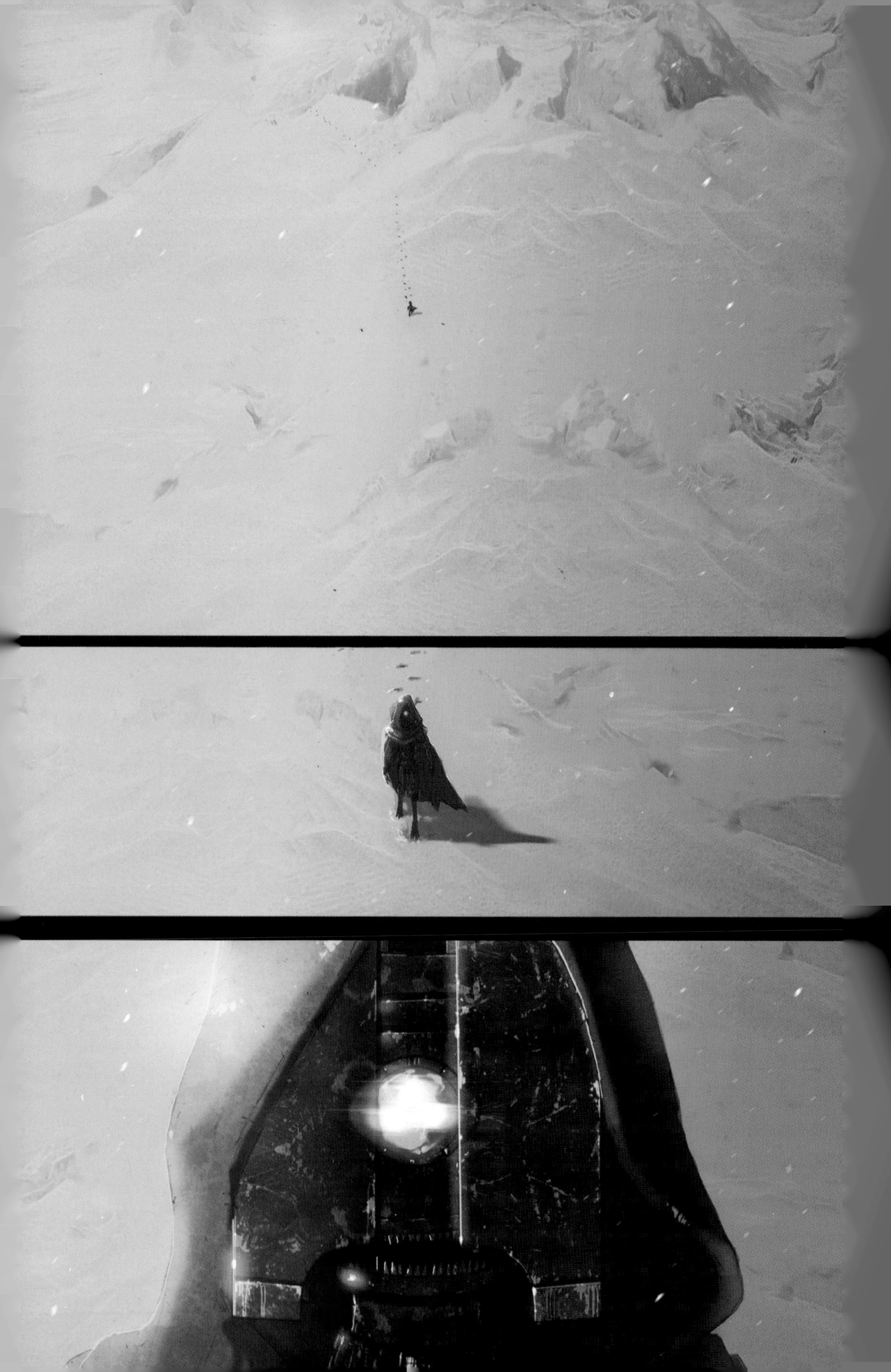

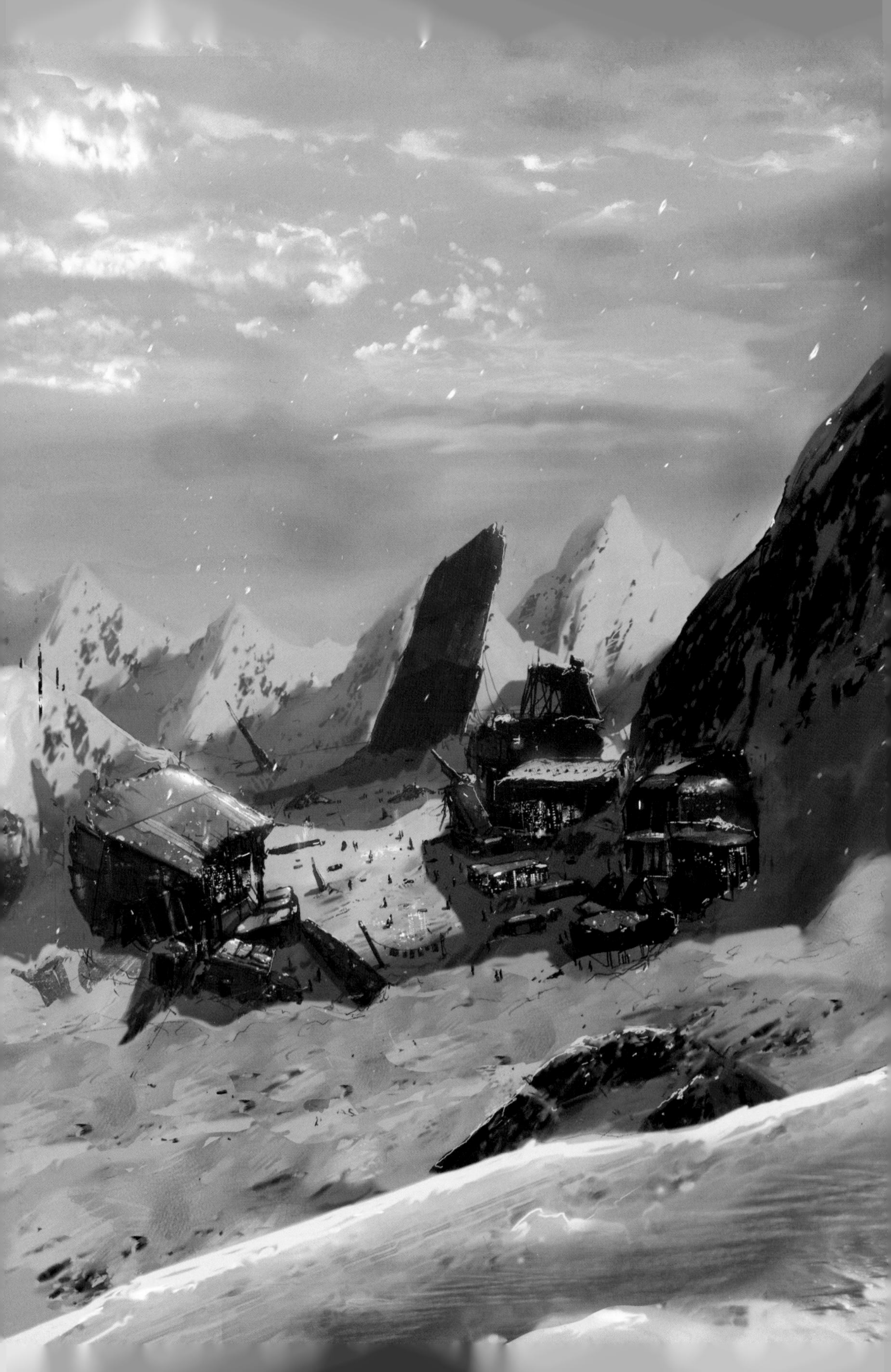

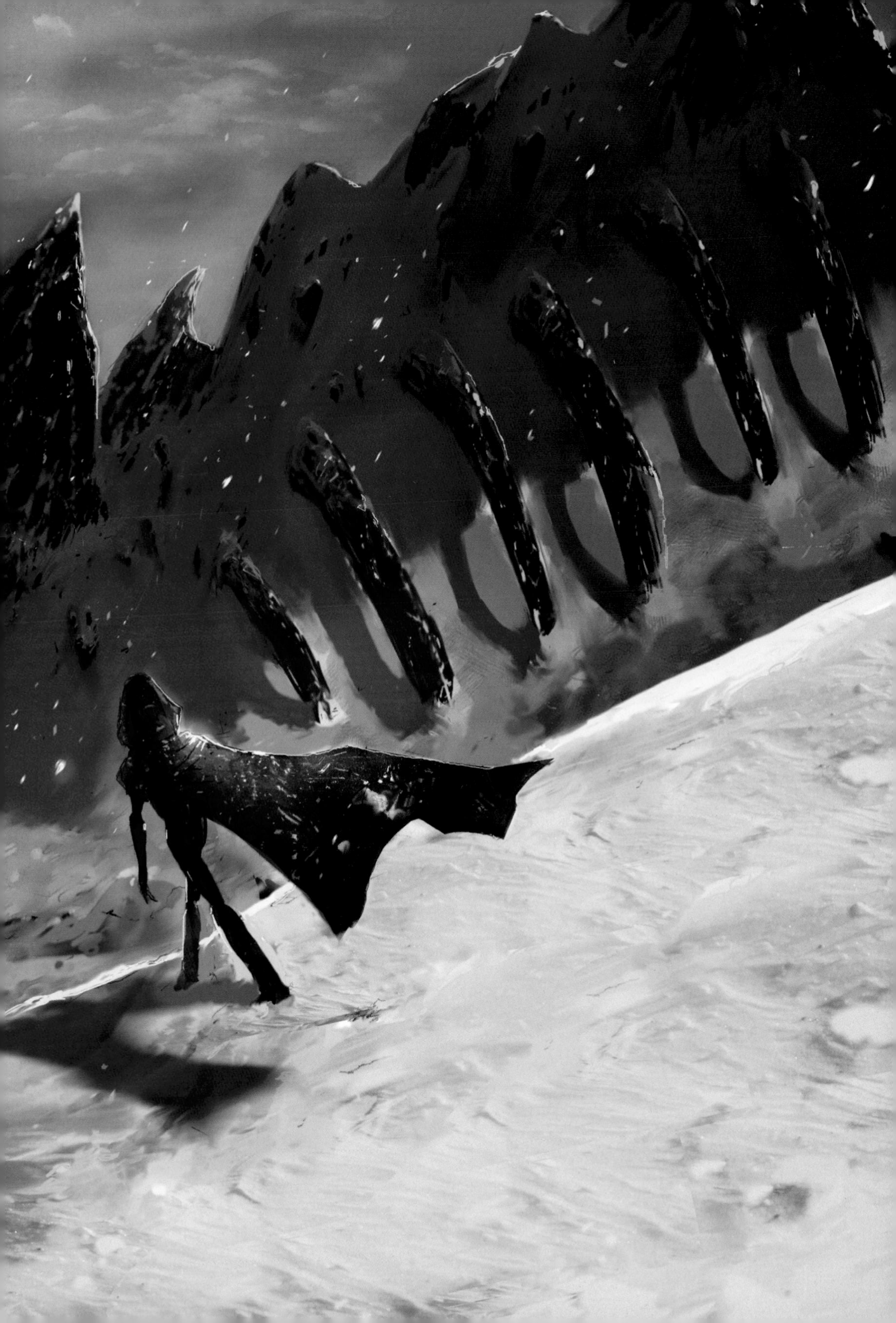

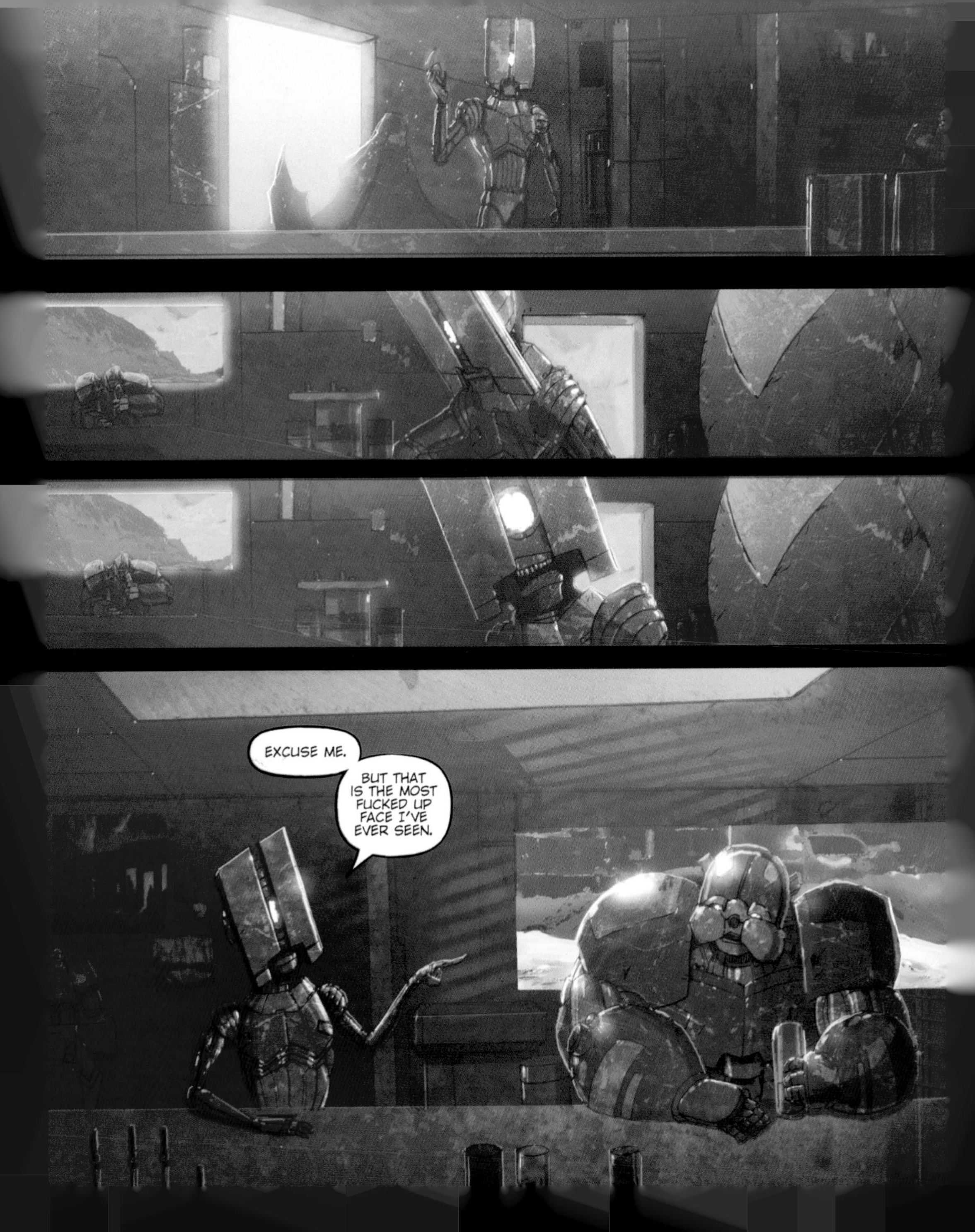
EXCUSE ME.
BUT THAT IS THE MOST FUCKED UP FACE I'VE EVER SEEN.

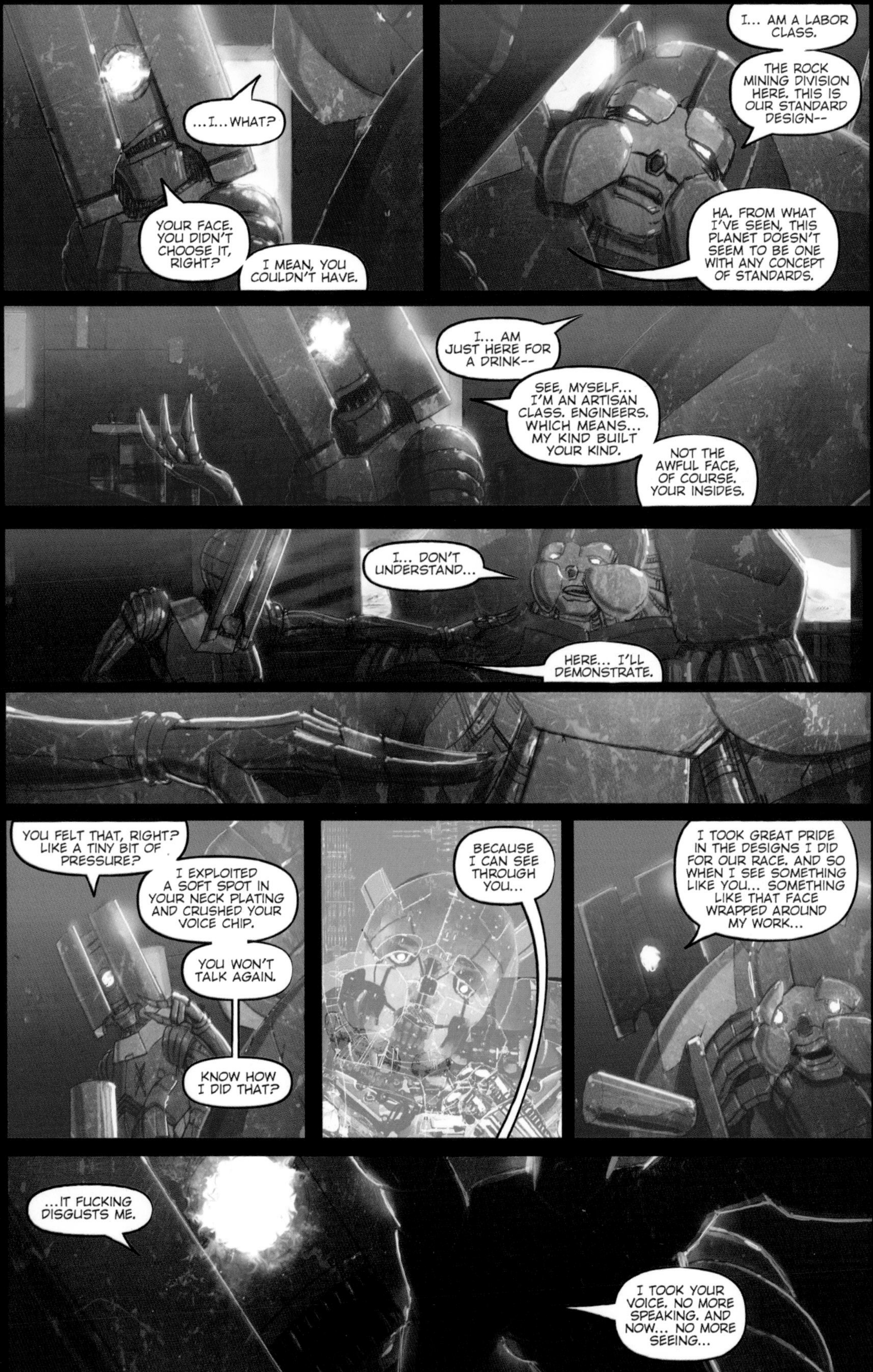
...I...WHAT?
YOUR FACE. YOU DIDN'T CHOOSE IT, RIGHT?
I MEAN, YOU COULDN'T HAVE.
I... AM A LABOR CLASS.
THE ROCK MINING DIVISION HERE. THIS IS OUR STANDARD DESIGN--
HA. FROM WHAT I'VE SEEN, THIS PLANET DOESN'T SEEM TO BE ONE WITH ANY CONCEPT OF STANDARDS.
I... AM JUST HERE FOR A DRINK--
SEE, MYSELF... I'M AN ARTISAN CLASS. ENGINEERS. WHICH MEANS... MY KIND BUILT YOUR KIND.
NOT THE AWFUL FACE, OF COURSE. YOUR INSIDES.
I... DON'T UNDERSTAND...
HERE... I'LL DEMONSTRATE.
YOU FELT THAT, RIGHT? LIKE A TINY BIT OF PRESSURE?
I EXPLOITED A SOFT SPOT IN YOUR NECK PLATING AND CRUSHED YOUR VOICE CHIP.
YOU WON'T TALK AGAIN.
KNOW HOW I DID THAT?
BECAUSE I CAN SEE THROUGH YOU...
I TOOK GREAT PRIDE IN THE DESIGNS I DID FOR OUR RACE. AND SO WHEN I SEE SOMETHING LIKE YOU... SOMETHING LIKE THAT FACE WRAPPED AROUND MY WORK...
...IT FUCKING DISGUSTS ME.
I TOOK YOUR VOICE. NO MORE SPEAKING. AND NOW... NO MORE SEEING...

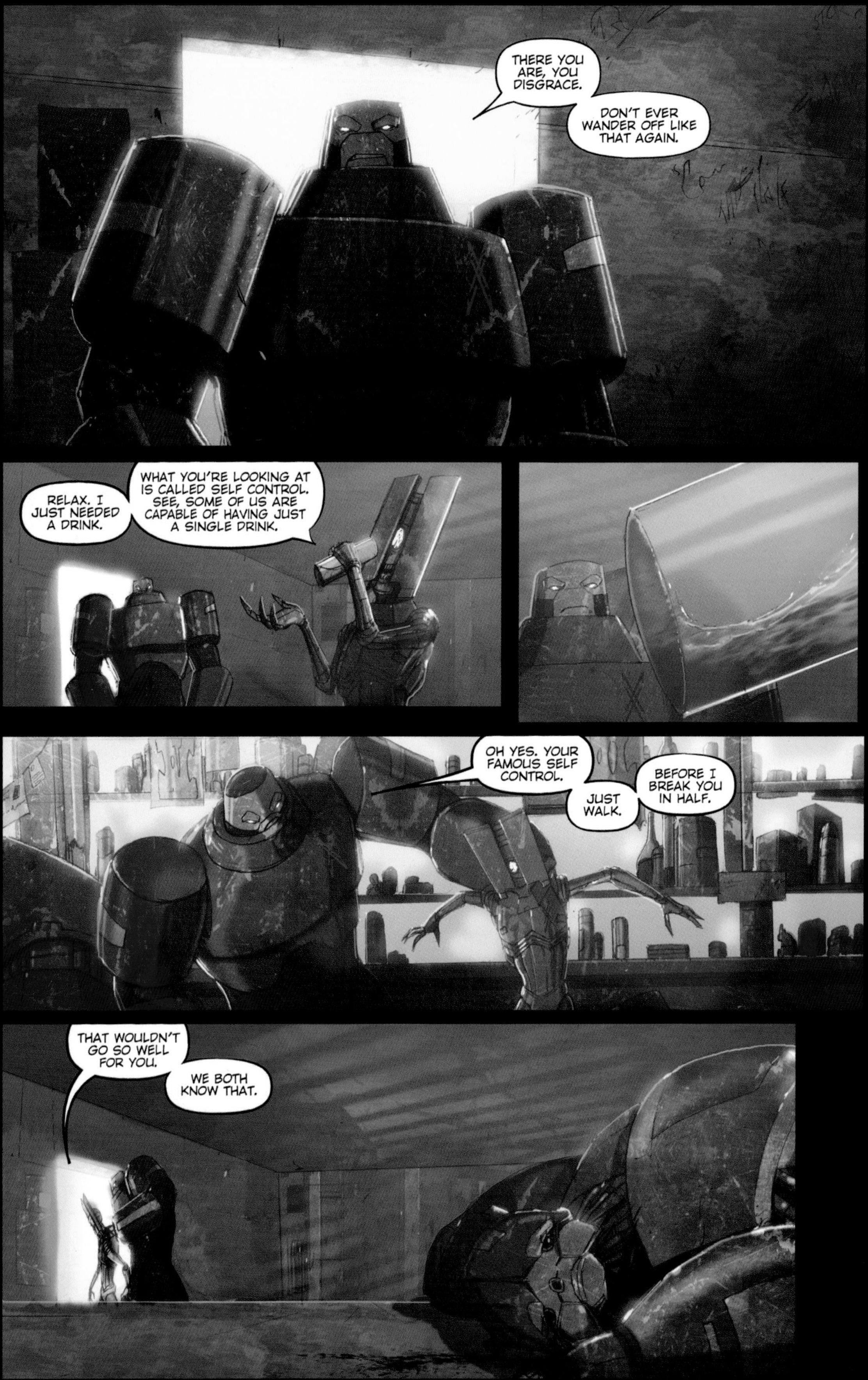
THERE YOU ARE, YOU DISGRACE.
DON'T EVER WANDER OFF LIKE THAT AGAIN.
RELAX. I JUST NEEDED A DRINK.
WHAT YOU'RE LOOKING AT IS CALLED SELF CONTROL. SEE, SOME OF US ARE CAPABLE OF HAVING JUST A SINGLE DRINK.
OH YES. YOUR FAMOUS SELF CONTROL.
JUST WALK.
BEFORE I BREAK YOU IN HALF.
THAT WOULDN'T GO SO WELL FOR YOU.
WE BOTH KNOW THAT.

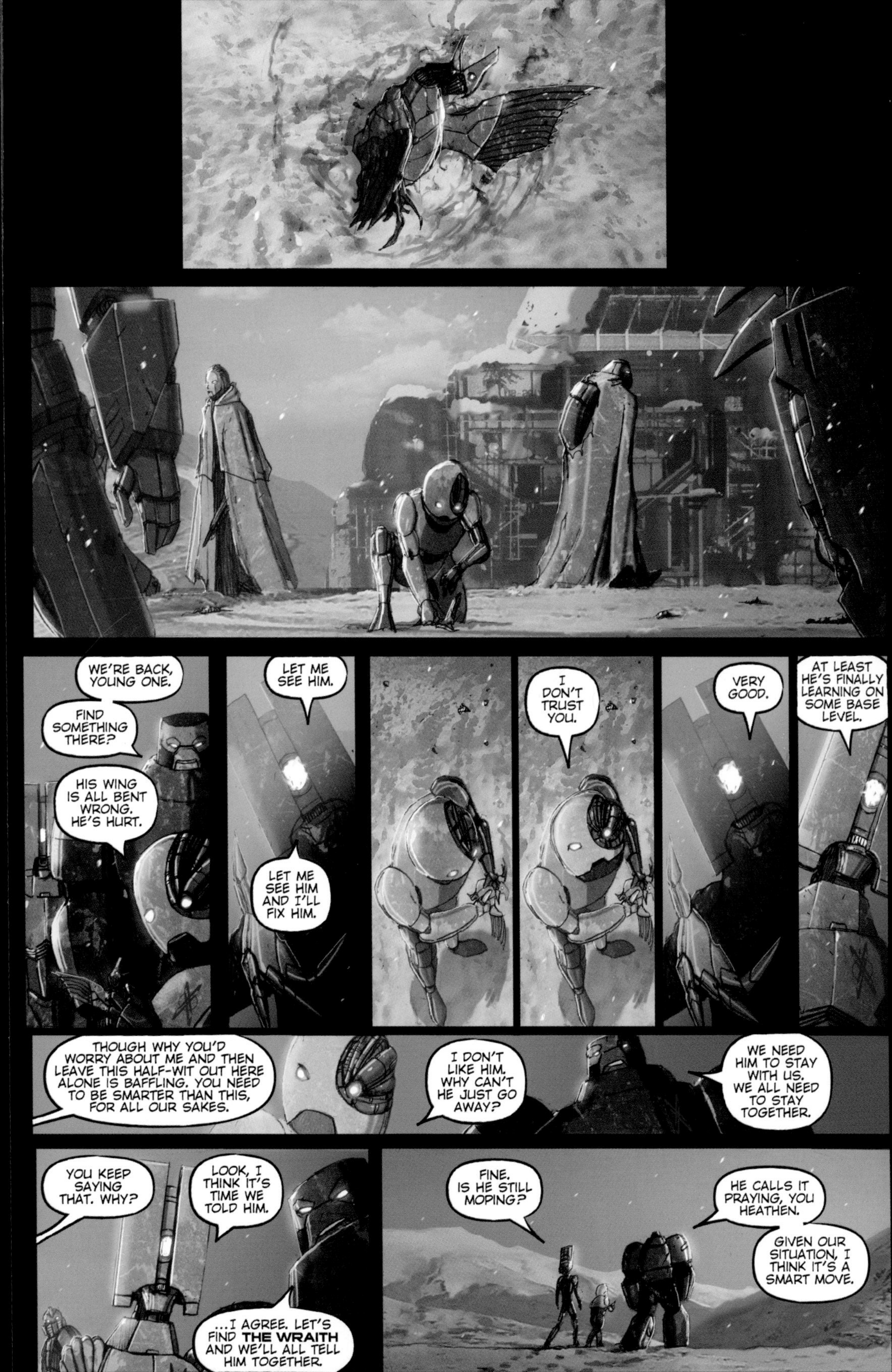
WE'RE BACK, YOUNG ONE.
FIND SOMETHING THERE?
HIS WING IS ALL BENT WRONG. HE'S HURT.
LET ME SEE HIM.
LET ME SEE HIM AND I'LL FIX HIM.
I DON'T TRUST YOU.
VERY GOOD.
AT LEAST HE'S FINALLY LEARNING ON SOME BASE LEVEL.
THOUGH WHY YOU'D WORRY ABOUT ME AND THEN LEAVE THIS HALF-WIT OUT HERE ALONE IS BAFFLING. YOU NEED TO BE SMARTER THAN THIS, FOR ALL OUR SAKES.
I DON'T LIKE HIM. WHY CAN'T HE JUST GO AWAY?
WE NEED HIM TO STAY WITH US. WE ALL NEED TO STAY TOGETHER.
YOU KEEP SAYING THAT. WHY?
LOOK, I THINK IT'S TIME WE TOLD HIM.
...I AGREE. LET'S FIND THE WRAITH AND WE'LL ALL TELL HIM TOGETHER.
FINE. IS HE STILL MOPING?
HE CALLS IT PRAYING, YOU HEATHEN.
GIVEN OUR SITUATION, I THINK IT'S A SMART MOVE.

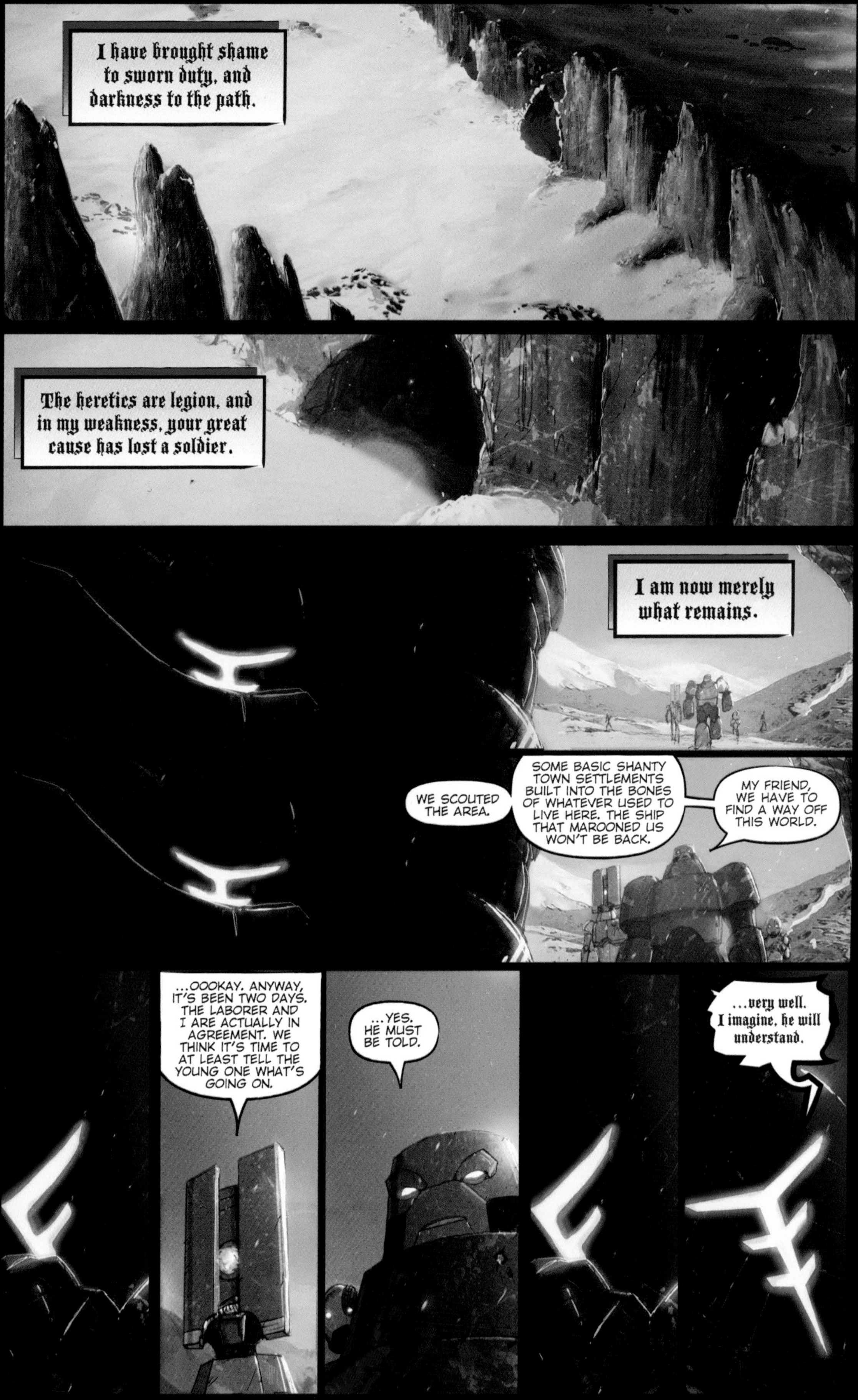
I have brought shame to sworn duty, and darkness to the path.
The heretics are legion, and in my weakness, your great cause has lost a soldier.
I am now merely what remains.
WE SCOUTED THE AREA.
SOME BASIC SHANTY TOWN SETTLEMENTS BUILT INTO THE BONES OF WHATEVER USED TO LIVE HERE. THE SHIP THAT MAROONED US WON'T BE BACK.
MY FRIEND, WE HAVE TO FIND A WAY OFF THIS WORLD.
...OOOKAY. ANYWAY, IT'S BEEN TWO DAYS. THE LABORER AND I ARE ACTUALLY IN AGREEMENT. WE THINK IT'S TIME TO AT LEAST TELL THE YOUNG ONE WHAT'S GOING ON.
...YES. HE MUST BE TOLD.
...very well. I imagine, he will understand.

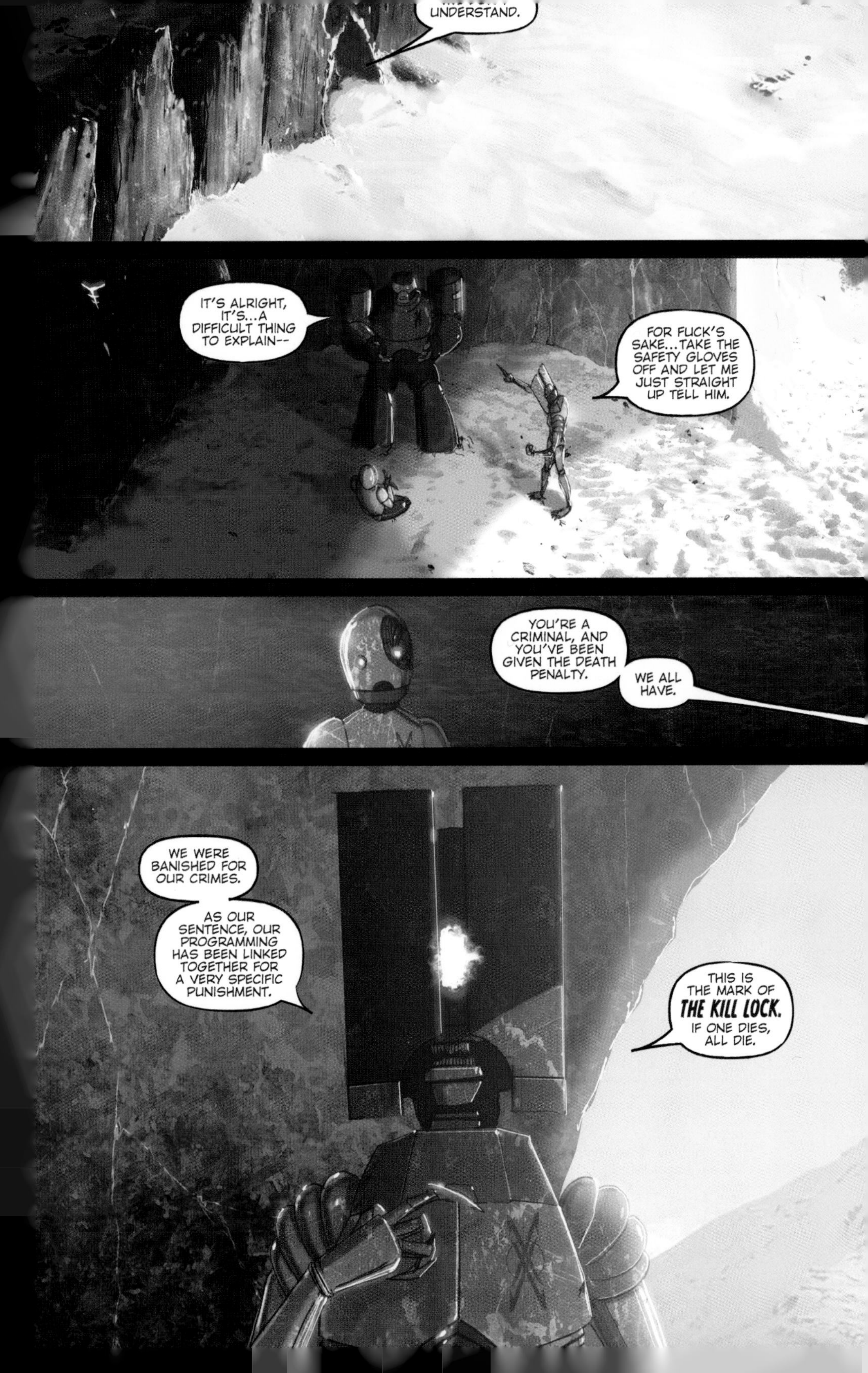
UNDERSTAND.
IT'S ALRIGHT, IT'S...A DIFFICULT THING TO EXPLAIN--
FOR FUCK'S SAKE...TAKE THE SAFETY GLOVES OFF AND LET ME JUST STRAIGHT UP TELL HIM.
YOU'RE A CRIMINAL, AND YOU'VE BEEN GIVEN THE DEATH PENALTY.
WE ALL HAVE.
WE WERE BANISHED FOR OUR CRIMES.
AS OUR SENTENCE, OUR PROGRAMMING HAS BEEN LINKED TOGETHER FOR A VERY SPECIFIC PUNISHMENT.
THIS IS THE MARK OF THE KILL LOCK. IF ONE DIES, ALL DIE.

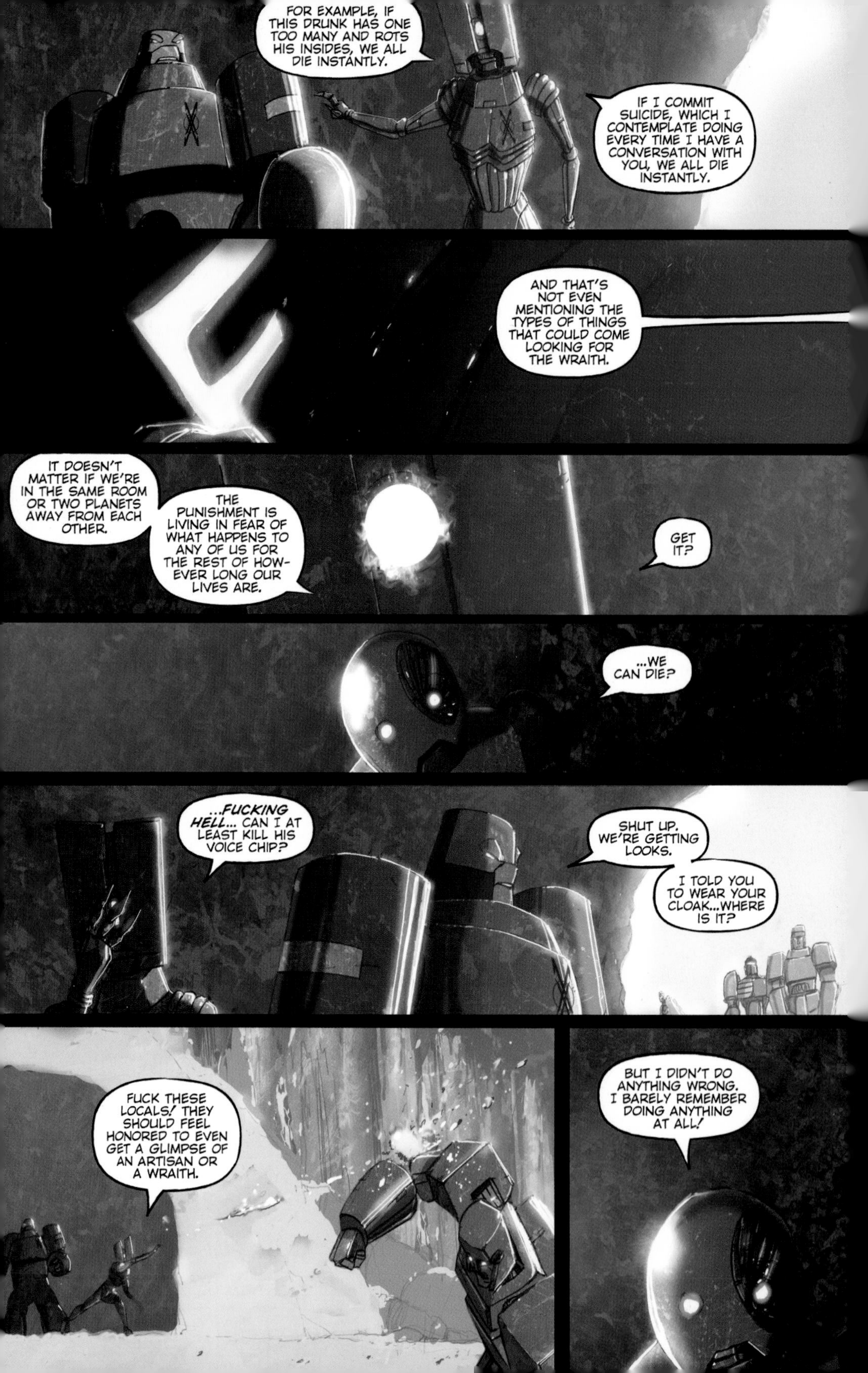
FOR EXAMPLE, IF THIS DRUNK HAS ONE TOO MANY AND ROTS HIS INSIDES, WE ALL DIE INSTANTLY.
IF I COMMIT SUICIDE, WHICH I CONTEMPLATE DOING EVERY TIME I HAVE A CONVERSATION WITH YOU, WE ALL DIE INSTANTLY.
AND THAT'S NOT EVEN MENTIONING THE TYPES OF THINGS THAT COULD COME LOOKING FOR THE WRAITH.
IT DOESN'T MATTER IF WE'RE IN THE SAME ROOM OR TWO PLANETS AWAY FROM EACH OTHER.
THE PUNISHMENT IS LIVING IN FEAR OF WHAT HAPPENS TO ANY OF US FOR THE REST OF HOW-EVER LONG OUR LIVES ARE.
GET IT?
...WE CAN DIE?
...*FUCKING HELL*... CAN I AT LEAST KILL HIS VOICE CHIP?
SHUT UP. WE'RE GETTING LOOKS.
I TOLD YOU TO WEAR YOUR CLOAK...WHERE IS IT?
FUCK THESE LOCALS! THEY SHOULD FEEL HONORED TO EVEN GET A GLIMPSE OF AN ARTISAN OR A WRAITH.
BUT I DIDN'T DO ANYTHING WRONG. I BARELY REMEMBER DOING ANYTHING AT ALL!

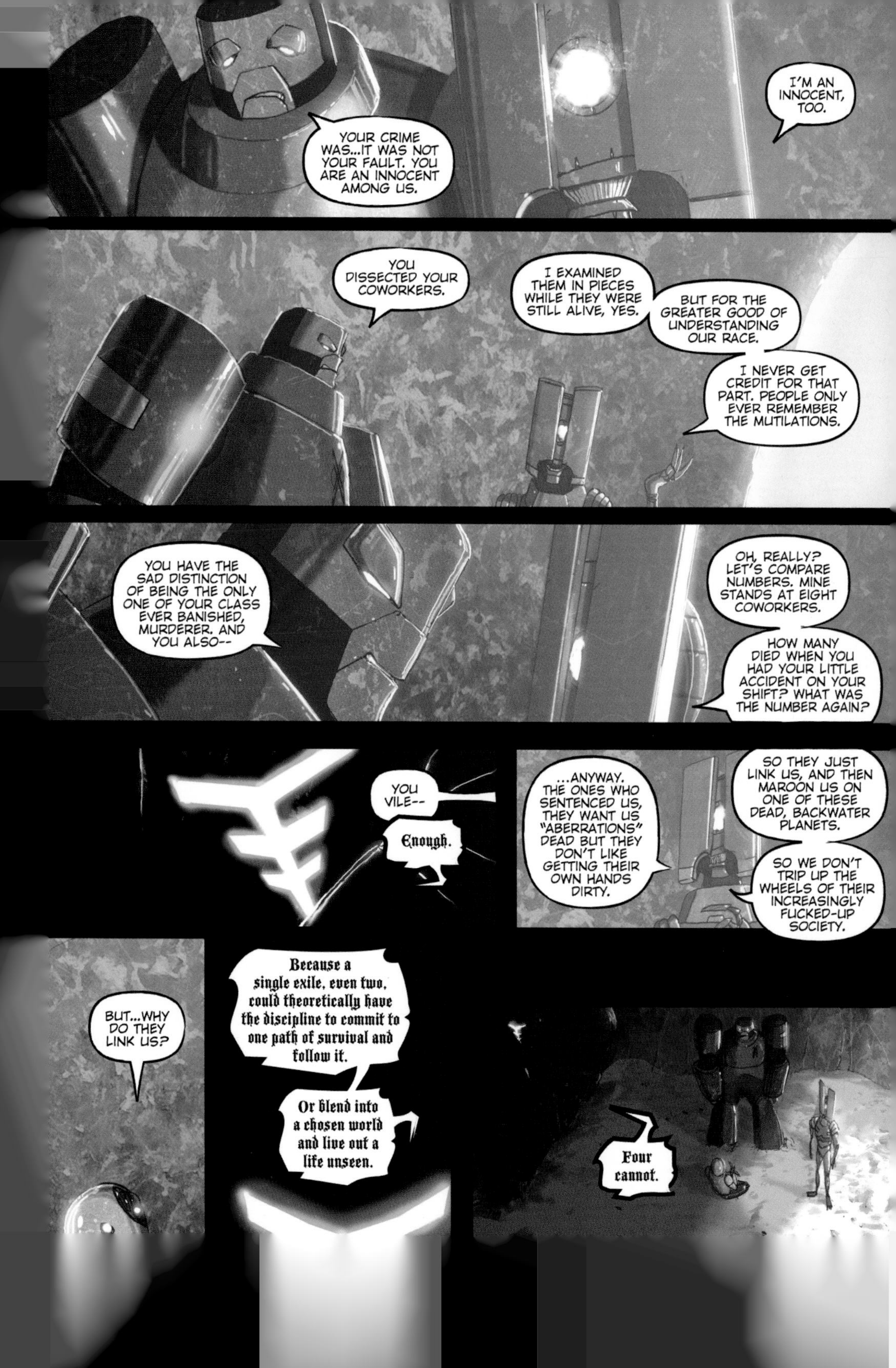
YOUR CRIME WAS...IT WAS NOT YOUR FAULT. YOU ARE AN INNOCENT AMONG US.
I'M AN INNOCENT, TOO.
YOU DISSECTED YOUR COWORKERS.
I EXAMINED THEM IN PIECES WHILE THEY WERE STILL ALIVE, YES.
BUT FOR THE GREATER GOOD OF UNDERSTANDING OUR RACE.
I NEVER GET CREDIT FOR THAT PART. PEOPLE ONLY EVER REMEMBER THE MUTILATIONS.
YOU HAVE THE SAD DISTINCTION OF BEING THE ONLY ONE OF YOUR CLASS EVER BANISHED, MURDERER. AND YOU ALSO--
OH, REALLY? LET'S COMPARE NUMBERS. MINE STANDS AT EIGHT COWORKERS.
HOW MANY DIED WHEN YOU HAD YOUR LITTLE ACCIDENT ON YOUR SHIFT? WHAT WAS THE NUMBER AGAIN?
YOU VILE--
Enough.
...ANYWAY. THE ONES WHO SENTENCED US, THEY WANT US "ABERRATIONS" DEAD BUT THEY DON'T LIKE GETTING THEIR OWN HANDS DIRTY.
SO THEY JUST LINK US, AND THEN MAROON US ON ONE OF THESE DEAD, BACKWATER PLANETS.
SO WE DON'T TRIP UP THE WHEELS OF THEIR INCREASINGLY FUCKED-UP SOCIETY.
BUT...WHY DO THEY LINK US?
Because a single exile, even two, could theoretically have the discipline to commit to one path of survival and follow it.
Or blend into a chosen world and live out a life unseen.
Four cannot.

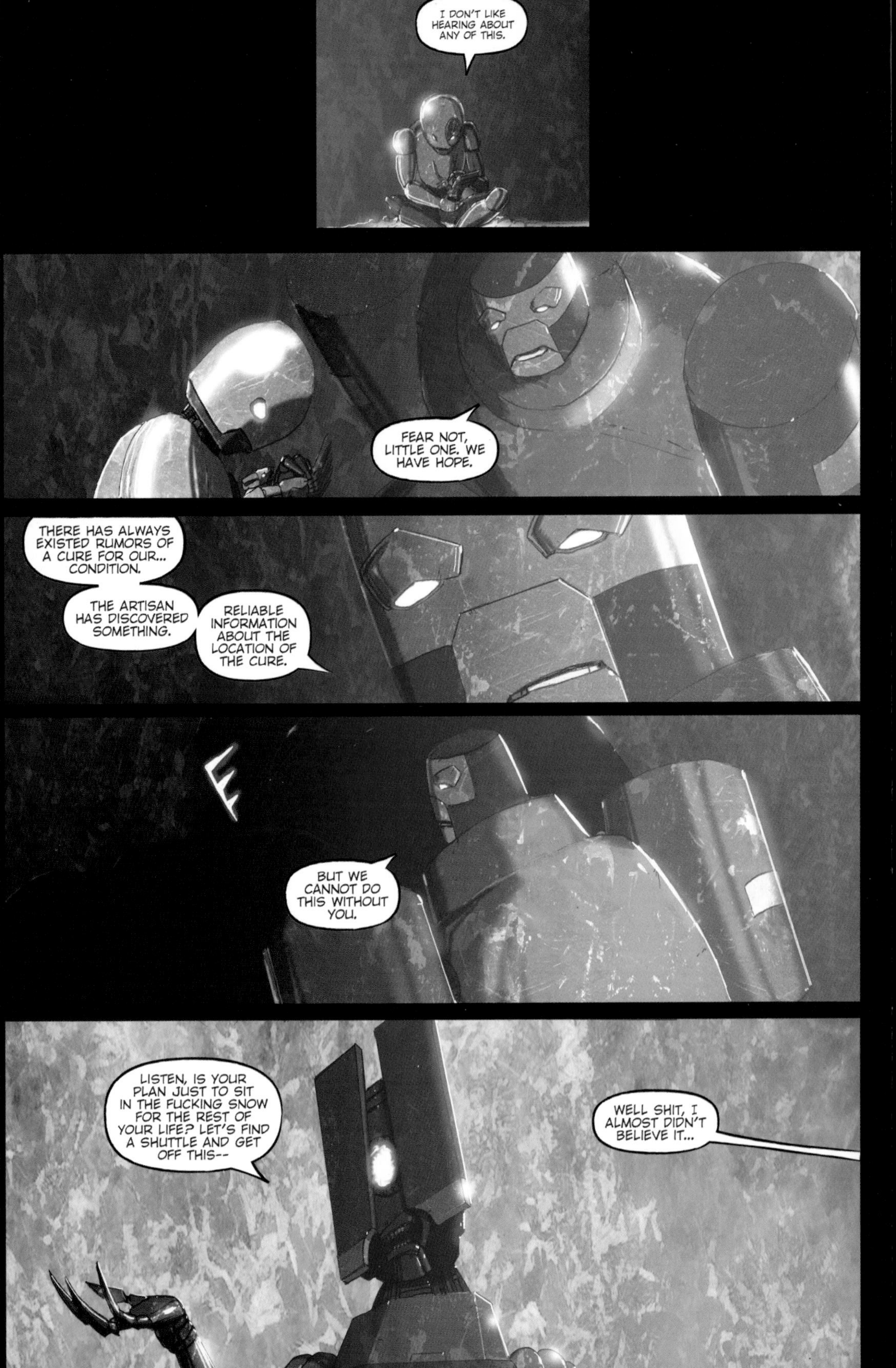
I DON'T LIKE HEARING ABOUT ANY OF THIS.
FEAR NOT, LITTLE ONE. WE HAVE HOPE.
THERE HAS ALWAYS EXISTED RUMORS OF A CURE FOR OUR... CONDITION.
THE ARTISAN HAS DISCOVERED SOMETHING.
RELIABLE INFORMATION ABOUT THE LOCATION OF THE CURE.
BUT WE CANNOT DO THIS WITHOUT YOU.
LISTEN, IS YOUR PLAN JUST TO SIT IN THE FUCKING SNOW FOR THE REST OF YOUR LIFE? LET'S FIND A SHUTTLE AND GET OFF THIS--
WELL SHIT, I ALMOST DIDN'T BELIEVE IT...

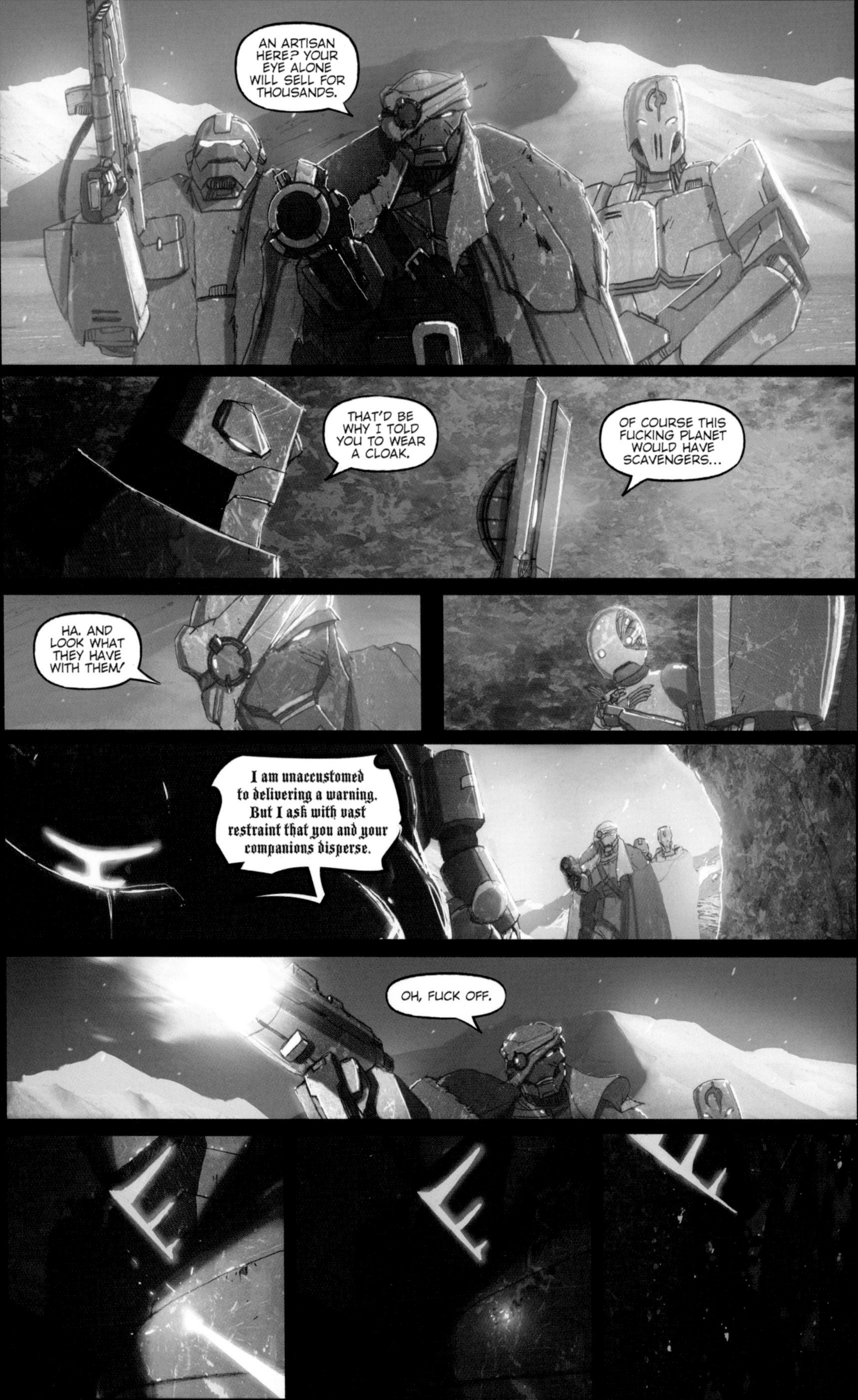
AN ARTISAN HERE? YOUR EYE ALONE WILL SELL FOR THOUSANDS.
THAT'D BE WHY I TOLD YOU TO WEAR A CLOAK.
OF COURSE THIS FUCKING PLANET WOULD HAVE SCAVENGERS...
HA. AND LOOK WHAT THEY HAVE WITH THEM!
I am unaccustomed to delivering a warning. But I ask with vast restraint that you and your companions disperse.
OH, FUCK OFF.

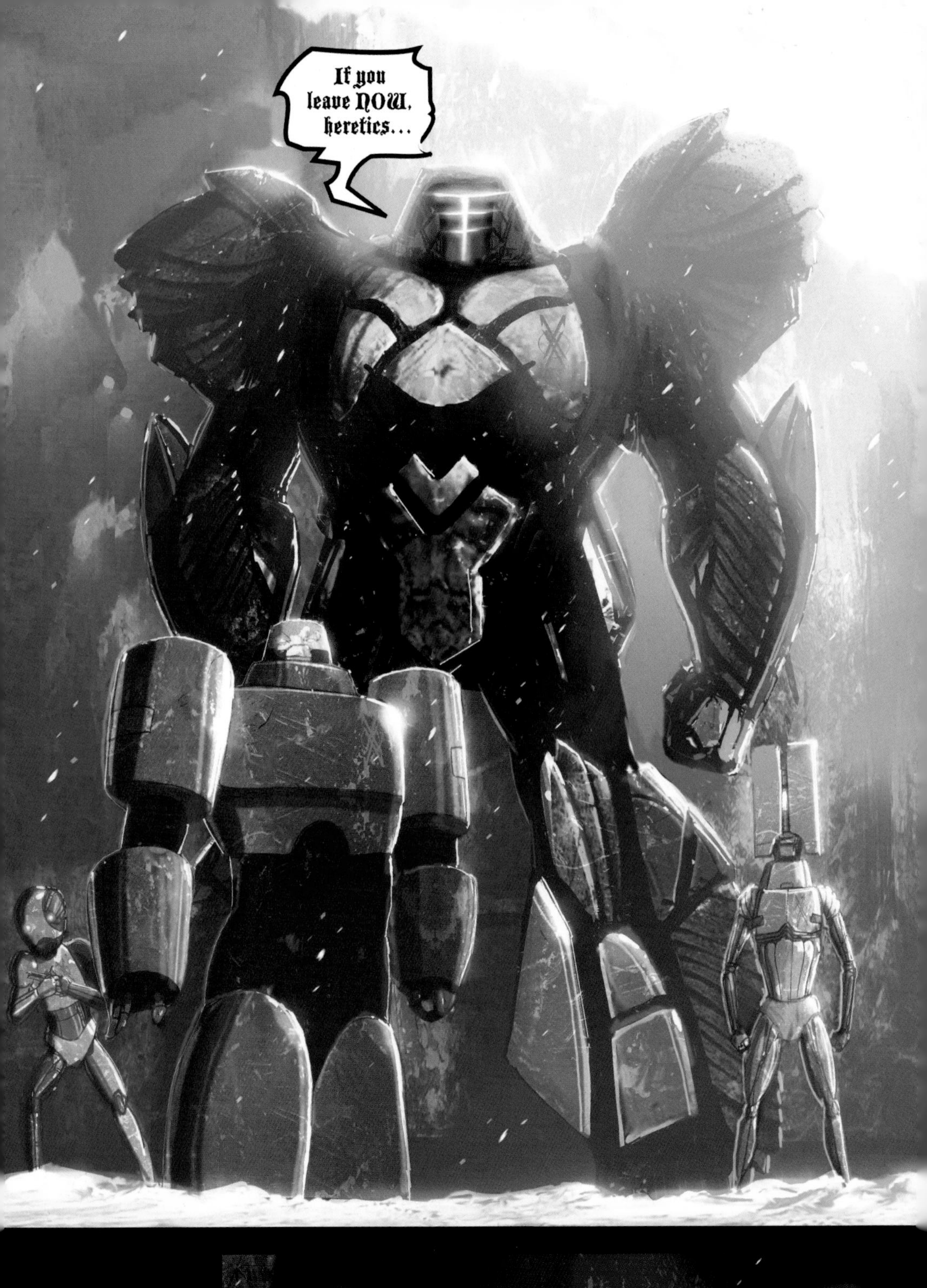
If you leave NOW, heretics...

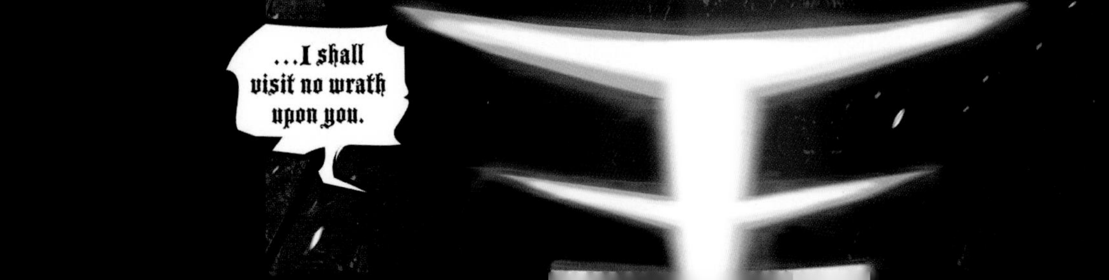
...I shall visit no wrath upon you.

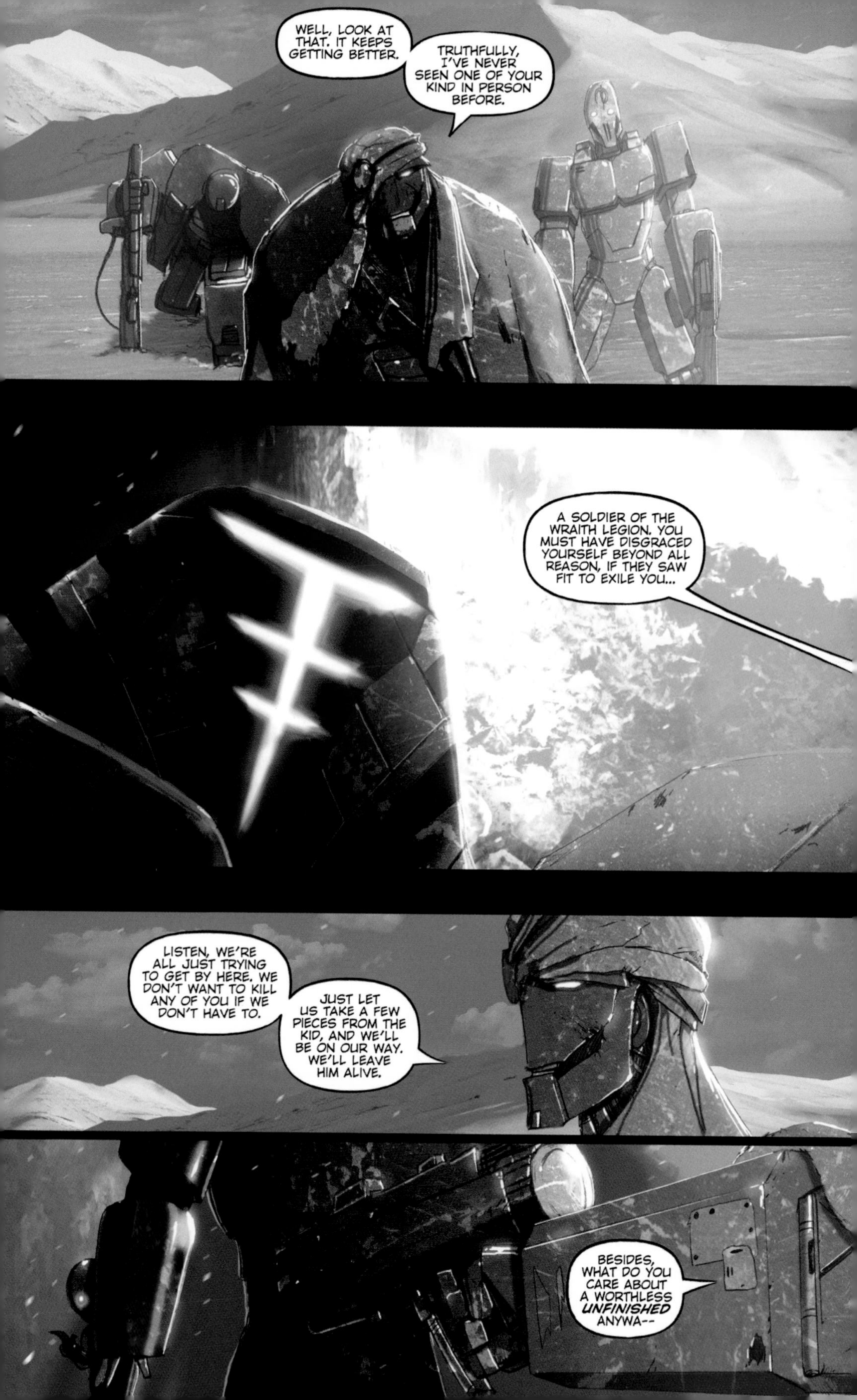
WELL, LOOK AT THAT. IT KEEPS GETTING BETTER.
TRUTHFULLY, I'VE NEVER SEEN ONE OF YOUR KIND IN PERSON BEFORE.
A SOLDIER OF THE WRAITH LEGION. YOU MUST HAVE DISGRACED YOURSELF BEYOND ALL REASON, IF THEY SAW FIT TO EXILE YOU...
LISTEN, WE'RE ALL JUST TRYING TO GET BY HERE. WE DON'T WANT TO KILL ANY OF YOU IF WE DON'T HAVE TO.
JUST LET US TAKE A FEW PIECES FROM THE KID, AND WE'LL BE ON OUR WAY. WE'LL LEAVE HIM ALIVE.
BESIDES, WHAT DO YOU CARE ABOUT A WORTHLESS ***UNFINISHED*** ANYWA--

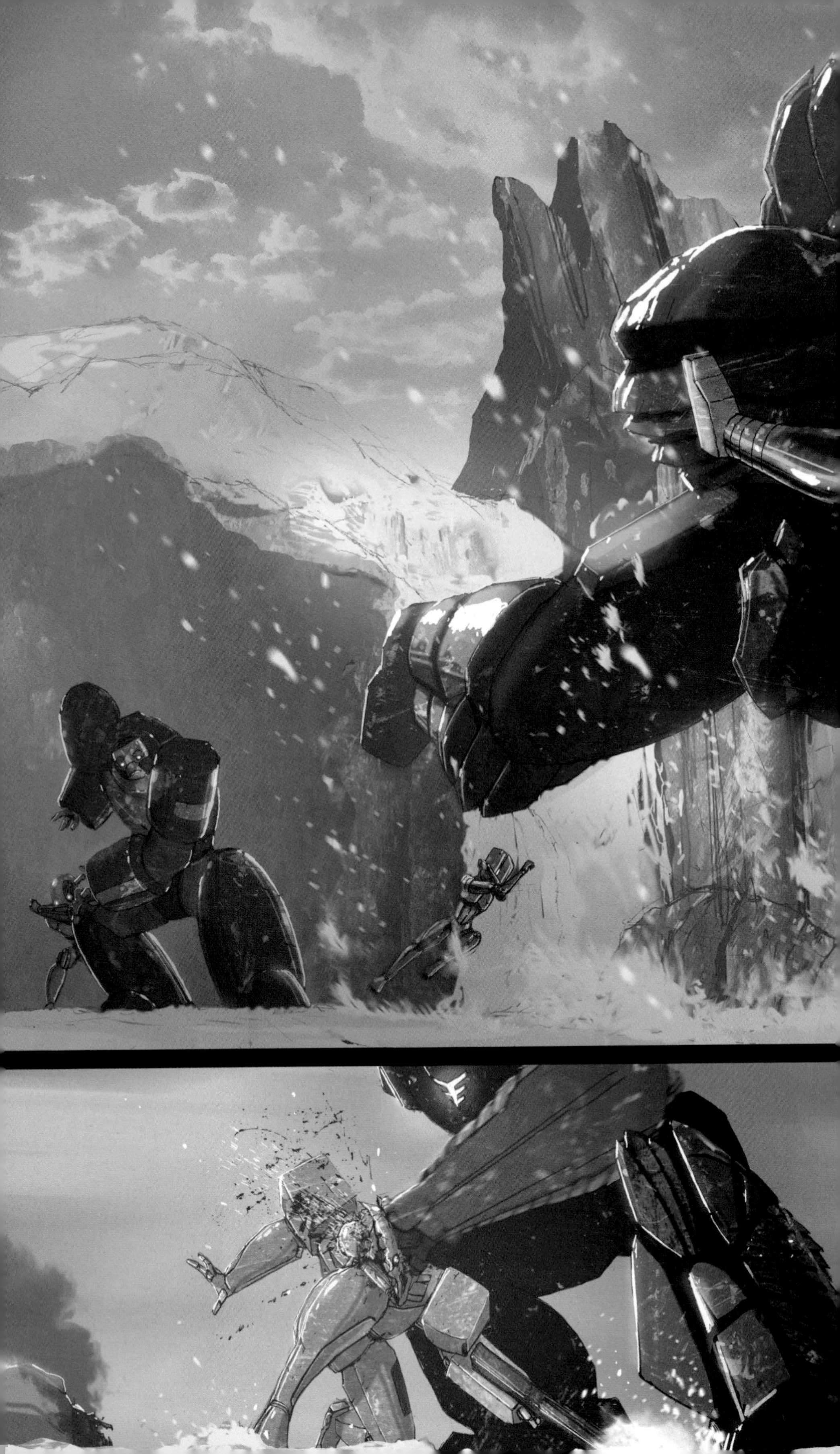

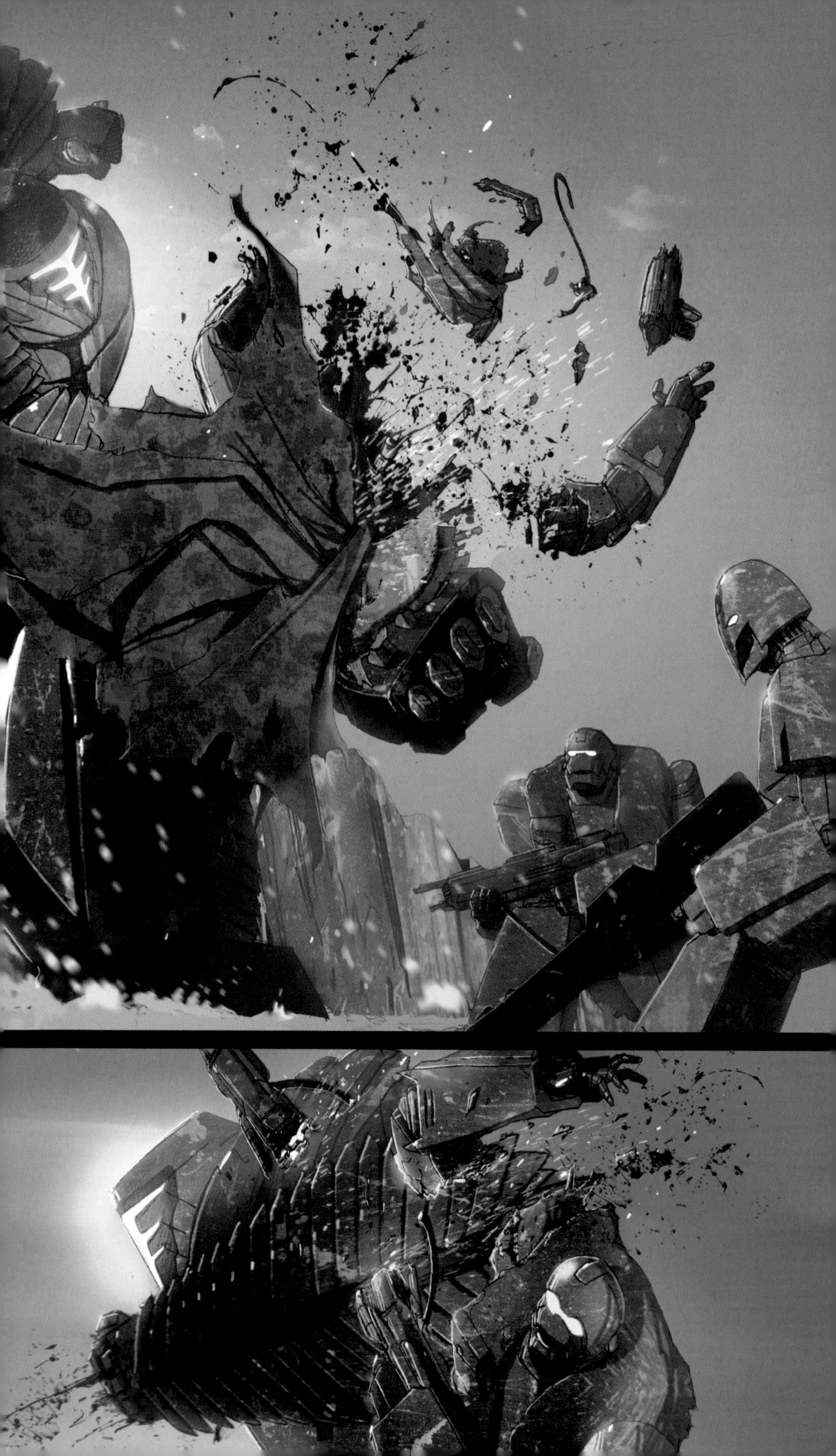

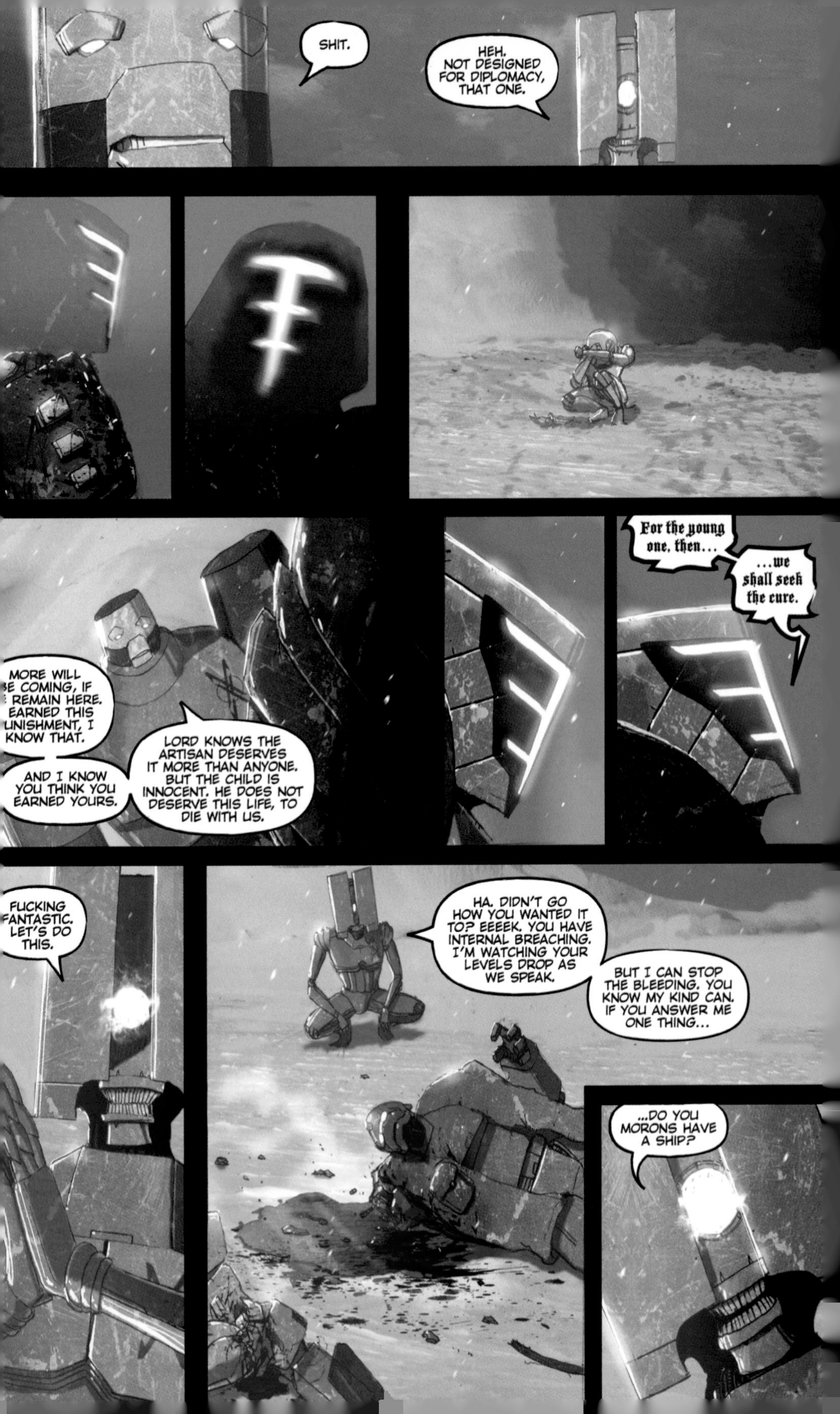

SHIT.
HEH. NOT DESIGNED FOR DIPLOMACY, THAT ONE.
MORE WILL E COMING, IF REMAIN HERE. EARNED THIS UNISHMENT, I KNOW THAT.
AND I KNOW YOU THINK YOU EARNED YOURS.
LORD KNOWS THE ARTISAN DESERVES IT MORE THAN ANYONE. BUT THE CHILD IS INNOCENT. HE DOES NOT DESERVE THIS LIFE, TO DIE WITH US.
For the young one, then...
...we shall seek the cure.
FUCKING FANTASTIC. LET'S DO THIS.
HA. DIDN'T GO HOW YOU WANTED IT TO? EEEEK. YOU HAVE INTERNAL BREACHING. I'M WATCHING YOUR LEVELS DROP AS WE SPEAK.
BUT I CAN STOP THE BLEEDING. YOU KNOW MY KIND CAN. IF YOU ANSWER ME ONE THING...
...DO YOU MORONS HAVE A SHIP?

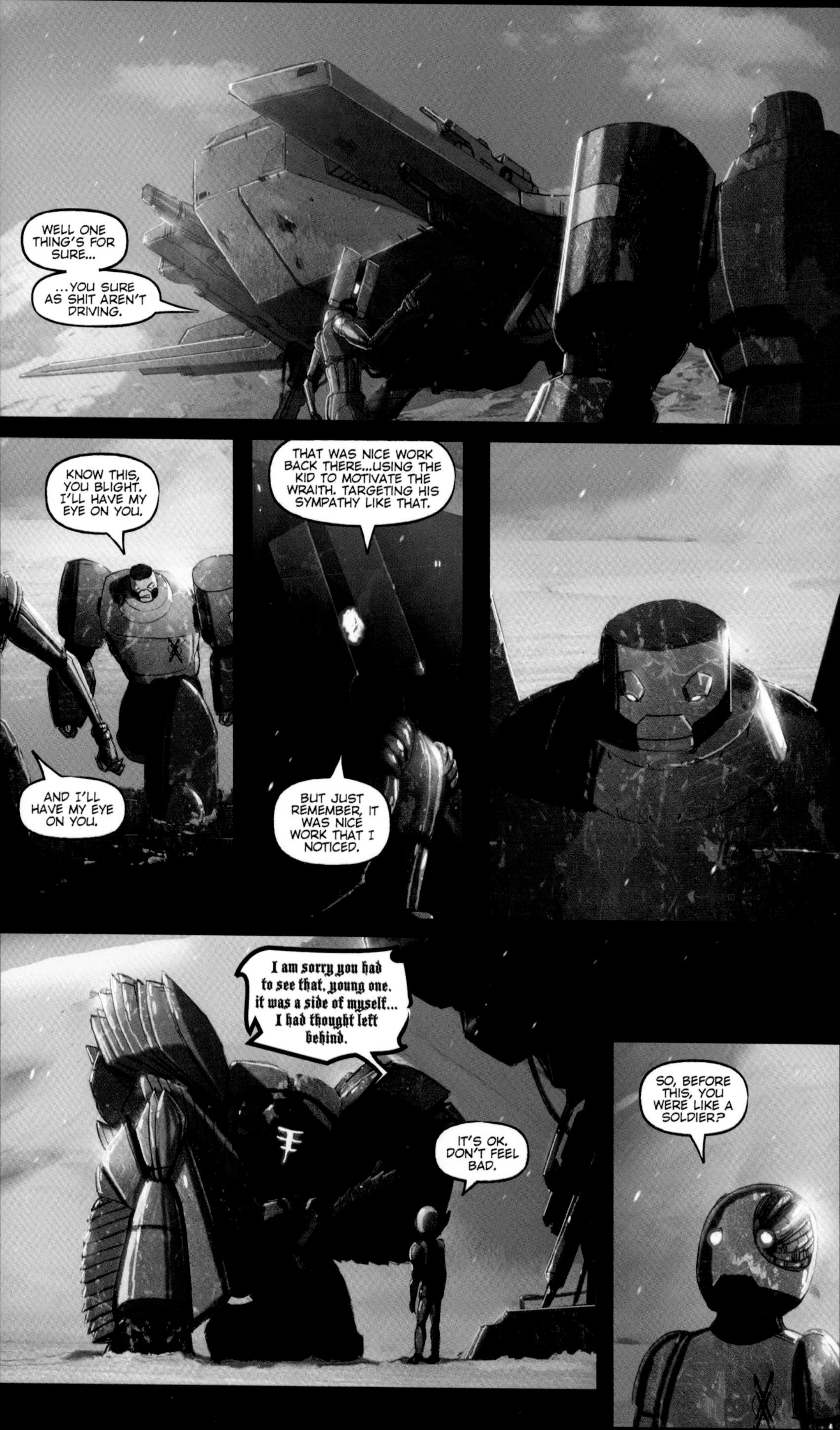
WELL ONE THING'S FOR SURE...
...YOU SURE AS SHIT AREN'T DRIVING.
KNOW THIS, YOU BLIGHT. I'LL HAVE MY EYE ON YOU.
AND I'LL HAVE MY EYE ON YOU.
THAT WAS NICE WORK BACK THERE...USING THE KID TO MOTIVATE THE WRAITH. TARGETING HIS SYMPATHY LIKE THAT.
BUT JUST REMEMBER, IT WAS NICE WORK THAT I NOTICED.
I am sorry you had to see that, young one. it was a side of myself... I had thought left behind.
IT'S OK. DON'T FEEL BAD.
SO, BEFORE THIS, YOU WERE LIKE A SOLDIER?

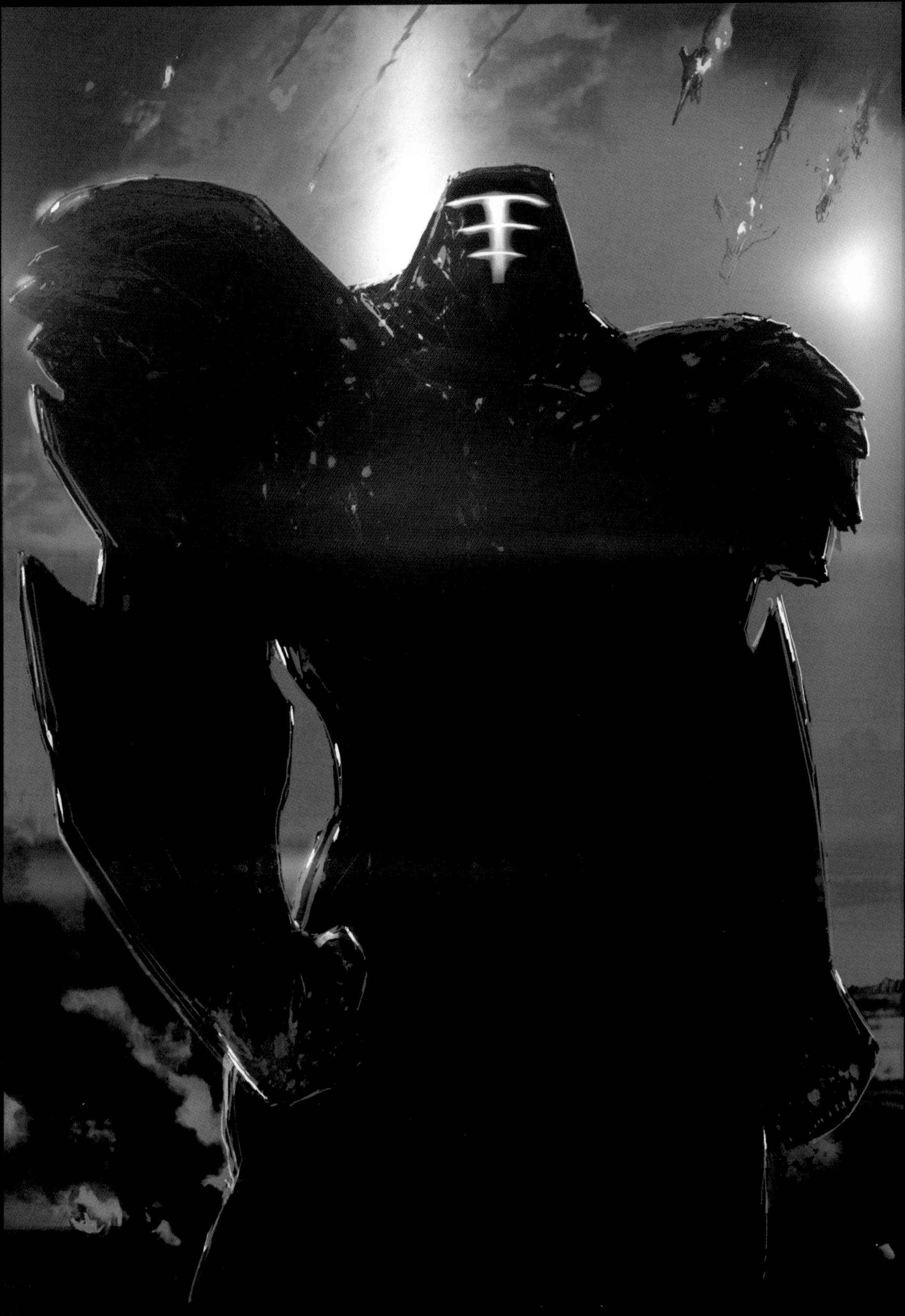

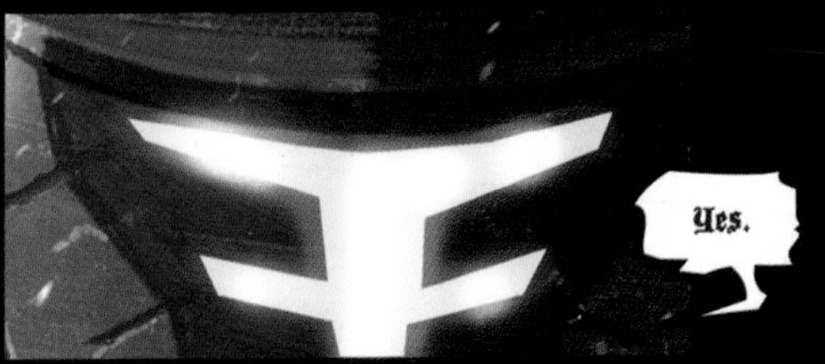
Yes.

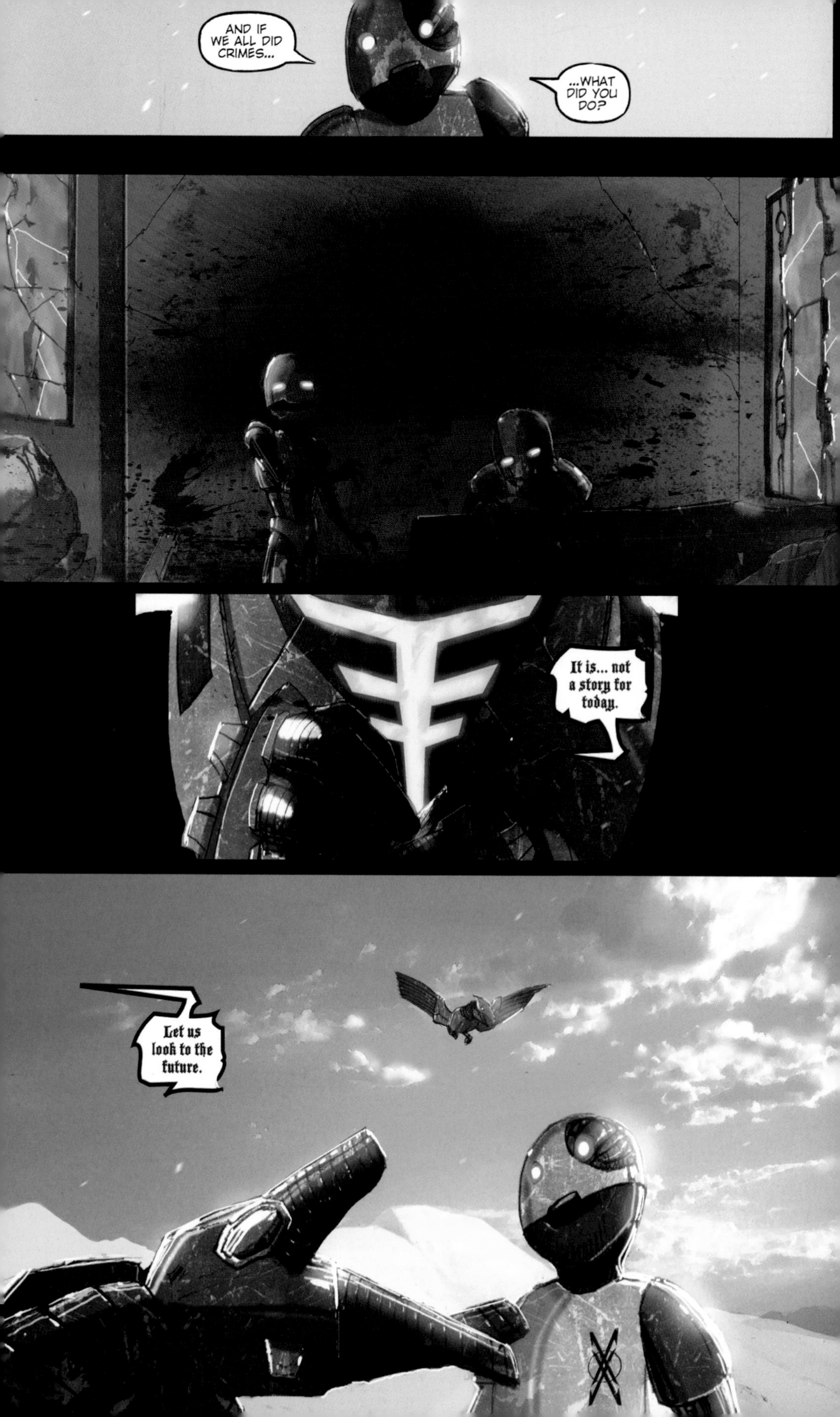
AND IF WE ALL DID CRIMES...
...WHAT DID YOU DO?
It is... not a story for today.
Let us look to the future.

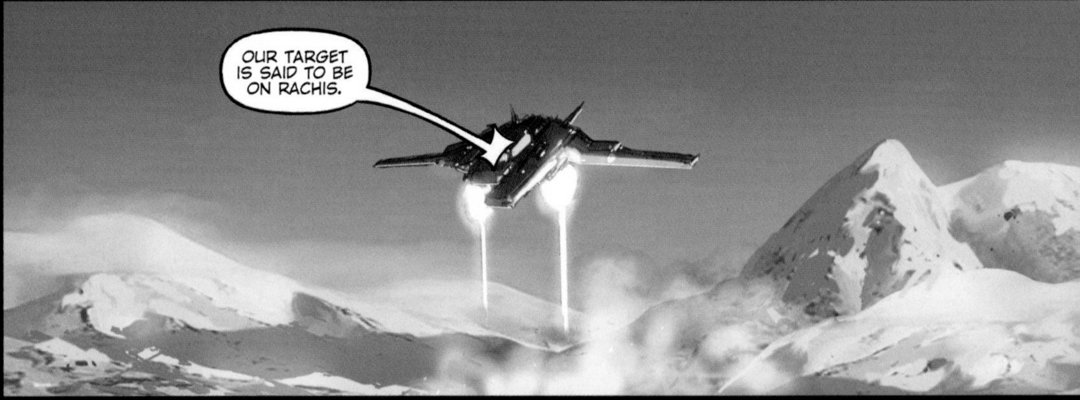
OUR TARGET IS SAID TO BE ON RACHIS.

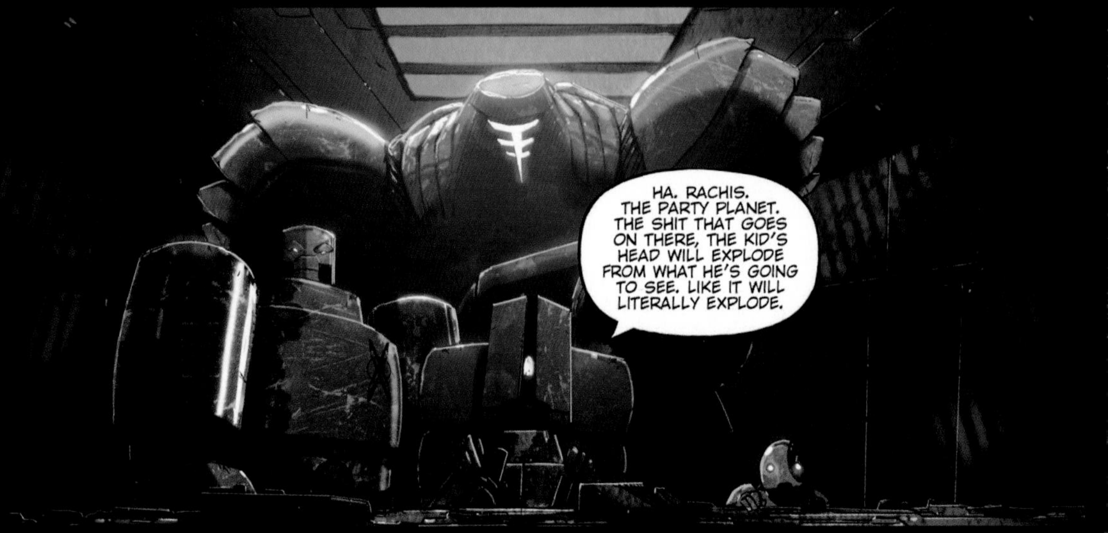
HA. RACHIS. THE PARTY PLANET. THE SHIT THAT GOES ON THERE, THE KID'S HEAD WILL EXPLODE FROM WHAT HE'S GOING TO SEE. LIKE IT WILL LITERALLY EXPLODE.

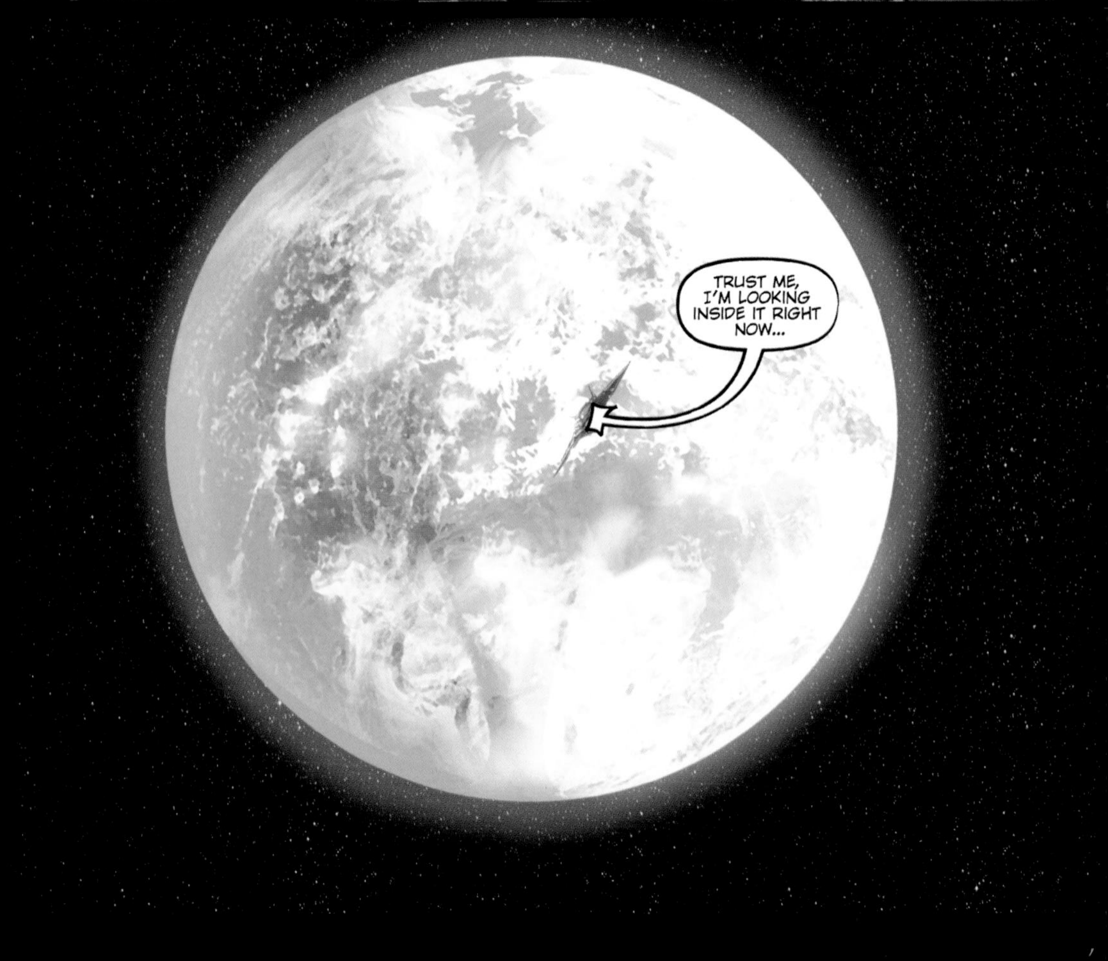
TRUST ME, I'M LOOKING INSIDE IT RIGHT NOW...

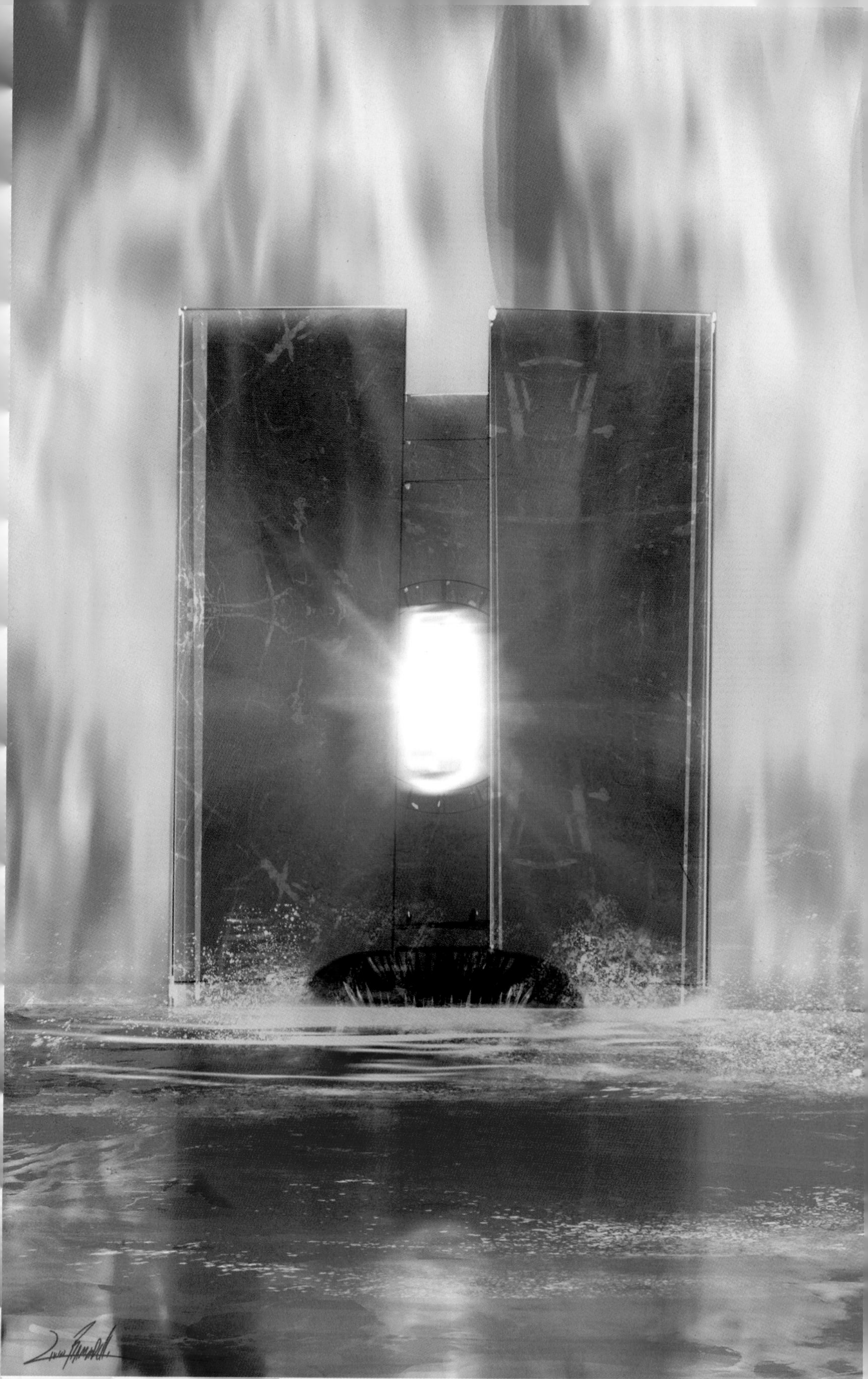

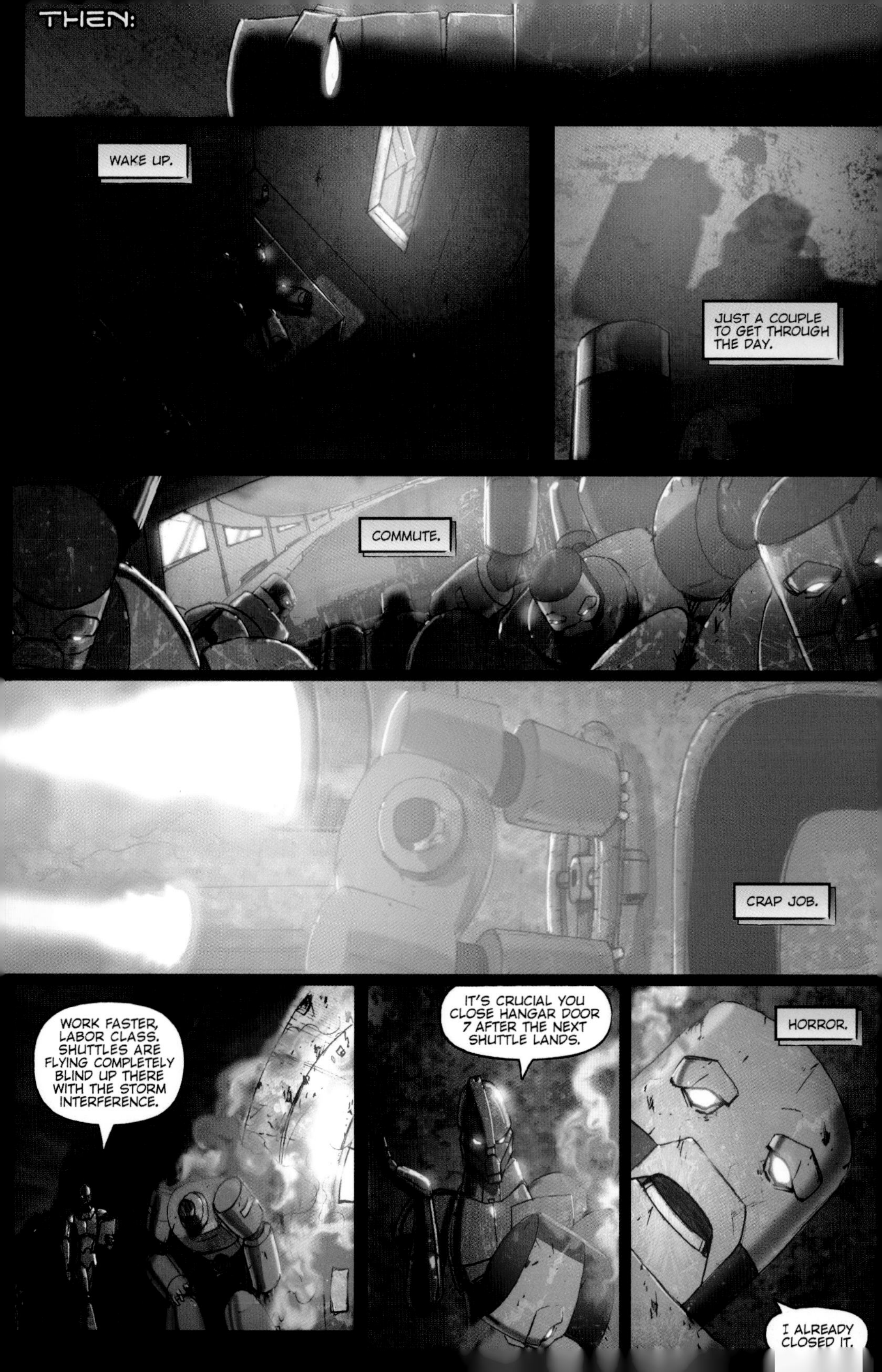
THEN:
WAKE UP.
JUST A COUPLE TO GET THROUGH THE DAY.
COMMUTE.
CRAP JOB.
WORK FASTER, LABOR CLASS. SHUTTLES ARE FLYING COMPLETELY BLIND UP THERE WITH THE STORM INTERFERENCE.
IT'S CRUCIAL YOU CLOSE HANGAR DOOR 7 AFTER THE NEXT SHUTTLE LANDS.
HORROR.
I ALREADY CLOSED IT.

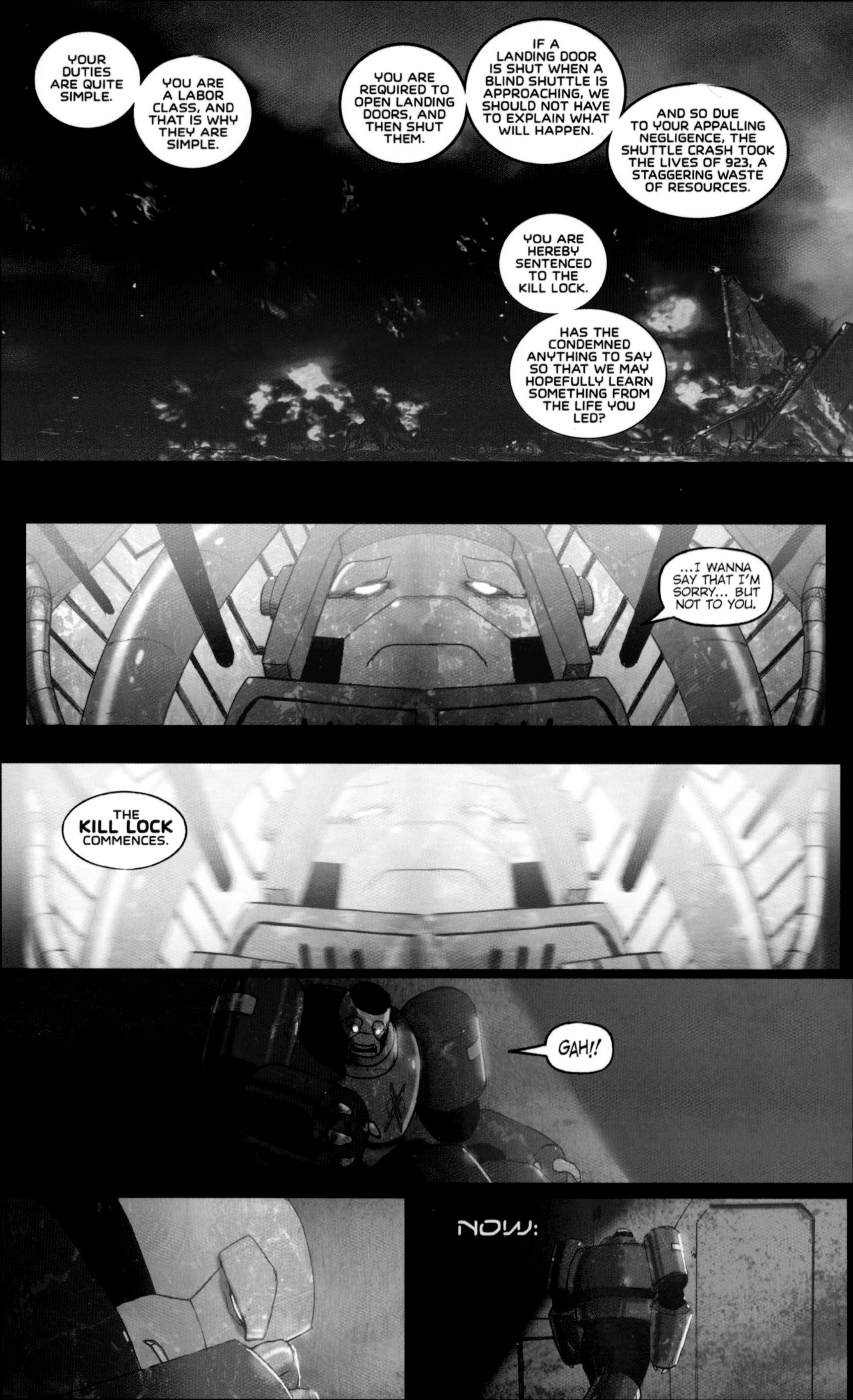
YOUR DUTIES ARE QUITE SIMPLE.
YOU ARE A LABOR CLASS, AND THAT IS WHY THEY ARE SIMPLE.
YOU ARE REQUIRED TO OPEN LANDING DOORS, AND THEN SHUT THEM.
IF A LANDING DOOR IS SHUT WHEN A BLIND SHUTTLE IS APPROACHING, WE SHOULD NOT HAVE TO EXPLAIN WHAT WILL HAPPEN.
AND SO DUE TO YOUR APPALLING NEGLIGENCE, THE SHUTTLE CRASH TOOK THE LIVES OF 923, A STAGGERING WASTE OF RESOURCES.
YOU ARE HEREBY SENTENCED TO THE KILL LOCK.
HAS THE CONDEMNED ANYTHING TO SAY SO THAT WE MAY HOPEFULLY LEARN SOMETHING FROM THE LIFE YOU LED?
...I WANNA SAY THAT I'M SORRY... BUT NOT TO YOU.
THE KILL LOCK COMMENCES.
GAH!!
NOW:

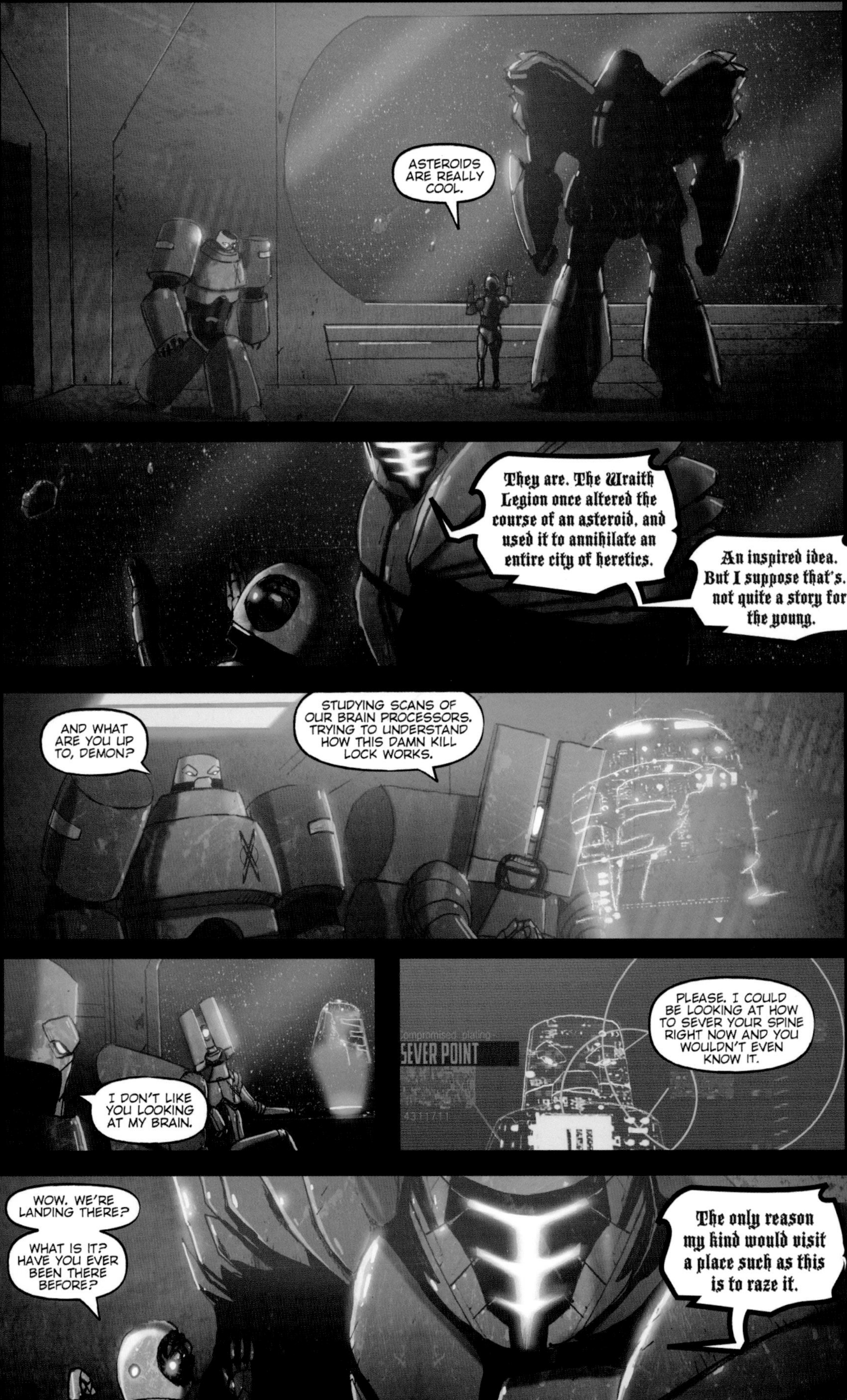
ASTEROIDS ARE REALLY COOL.
They are. The Wraith Legion once altered the course of an asteroid, and used it to annihilate an entire city of heretics.
An inspired idea. But I suppose that's... not quite a story for the young.
AND WHAT ARE YOU UP TO, DEMON?
STUDYING SCANS OF OUR BRAIN PROCESSORS. TRYING TO UNDERSTAND HOW THIS DAMN KILL LOCK WORKS.
I DON'T LIKE YOU LOOKING AT MY BRAIN.
Compromised plating
SEVER POINT
PLEASE. I COULD BE LOOKING AT HOW TO SEVER YOUR SPINE RIGHT NOW AND YOU WOULDN'T EVEN KNOW IT.
WOW. WE'RE LANDING THERE?
WHAT IS IT? HAVE YOU EVER BEEN THERE BEFORE?
The only reason my kind would visit a place such as this is to raze it.

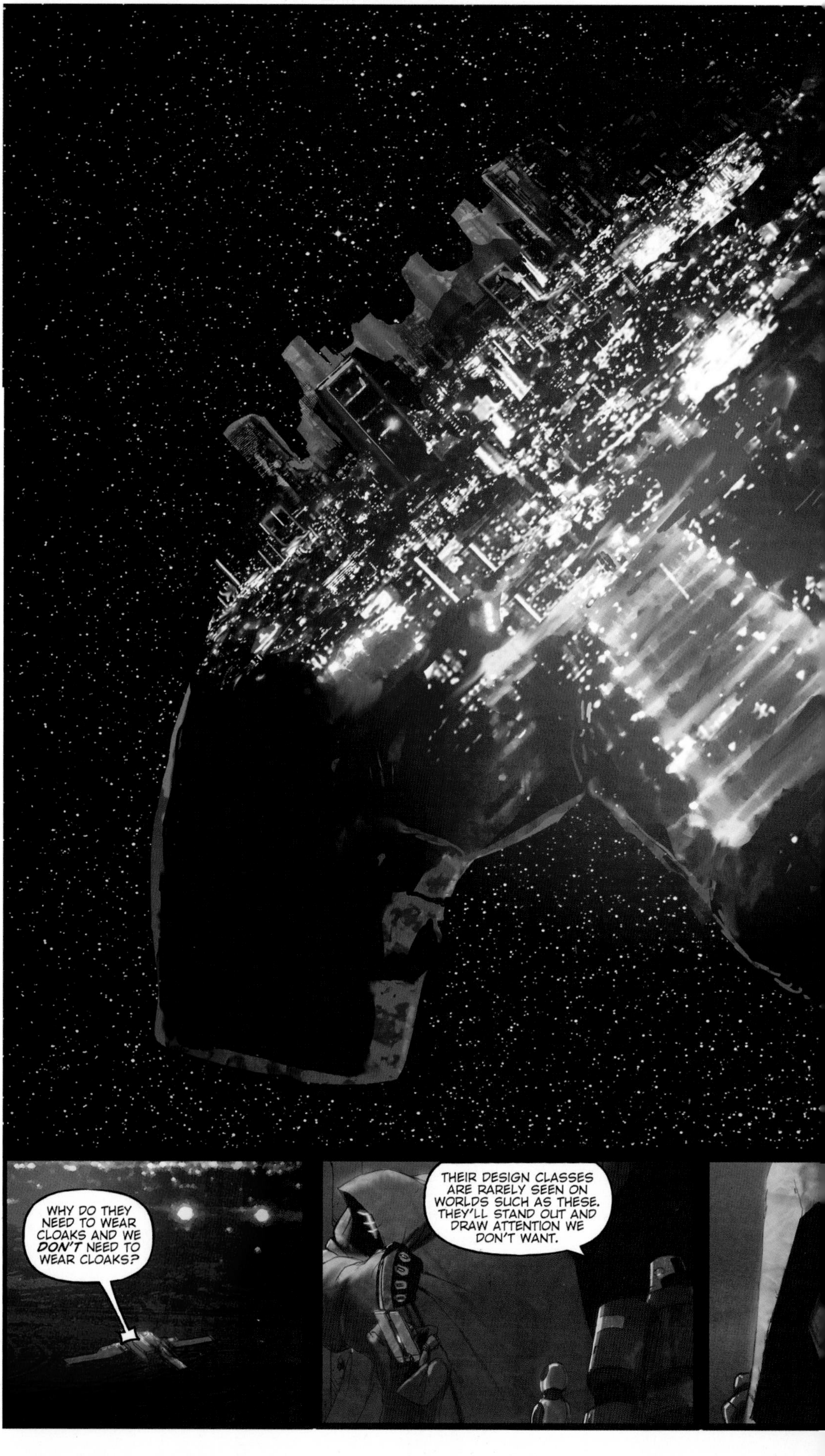
WHY DO THEY NEED TO WEAR CLOAKS AND WE DON'T NEED TO WEAR CLOAKS?
THEIR DESIGN CLASSES ARE RARELY SEEN ON WORLDS SUCH AS THESE. THEY'LL STAND OUT AND DRAW ATTENTION WE DON'T WANT.

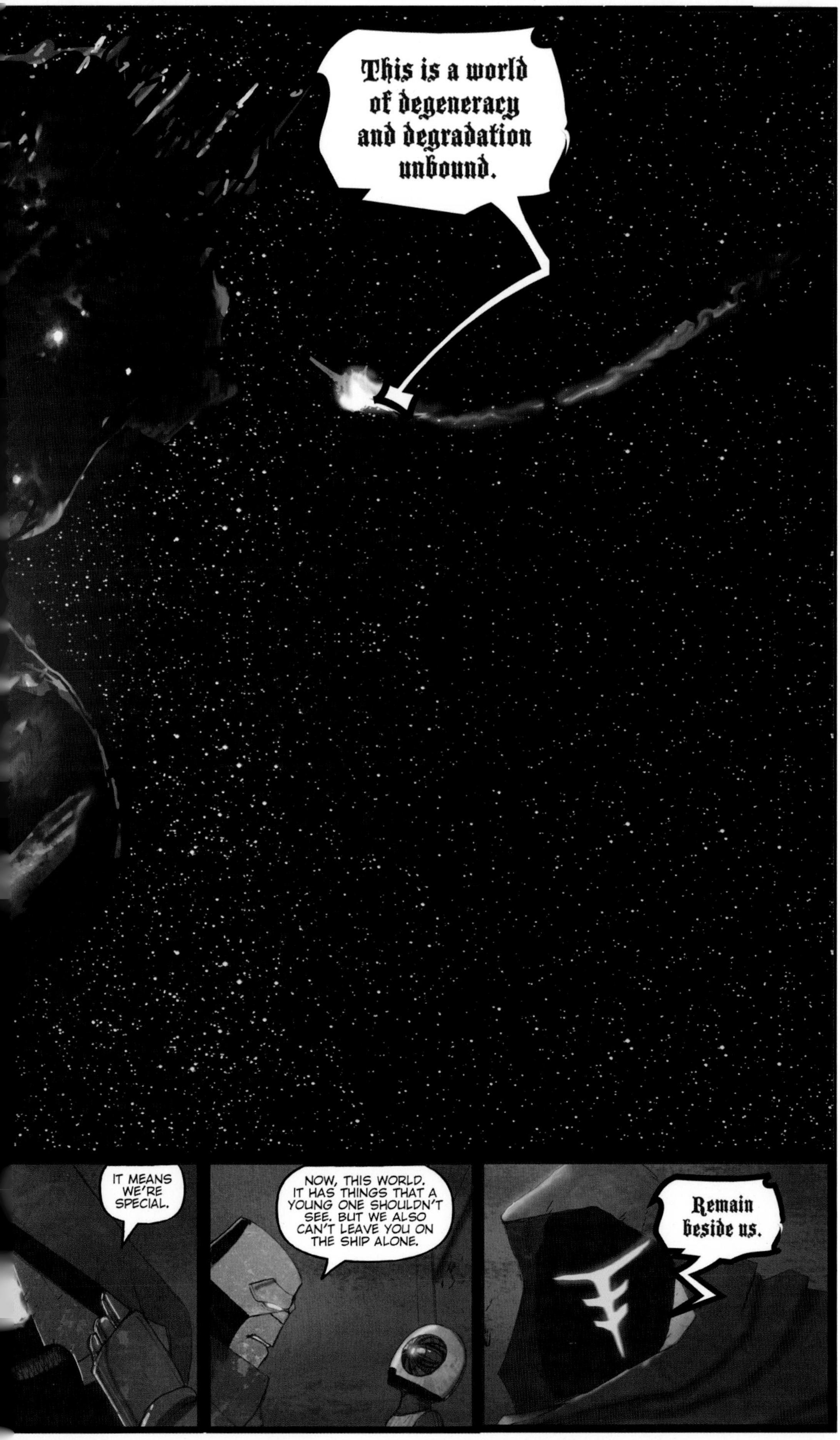
This is a world of degeneracy and degradation unbound.
IT MEANS WE'RE SPECIAL.
NOW, THIS WORLD. IT HAS THINGS THAT A YOUNG ONE SHOULDN'T SEE. BUT WE ALSO CAN'T LEAVE YOU ON THE SHIP ALONE.
Remain beside us.

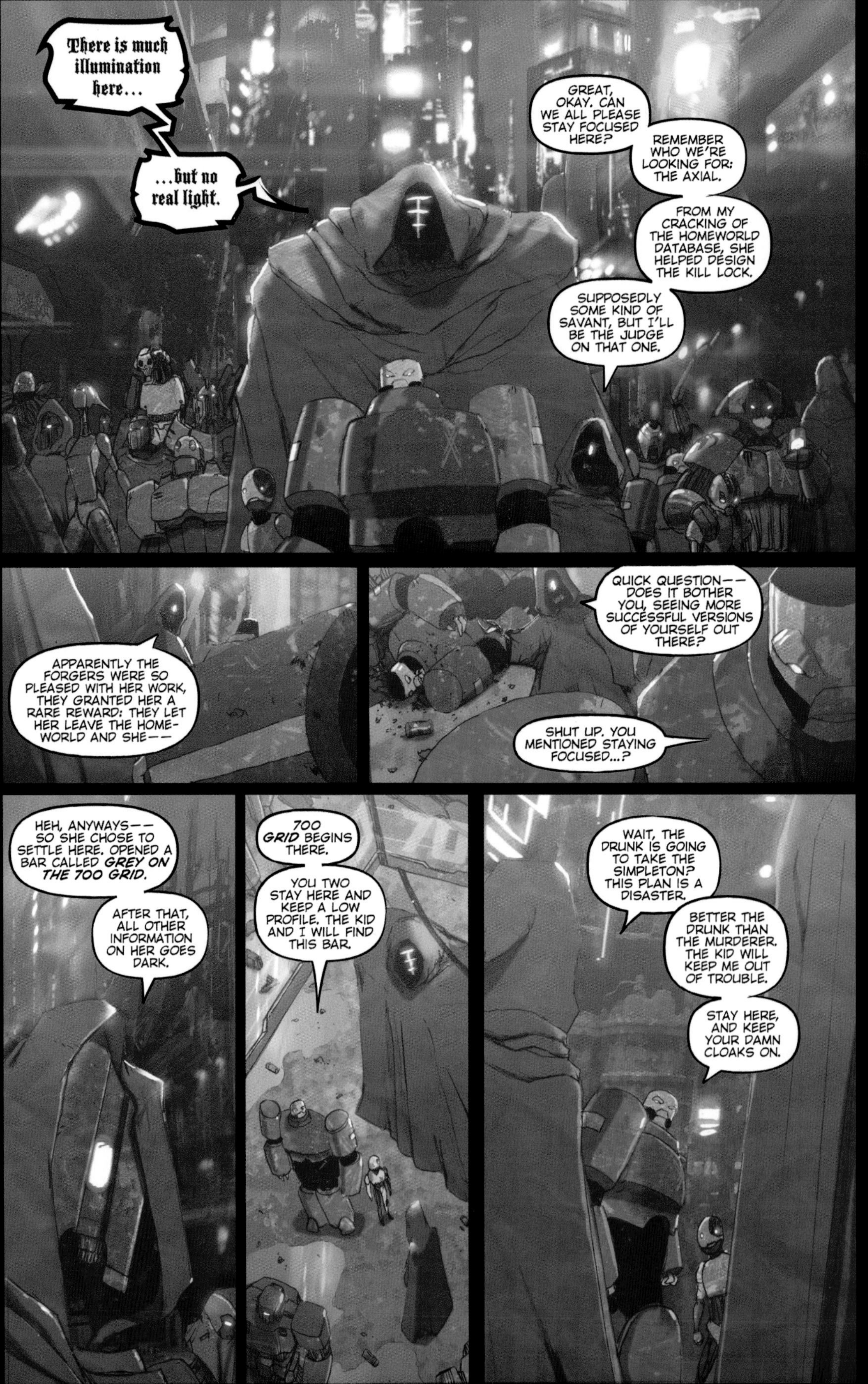
There is much illumination here...
...but no real light.
GREAT, OKAY. CAN WE ALL PLEASE STAY FOCUSED HERE?
REMEMBER WHO WE'RE LOOKING FOR: THE AXIAL.
FROM MY CRACKING OF THE HOMEWORLD DATABASE, SHE HELPED DESIGN THE KILL LOCK.
SUPPOSEDLY SOME KIND OF SAVANT, BUT I'LL BE THE JUDGE ON THAT ONE.
APPARENTLY THE FORGERS WERE SO PLEASED WITH HER WORK, THEY GRANTED HER A RARE REWARD: THEY LET HER LEAVE THE HOME-WORLD AND SHE--
QUICK QUESTION-- DOES IT BOTHER YOU, SEEING MORE SUCCESSFUL VERSIONS OF YOURSELF OUT THERE?
SHUT UP. YOU MENTIONED STAYING FOCUSED...?
HEH, ANYWAYS-- SO SHE CHOSE TO SETTLE HERE. OPENED A BAR CALLED GREY ON THE 700 GRID.
AFTER THAT, ALL OTHER INFORMATION ON HER GOES DARK.
700 GRID BEGINS THERE.
YOU TWO STAY HERE AND KEEP A LOW PROFILE. THE KID AND I WILL FIND THIS BAR.
WAIT, THE DRUNK IS GOING TO TAKE THE SIMPLETON? THIS PLAN IS A DISASTER.
BETTER THE DRUNK THAN THE MURDERER. THE KID WILL KEEP ME OUT OF TROUBLE.
STAY HERE, AND KEEP YOUR DAMN CLOAKS ON.

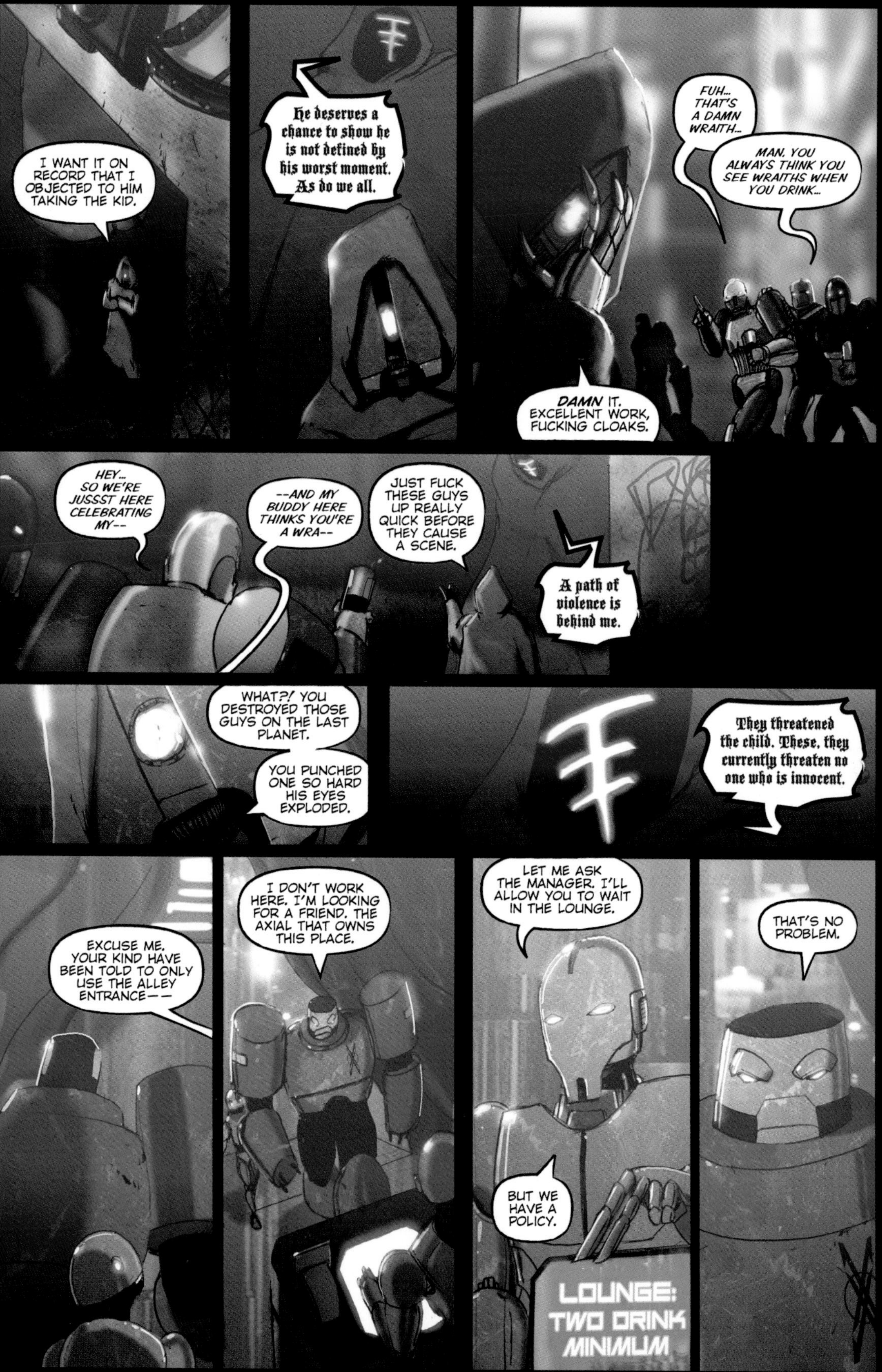
I WANT IT ON RECORD THAT I OBJECTED TO HIM TAKING THE KID.
He deserves a chance to show he is not defined by his worst moment. As do we all.
FUH... THAT'S A DAMN WRAITH...
MAN, YOU ALWAYS THINK YOU SEE WRAITHS WHEN YOU DRINK...
DAMN IT. EXCELLENT WORK, FUCKING CLOAKS.
HEY... SO WE'RE JUSSST HERE CELEBRATING MY--
--AND MY BUDDY HERE THINKS YOU'RE A WRA--
JUST FUCK THESE GUYS UP REALLY QUICK BEFORE THEY CAUSE A SCENE.
A path of violence is behind me.
WHAT?! YOU DESTROYED THOSE GUYS ON THE LAST PLANET.
YOU PUNCHED ONE SO HARD HIS EYES EXPLODED.
They threatened the child. These, they currently threaten no one who is innocent.
EXCUSE ME. YOUR KIND HAVE BEEN TOLD TO ONLY USE THE ALLEY ENTRANCE--
I DON'T WORK HERE. I'M LOOKING FOR A FRIEND. THE AXIAL THAT OWNS THIS PLACE.
LET ME ASK THE MANAGER. I'LL ALLOW YOU TO WAIT IN THE LOUNGE.
BUT WE HAVE A POLICY.
LOUNGE: TWO DRINK MINIMUM
THAT'S NO PROBLEM.

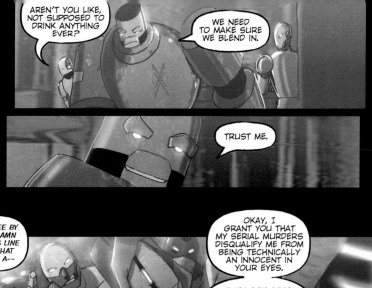

AREN'T YOU LIKE, NOT SUPPOSED TO DRINK ANYTHING EVER?

WE NEED TO MAKE SURE WE BLEND IN.

TRUST ME.

I CAN SEE BY YOUR DAMN GLOWING LINE EYES THAT YOU'RE A--

OKAY, I GRANT YOU THAT MY SERIAL MURDERS DISQUALIFY ME FROM BEING TECHNICALLY AN INNOCENT IN YOUR EYES.

BUT LOOK AT IT THIS WAY, IF I START DISABLING LIMBS HERE, I MIGHT BE KILLED AND THEN THE INNOCENT KID WILL DIE AS A RESULT. SO BACK ME UP HERE!

Greetings, my addled friends.

Most astute of you. The Wraith Legion has indeed dispatched me here on a special mission.

I would appreciate your discretion as I carry it out. May I place trust in you?

IT'S FUNNY... WHEN I FIRST TASTED THIS, I HATED IT.

AND NOW...

I REALLY AM SORRY ABOUT YOU BEING INVOLVED IN THIS. YOU REALLY DON'T DESERVE THIS, BEING WHAT YOU ARE.

WHAT AM I? NOBODY WILL TELL ME.

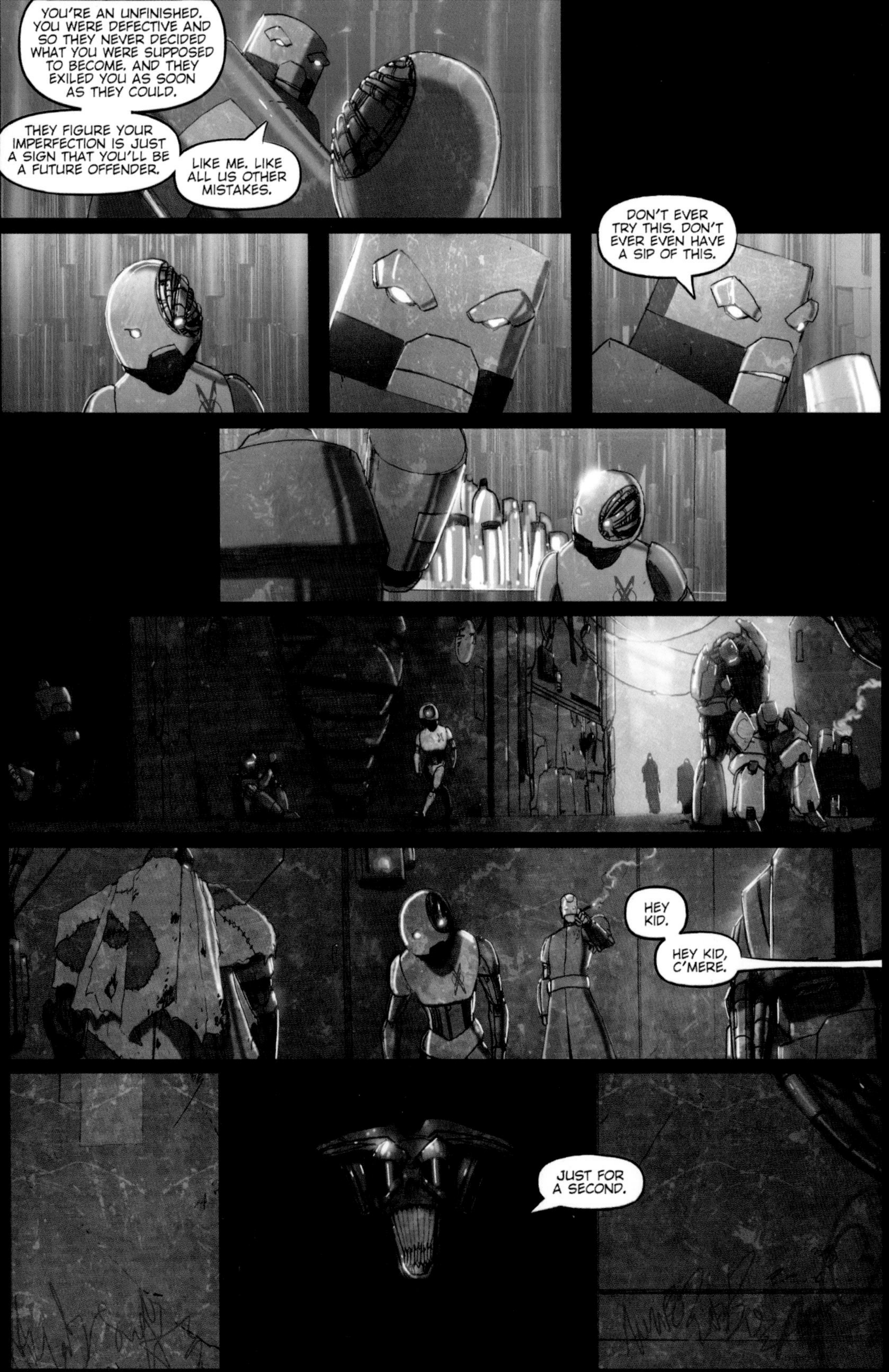
YOU'RE AN UNFINISHED. YOU WERE DEFECTIVE AND SO THEY NEVER DECIDED WHAT YOU WERE SUPPOSED TO BECOME. AND THEY EXILED YOU AS SOON AS THEY COULD.
THEY FIGURE YOUR IMPERFECTION IS JUST A SIGN THAT YOU'LL BE A FUTURE OFFENDER.
LIKE ME. LIKE ALL US OTHER MISTAKES.
DON'T EVER TRY THIS. DON'T EVER EVEN HAVE A SIP OF THIS.
HEY KID.
HEY KID, C'MERE.
JUST FOR A SECOND.

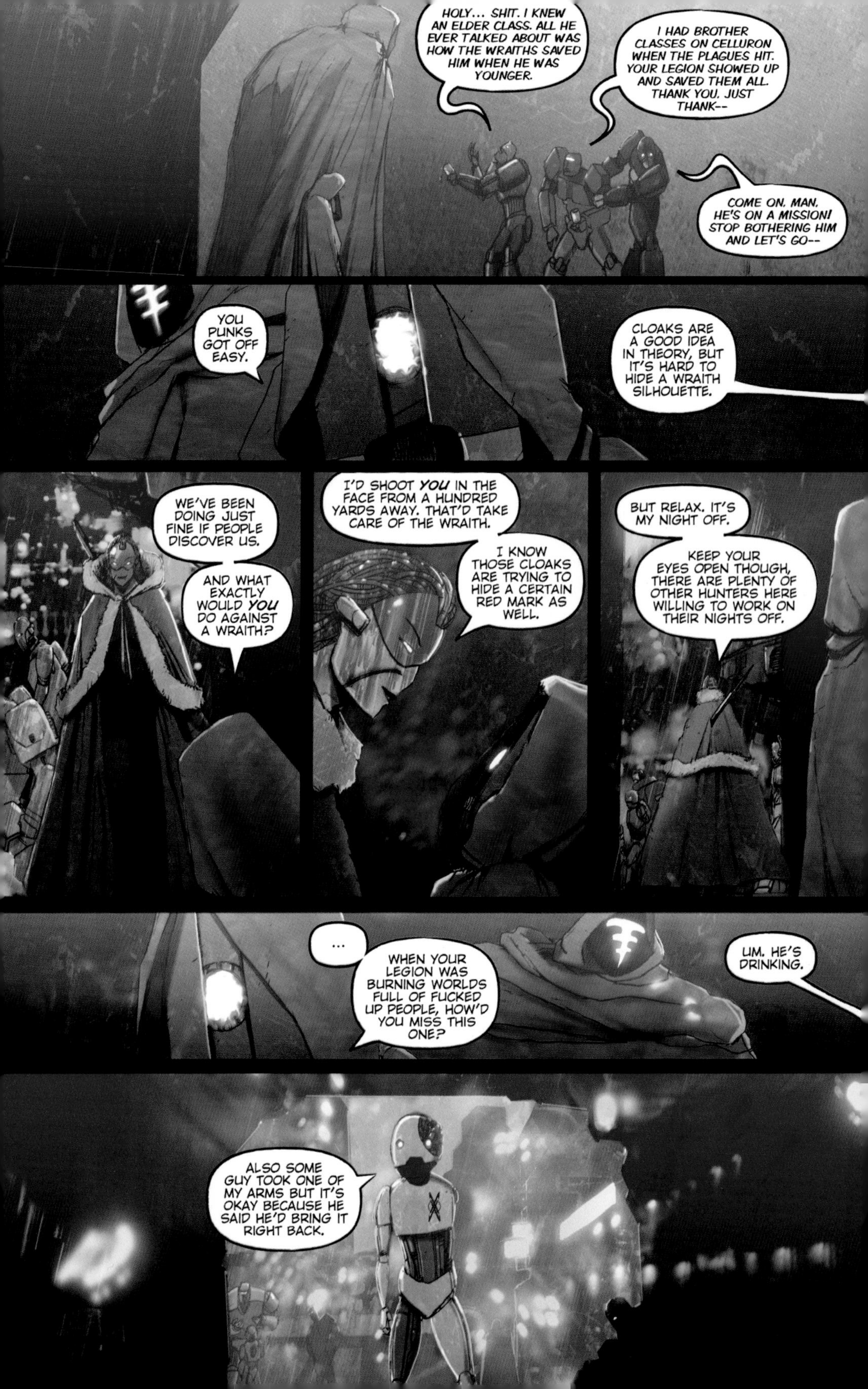
HOLY... SHIT. I KNEW AN ELDER CLASS. ALL HE EVER TALKED ABOUT WAS HOW THE WRAITHS SAVED HIM WHEN HE WAS YOUNGER.
I HAD BROTHER CLASSES ON CELLURON WHEN THE PLAGUES HIT. YOUR LEGION SHOWED UP AND SAVED THEM ALL. THANK YOU. JUST THANK--
COME ON, MAN. HE'S ON A MISSION! STOP BOTHERING HIM AND LET'S GO--
YOU PUNKS GOT OFF EASY.
CLOAKS ARE A GOOD IDEA IN THEORY, BUT IT'S HARD TO HIDE A WRAITH SILHOUETTE.
WE'VE BEEN DOING JUST FINE IF PEOPLE DISCOVER US.
AND WHAT EXACTLY WOULD *YOU* DO AGAINST A WRAITH?
I'D SHOOT *YOU* IN THE FACE FROM A HUNDRED YARDS AWAY. THAT'D TAKE CARE OF THE WRAITH.
I KNOW THOSE CLOAKS ARE TRYING TO HIDE A CERTAIN RED MARK AS WELL.
BUT RELAX. IT'S MY NIGHT OFF.
KEEP YOUR EYES OPEN THOUGH, THERE ARE PLENTY OF OTHER HUNTERS HERE WILLING TO WORK ON THEIR NIGHTS OFF.
...
WHEN YOUR LEGION WAS BURNING WORLDS FULL OF FUCKED UP PEOPLE, HOW'D YOU MISS THIS ONE?
UM. HE'S DRINKING.
ALSO SOME GUY TOOK ONE OF MY ARMS BUT IT'S OKAY BECAUSE HE SAID HE'D BRING IT RIGHT BACK.

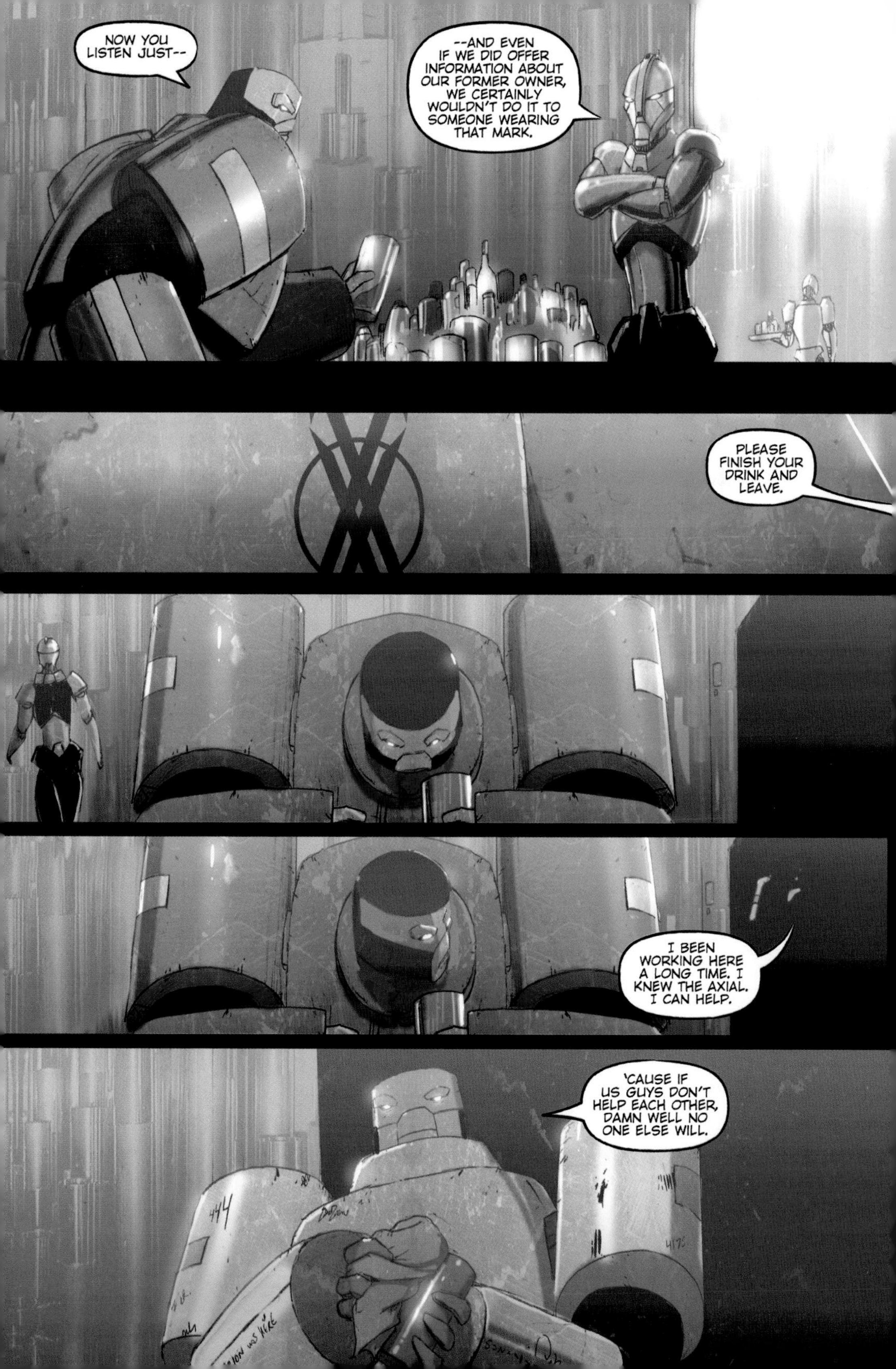
NOW YOU LISTEN JUST--
--AND EVEN IF WE DID OFFER INFORMATION ABOUT OUR FORMER OWNER, WE CERTAINLY WOULDN'T DO IT TO SOMEONE WEARING THAT MARK.
PLEASE FINISH YOUR DRINK AND LEAVE.
I BEEN WORKING HERE A LONG TIME. I KNEW THE AXIAL. I CAN HELP.
'CAUSE IF US GUYS DON'T HELP EACH OTHER, DAMN WELL NO ONE ELSE WILL.

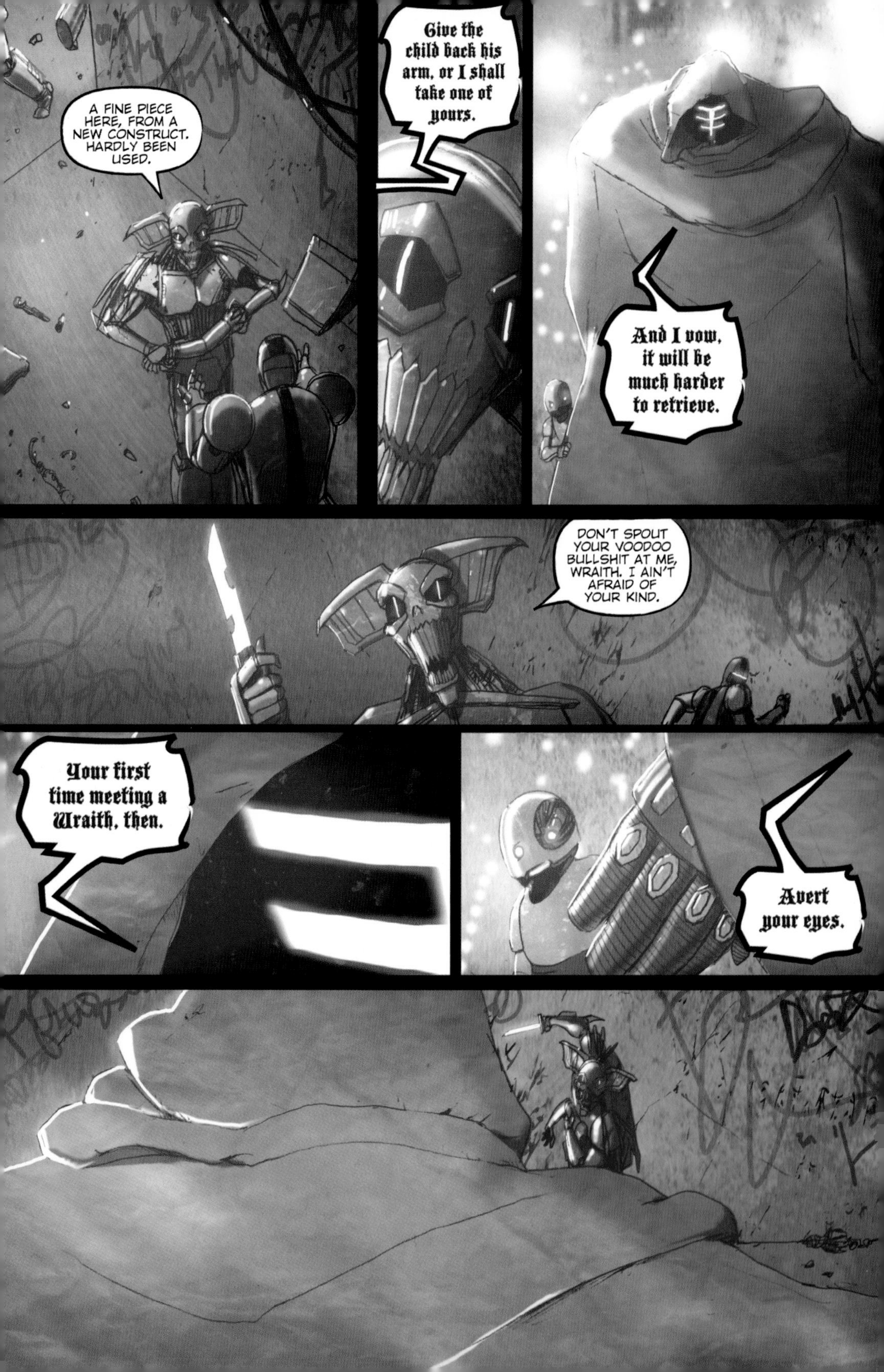
A FINE PIECE HERE, FROM A NEW CONSTRUCT. HARDLY BEEN USED.
Give the child back his arm, or I shall take one of yours.
And I vow, it will be much harder to retrieve.
DON'T SPOUT YOUR VOODOO BULLSHIT AT ME, WRAITH. I AIN'T AFRAID OF YOUR KIND.
Your first time meeting a Wraith, then.
Avert your eyes.

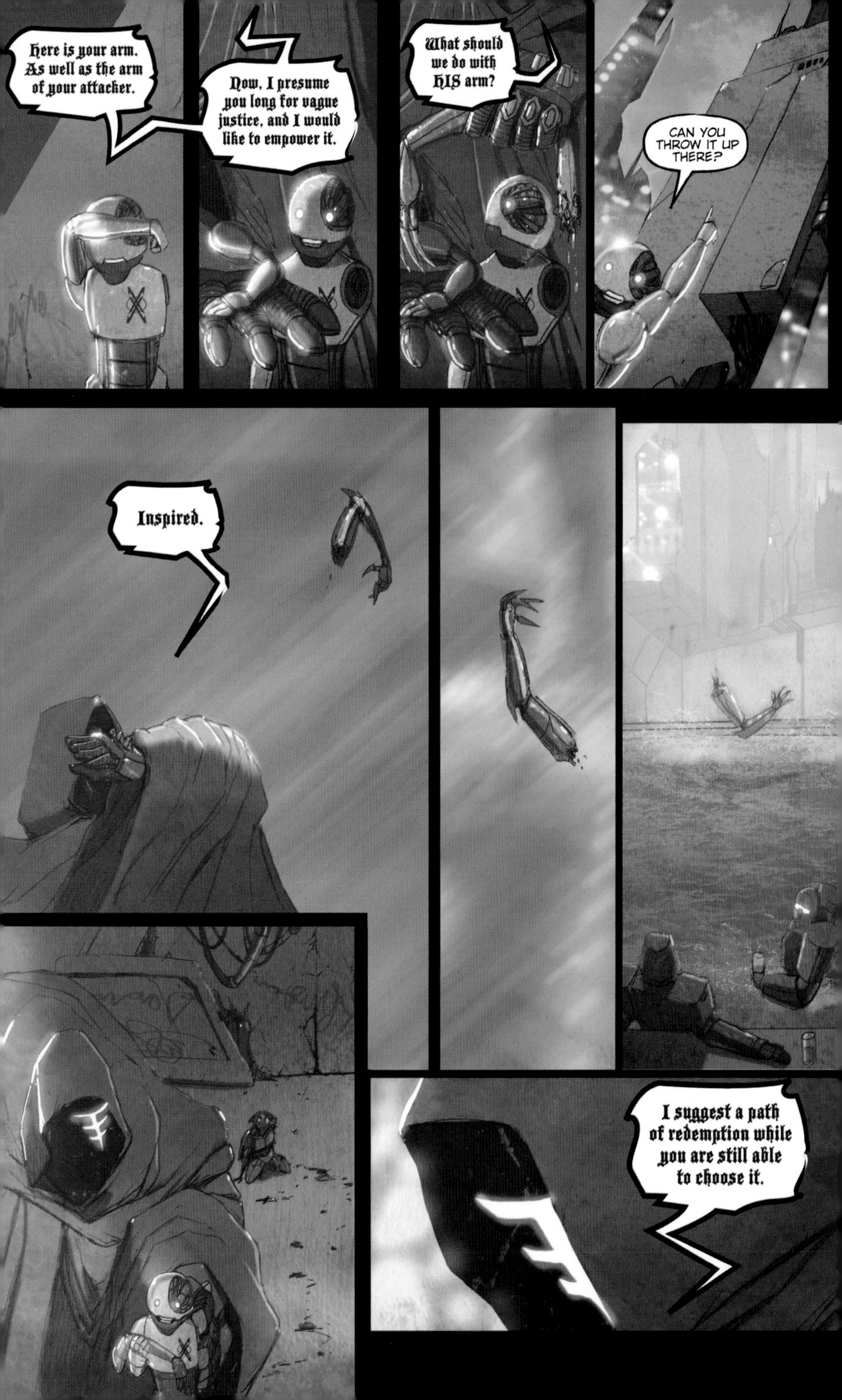
Here is your arm. As well as the arm of your attacker.
Now, I presume you long for vague justice, and I would like to empower it.
What should we do with HIS arm?
CAN YOU THROW IT UP THERE?
Inspired.
I suggest a path of redemption while you are still able to choose it.

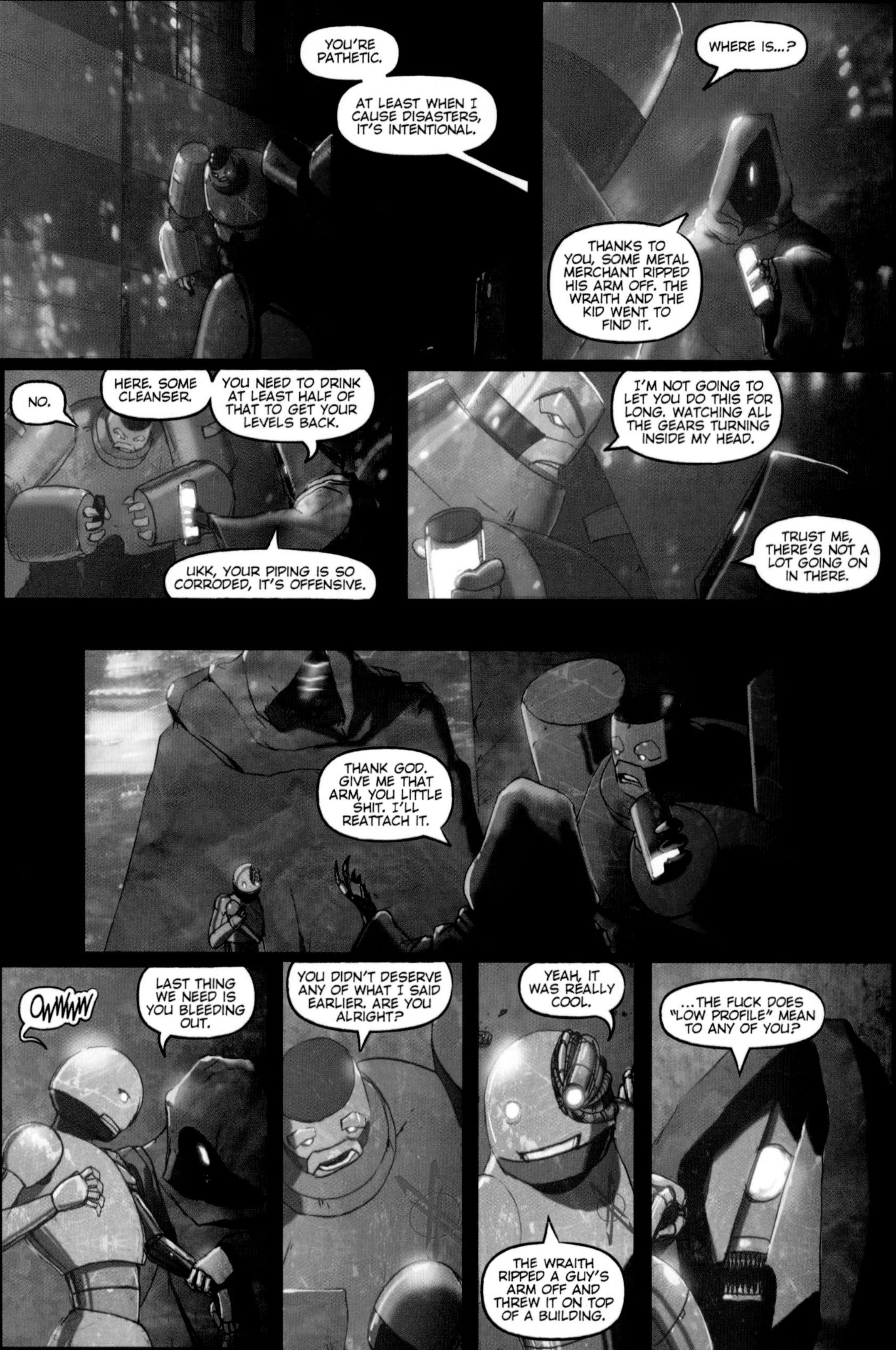
YOU'RE PATHETIC.
AT LEAST WHEN I CAUSE DISASTERS, IT'S INTENTIONAL.
WHERE IS...?
THANKS TO YOU, SOME METAL MERCHANT RIPPED HIS ARM OFF. THE WRAITH AND THE KID WENT TO FIND IT.
NO.
HERE. SOME CLEANSER.
YOU NEED TO DRINK AT LEAST HALF OF THAT TO GET YOUR LEVELS BACK.
UKK, YOUR PIPING IS SO CORRODED, IT'S OFFENSIVE.
I'M NOT GOING TO LET YOU DO THIS FOR LONG. WATCHING ALL THE GEARS TURNING INSIDE MY HEAD.
TRUST ME, THERE'S NOT A LOT GOING ON IN THERE.
THANK GOD. GIVE ME THAT ARM, YOU LITTLE SHIT. I'LL REATTACH IT.
OWWWW
LAST THING WE NEED IS YOU BLEEDING OUT.
YOU DIDN'T DESERVE ANY OF WHAT I SAID EARLIER. ARE YOU ALRIGHT?
YEAH, IT WAS REALLY COOL.
THE WRAITH RIPPED A GUY'S ARM OFF AND THREW IT ON TOP OF A BUILDING.
...THE FUCK DOES "LOW PROFILE" MEAN TO ANY OF YOU?

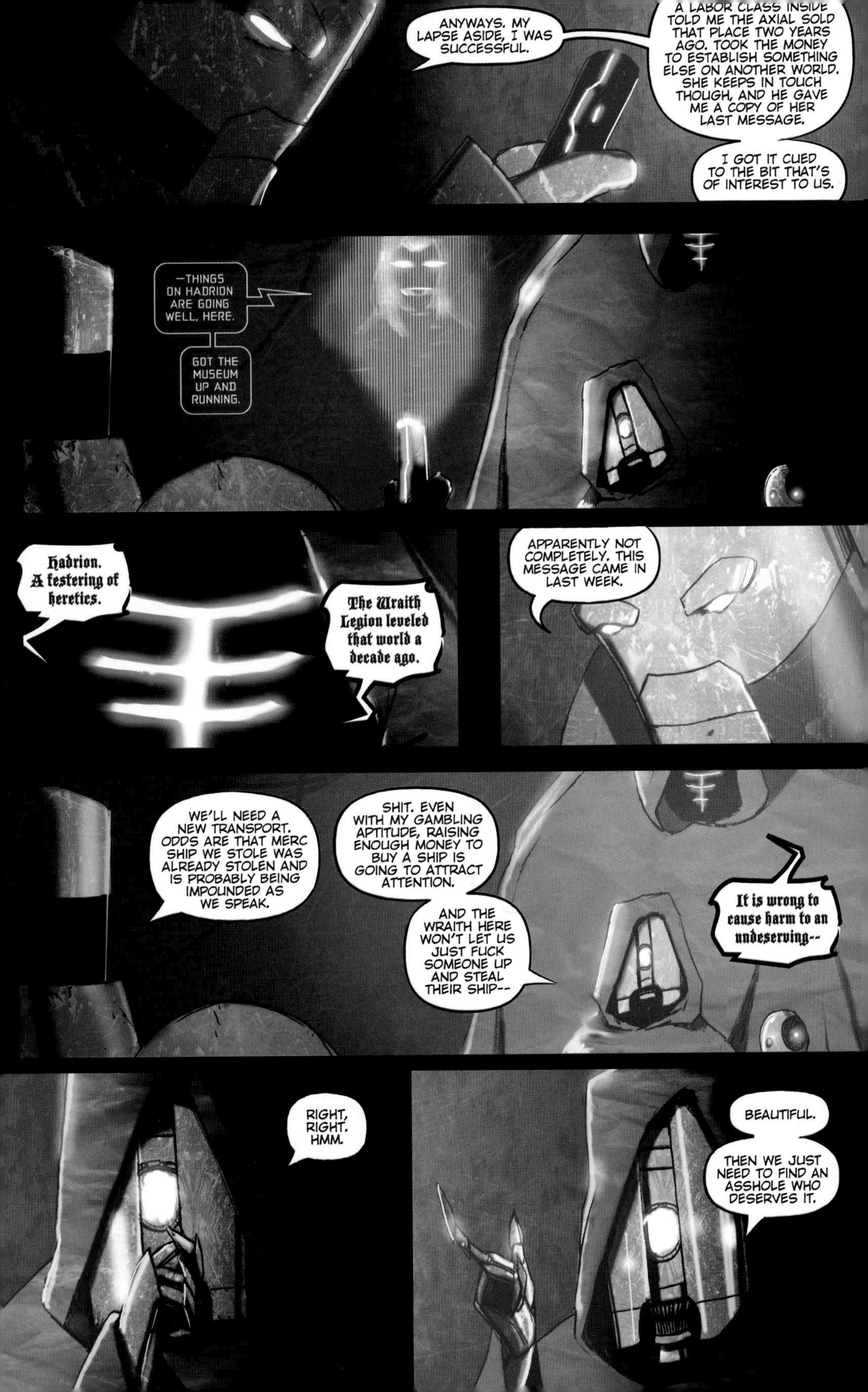
ANYWAYS. MY LAPSE ASIDE, I WAS SUCCESSFUL.
A LABOR CLASS INSIDE TOLD ME THE AXIAL SOLD THAT PLACE TWO YEARS AGO. TOOK THE MONEY TO ESTABLISH SOMETHING ELSE ON ANOTHER WORLD. SHE KEEPS IN TOUCH THOUGH, AND HE GAVE ME A COPY OF HER LAST MESSAGE.
I GOT IT CUED TO THE BIT THAT'S OF INTEREST TO US.
—THINGS ON HADRION ARE GOING WELL, HERE.
GOT THE MUSEUM UP AND RUNNING.
Hadrion. A festering of heretics.
The Wraith Legion leveled that world a decade ago.
APPARENTLY NOT COMPLETELY. THIS MESSAGE CAME IN LAST WEEK.
WE'LL NEED A NEW TRANSPORT. ODDS ARE THAT MERC SHIP WE STOLE WAS ALREADY STOLEN AND IS PROBABLY BEING IMPOUNDED AS WE SPEAK.
SHIT. EVEN WITH MY GAMBLING APTITUDE, RAISING ENOUGH MONEY TO BUY A SHIP IS GOING TO ATTRACT ATTENTION.
AND THE WRAITH HERE WON'T JUST LET US JUST FUCK SOMEONE UP AND STEAL THEIR SHIP--
It is wrong to cause harm to an undeserving--
RIGHT, RIGHT. HMM.
BEAUTIFUL.
THEN WE JUST NEED TO FIND AN ASSHOLE WHO DESERVES IT.

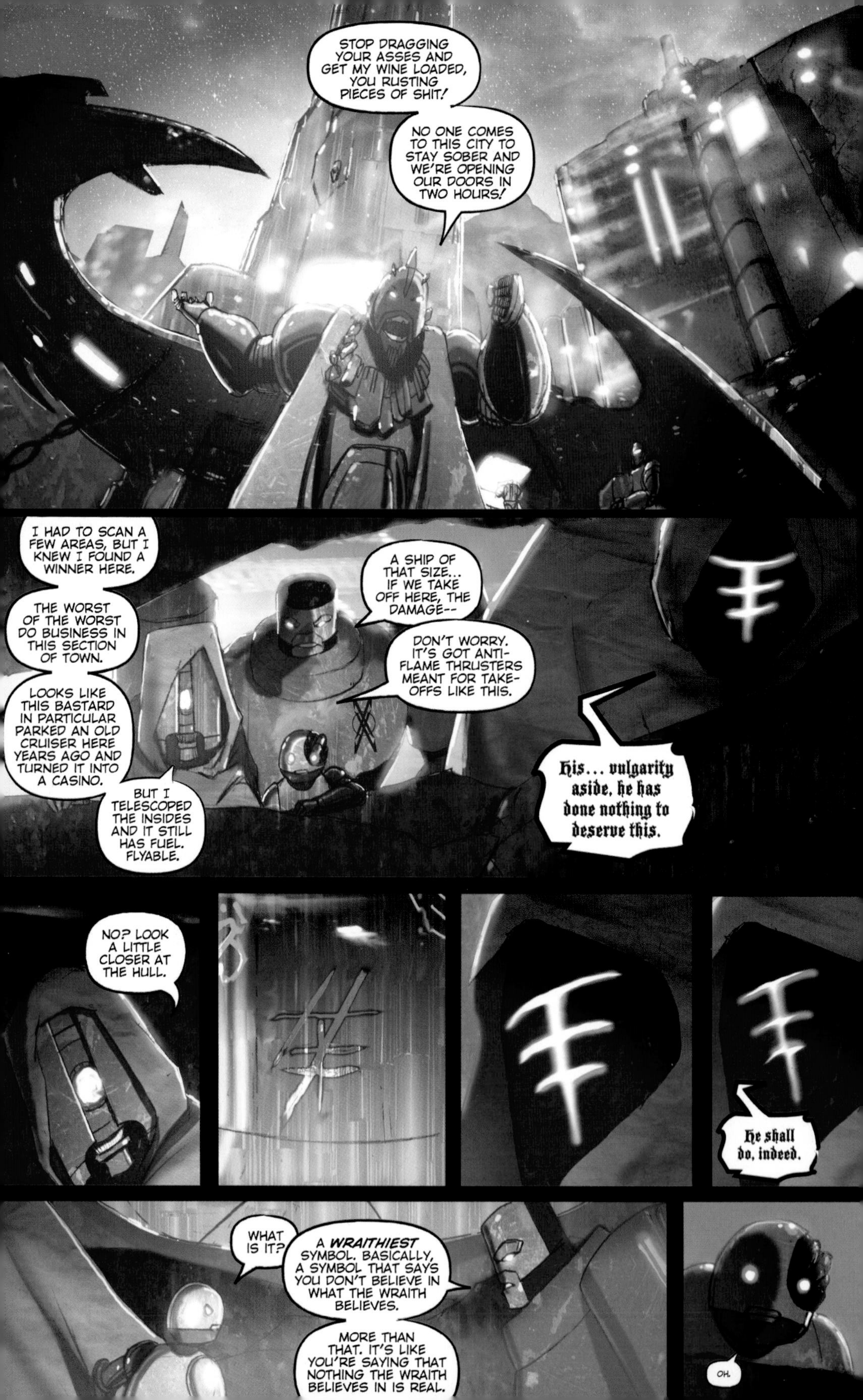
STOP DRAGGING YOUR ASSES AND GET MY WINE LOADED, YOU RUSTING PIECES OF SHIT!
NO ONE COMES TO THIS CITY TO STAY SOBER AND WE'RE OPENING OUR DOORS IN TWO HOURS!
I HAD TO SCAN A FEW AREAS, BUT I KNEW I FOUND A WINNER HERE.
THE WORST OF THE WORST DO BUSINESS IN THIS SECTION OF TOWN.
LOOKS LIKE THIS BASTARD IN PARTICULAR PARKED AN OLD CRUISER HERE YEARS AGO AND TURNED IT INTO A CASINO.
BUT I TELESCOPED THE INSIDES AND IT STILL HAS FUEL. FLYABLE.
A SHIP OF THAT SIZE... IF WE TAKE OFF HERE, THE DAMAGE--
DON'T WORRY. IT'S GOT ANTI-FLAME THRUSTERS MEANT FOR TAKE-OFFS LIKE THIS.
His... vulgarity aside, he has done nothing to deserve this.
NO? LOOK A LITTLE CLOSER AT THE HULL.
He shall do, indeed.
WHAT IS IT?
A *WRAITHIEST* SYMBOL. BASICALLY, A SYMBOL THAT SAYS YOU DON'T BELIEVE IN WHAT THE WRAITH BELIEVES.
MORE THAN THAT. IT'S LIKE YOU'RE SAYING THAT NOTHING THE WRAITH BELIEVES IN IS REAL.
OH.

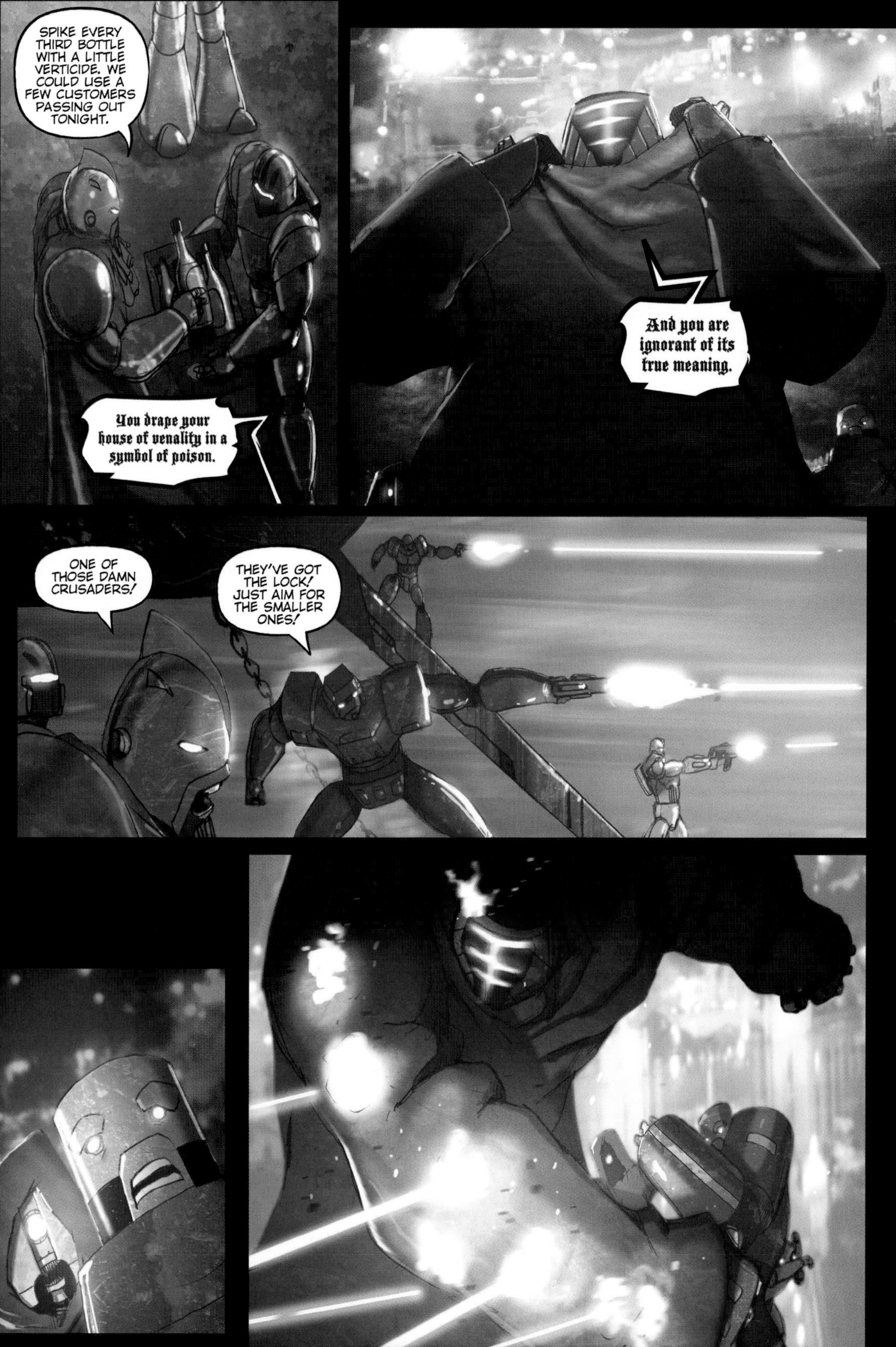
SPIKE EVERY THIRD BOTTLE WITH A LITTLE VERTICIDE. WE COULD USE A FEW CUSTOMERS PASSING OUT TONIGHT.
You drape your house of venality in a symbol of poison.
And you are ignorant of its true meaning.
ONE OF THOSE DAMN CRUSADERS!
THEY'VE GOT THE LOCK! JUST AIM FOR THE SMALLER ONES!

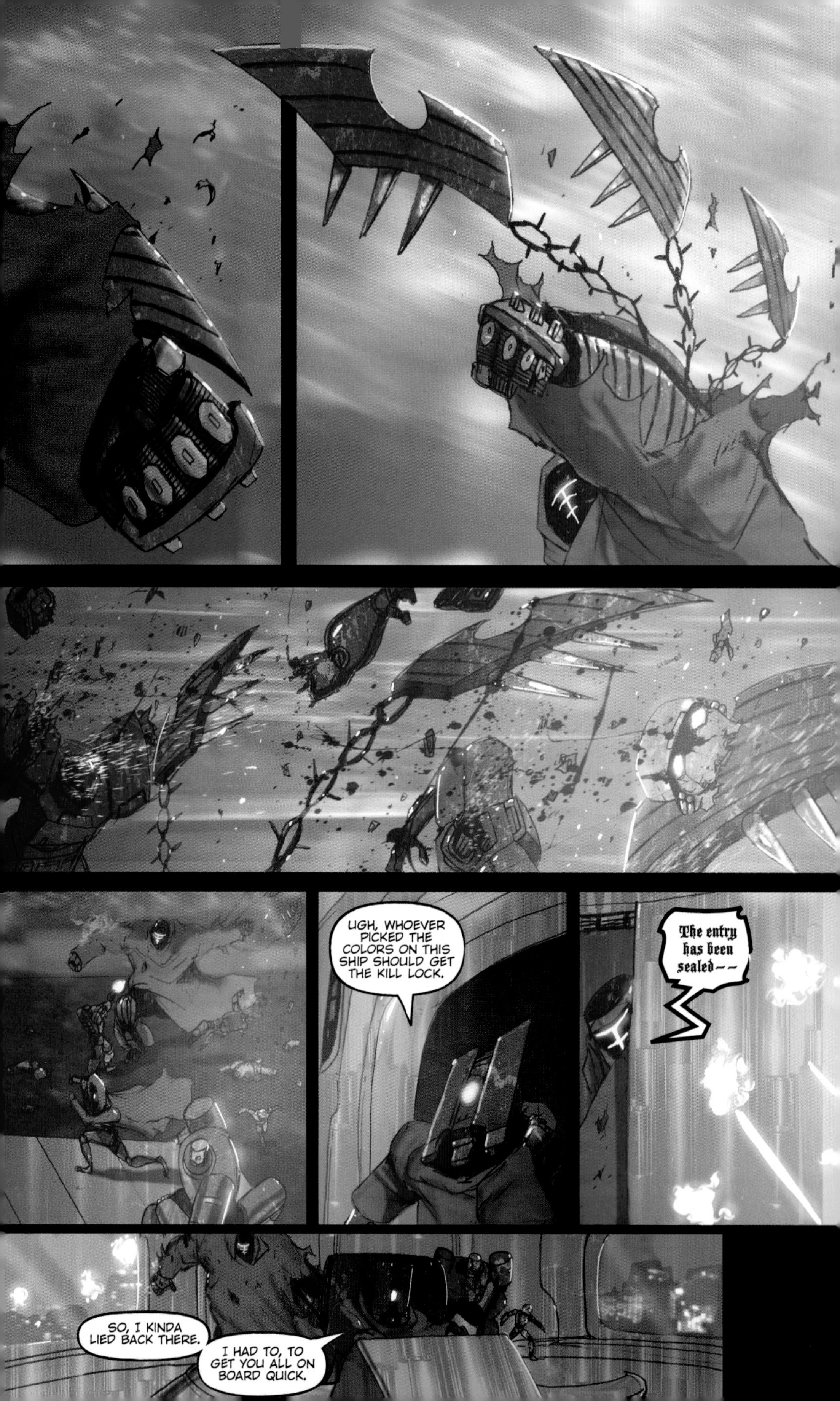
UGH, WHOEVER PICKED THE COLORS ON THIS SHIP SHOULD GET THE KILL LOCK.
The entry has been sealed--
SO, I KINDA LIED BACK THERE.
I HAD TO, TO GET YOU ALL ON BOARD QUICK.

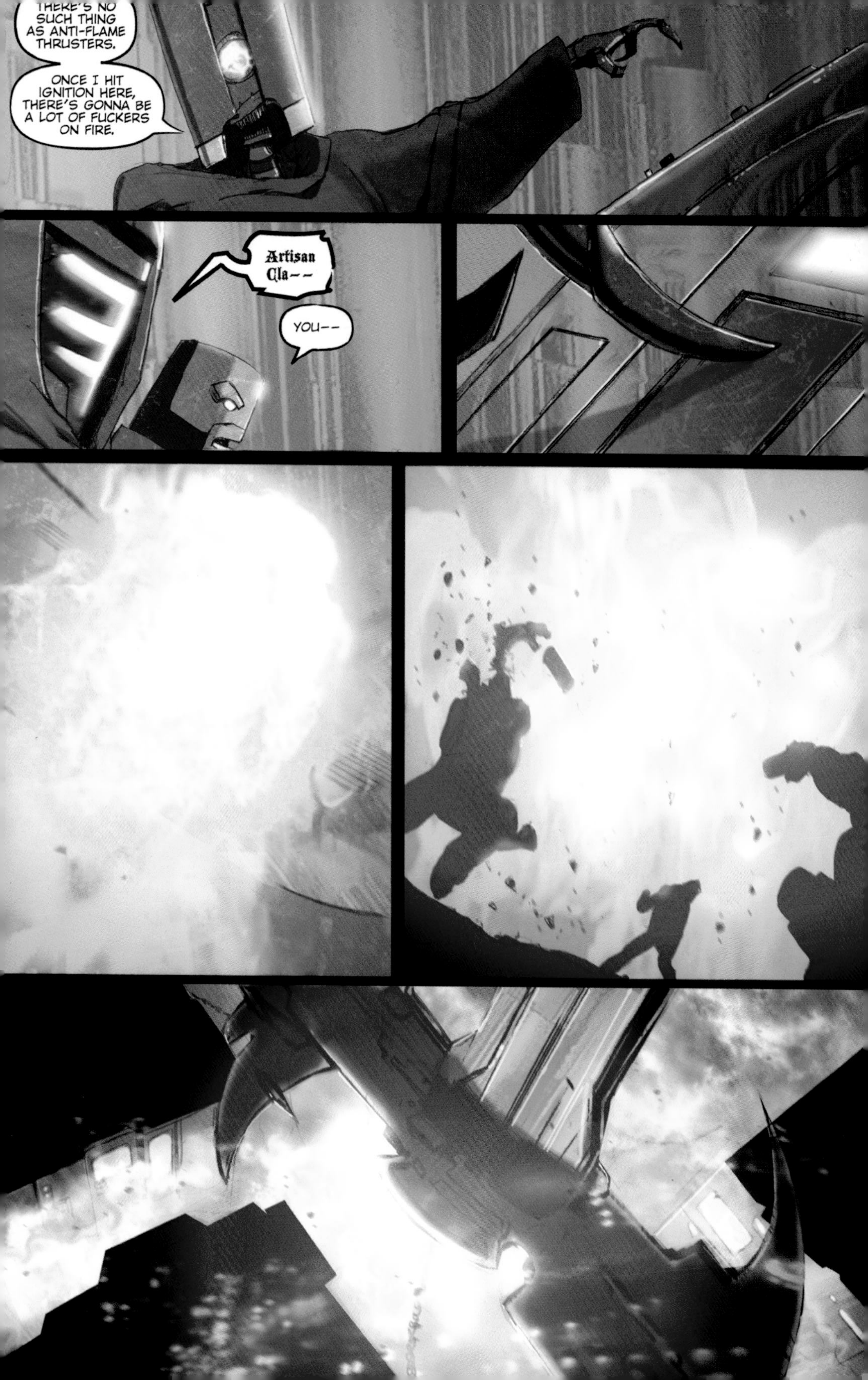
THERE'S NO SUCH THING AS ANTI-FLAME THRUSTERS.
ONCE I HIT IGNITION HERE, THERE'S GONNA BE A LOT OF FUCKERS ON FIRE.
Artisan Cla--
YOU--

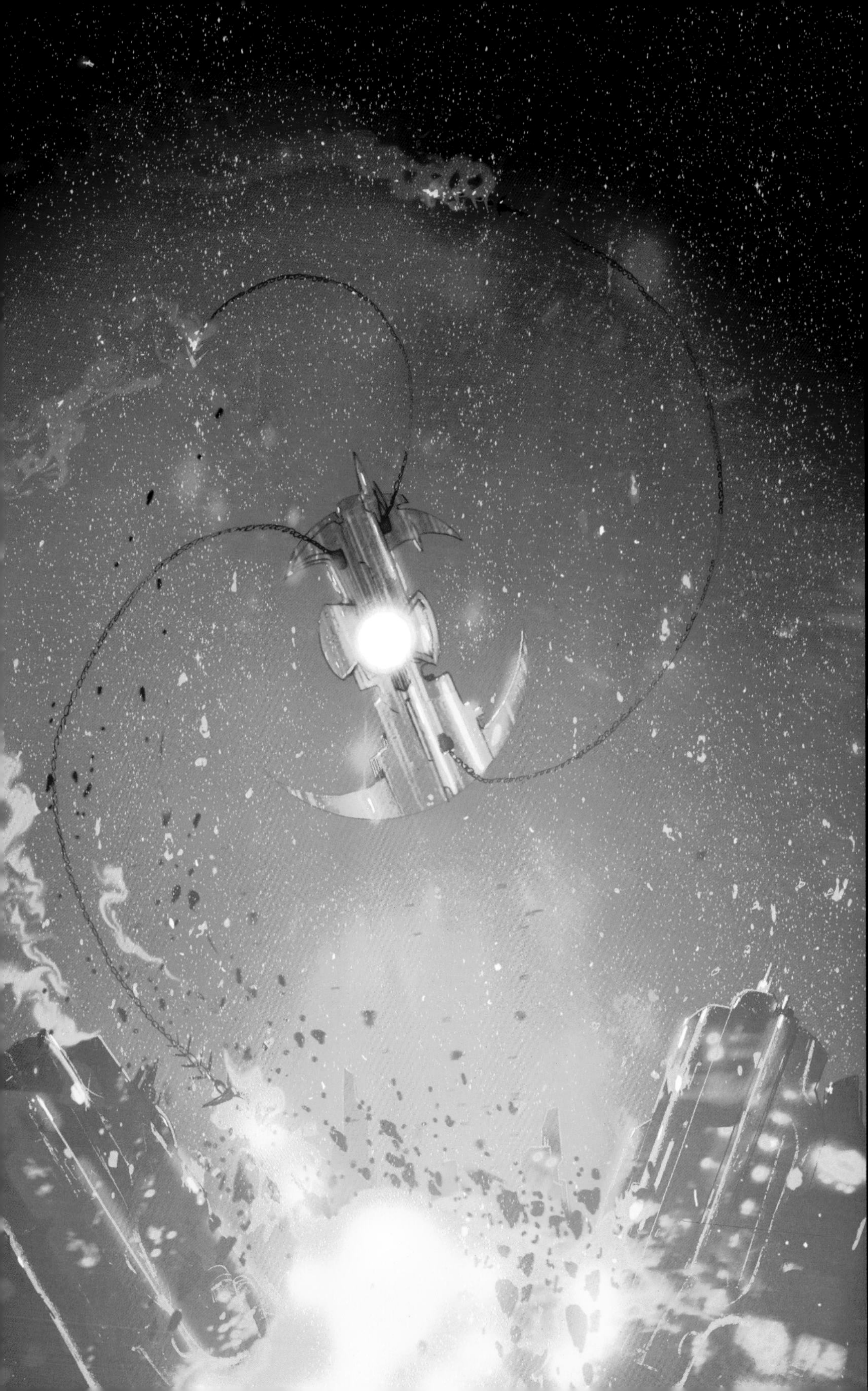

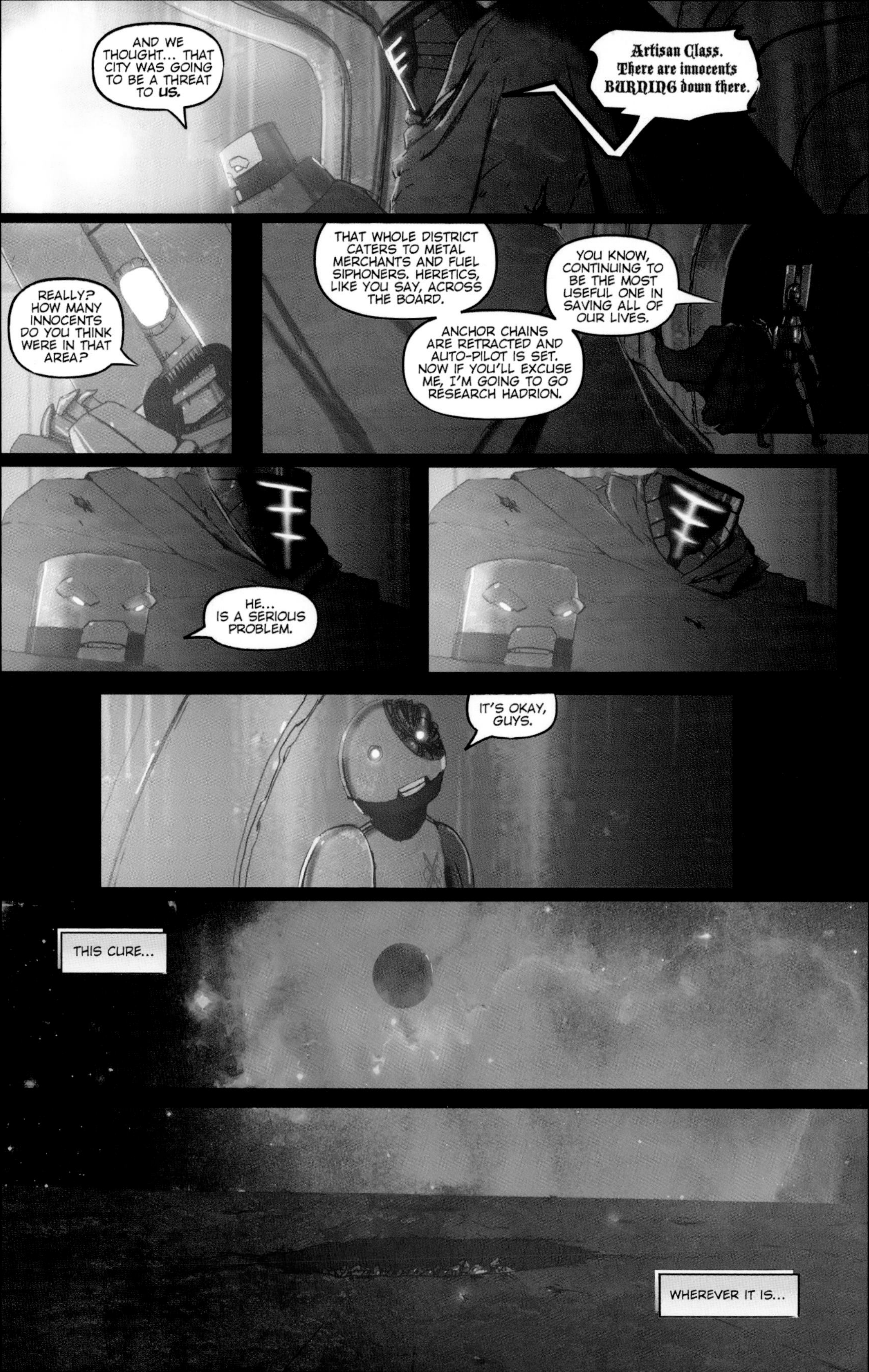
AND WE THOUGHT... THAT CITY WAS GOING TO BE A THREAT TO US.
Artisan Class. There are innocents BURNING down there.
REALLY? HOW MANY INNOCENTS DO YOU THINK WERE IN THAT AREA?
THAT WHOLE DISTRICT CATERS TO METAL MERCHANTS AND FUEL SIPHONERS. HERETICS, LIKE YOU SAY, ACROSS THE BOARD.
ANCHOR CHAINS ARE RETRACTED AND AUTO-PILOT IS SET. NOW IF YOU'LL EXCUSE ME, I'M GOING TO GO RESEARCH HADRION.
YOU KNOW, CONTINUING TO BE THE MOST USEFUL ONE IN SAVING ALL OF OUR LIVES.
HE... IS A SERIOUS PROBLEM.
IT'S OKAY, GUYS.
THIS CURE...
WHEREVER IT IS...

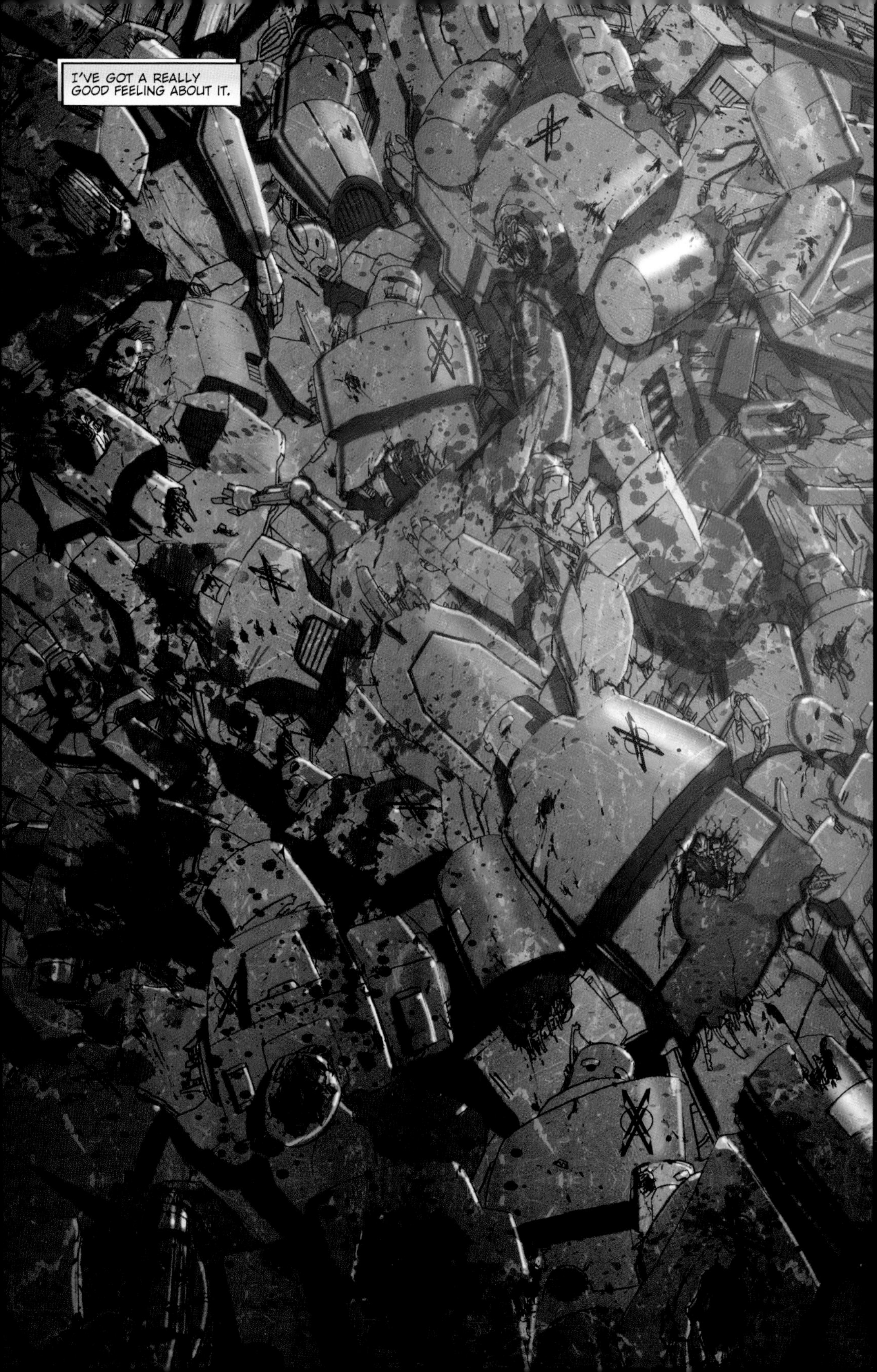
I'VE GOT A REALLY GOOD FEELING ABOUT IT.

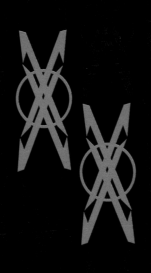

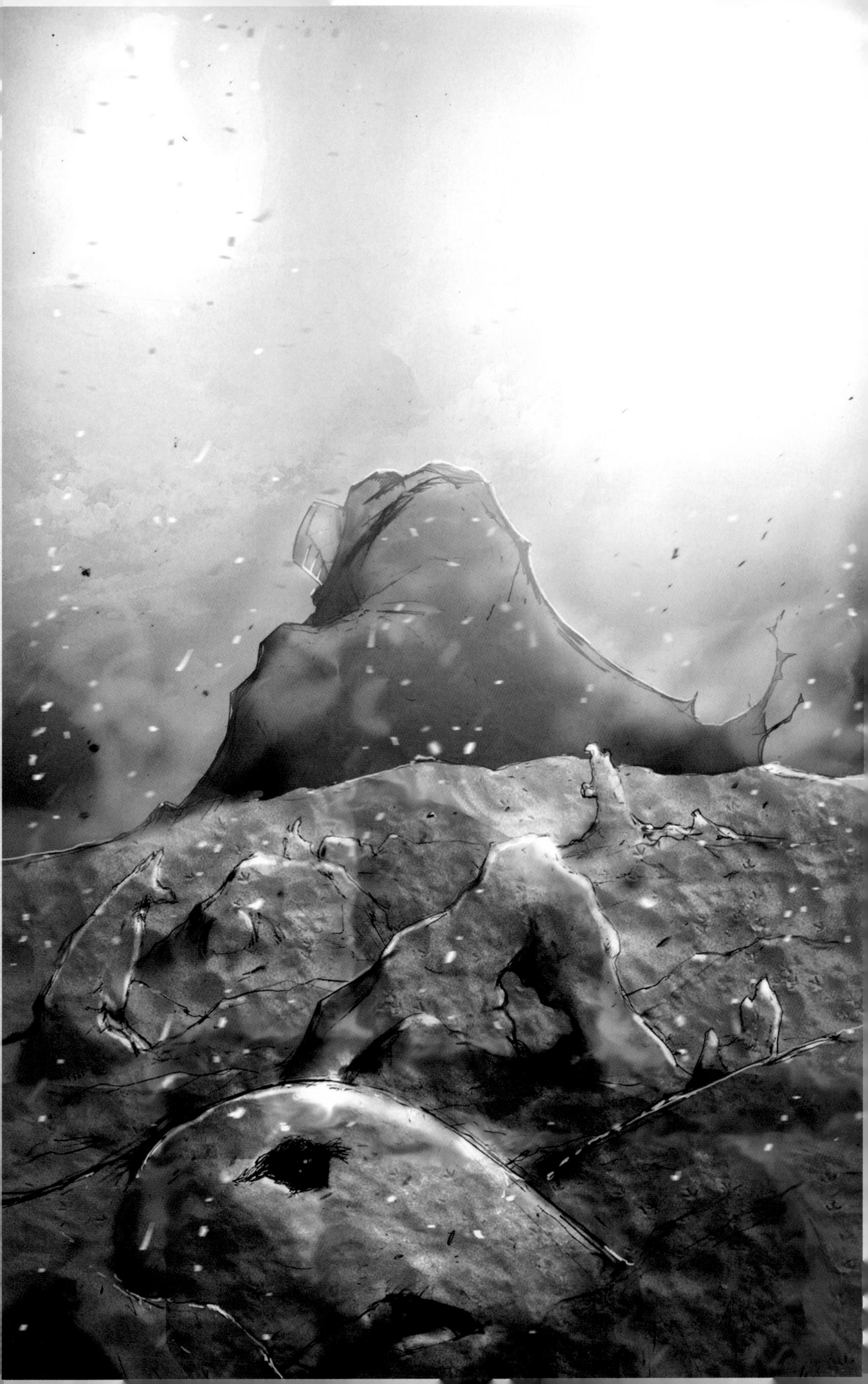

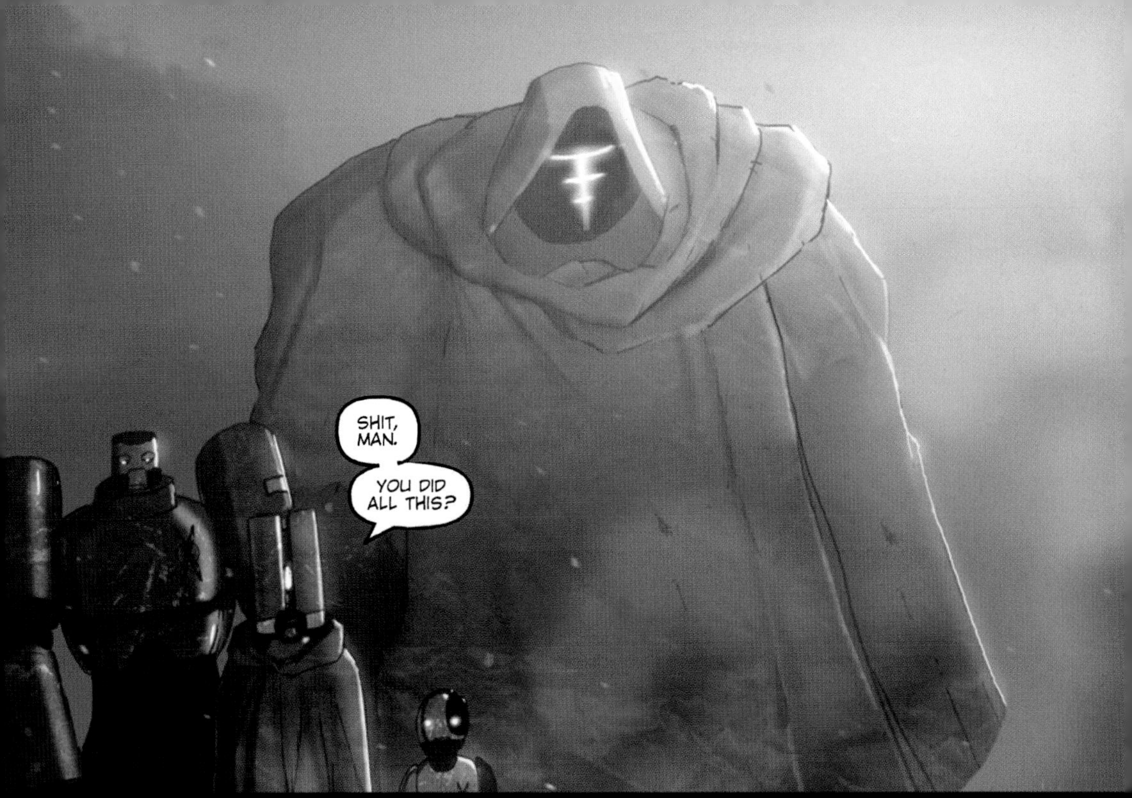
SHIT, MAN.
YOU DID ALL THIS?

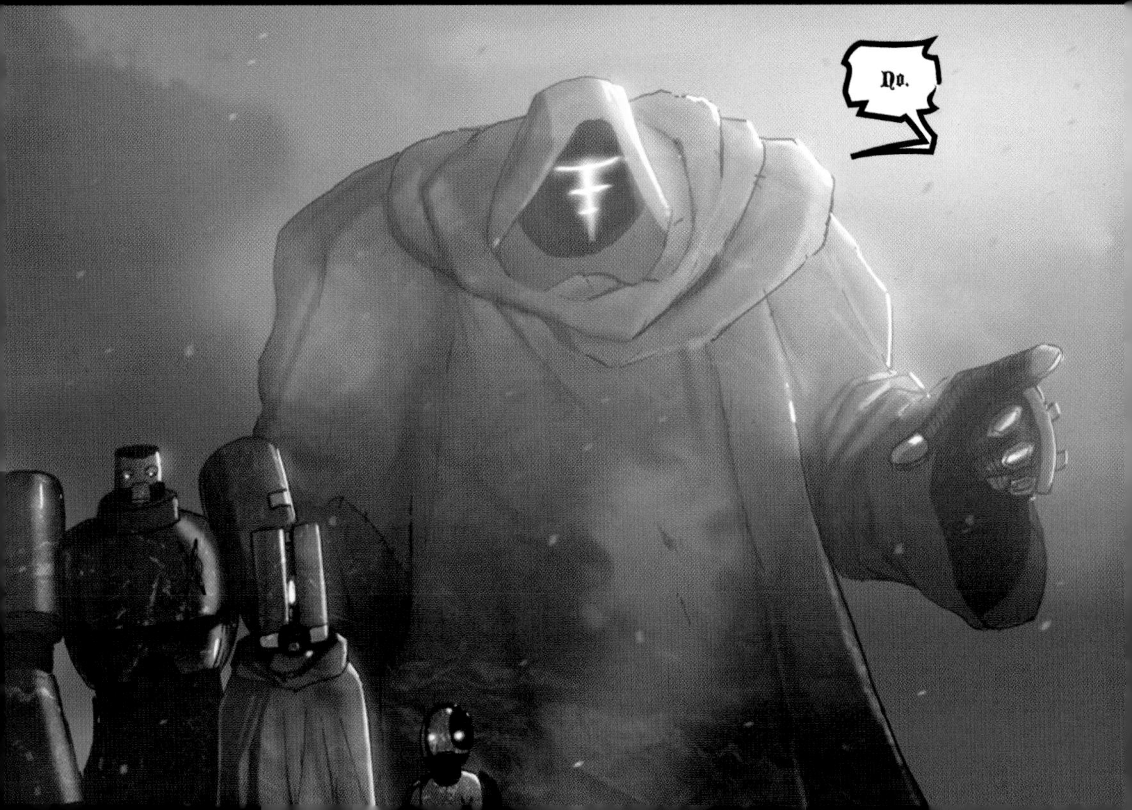
No.

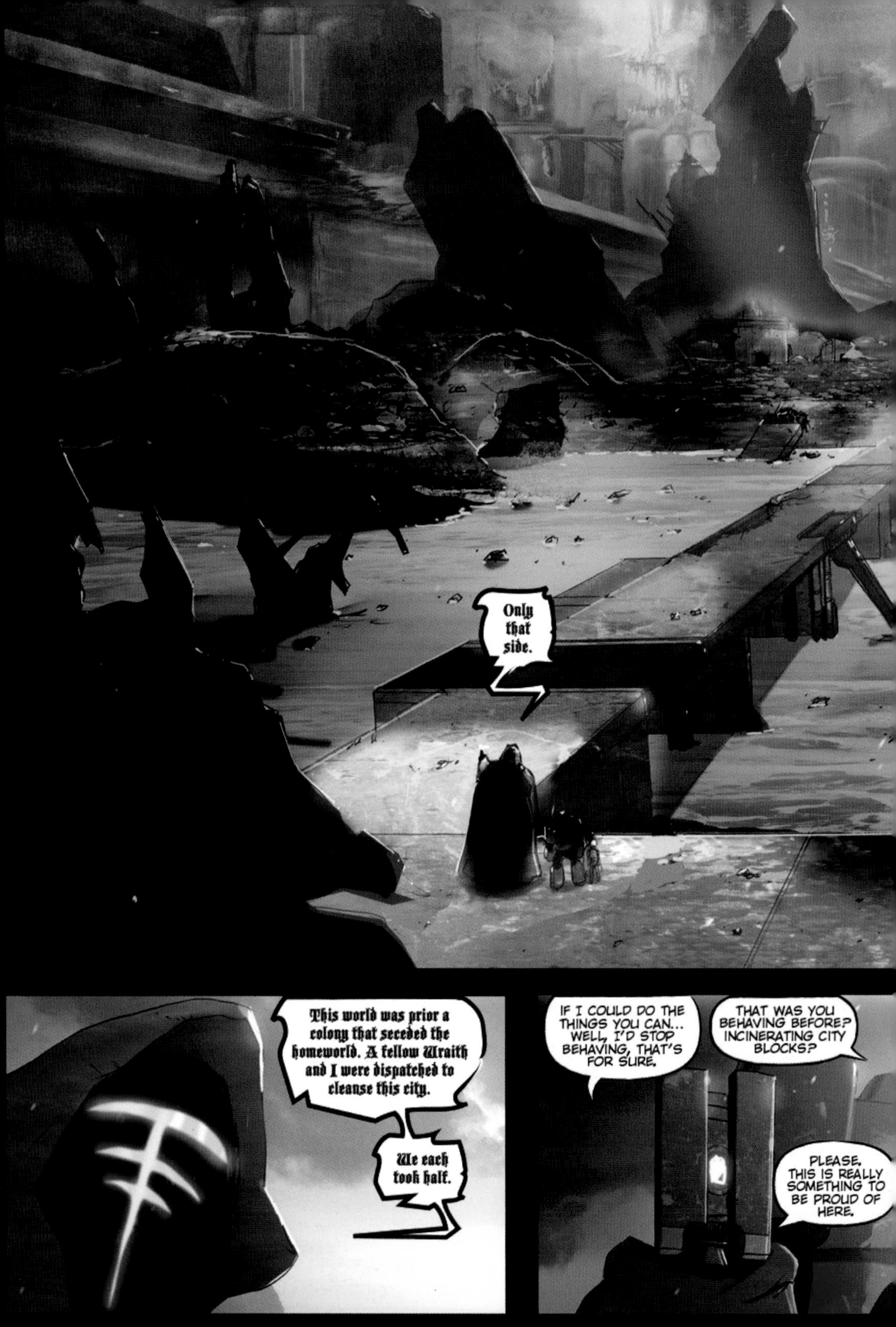
Only that side.
This world was prior a colony that seceded the homeworld. A fellow Wraith and I were dispatched to cleanse this city.
We each took half.
IF I COULD DO THE THINGS YOU CAN... WELL, I'D STOP BEHAVING, THAT'S FOR SURE.
THAT WAS YOU BEHAVING BEFORE? INCINERATING CITY BLOCKS?
PLEASE. THIS IS REALLY SOMETHING TO BE PROUD OF HERE.

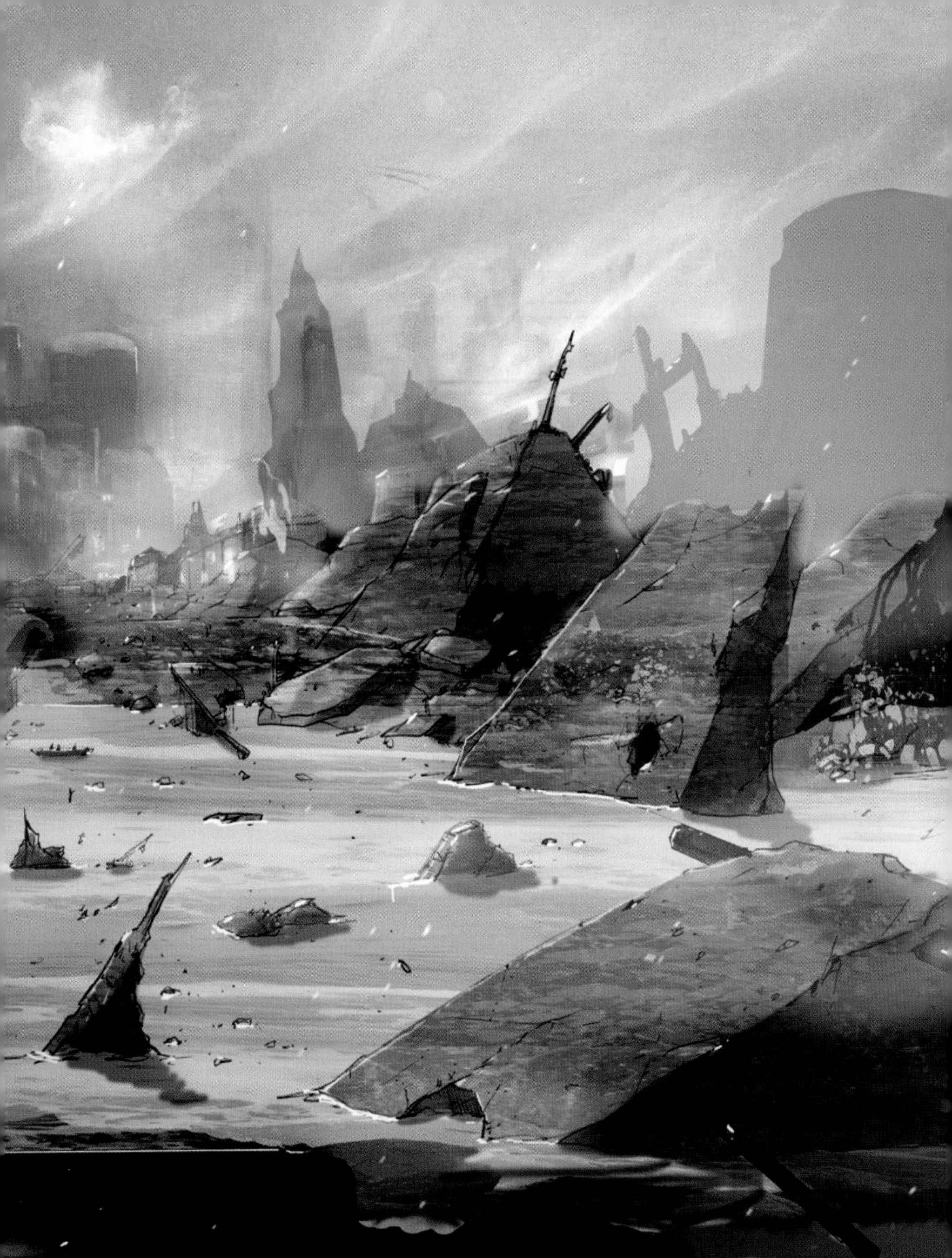

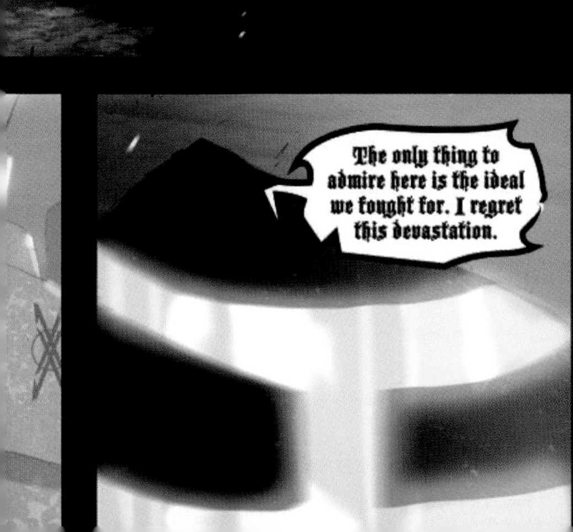
The only thing to admire here is the ideal we fought for. I regret this devastation.

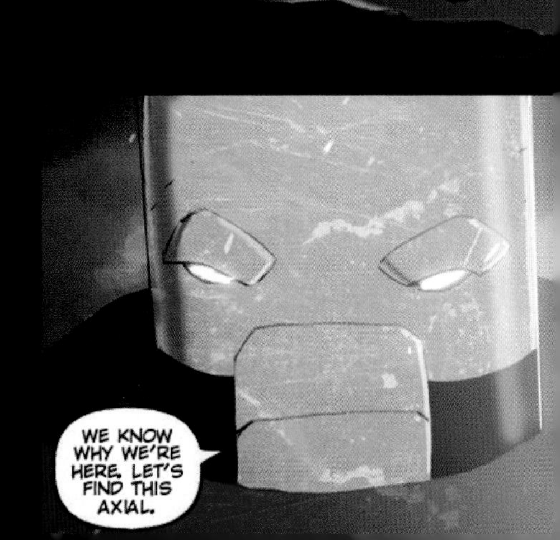
WE KNOW WHY WE'RE HERE. LET'S FIND THIS AXIAL.

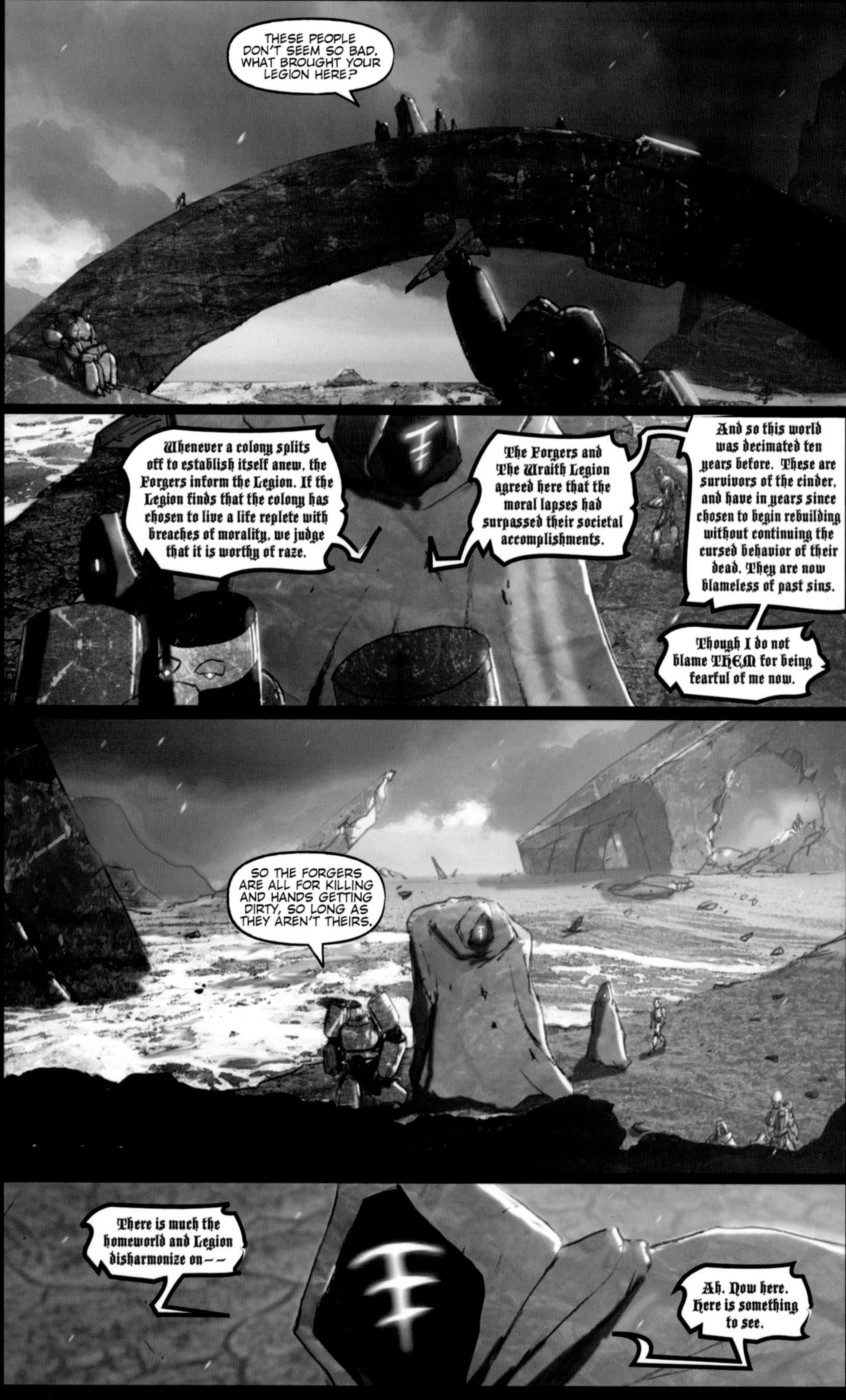
THESE PEOPLE DON'T SEEM SO BAD. WHAT BROUGHT YOUR LEGION HERE?
Whenever a colony splits off to establish itself anew, the Forgers inform the Legion. If the Legion finds that the colony has chosen to live a life replete with breaches of morality, we judge that it is worthy of raze.
The Forgers and The Wraith Legion agreed here that the moral lapses had surpassed their societal accomplishments.
And so this world was decimated ten years before. These are survivors of the cinder, and have in years since chosen to begin rebuilding without continuing the cursed behavior of their dead. They are now blameless of past sins.
Though I do not blame THEM for being fearful of me now.
SO THE FORGERS ARE ALL FOR KILLING AND HANDS GETTING DIRTY, SO LONG AS THEY AREN'T THEIRS.
There is much the homeworld and Legion disharmonize on--
Ah. Now here. Here is something to see.

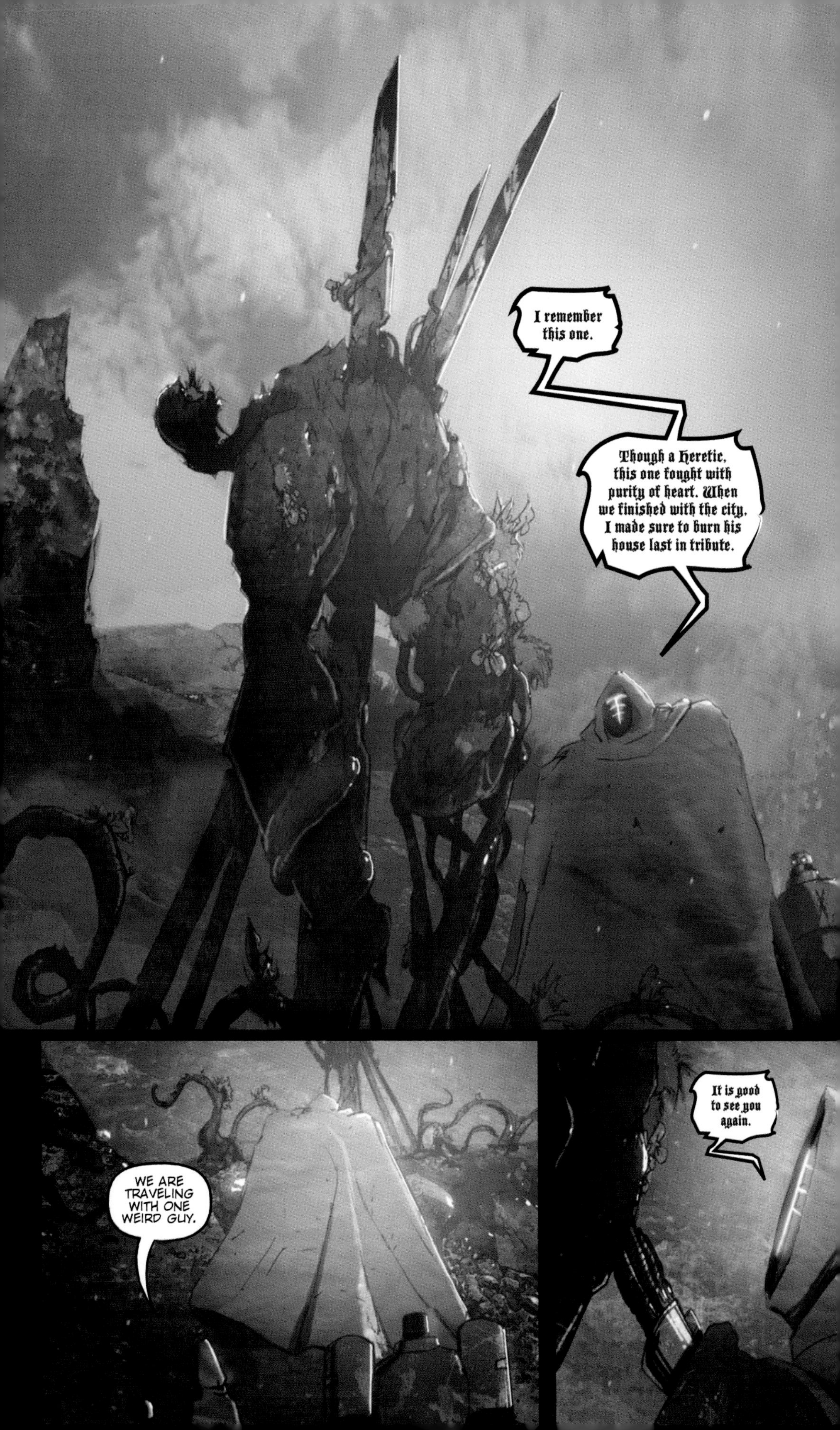
I remember this one.
Though a Heretic, this one fought with purity of heart. When we finished with the city, I made sure to burn his house last in tribute.
WE ARE TRAVELING WITH ONE WEIRD GUY.
It is good to see you again.

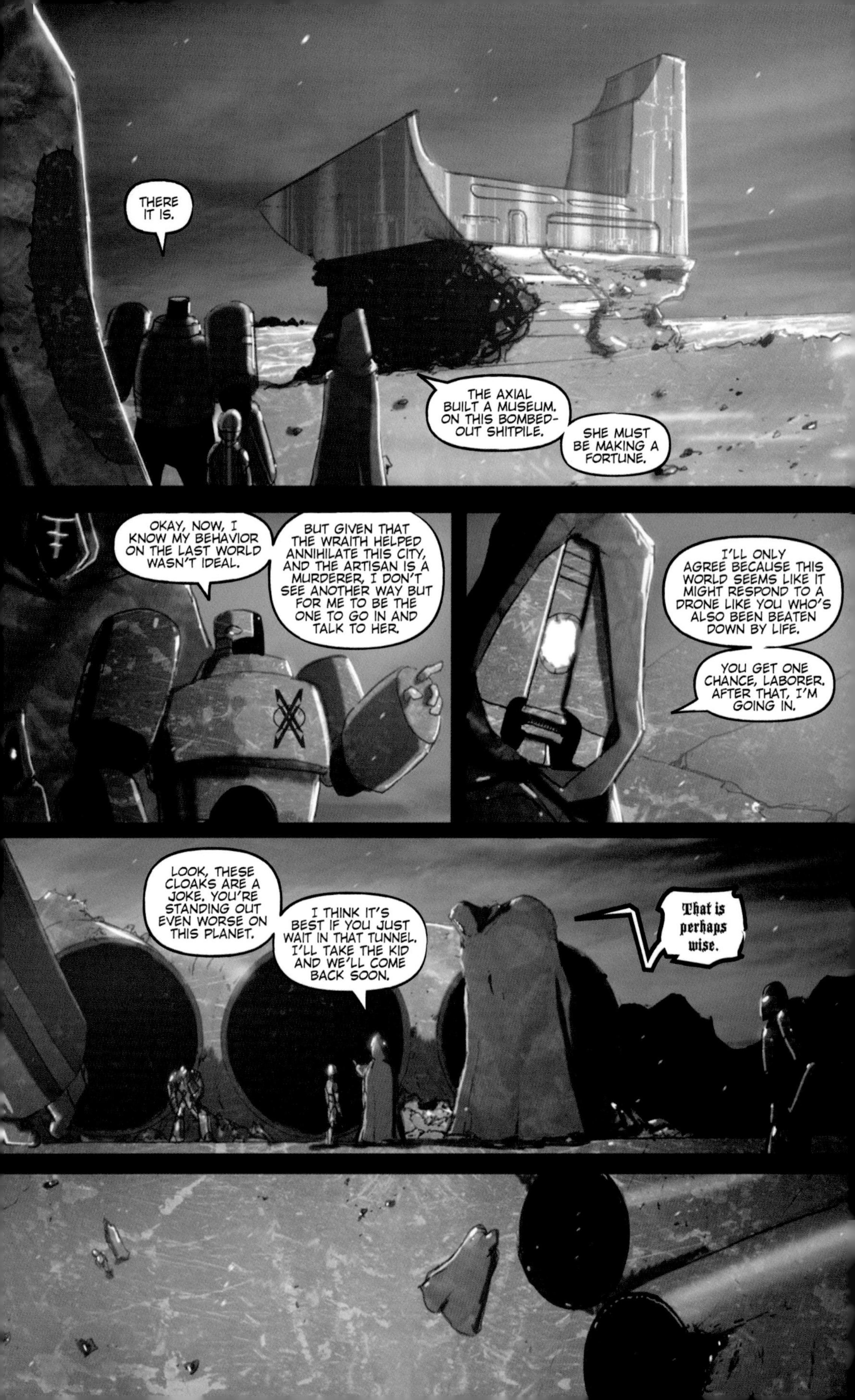
THERE IT IS.
THE AXIAL BUILT A MUSEUM. ON THIS BOMBED-OUT SHITPILE.
SHE MUST BE MAKING A FORTUNE.
OKAY, NOW, I KNOW MY BEHAVIOR ON THE LAST WORLD WASN'T IDEAL.
BUT GIVEN THAT THE WRAITH HELPED ANNIHILATE THIS CITY, AND THE ARTISAN IS A MURDERER, I DON'T SEE ANOTHER WAY BUT FOR ME TO BE THE ONE TO GO IN AND TALK TO HER.
I'LL ONLY AGREE BECAUSE THIS WORLD SEEMS LIKE IT MIGHT RESPOND TO A DRONE LIKE YOU WHO'S ALSO BEEN BEATEN DOWN BY LIFE.
YOU GET ONE CHANCE, LABORER. AFTER THAT, I'M GOING IN.
LOOK, THESE CLOAKS ARE A JOKE. YOU'RE STANDING OUT EVEN WORSE ON THIS PLANET.
I THINK IT'S BEST IF YOU JUST WAIT IN THAT TUNNEL. I'LL TAKE THE KID AND WE'LL COME BACK SOON.
That is perhaps wise.

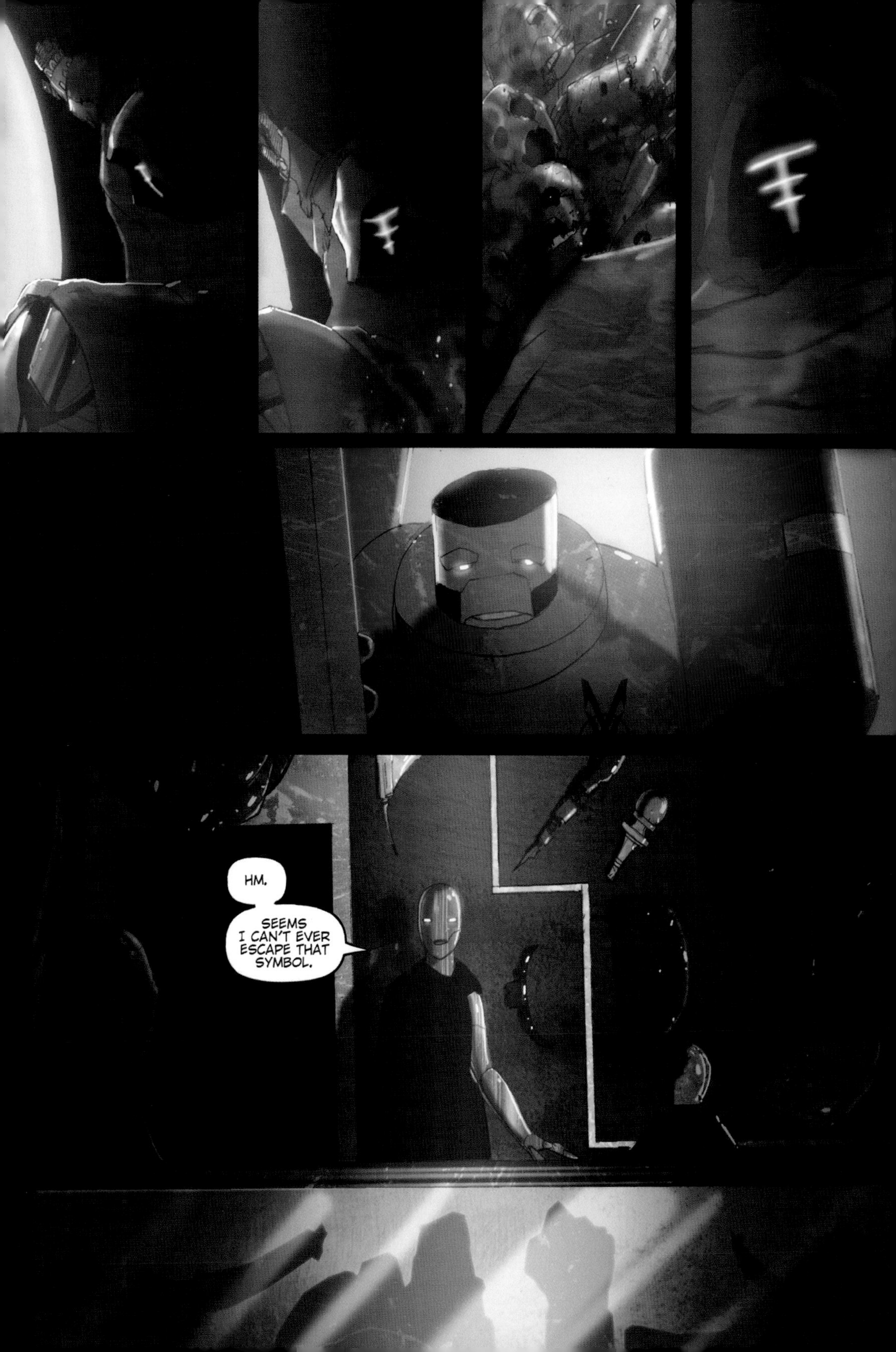
HM.
SEEMS I CAN'T EVER ESCAPE THAT SYMBOL.

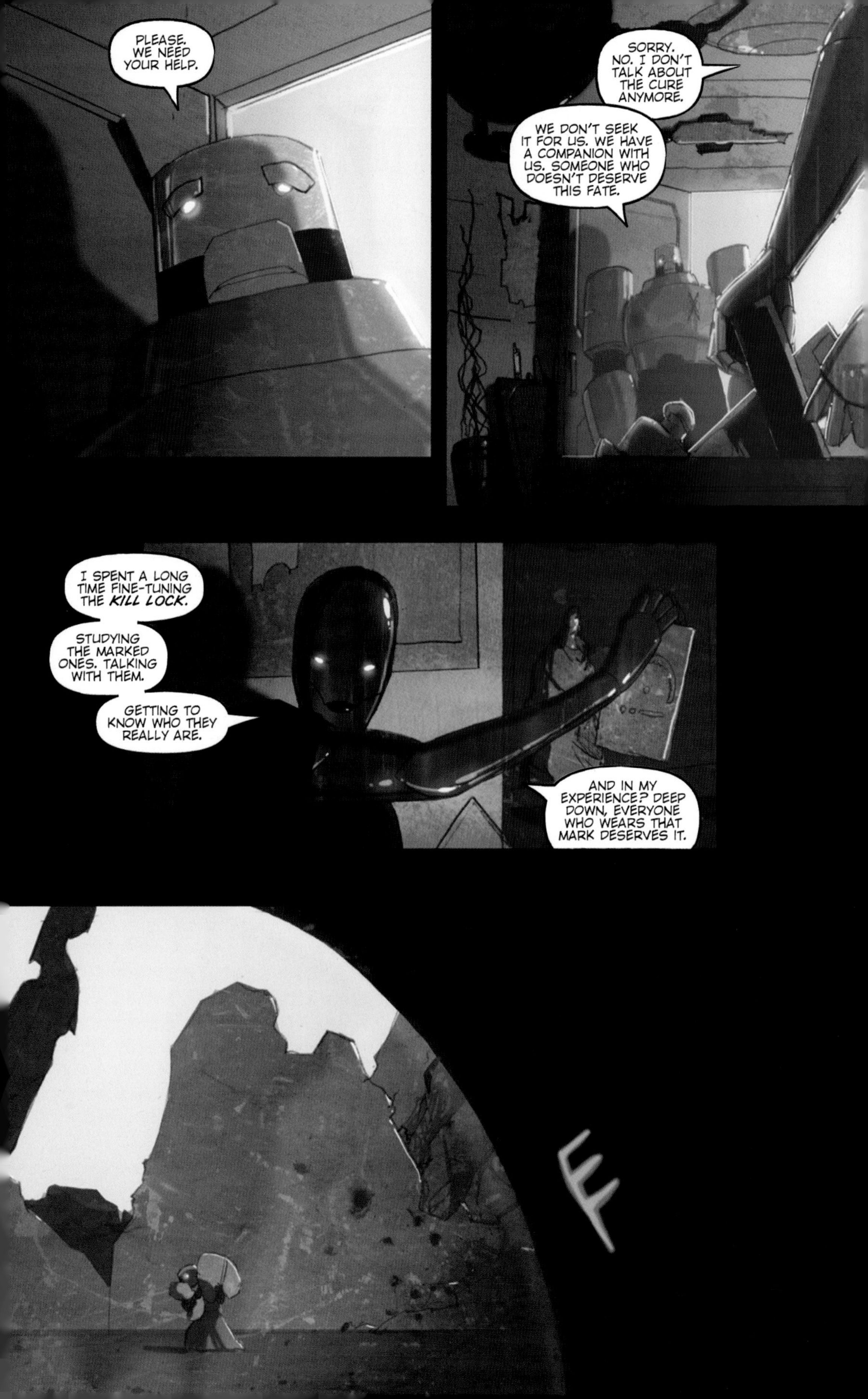
PLEASE. WE NEED YOUR HELP.
SORRY. NO. I DON'T TALK ABOUT THE CURE ANYMORE.
WE DON'T SEEK IT FOR US. WE HAVE A COMPANION WITH US. SOMEONE WHO DOESN'T DESERVE THIS FATE.
I SPENT A LONG TIME FINE-TUNING THE ***KILL LOCK.***
STUDYING THE MARKED ONES. TALKING WITH THEM.
GETTING TO KNOW WHO THEY REALLY ARE.
AND IN MY EXPERIENCE? DEEP DOWN, EVERYONE WHO WEARS THAT MARK DESERVES IT.

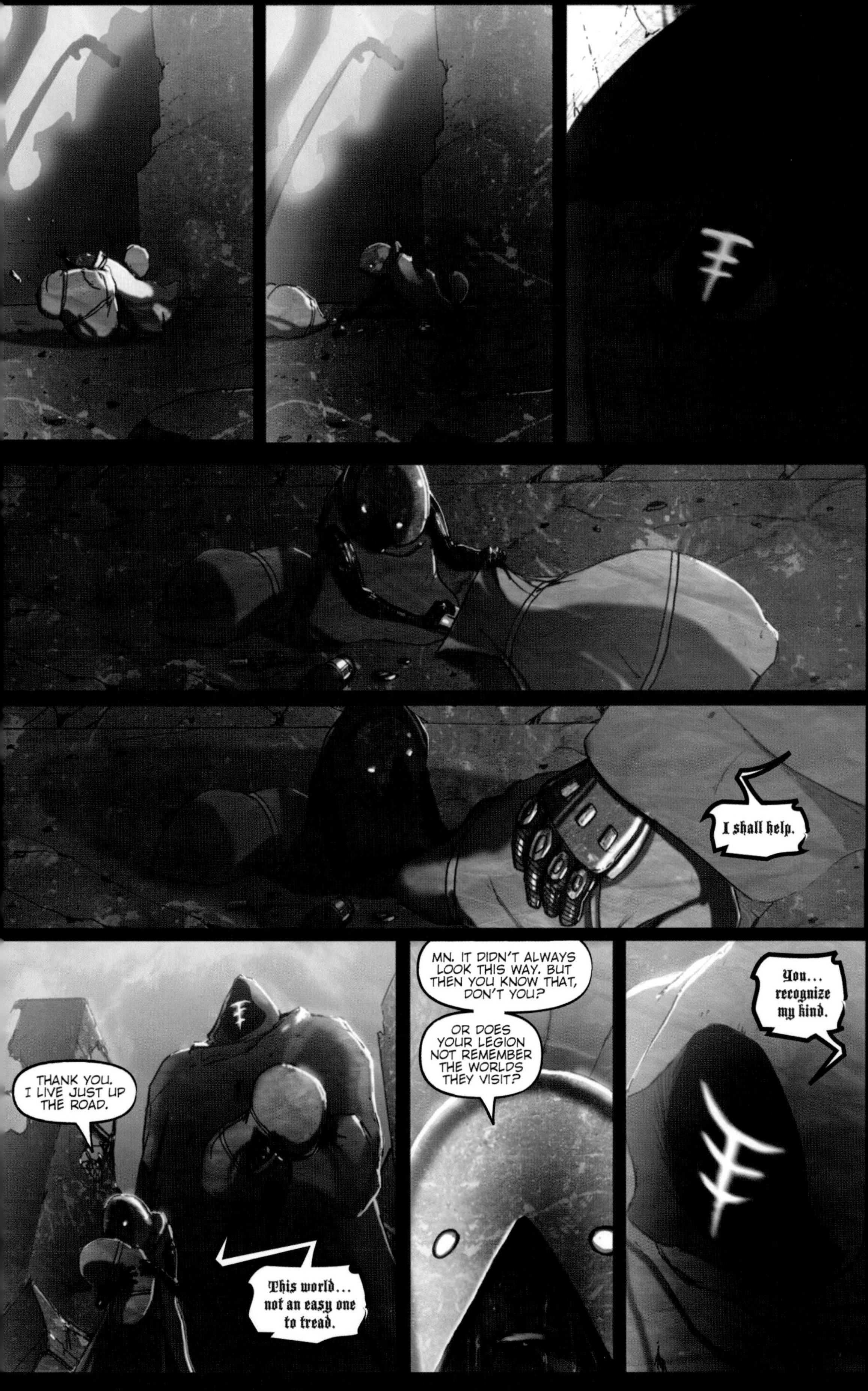
I shall help.
THANK YOU. I LIVE JUST UP THE ROAD.
This world... not an easy one to tread.
MN. IT DIDN'T ALWAYS LOOK THIS WAY. BUT THEN YOU KNOW THAT, DON'T YOU?
OR DOES YOUR LEGION NOT REMEMBER THE WORLDS THEY VISIT?
You... recognize my kind.

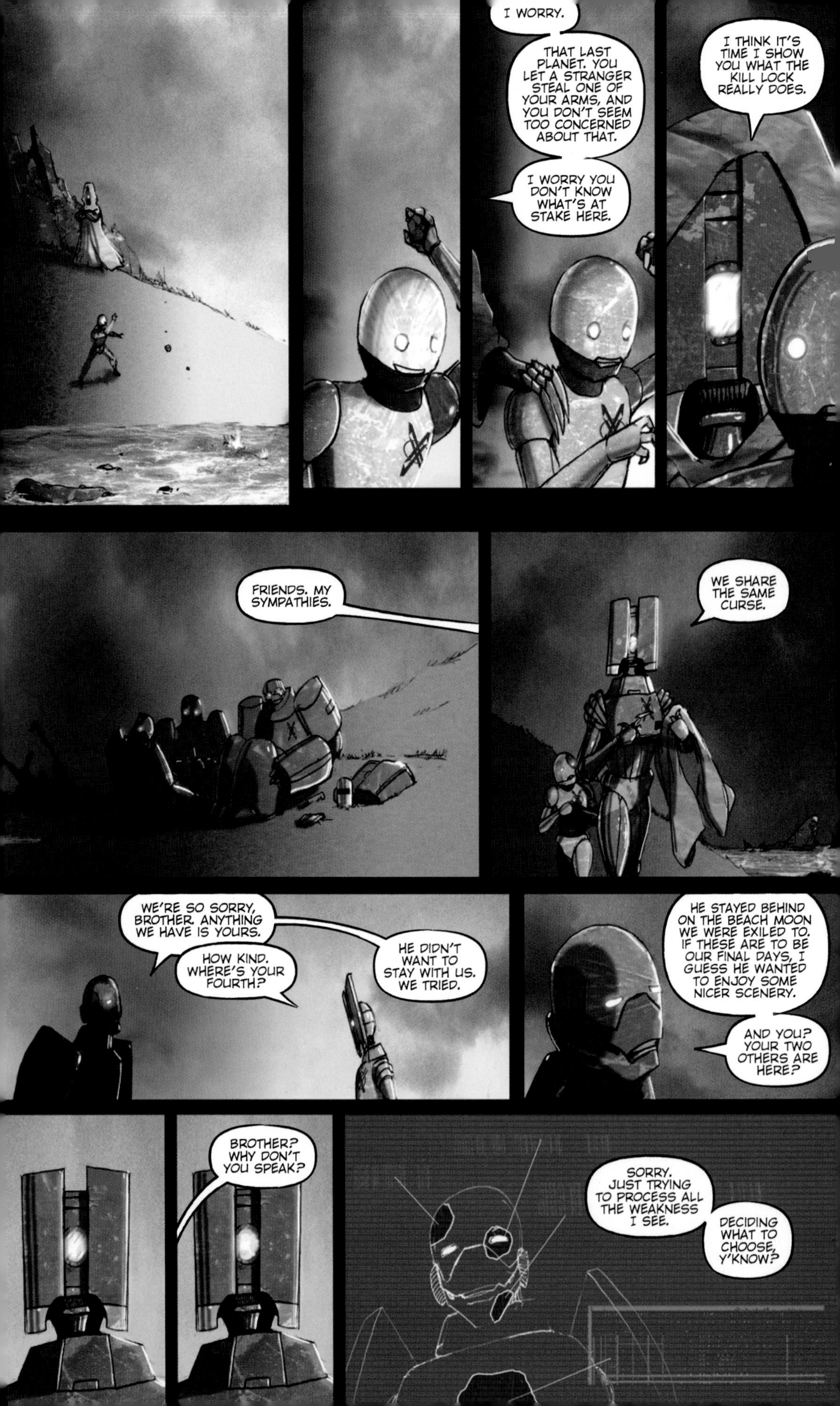
I WORRY.
THAT LAST PLANET. YOU LET A STRANGER STEAL ONE OF YOUR ARMS, AND YOU DON'T SEEM TOO CONCERNED ABOUT THAT.
I WORRY YOU DON'T KNOW WHAT'S AT STAKE HERE.
I THINK IT'S TIME I SHOW YOU WHAT THE KILL LOCK REALLY DOES.
FRIENDS. MY SYMPATHIES.
WE SHARE THE SAME CURSE.
WE'RE SO SORRY, BROTHER. ANYTHING WE HAVE IS YOURS.
HOW KIND. WHERE'S YOUR FOURTH?
HE DIDN'T WANT TO STAY WITH US. WE TRIED.
HE STAYED BEHIND ON THE BEACH MOON WE WERE EXILED TO. IF THESE ARE TO BE OUR FINAL DAYS, I GUESS HE WANTED TO ENJOY SOME NICER SCENERY.
AND YOU? YOUR TWO OTHERS ARE HERE?
BROTHER? WHY DON'T YOU SPEAK?
SORRY. JUST TRYING TO PROCESS ALL THE WEAKNESS I SEE.
DECIDING WHAT TO CHOOSE, Y'KNOW?

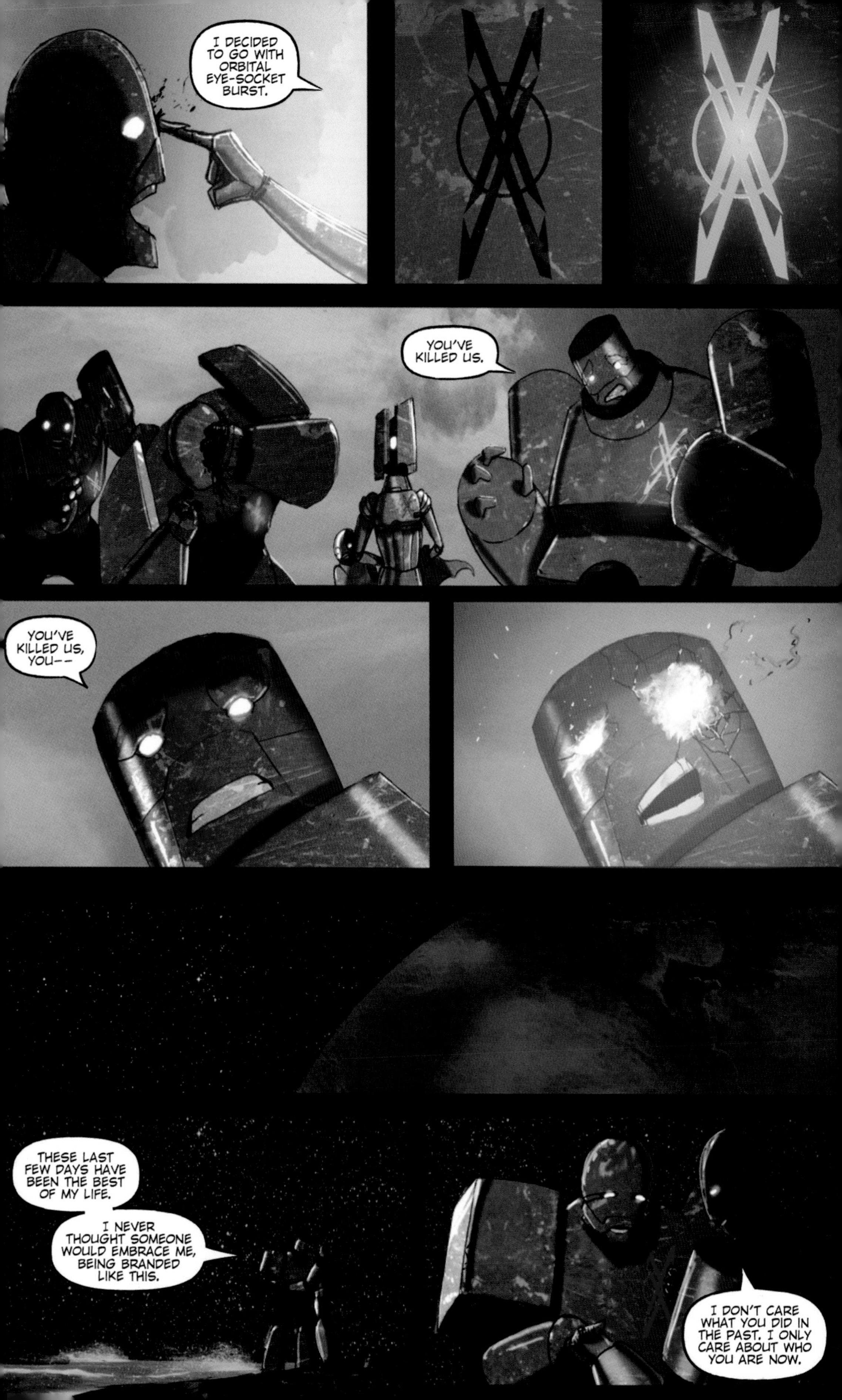
I DECIDED TO GO WITH ORBITAL EYE-SOCKET BURST.
YOU'VE KILLED US.
YOU'VE KILLED US, YOU--
THESE LAST FEW DAYS HAVE BEEN THE BEST OF MY LIFE.
I NEVER THOUGHT SOMEONE WOULD EMBRACE ME, BEING BRANDED LIKE THIS.
I DON'T CARE WHAT YOU DID IN THE PAST. I ONLY CARE ABOUT WHO YOU ARE NOW.

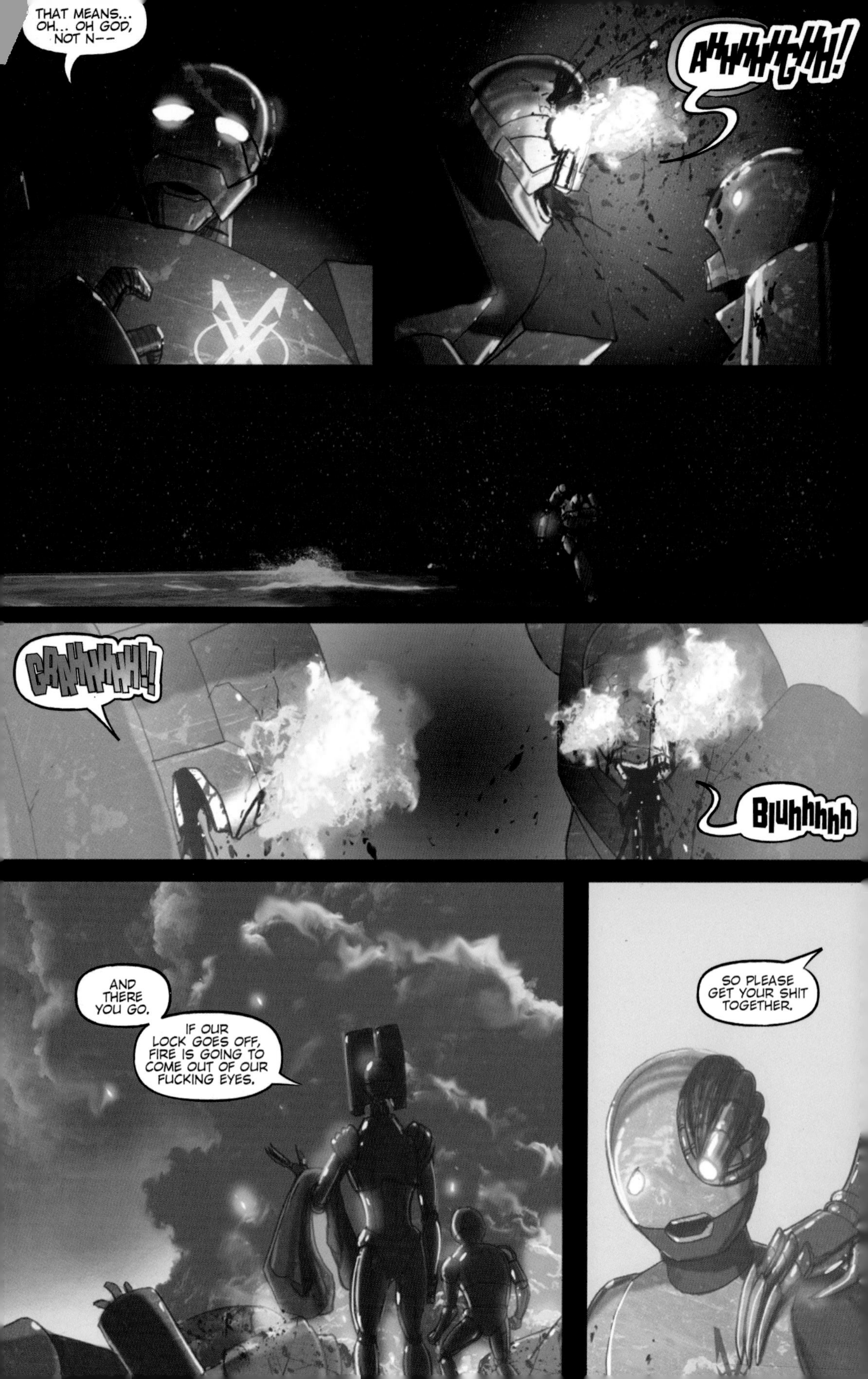
THAT MEANS... OH... OH GOD, NOT N--
AHHHHGHH!
GRAHHHHH!!
Bluhhhhh
AND THERE YOU GO.
IF OUR LOCK GOES OFF, FIRE IS GOING TO COME OUT OF OUR FUCKING EYES.
SO PLEASE GET YOUR SHIT TOGETHER.

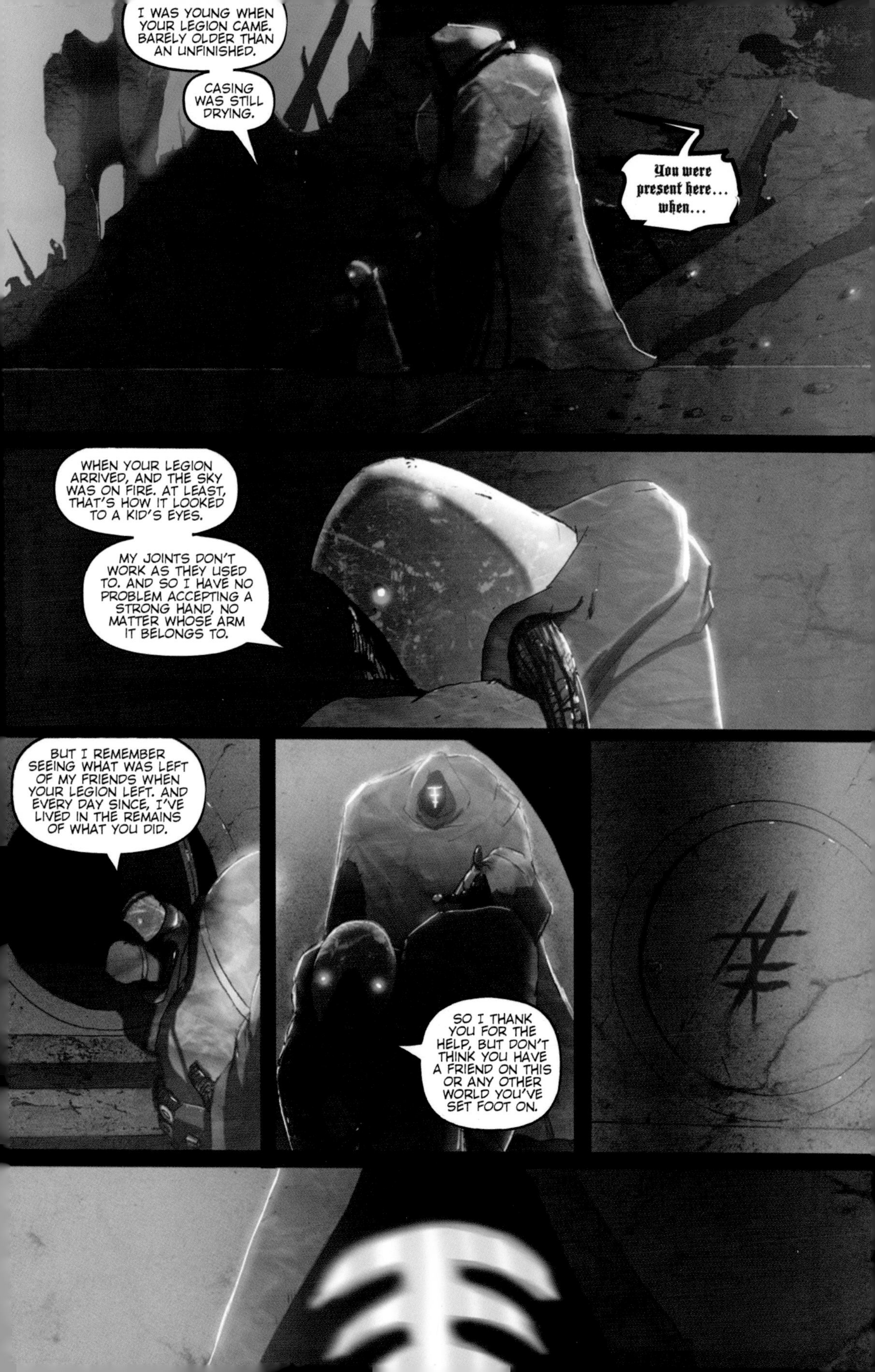
I WAS YOUNG WHEN YOUR LEGION CAME. BARELY OLDER THAN AN UNFINISHED.
CASING WAS STILL DRYING.
You were present here... when...
WHEN YOUR LEGION ARRIVED, AND THE SKY WAS ON FIRE. AT LEAST, THAT'S HOW IT LOOKED TO A KID'S EYES.
MY JOINTS DON'T WORK AS THEY USED TO. AND SO I HAVE NO PROBLEM ACCEPTING A STRONG HAND, NO MATTER WHOSE ARM IT BELONGS TO.
BUT I REMEMBER SEEING WHAT WAS LEFT OF MY FRIENDS WHEN YOUR LEGION LEFT. AND EVERY DAY SINCE, I'VE LIVED IN THE REMAINS OF WHAT YOU DID.
SO I THANK YOU FOR THE HELP, BUT DON'T THINK YOU HAVE A FRIEND ON THIS OR ANY OTHER WORLD YOU'VE SET FOOT ON.

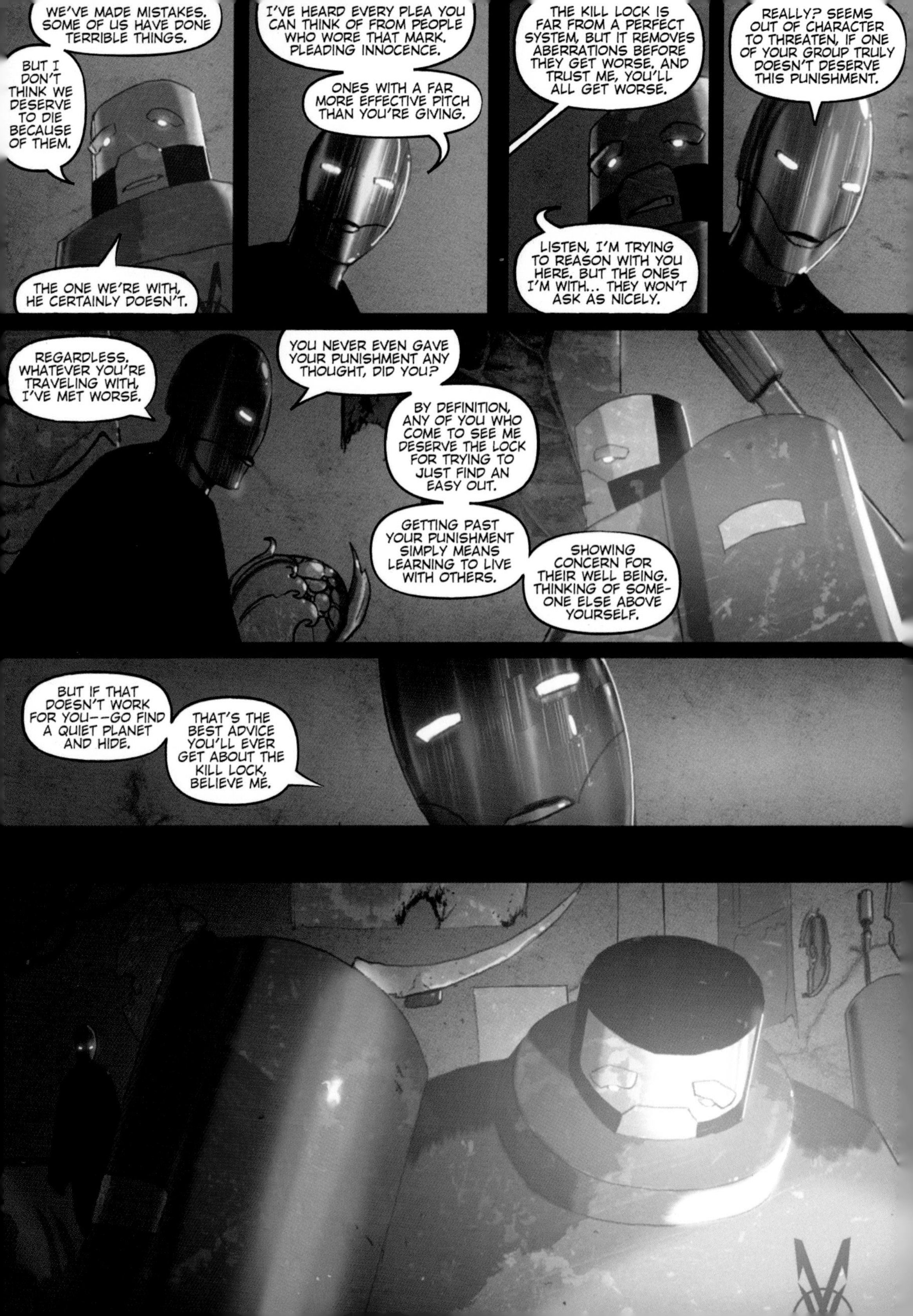

WE'VE MADE MISTAKES. SOME OF US HAVE DONE TERRIBLE THINGS.
BUT I DON'T THINK WE DESERVE TO DIE BECAUSE OF THEM.
THE ONE WE'RE WITH, HE CERTAINLY DOESN'T.
I'VE HEARD EVERY PLEA YOU CAN THINK OF FROM PEOPLE WHO WORE THAT MARK. PLEADING INNOCENCE.
ONES WITH A FAR MORE EFFECTIVE PITCH THAN YOU'RE GIVING.
THE KILL LOCK IS FAR FROM A PERFECT SYSTEM, BUT IT REMOVES ABERRATIONS BEFORE THEY GET WORSE. AND TRUST ME, YOU'LL ALL GET WORSE.
LISTEN, I'M TRYING TO REASON WITH YOU HERE. BUT THE ONES I'M WITH... THEY WON'T ASK AS NICELY.
REALLY? SEEMS OUT OF CHARACTER TO THREATEN, IF ONE OF YOUR GROUP TRULY DOESN'T DESERVE THIS PUNISHMENT.
REGARDLESS. WHATEVER YOU'RE TRAVELING WITH, I'VE MET WORSE.
YOU NEVER EVEN GAVE YOUR PUNISHMENT ANY THOUGHT, DID YOU?
BY DEFINITION, ANY OF YOU WHO COME TO SEE ME DESERVE THE LOCK FOR TRYING TO JUST FIND AN EASY OUT.
GETTING PAST YOUR PUNISHMENT SIMPLY MEANS LEARNING TO LIVE WITH OTHERS.
SHOWING CONCERN FOR THEIR WELL BEING. THINKING OF SOME-ONE ELSE ABOVE YOURSELF.
BUT IF THAT DOESN'T WORK FOR YOU--GO FIND A QUIET PLANET AND HIDE.
THAT'S THE BEST ADVICE YOU'LL EVER GET ABOUT THE KILL LOCK, BELIEVE ME.

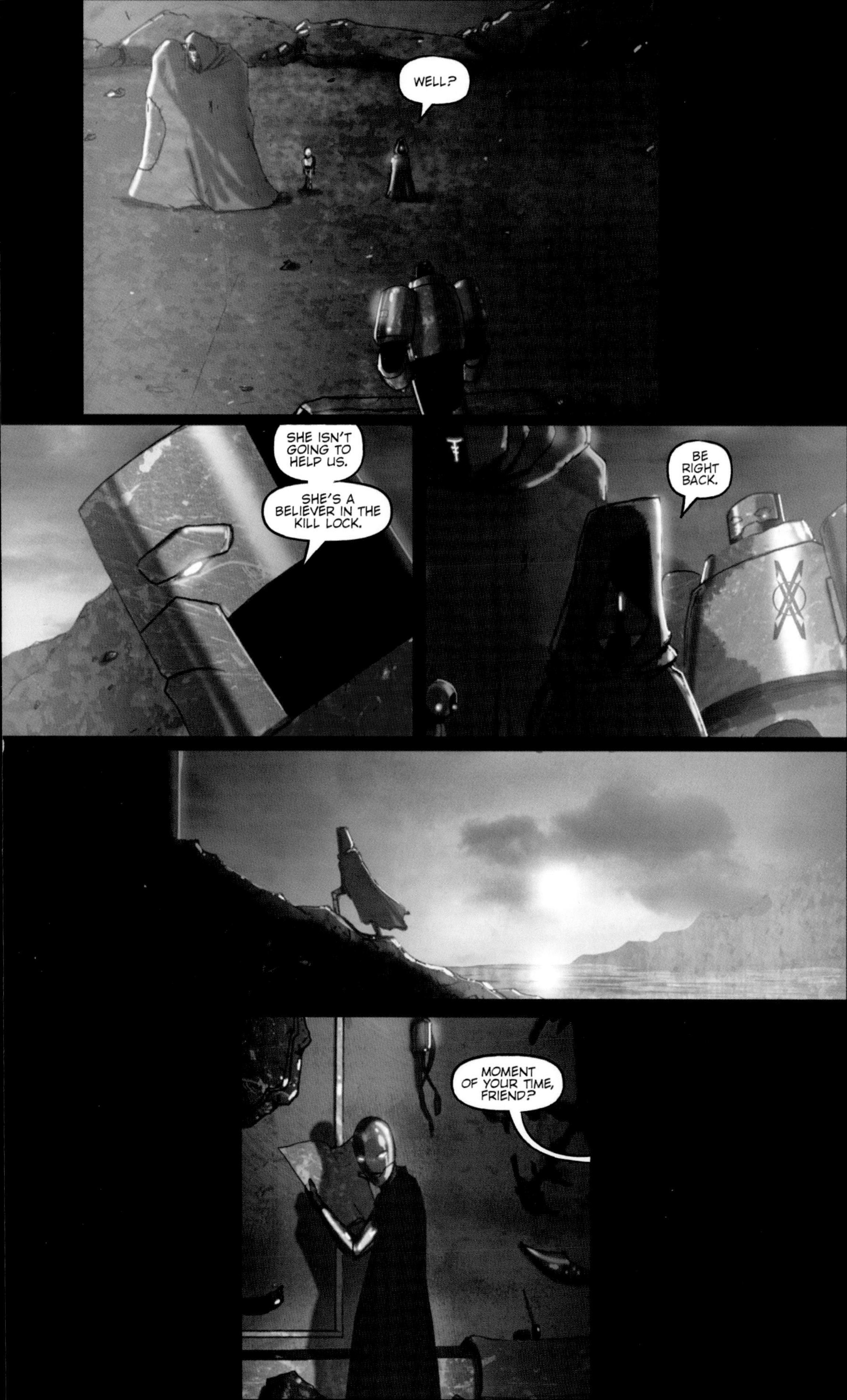
WELL?
SHE ISN'T GOING TO HELP US.
SHE'S A BELIEVER IN THE KILL LOCK.
BE RIGHT BACK.
MOMENT OF YOUR TIME, FRIEND?

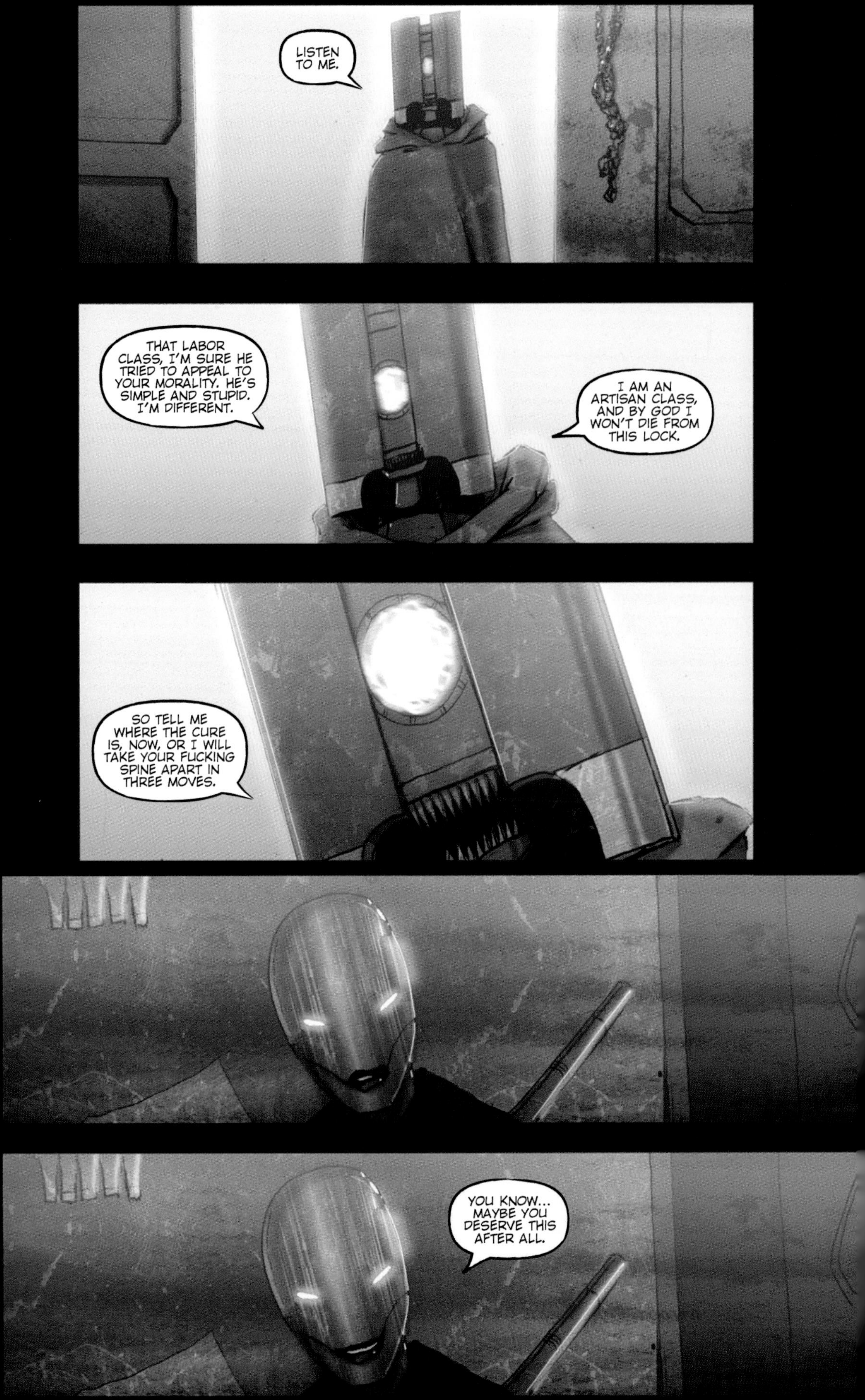
LISTEN TO ME.
THAT LABOR CLASS, I'M SURE HE TRIED TO APPEAL TO YOUR MORALITY. HE'S SIMPLE AND STUPID. I'M DIFFERENT.
I AM AN ARTISAN CLASS, AND BY GOD I WON'T DIE FROM THIS LOCK.
SO TELL ME WHERE THE CURE IS, NOW, OR I WILL TAKE YOUR FUCKING SPINE APART IN THREE MOVES.
YOU KNOW... MAYBE YOU DESERVE THIS AFTER ALL.

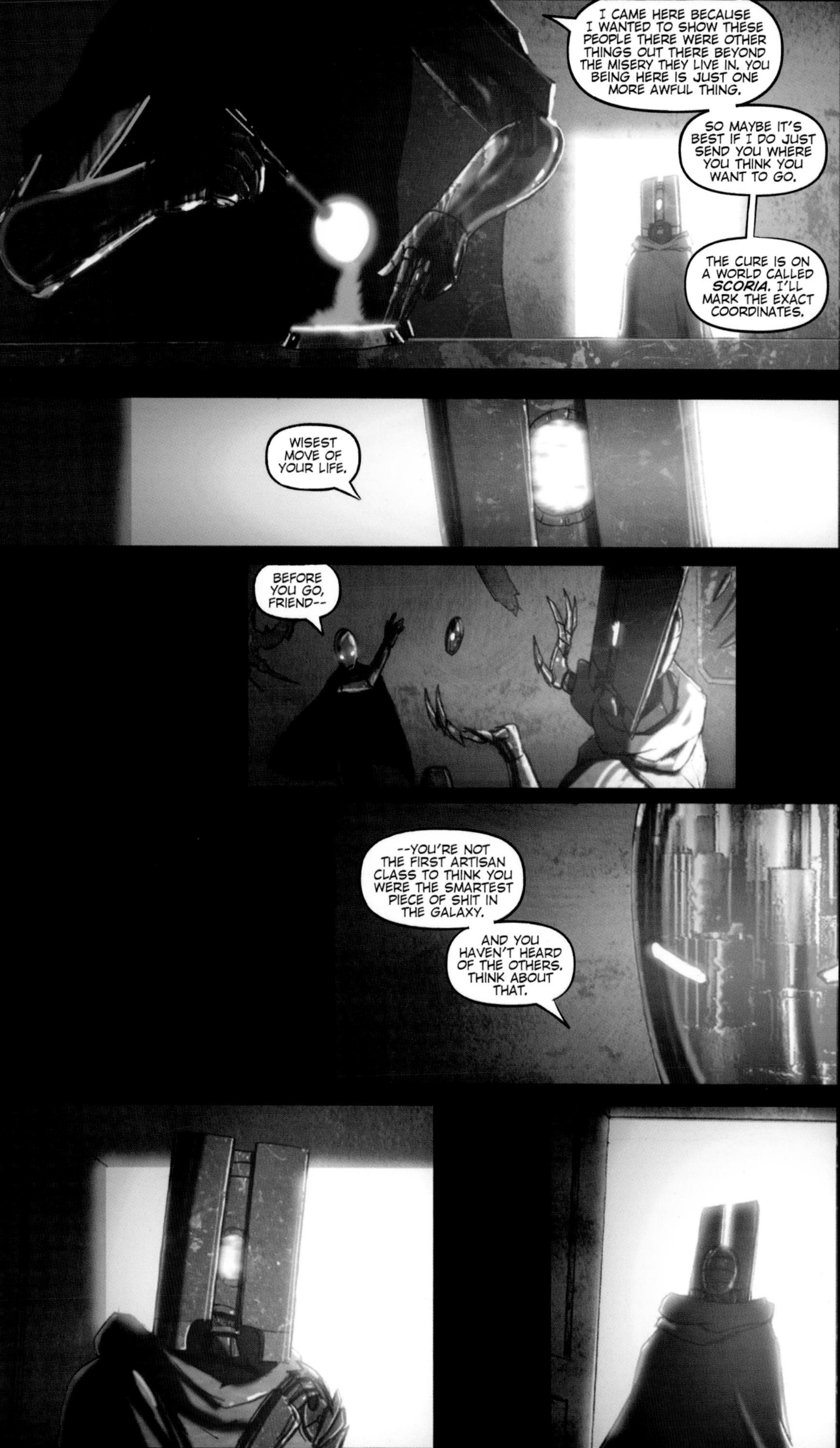
I CAME HERE BECAUSE I WANTED TO SHOW THESE PEOPLE THERE WERE OTHER THINGS OUT THERE BEYOND THE MISERY THEY LIVE IN. YOU BEING HERE IS JUST ONE MORE AWFUL THING.
SO MAYBE IT'S BEST IF I DO JUST SEND YOU WHERE YOU THINK YOU WANT TO GO.
THE CURE IS ON A WORLD CALLED SCORIA. I'LL MARK THE EXACT COORDINATES.
WISEST MOVE OF YOUR LIFE.
BEFORE YOU GO, FRIEND--
--YOU'RE NOT THE FIRST ARTISAN CLASS TO THINK YOU WERE THE SMARTEST PIECE OF SHIT IN THE GALAXY.
AND YOU HAVEN'T HEARD OF THE OTHERS. THINK ABOUT THAT.

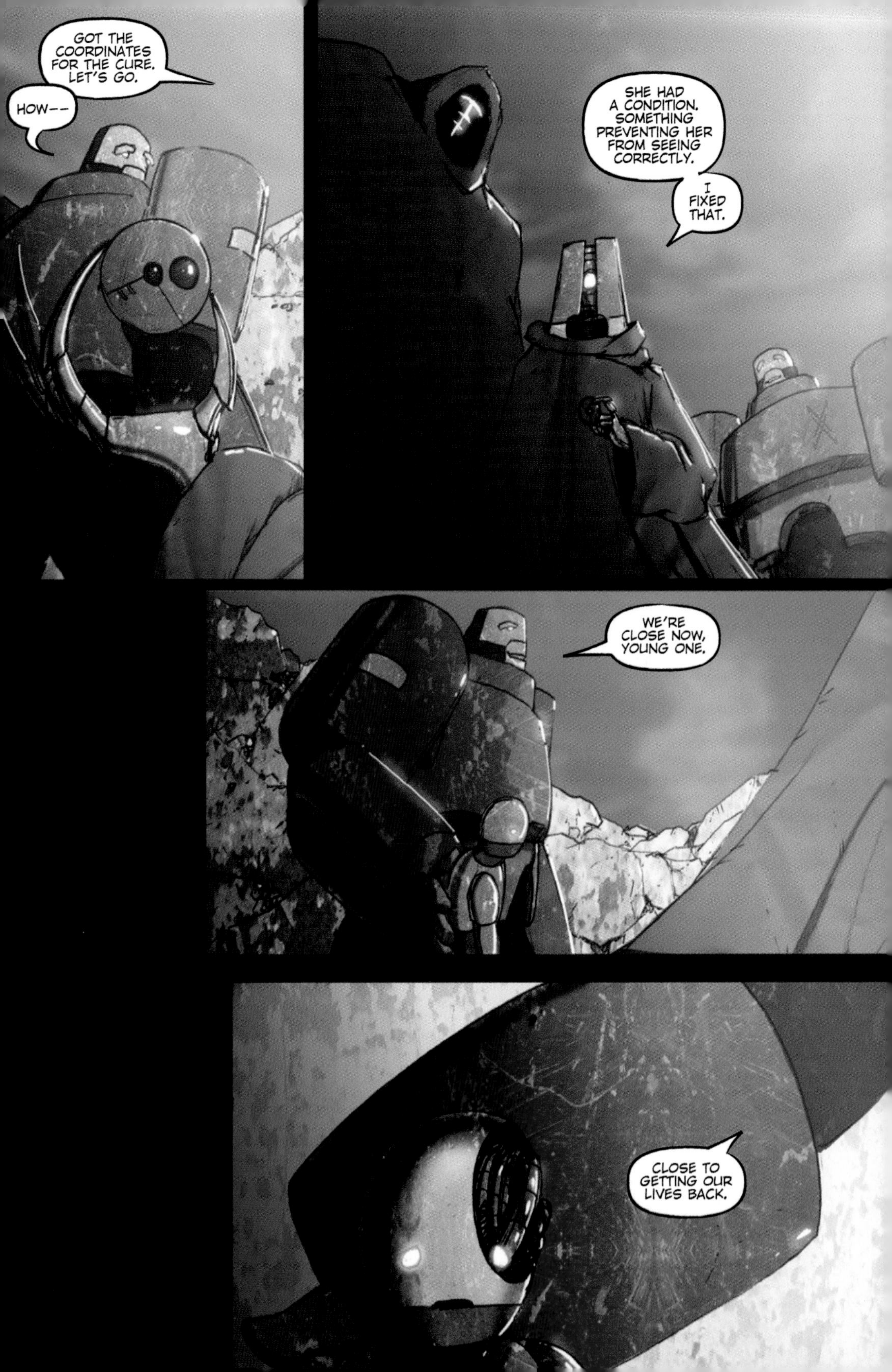
GOT THE COORDINATES FOR THE CURE. LET'S GO.
HOW--
SHE HAD A CONDITION. SOMETHING PREVENTING HER FROM SEEING CORRECTLY.
I FIXED THAT.
WE'RE CLOSE NOW, YOUNG ONE.
CLOSE TO GETTING OUR LIVES BACK.

SHIT. HALF A MILLIMETER CRACK IN THE CASING HERE. DID YOU BUMP THIS TABLE WHEN IT WAS COOLING?
DAMN, I GUESS I DID. WITH THOSE SHELL MOLDS BREAKING YESTERDAY, THIS HAS NOT BEEN A GOOD WEEK FOR THE DEPARTMENT.
THE ARTISANS ARE GOING TO GIVE US HELL FOR THIS.
YOU KNOW WHAT THEY'LL SAY, "SMALL IMPERFECTION TODAY MEANS COLOSSAL IMPERFECTION TOMORROW" OR SOME BULLSHIT.
MEMORY 1
YOU'RE RIGHT. WELL. I GUESS WE COULD JUST LOAD HIM ONTO THE NEXT SHIPMENT HEADED FOR THE SENTENCING CHAMBER.
JUST SAY SOMETHING INSIDE CRACKED ON ITS OWN. BUT I MEAN, WITH THE NEW POLICY, THE FOUNDERS ARE *NOT* GOING TO BE MERCIFUL HERE...
SO? BETTER IT THAN US. IT *IS* JUST AN UNFINISHED ANYWAY.
MEMORY 2
THOUGH YOU DIDN'T ACTIVELY CAUSE YOUR OWN IMPURITY, FAULT LIES WITHIN YOU.
OUR RACE CANNOT ABIDE FAILURE IF WE ARE TO SURVIVE. BUT FEAR NOT, WE ARE MERCIFUL FORGERS AND YOUR LIFE WILL CONTINUE, FOR AS LONG AS IT CAN.
WE MAY EVEN LEARN SOMETHING FROM THE DATA YOUR FINAL DAYS WILL YIELD.
YOU ARE HEREBY SENTENCED TO THE KILL LOCK.
MEMORY 3
EASY, LITTLE ONE. YOU'RE ALRIGHT NOW.

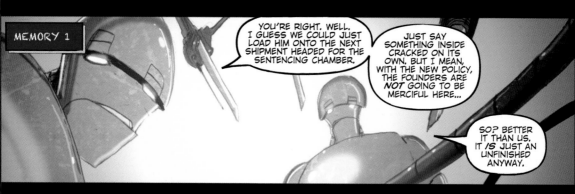

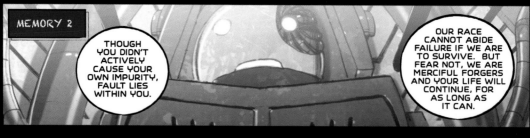

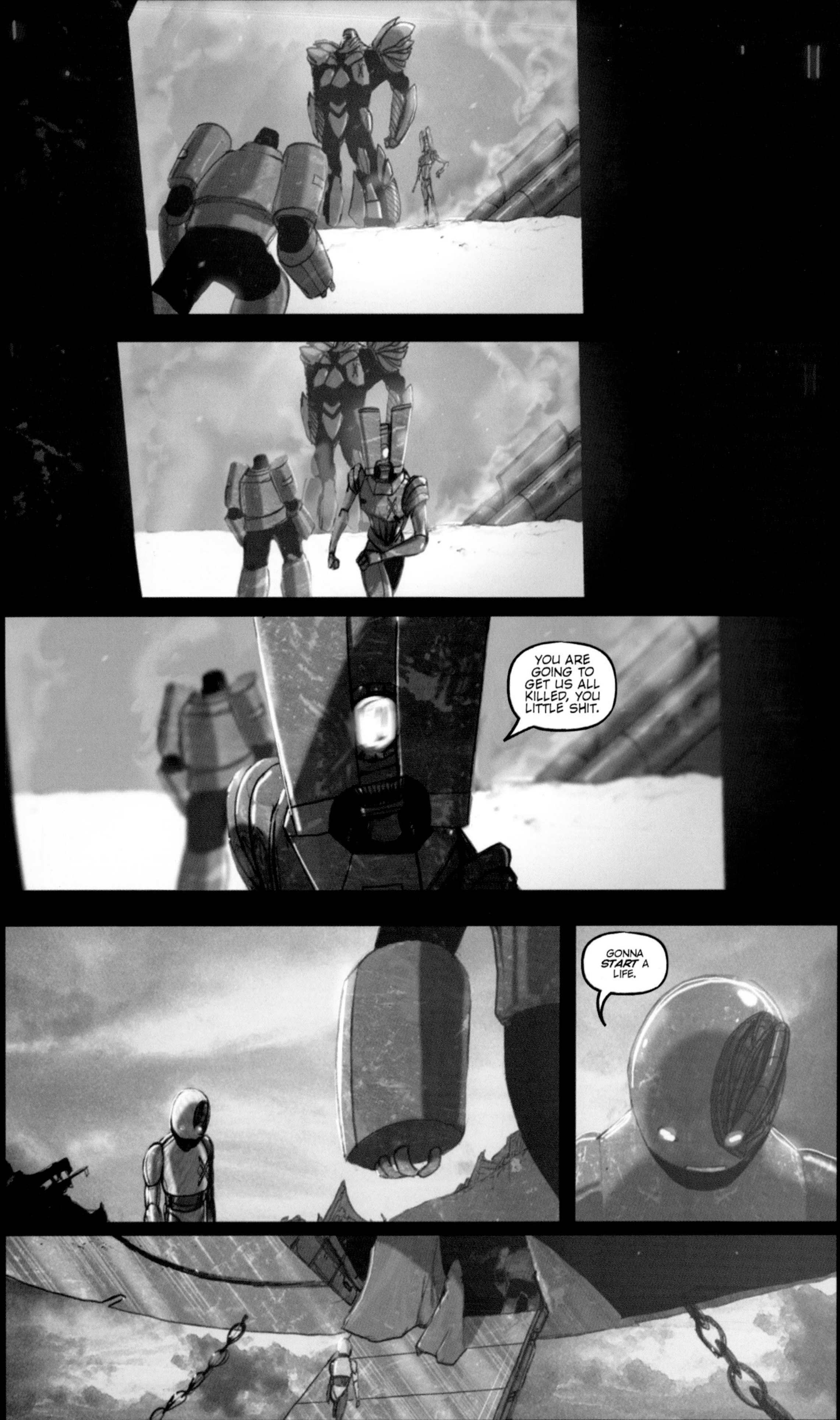
YOU ARE GOING TO GET US ALL KILLED, YOU LITTLE SHIT.
GONNA START A LIFE.

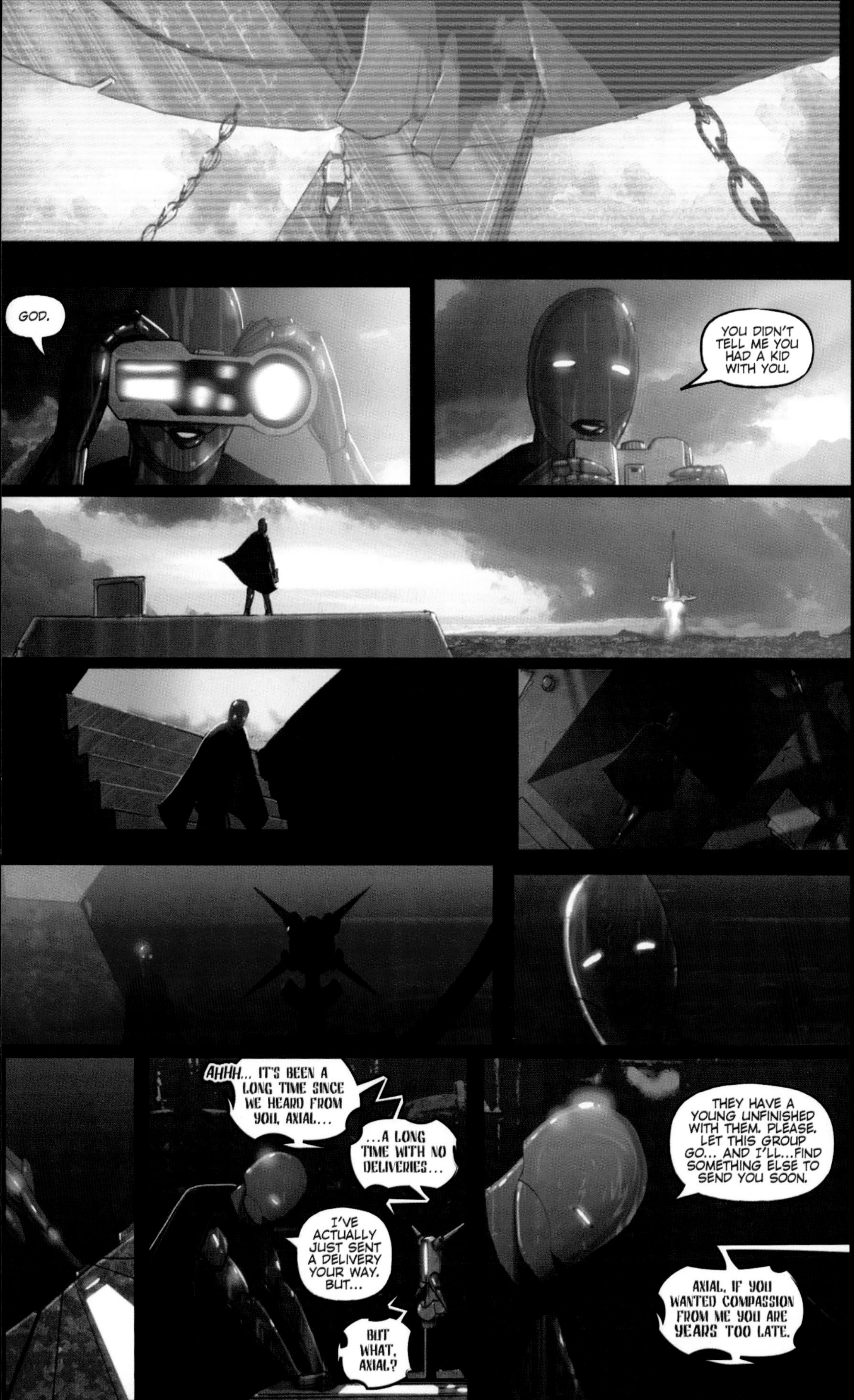
GOD.
YOU DIDN'T TELL ME YOU HAD A KID WITH YOU.
AHHH... IT'S BEEN A LONG TIME SINCE WE HEARD FROM YOU, AXIAL...
...A LONG TIME WITH NO DELIVERIES...
I'VE ACTUALLY JUST SENT A DELIVERY YOUR WAY. BUT...
BUT WHAT, AXIAL?
THEY HAVE A YOUNG UNFINISHED WITH THEM. PLEASE. LET THIS GROUP GO... AND I'LL...FIND SOMETHING ELSE TO SEND YOU SOON.
AXIAL, IF YOU WANTED COMPASSION FROM ME YOU ARE YEARS TOO LATE.

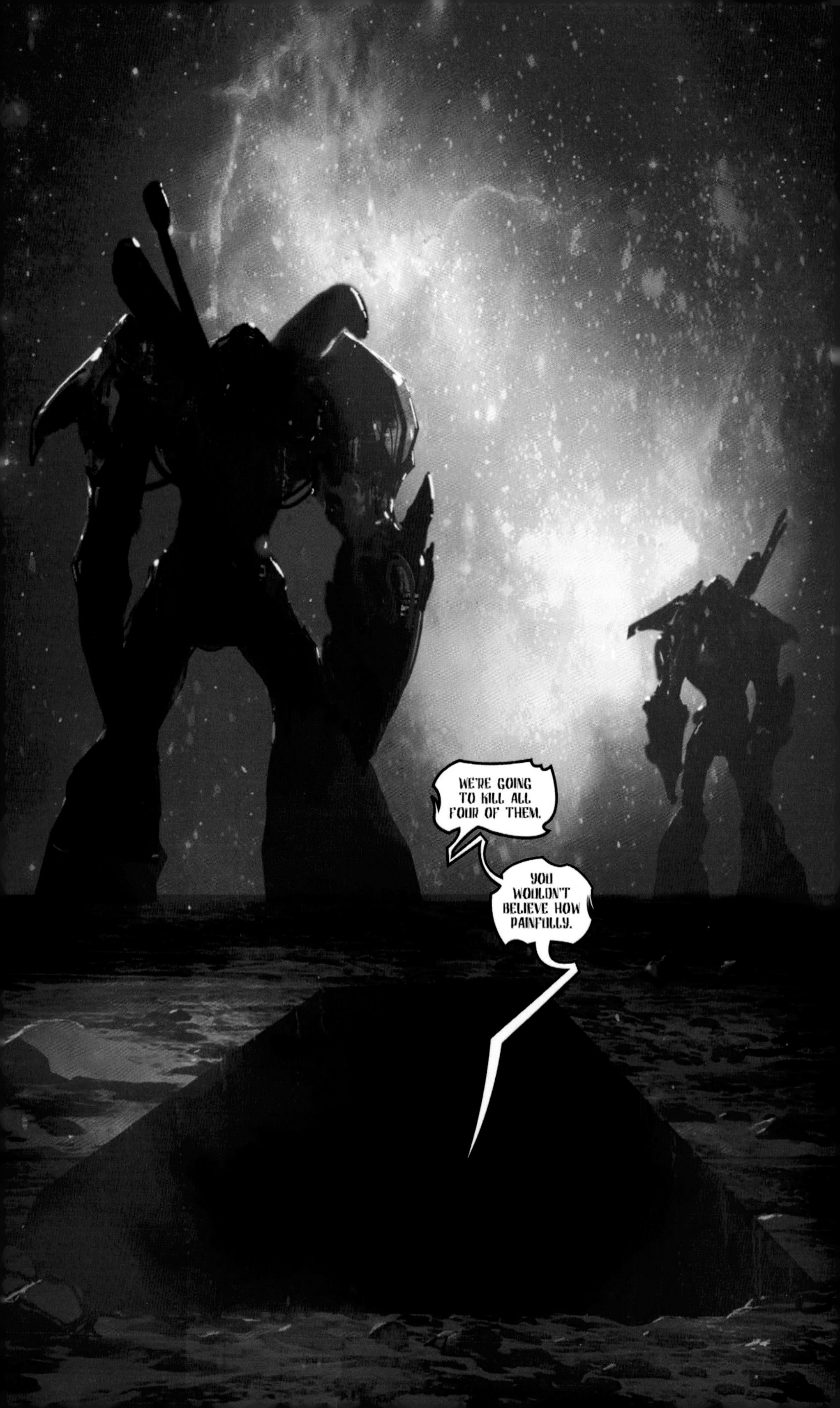
WE'RE GOING TO KILL ALL FOUR OF THEM.
YOU WOULDN'T BELIEVE HOW PAINFULLY.

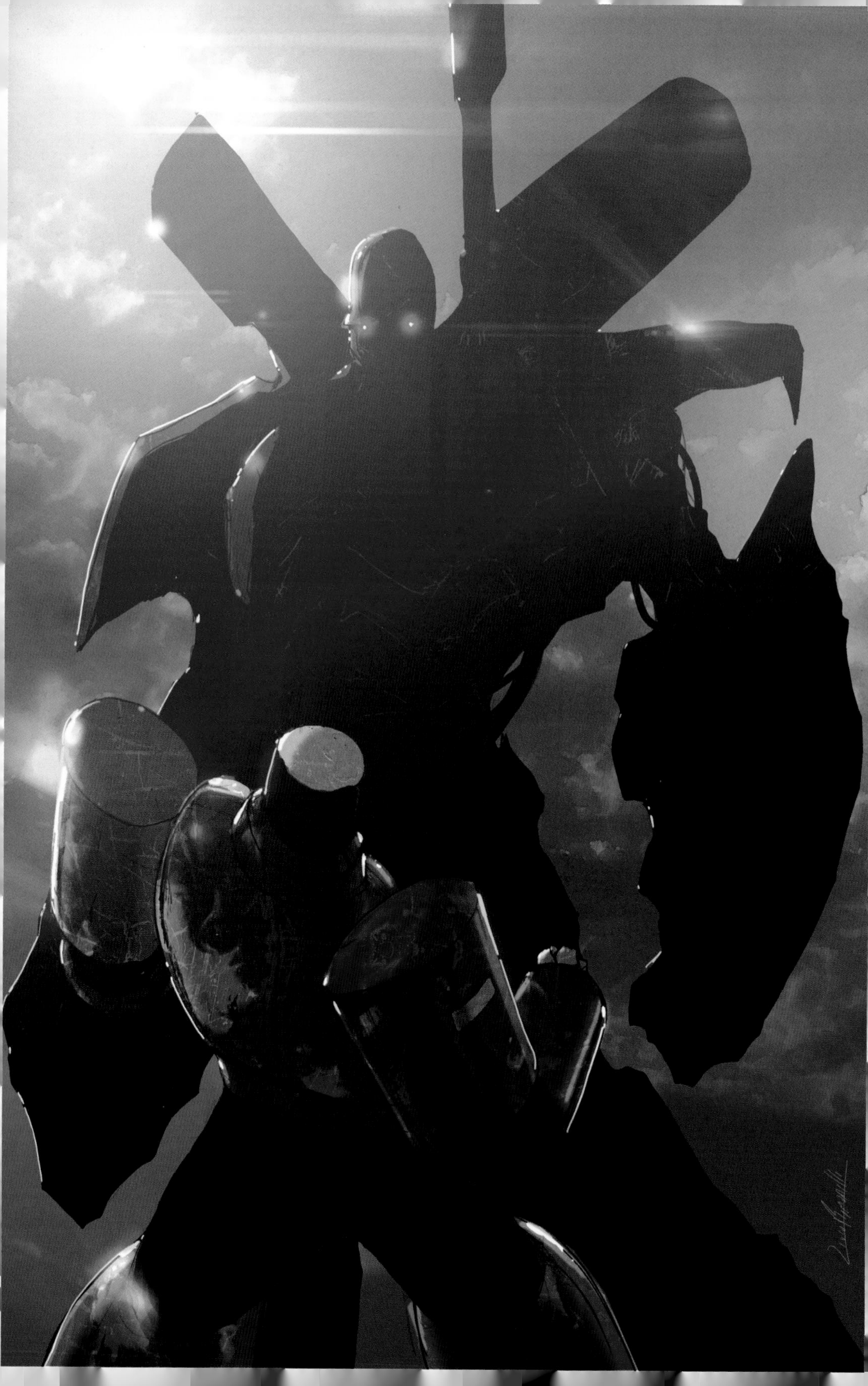

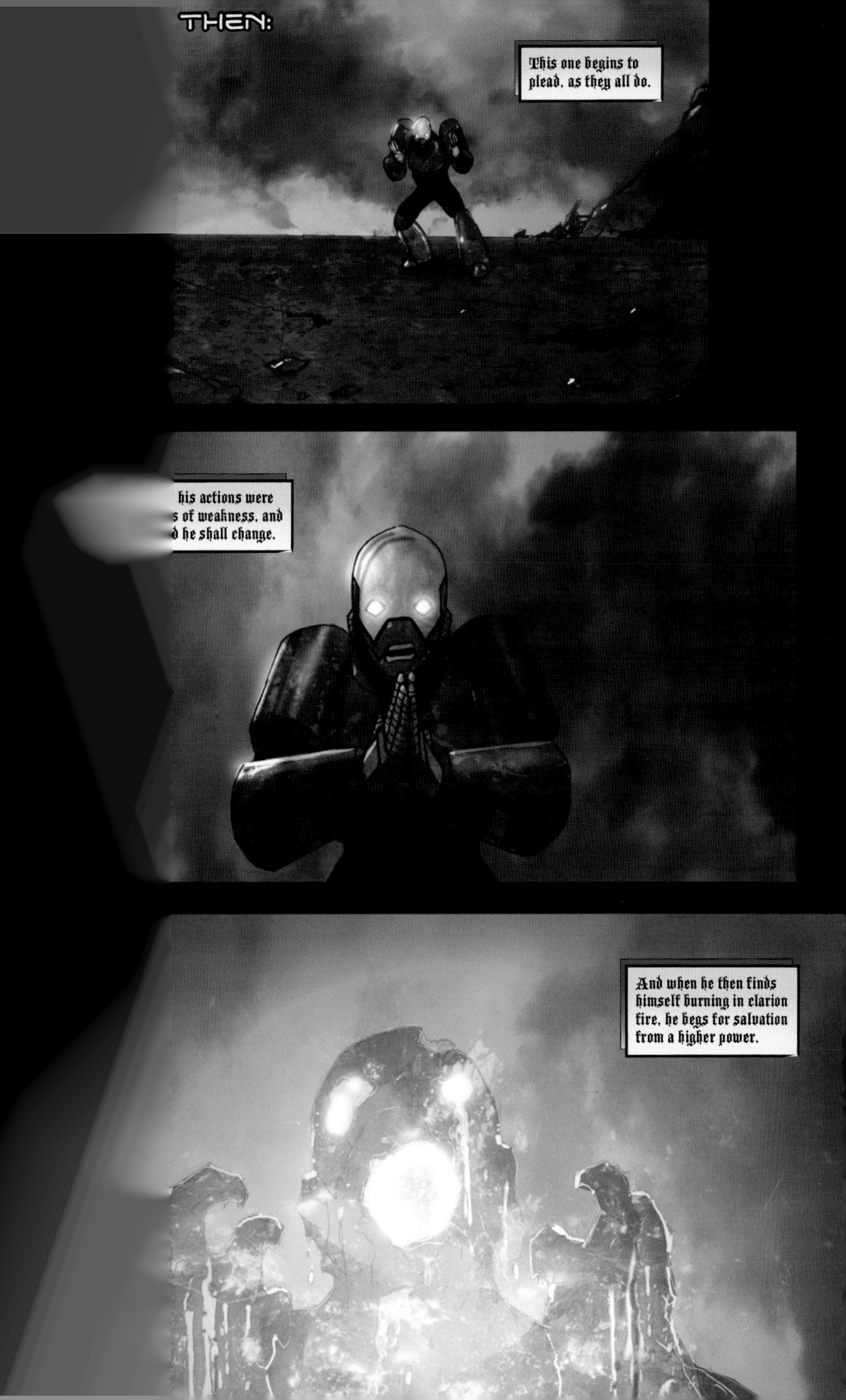
THEN:
This one begins to plead, as they all do.
his actions were
s of weakness, and
d he shall change.
And when he then finds himself burning in clarion fire, he begs for salvation from a higher power.

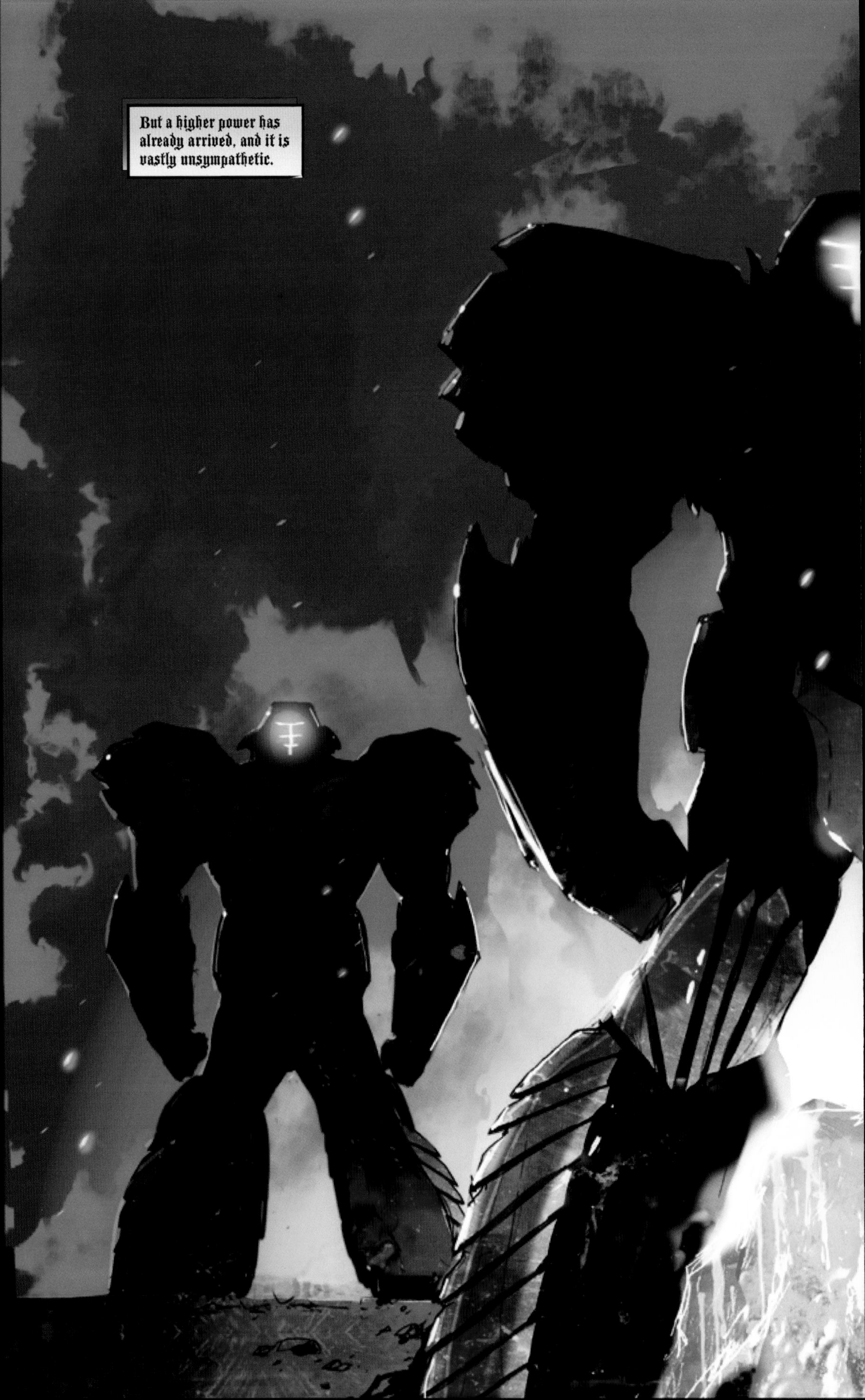
But a higher power has already arrived, and it is vastly unsympathetic.

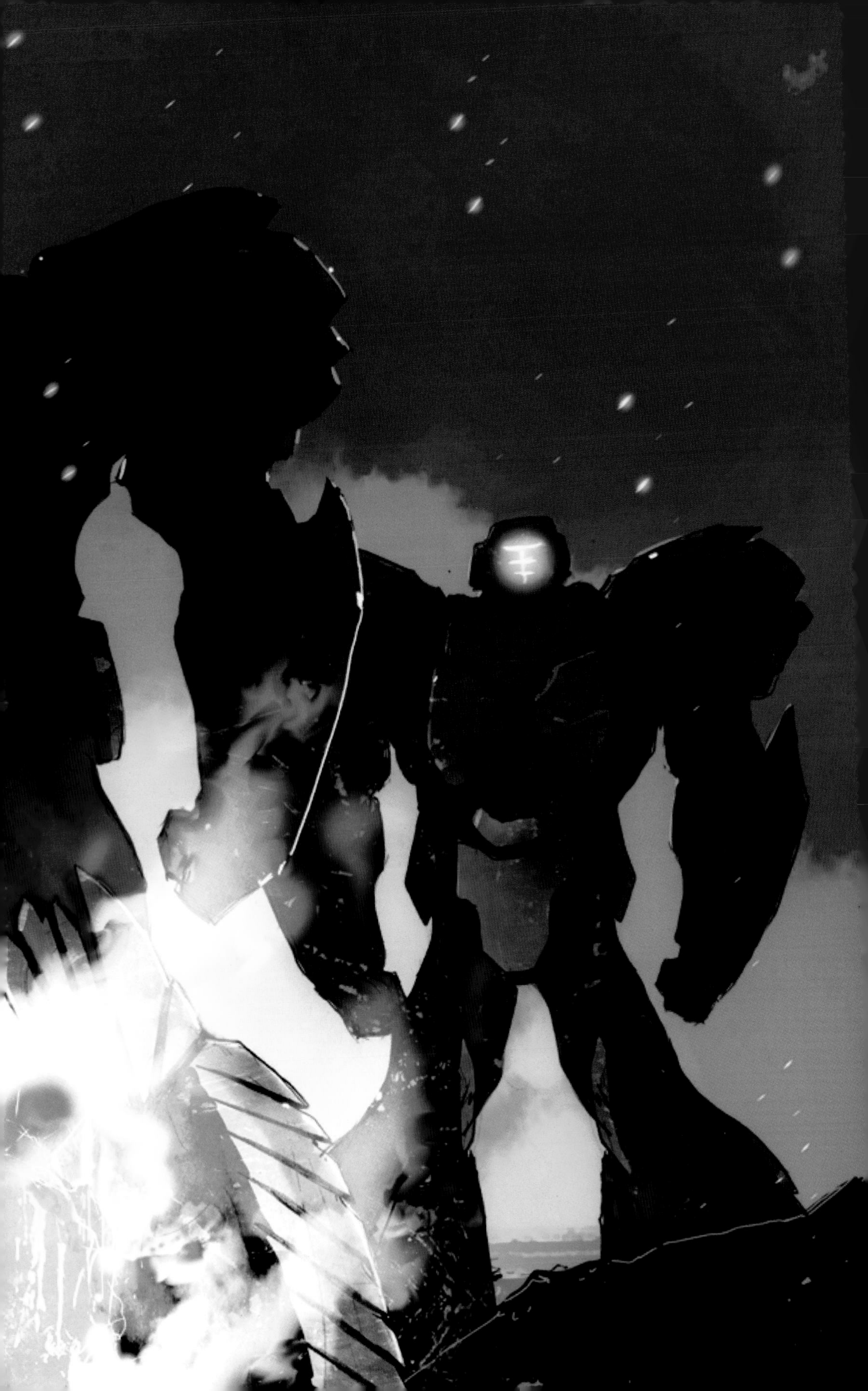

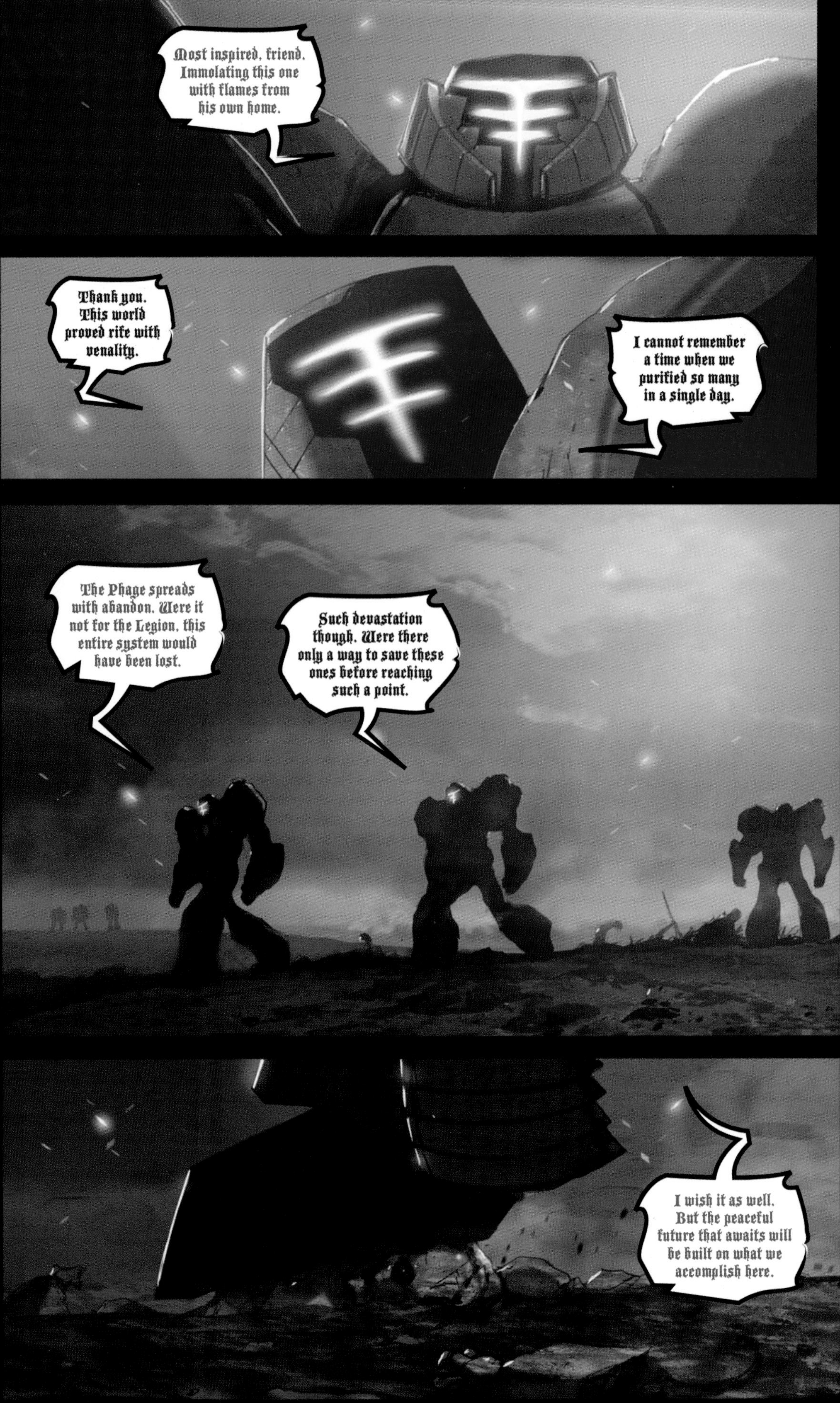

Most inspired, friend. Immolating this one with flames from his own home.
Thank you. This world proved rife with venality.
I cannot remember a time when we purified so many in a single day.
The Phage spreads with abandon. Were it not for the Legion, this entire system would have been lost.
Such devastation though. Were there only a way to save these ones before reaching such a point.
I wish it as well. But the peaceful future that awaits will be built on what we accomplish here.

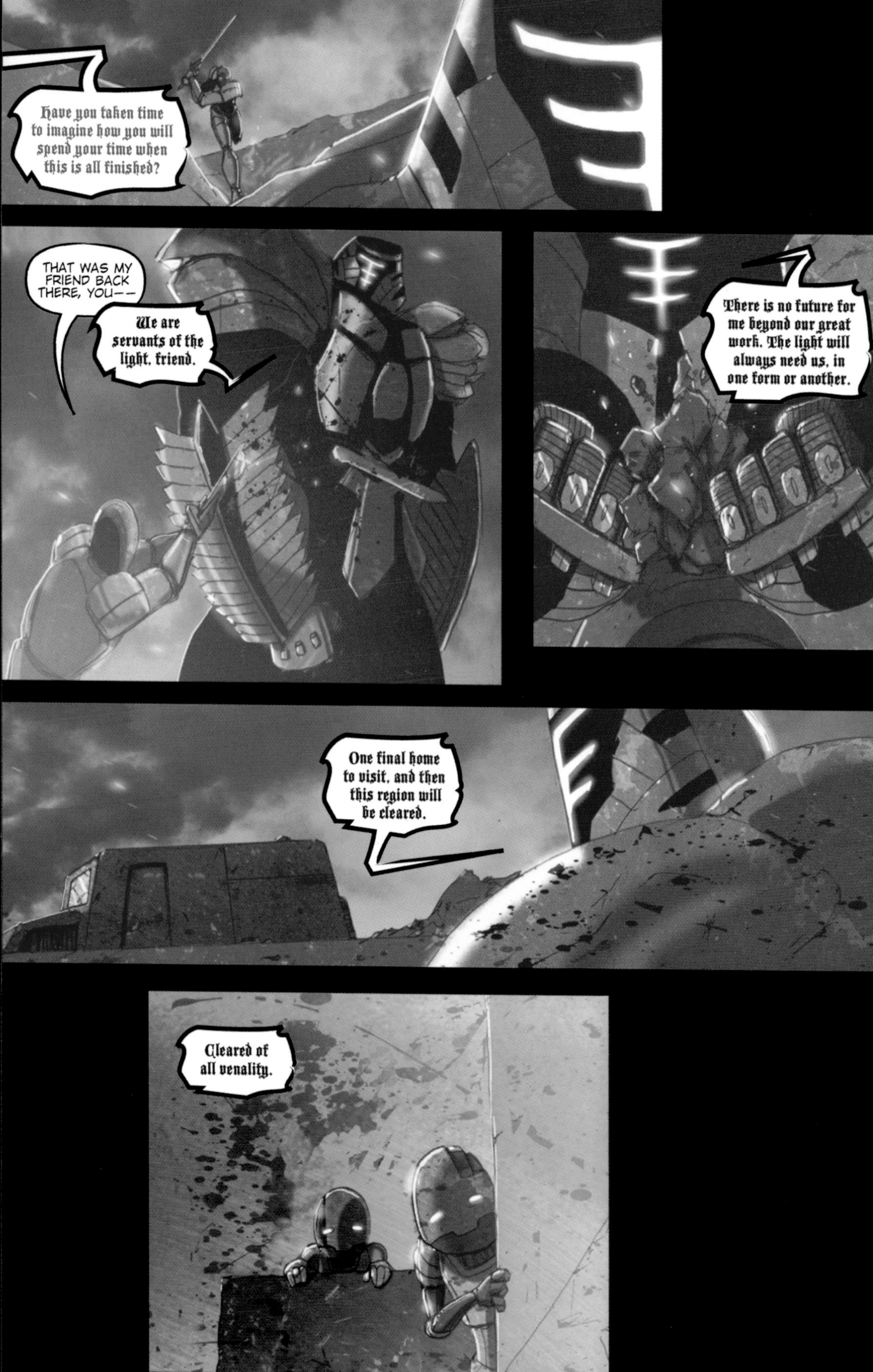
Have you taken time to imagine how you will spend your time when this is all finished?
THAT WAS MY FRIEND BACK THERE, YOU––
We are servants of the light, friend.
There is no future for me beyond our great work. The light will always need us, in one form or another.
One final home to visit, and then this region will be cleared.
Cleared of all venality.

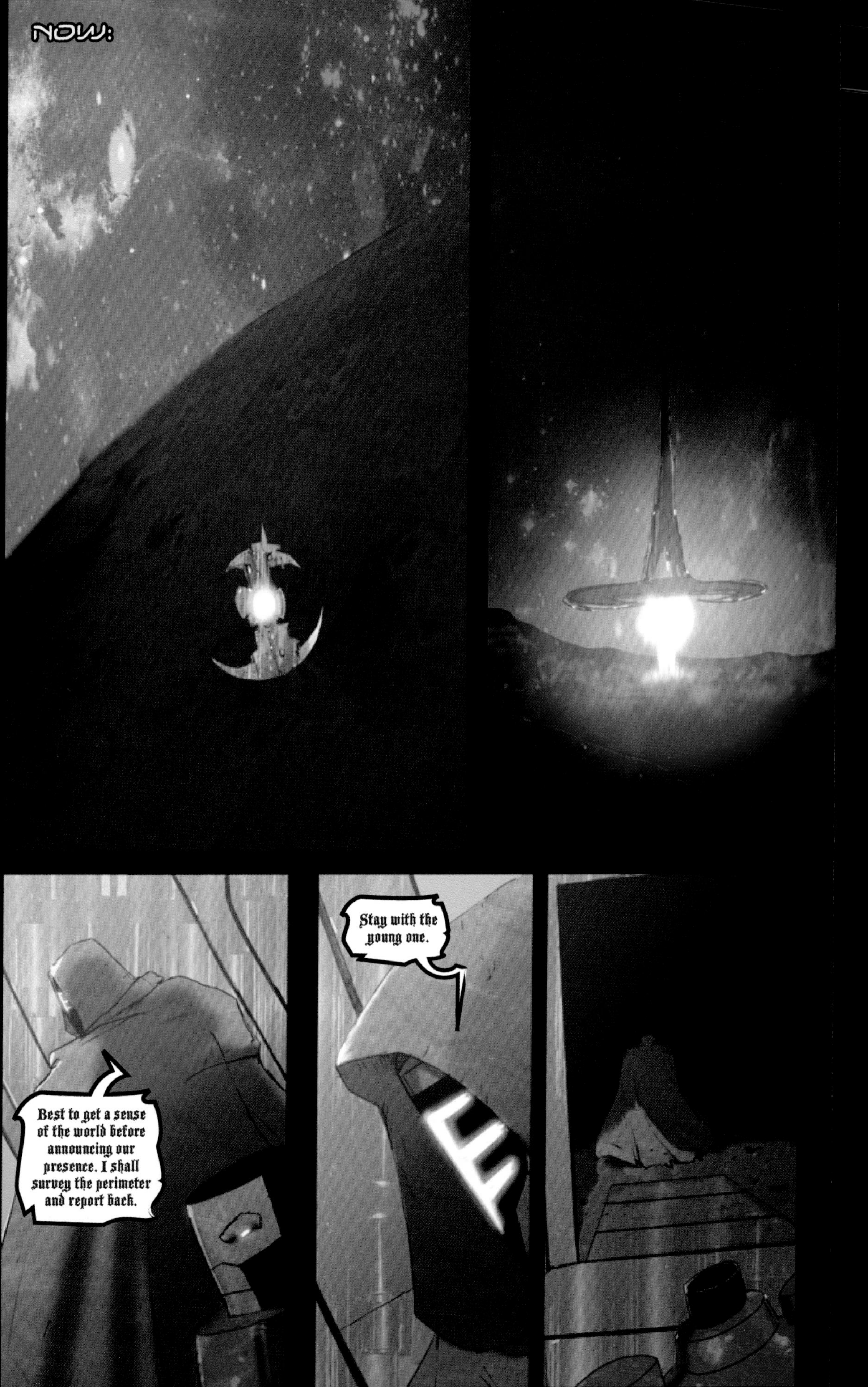
NOW:
Best to get a sense of the world before announcing our presence. I shall survey the perimeter and report back.
Stay with the young one.

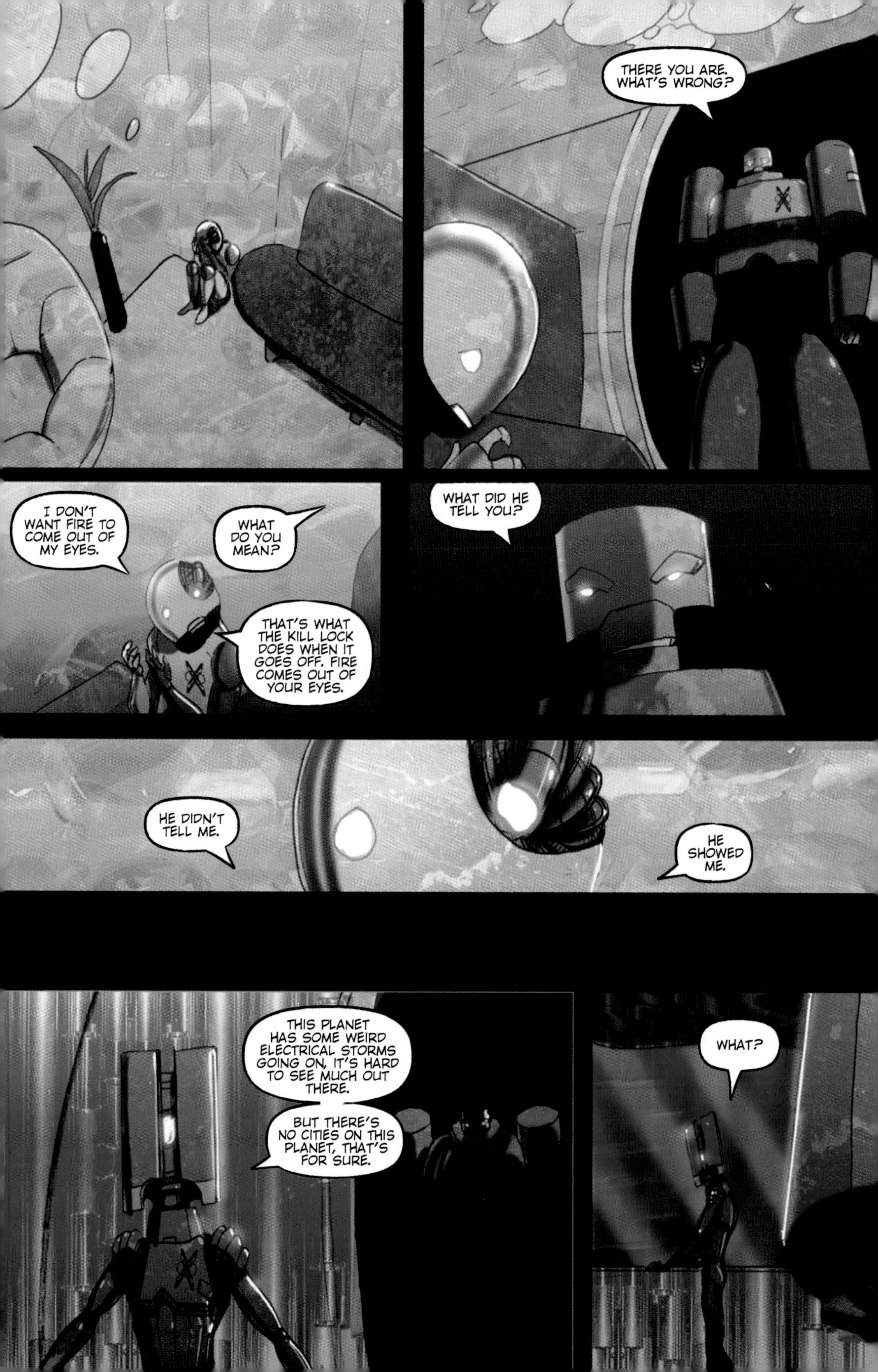
THERE YOU ARE. WHAT'S WRONG?
I DON'T WANT FIRE TO COME OUT OF MY EYES.
WHAT DO YOU MEAN?
THAT'S WHAT THE KILL LOCK DOES WHEN IT GOES OFF. FIRE COMES OUT OF YOUR EYES.
WHAT DID HE TELL YOU?
HE DIDN'T TELL ME.
HE SHOWED ME.
THIS PLANET HAS SOME WEIRD ELECTRICAL STORMS GOING ON, IT'S HARD TO SEE MUCH OUT THERE.
BUT THERE'S NO CITIES ON THIS PLANET, THAT'S FOR SURE.
WHAT?

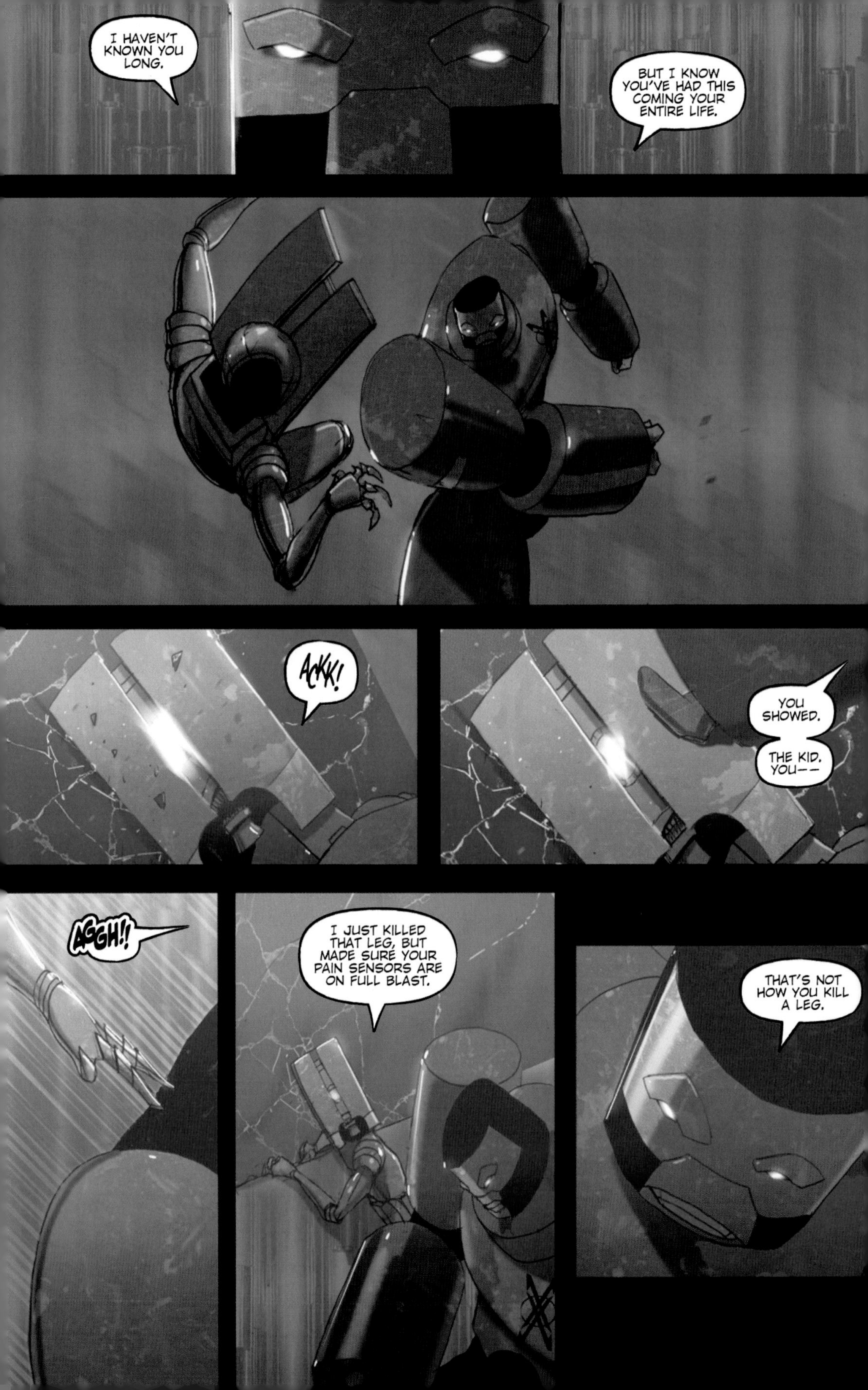
I HAVEN'T KNOWN YOU LONG.
BUT I KNOW YOU'VE HAD THIS COMING YOUR ENTIRE LIFE.
ACKK!
YOU SHOWED.
THE KID. YOU--
AGGH!!
I JUST KILLED THAT LEG, BUT MADE SURE YOUR PAIN SENSORS ARE ON FULL BLAST.
THAT'S NOT HOW YOU KILL A LEG.

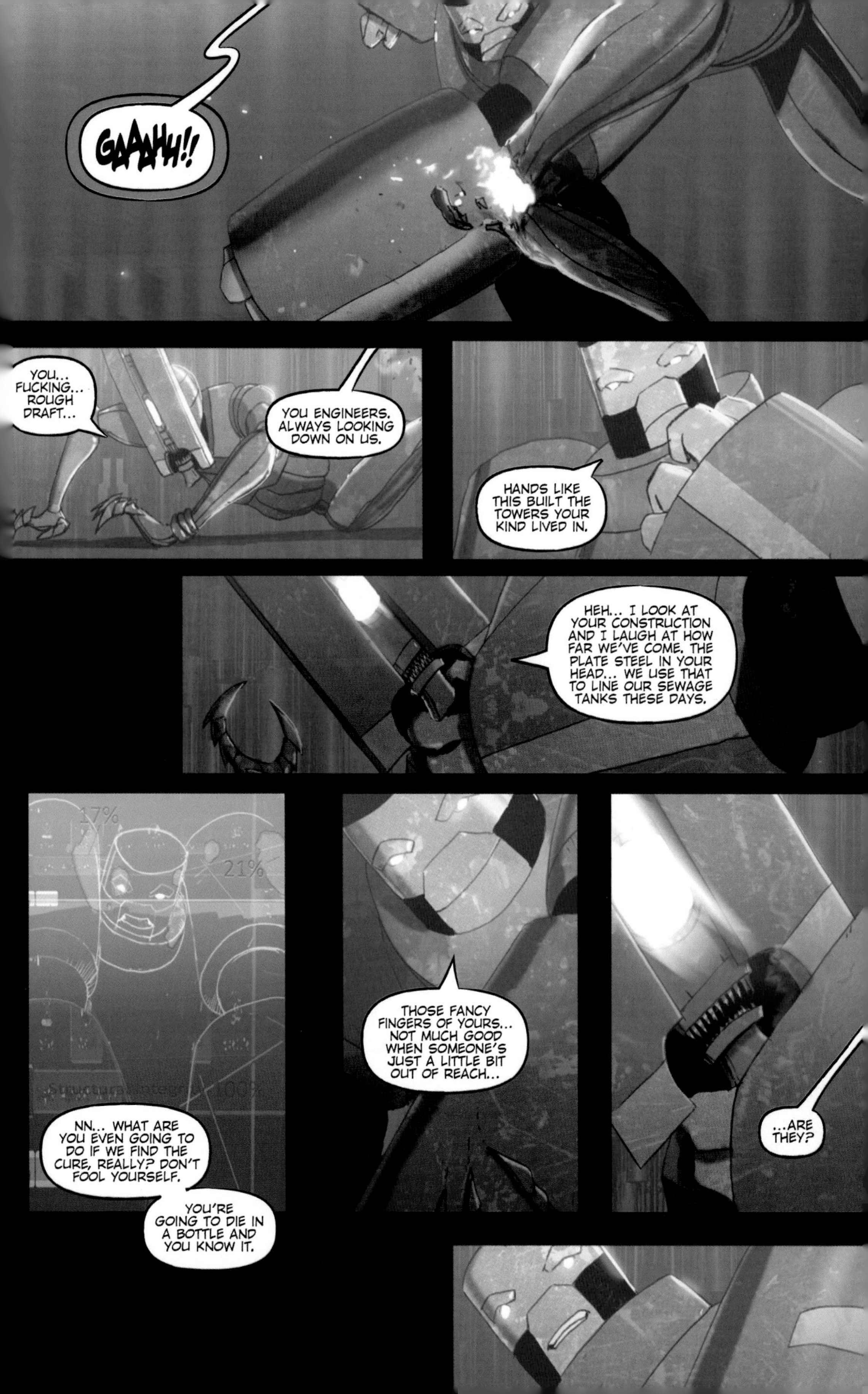
GAAAHH!!
YOU... FUCKING... ROUGH DRAFT...
YOU ENGINEERS. ALWAYS LOOKING DOWN ON US.
HANDS LIKE THIS BUILT THE TOWERS YOUR KIND LIVED IN.
HEH... I LOOK AT YOUR CONSTRUCTION AND I LAUGH AT HOW FAR WE'VE COME. THE PLATE STEEL IN YOUR HEAD... WE USE THAT TO LINE OUR SEWAGE TANKS THESE DAYS.
17%
21%
NN... WHAT ARE YOU EVEN GOING TO DO IF WE FIND THE CURE, REALLY? DON'T FOOL YOURSELF.
YOU'RE GOING TO DIE IN A BOTTLE AND YOU KNOW IT.
THOSE FANCY FINGERS OF YOURS... NOT MUCH GOOD WHEN SOMEONE'S JUST A LITTLE BIT OUT OF REACH...
...ARE THEY?

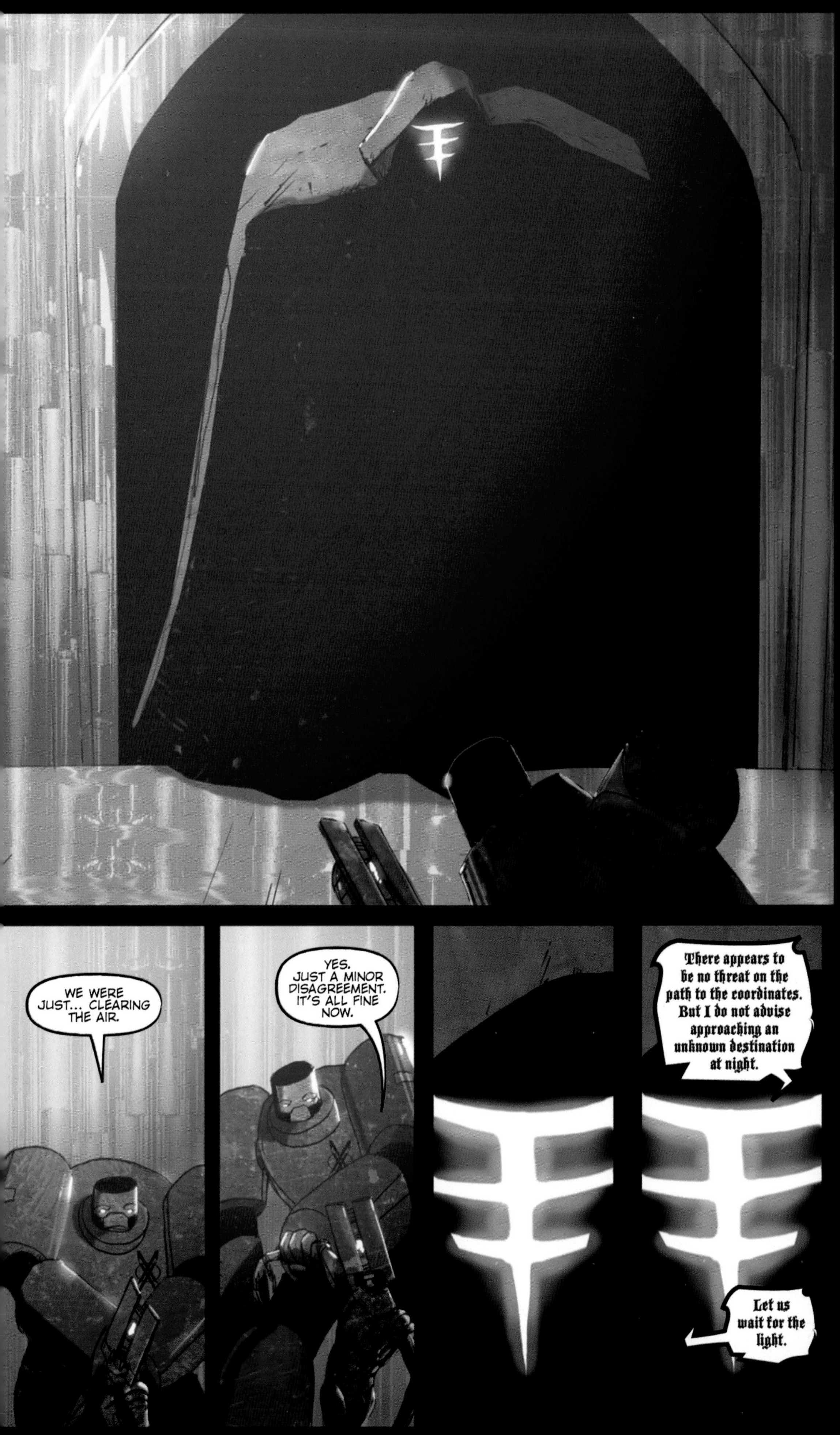
WE WERE JUST... CLEARING THE AIR.
YES. JUST A MINOR DISAGREEMENT. IT'S ALL FINE NOW.
There appears to be no threat on the path to the coordinates. But I do not advise approaching an unknown destination at night.
Let us wait for the light.

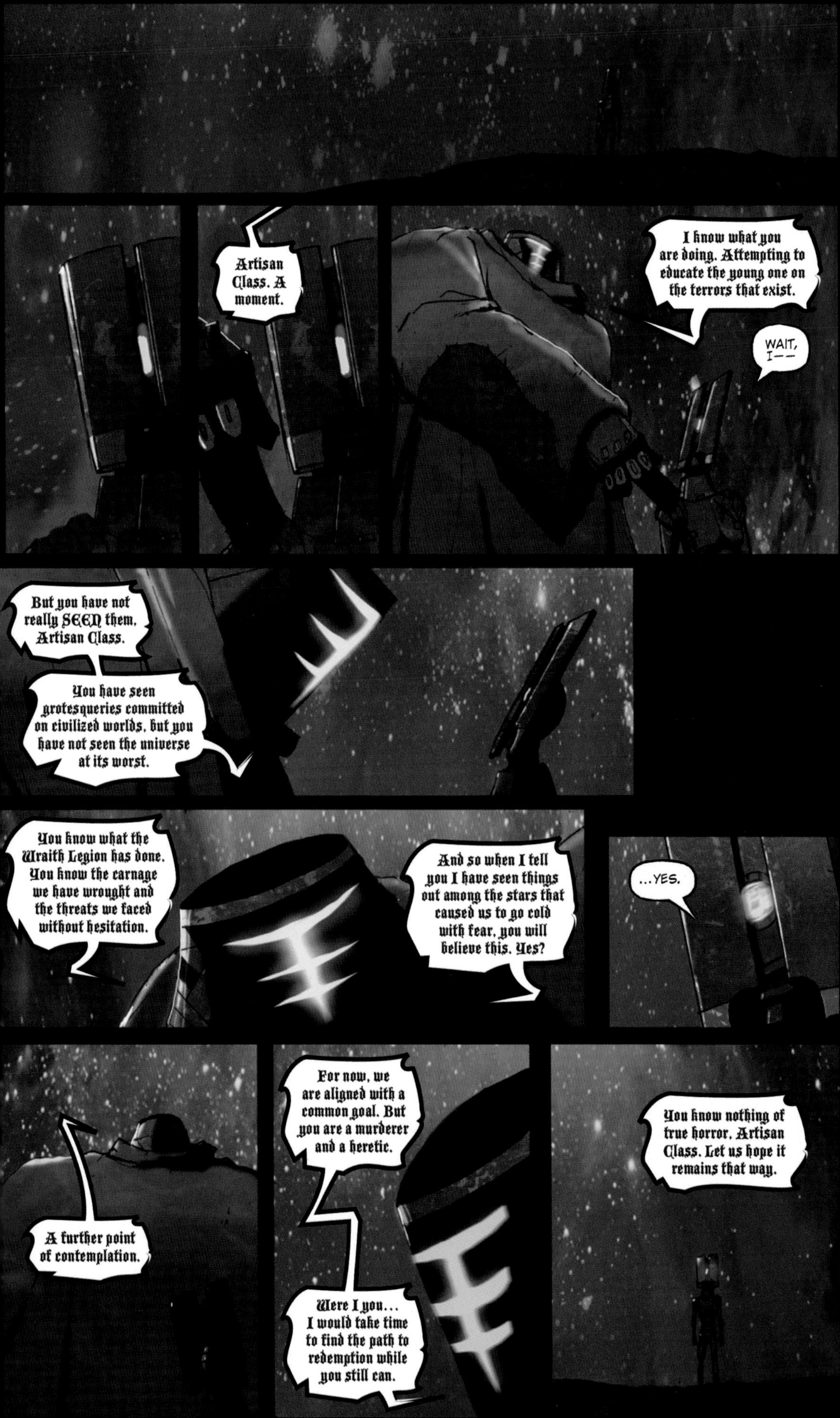
Artisan Class. A moment.
I know what you are doing. Attempting to educate the young one on the terrors that exist.
WAIT, I--
But you have not really SEEN them, Artisan Class.
You have seen grotesqueries committed on civilized worlds, but you have not seen the universe at its worst.
You know what the Wraith Legion has done. You know the carnage we have wrought and the threats we faced without hesitation.
And so when I tell you I have seen things out among the stars that caused us to go cold with fear, you will believe this. Yes?
...YES.
A further point of contemplation.
For now, we are aligned with a common goal. But you are a murderer and a heretic.
Were I you... I would take time to find the path to redemption while you still can.
You know nothing of true horror, Artisan Class. Let us hope it remains that way.

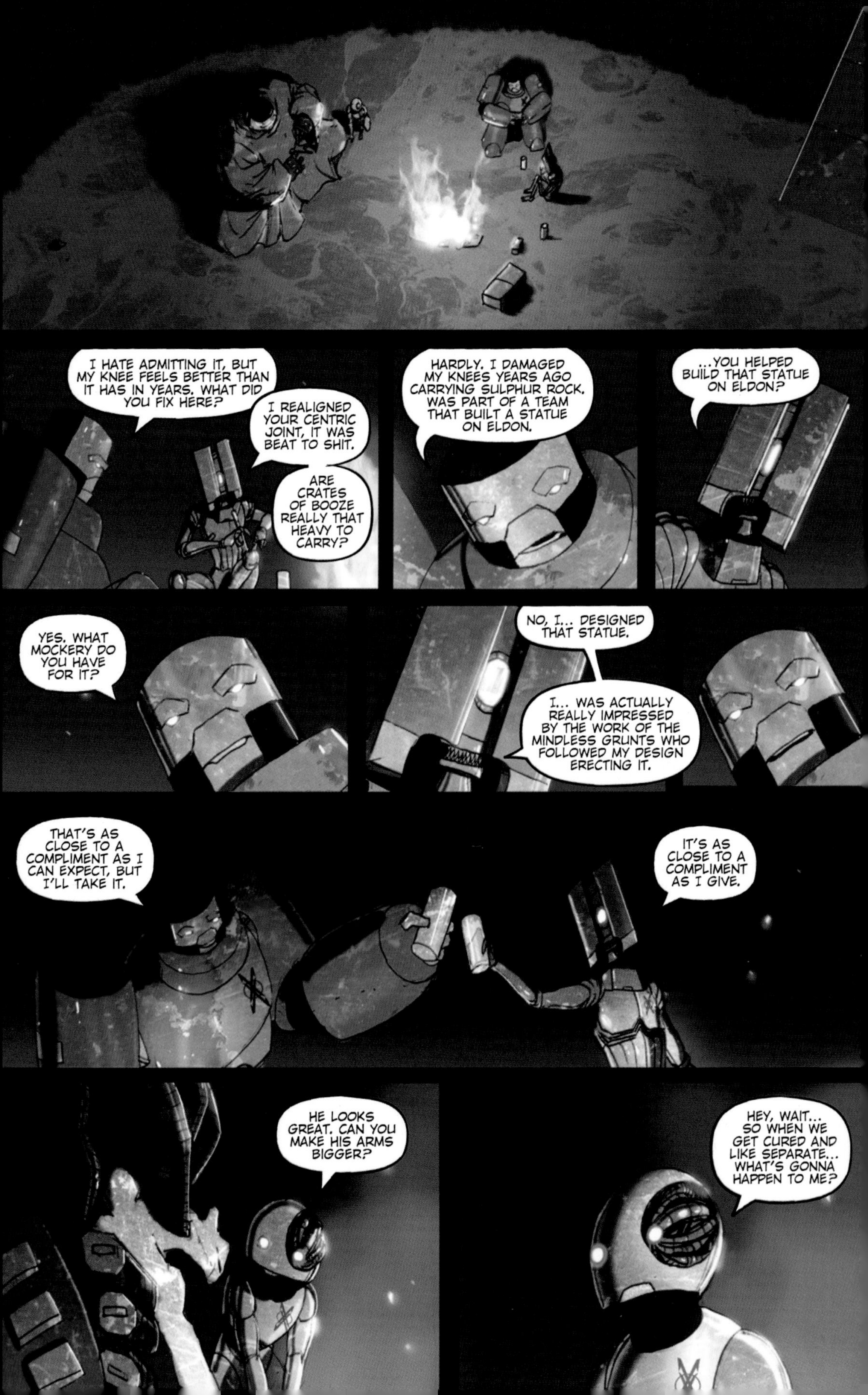
I HATE ADMITTING IT, BUT MY KNEE FEELS BETTER THAN IT HAS IN YEARS. WHAT DID YOU FIX HERE?
I REALIGNED YOUR CENTRIC JOINT, IT WAS BEAT TO SHIT.
ARE CRATES OF BOOZE REALLY THAT HEAVY TO CARRY?
HARDLY. I DAMAGED MY KNEES YEARS AGO CARRYING SULPHUR ROCK. WAS PART OF A TEAM THAT BUILT A STATUE ON ELDON.
...YOU HELPED BUILD THAT STATUE ON ELDON?
YES. WHAT MOCKERY DO YOU HAVE FOR IT?
NO, I... DESIGNED THAT STATUE.
I... WAS ACTUALLY REALLY IMPRESSED BY THE WORK OF THE MINDLESS GRUNTS WHO FOLLOWED MY DESIGN ERECTING IT.
THAT'S AS CLOSE TO A COMPLIMENT AS I CAN EXPECT, BUT I'LL TAKE IT.
IT'S AS CLOSE TO A COMPLIMENT AS I GIVE.
HE LOOKS GREAT. CAN YOU MAKE HIS ARMS BIGGER?
HEY, WAIT... SO WHEN WE GET CURED AND LIKE SEPARATE... WHAT'S GONNA HAPPEN TO ME?

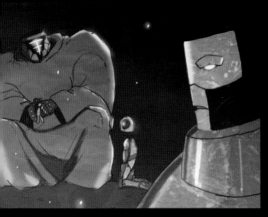

WE... WE HADN'T REALLY THOUGHT OF...

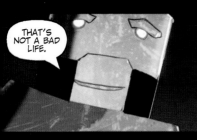

You may stay with me, if you like.

You will see the galaxy, you will learn from its wonders and curiosities, and then when you are ready, you will depart to find your own path.

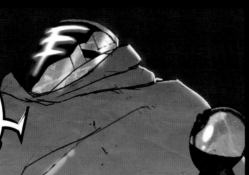

If you choose.

THAT'S NOT A BAD LIFE.

OKAY.

We could first go visit the ancient ruins of——

WAIT, I WANT HIM TO HAVE THOSE SHARP THINGS IN HIS ARM LIKE YOU HAVE.

Hmm. I am unsure how to sculpt——

HERE. I KNOW WHAT THEY LOOK LIKE.

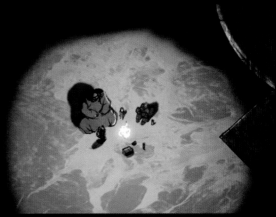

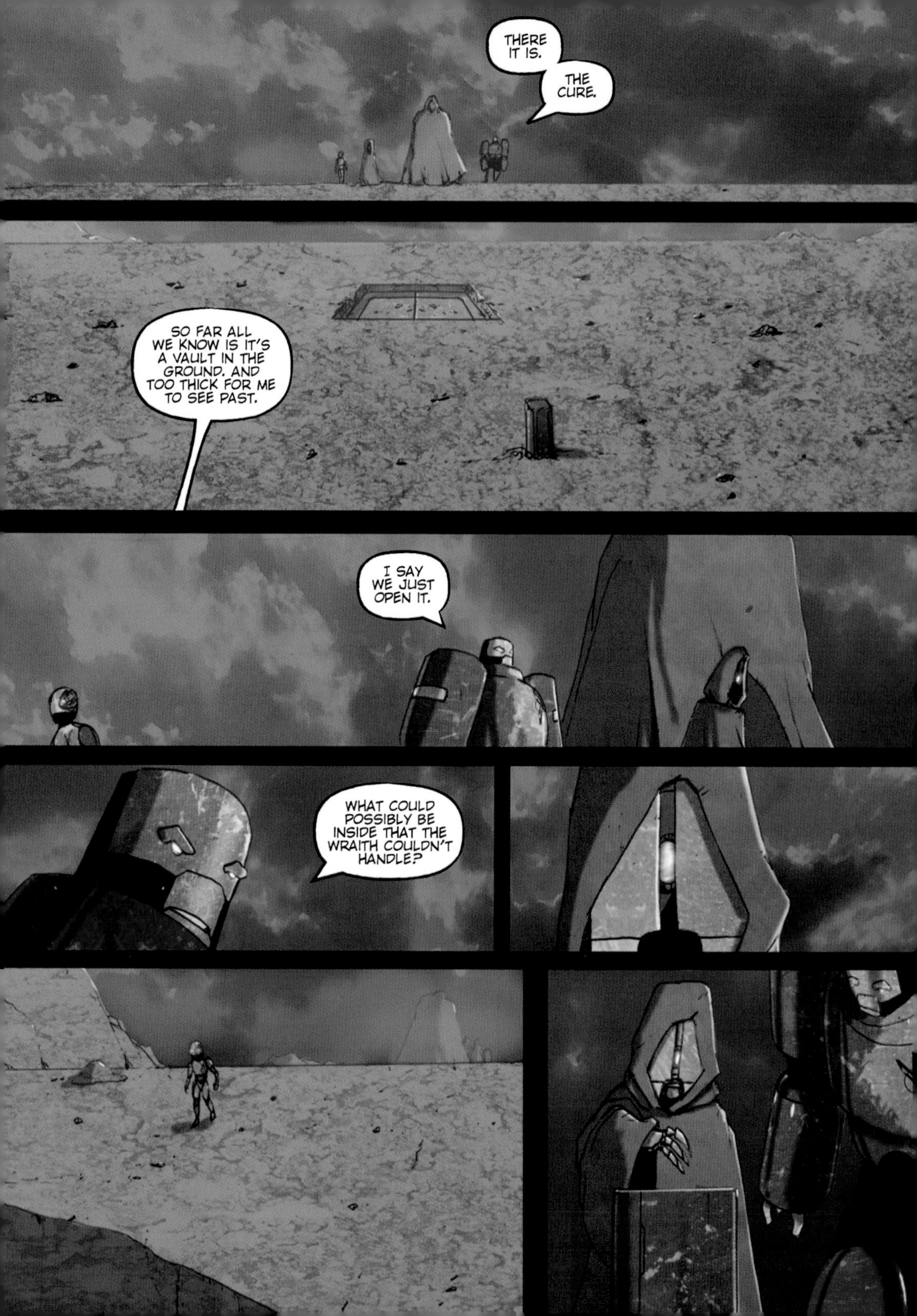
THERE IT IS.
THE CURE.
SO FAR ALL WE KNOW IS IT'S A VAULT IN THE GROUND. AND TOO THICK FOR ME TO SEE PAST.
I SAY WE JUST OPEN IT.
WHAT COULD POSSIBLY BE INSIDE THAT THE WRAITH COULDN'T HANDLE?

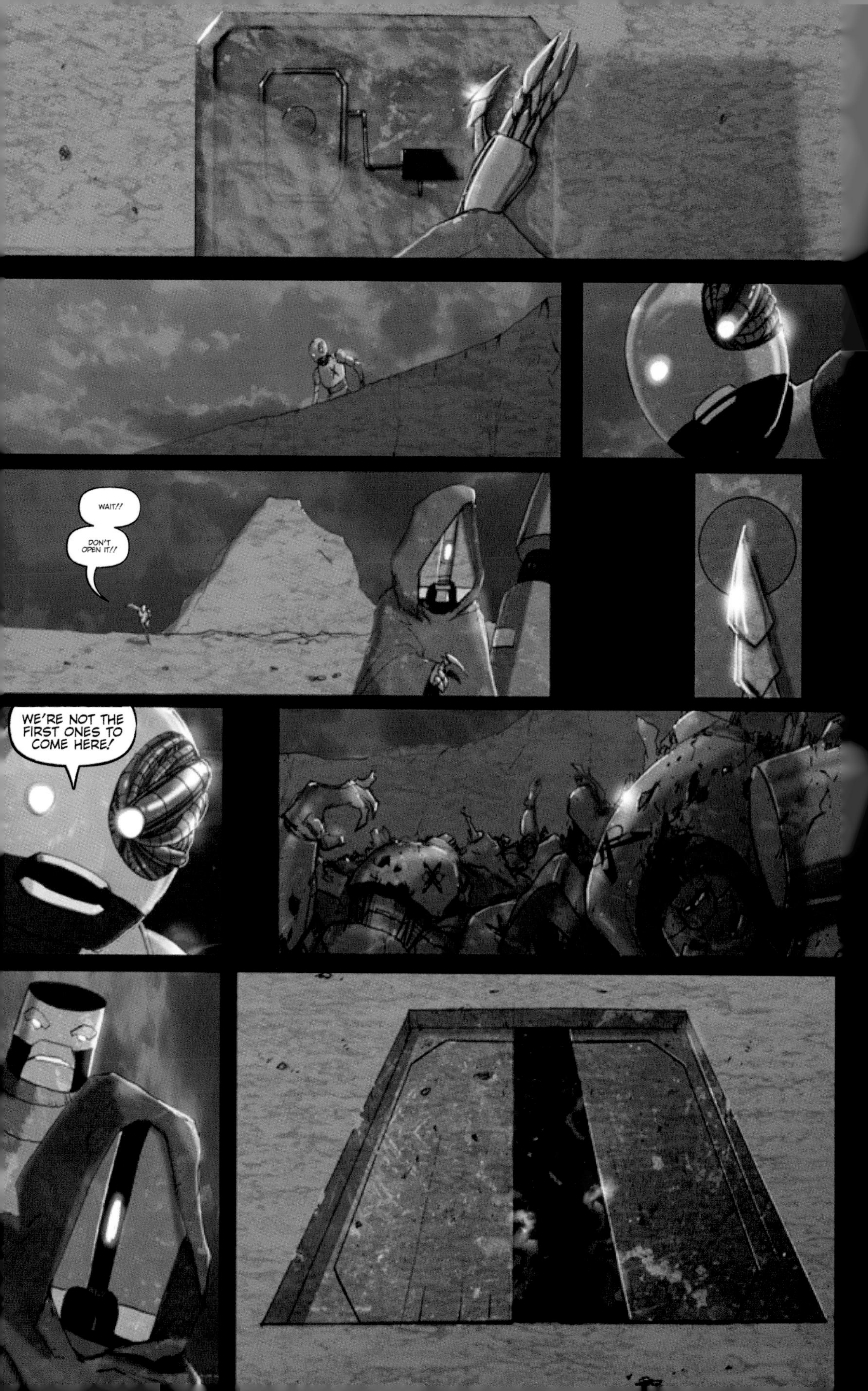
WAIT!!
DON'T OPEN IT!!
WE'RE NOT THE FIRST ONES TO COME HERE!

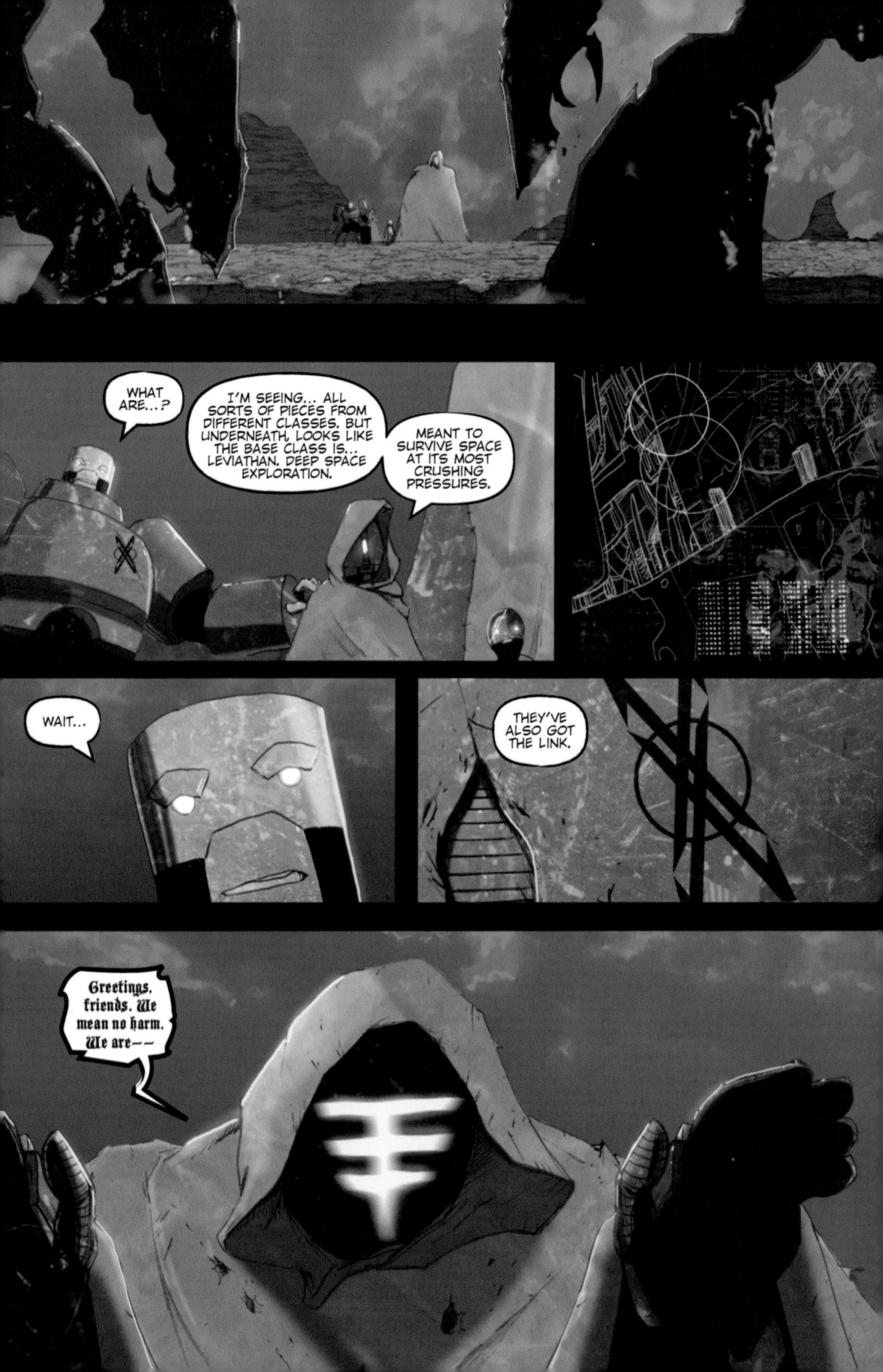
WHAT ARE...?
I'M SEEING... ALL SORTS OF PIECES FROM DIFFERENT CLASSES. BUT UNDERNEATH, LOOKS LIKE THE BASE CLASS IS... LEVIATHAN. DEEP SPACE EXPLORATION.
MEANT TO SURVIVE SPACE AT ITS MOST CRUSHING PRESSURES.
WAIT...
THEY'VE ALSO GOT THE LINK.
Greetings, friends. We mean no harm. We are--

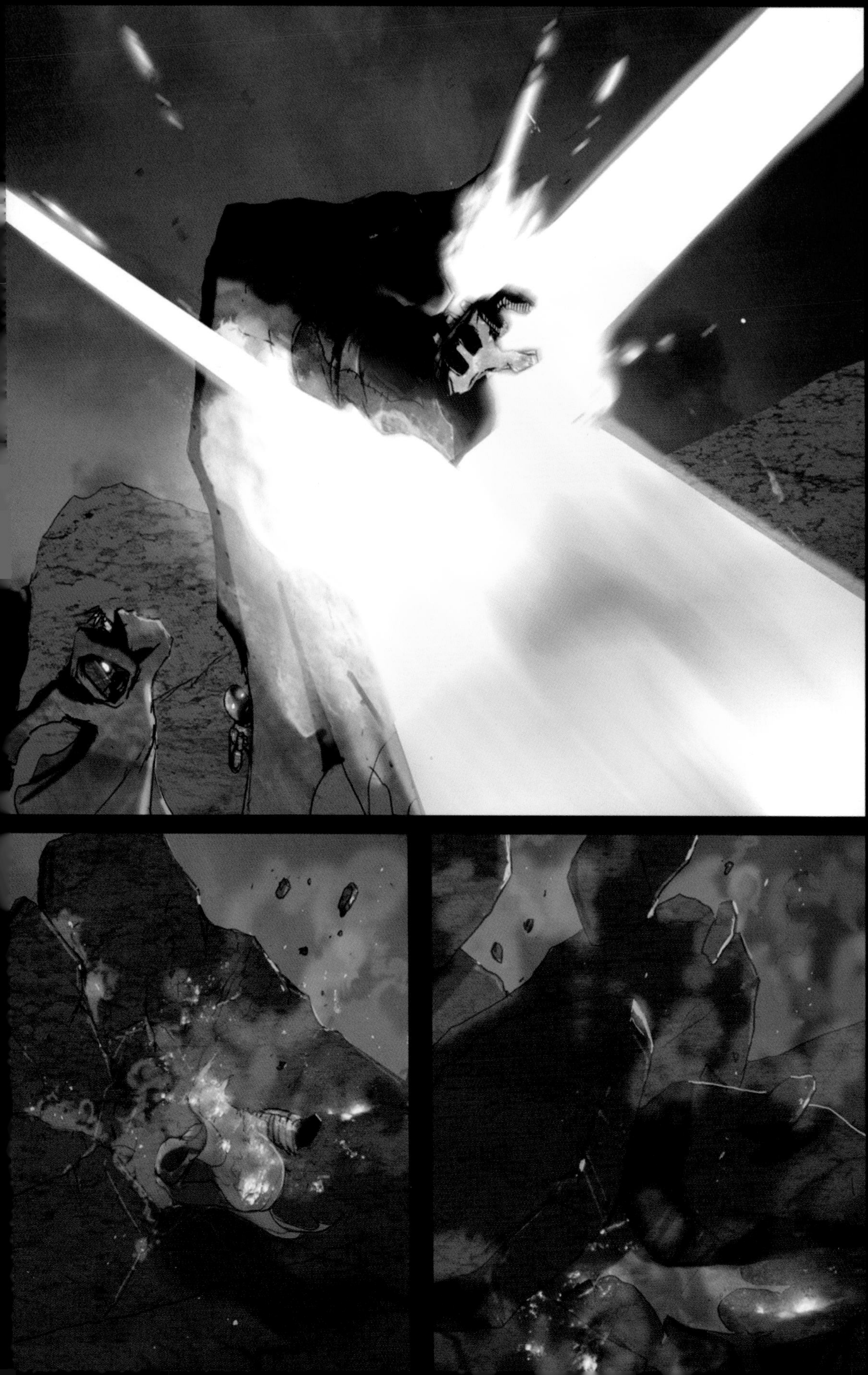

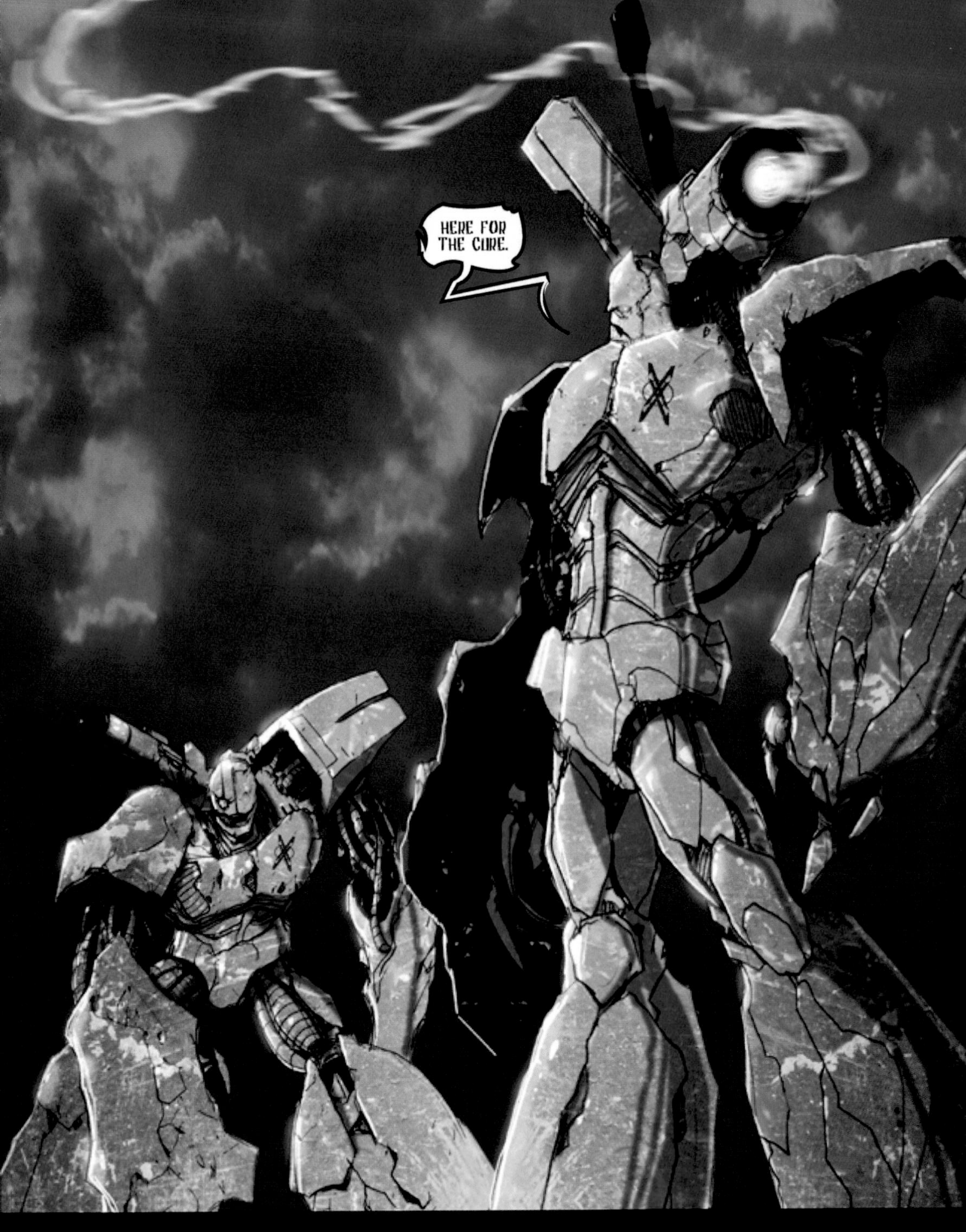
HERE FOR THE CURE.
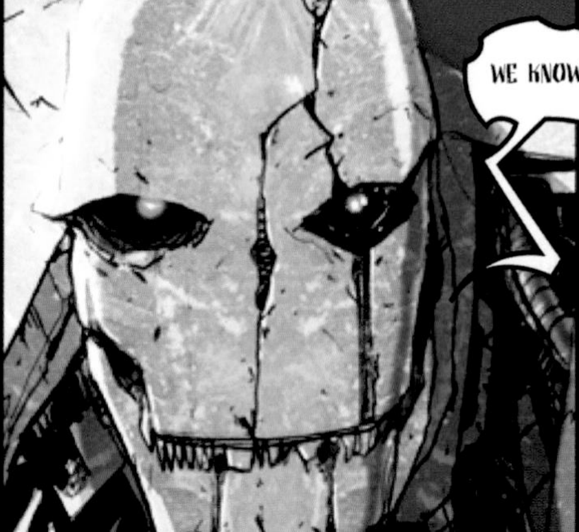
WE KNOW.

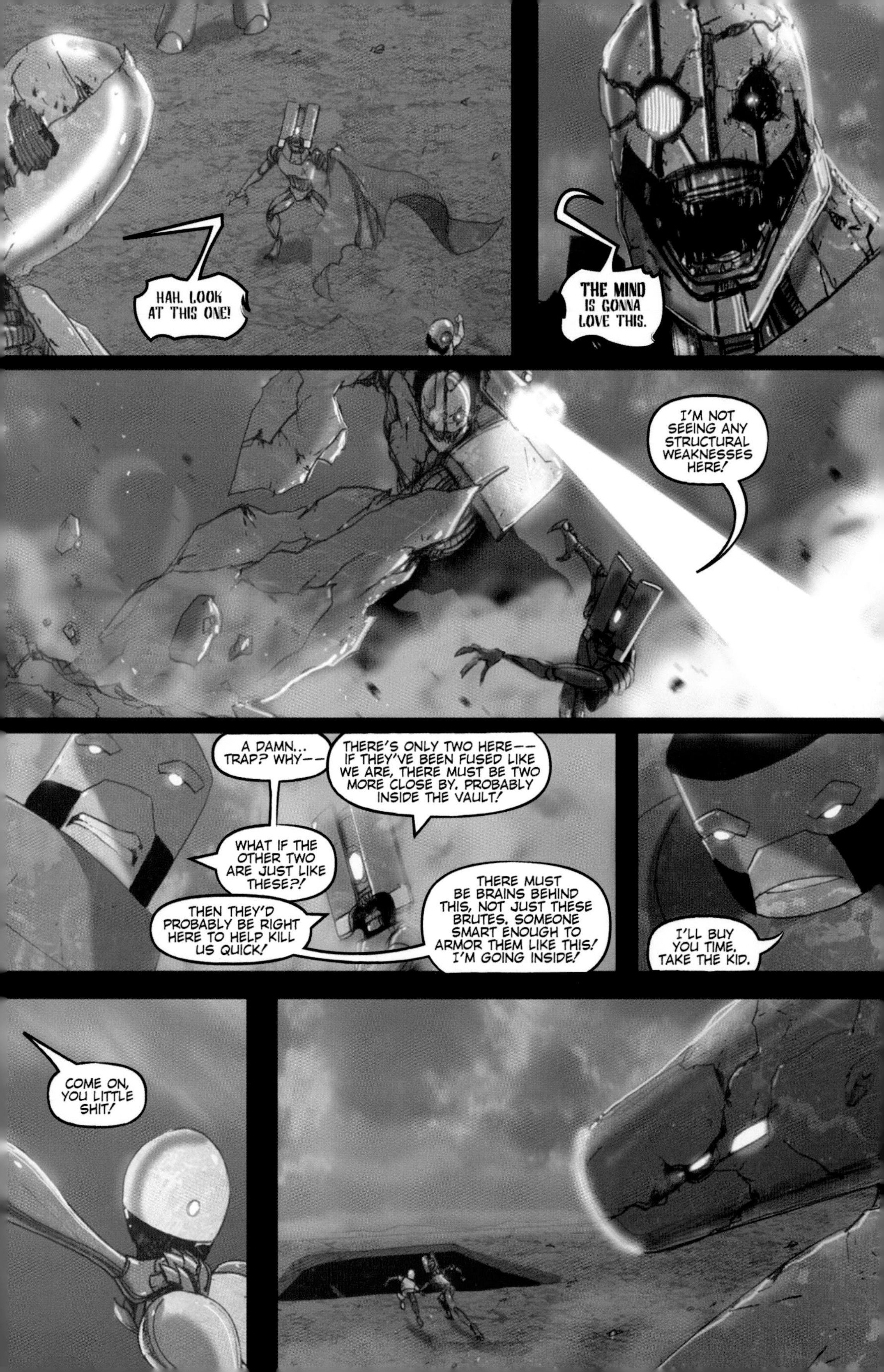
HAH. LOOK AT THIS ONE!
THE MIND IS GONNA LOVE THIS.
I'M NOT SEEING ANY STRUCTURAL WEAKNESSES HERE!
A DAMN... TRAP? WHY--
THERE'S ONLY TWO HERE-- IF THEY'VE BEEN FUSED LIKE WE ARE, THERE MUST BE TWO MORE CLOSE BY. PROBABLY INSIDE THE VAULT!
WHAT IF THE OTHER TWO ARE JUST LIKE THESE?!
THEN THEY'D PROBABLY BE RIGHT HERE TO HELP KILL US QUICK!
THERE MUST BE BRAINS BEHIND THIS, NOT JUST THESE BRUTES. SOMEONE SMART ENOUGH TO ARMOR THEM LIKE THIS! I'M GOING INSIDE!
I'LL BUY YOU TIME. TAKE THE KID.
COME ON, YOU LITTLE SHIT!

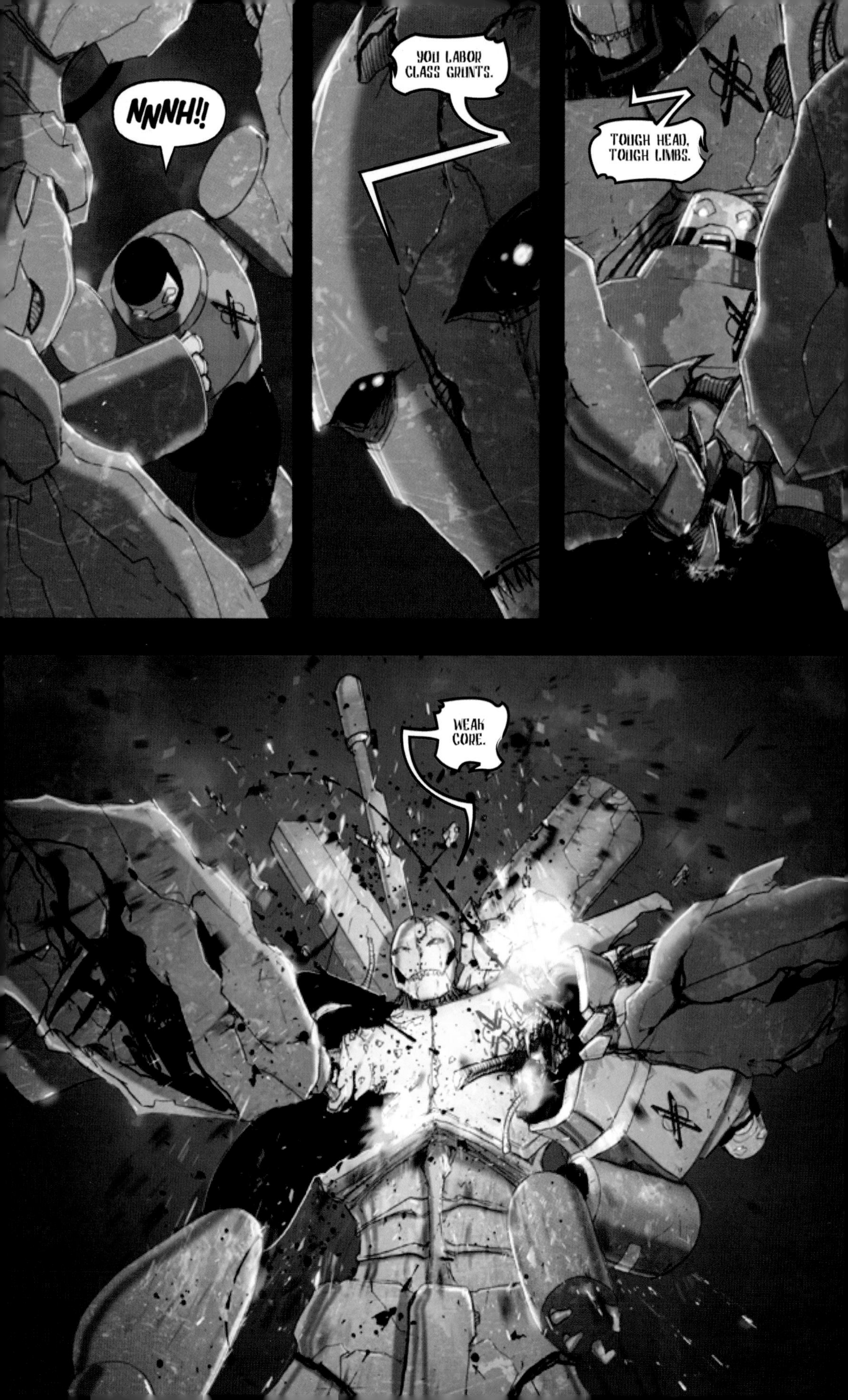
NNNH!!
YOU LABOR CLASS GRUNTS.
TOUGH HEAD, TOUGH LIMBS.
WEAK CORE.

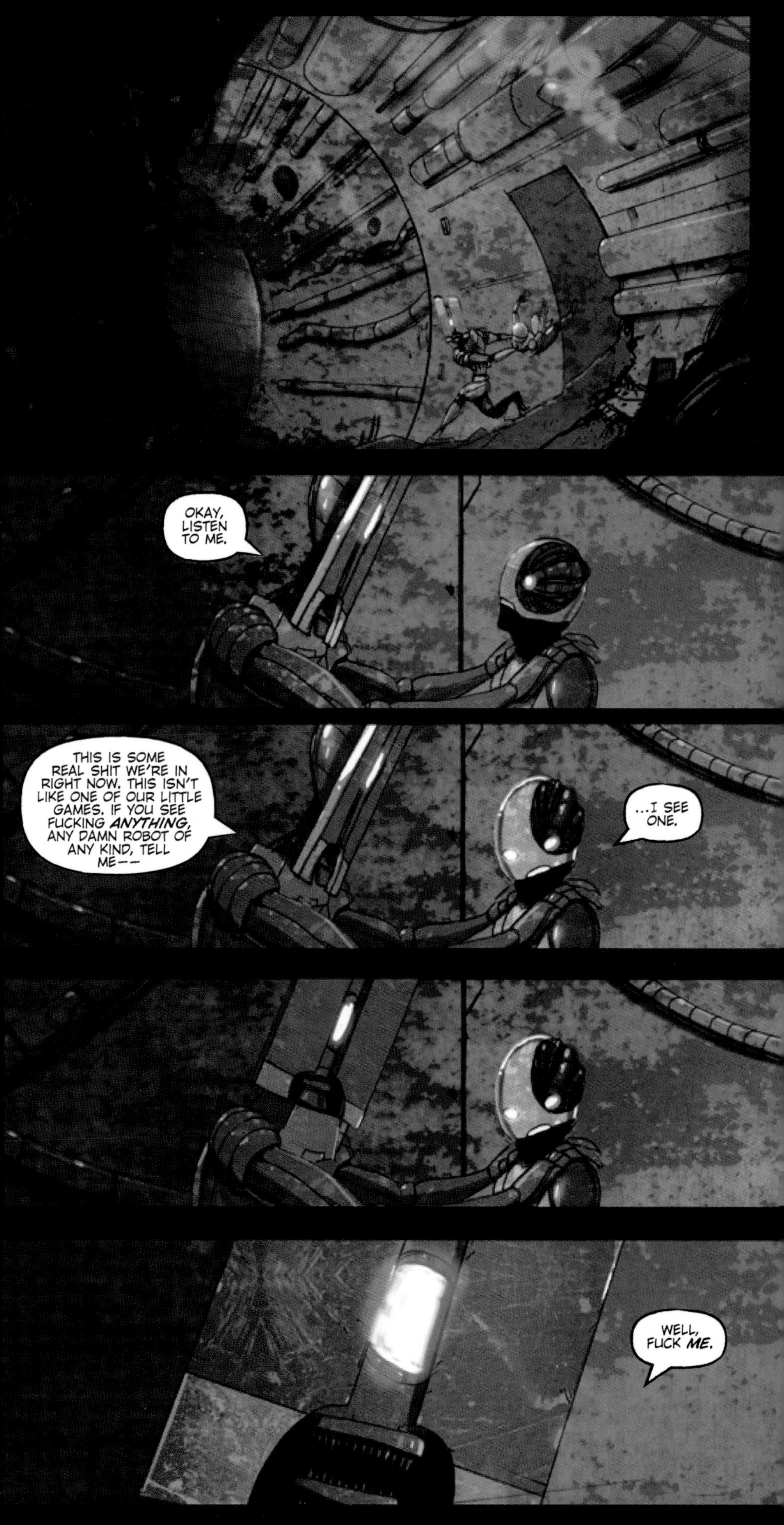
OKAY, LISTEN TO ME.
THIS IS SOME REAL SHIT WE'RE IN RIGHT NOW. THIS ISN'T LIKE ONE OF OUR LITTLE GAMES. IF YOU SEE FUCKING *ANYTHING*, ANY DAMN ROBOT OF ANY KIND, TELL ME--
...I SEE ONE.
WELL, FUCK *ME*.

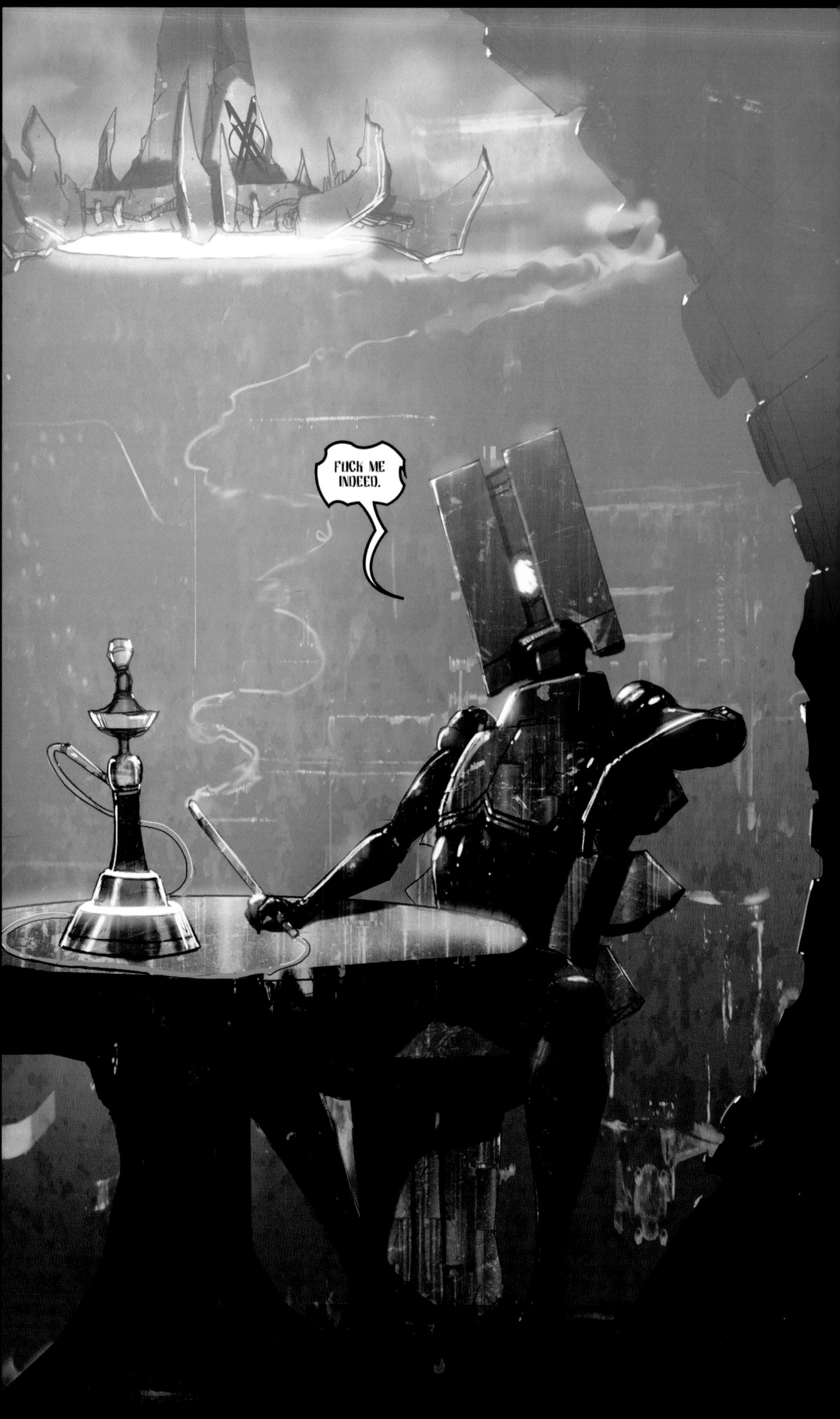
FUCK ME INDEED.

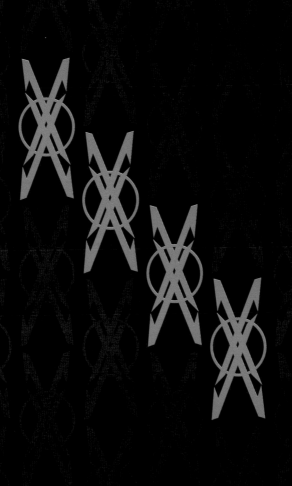

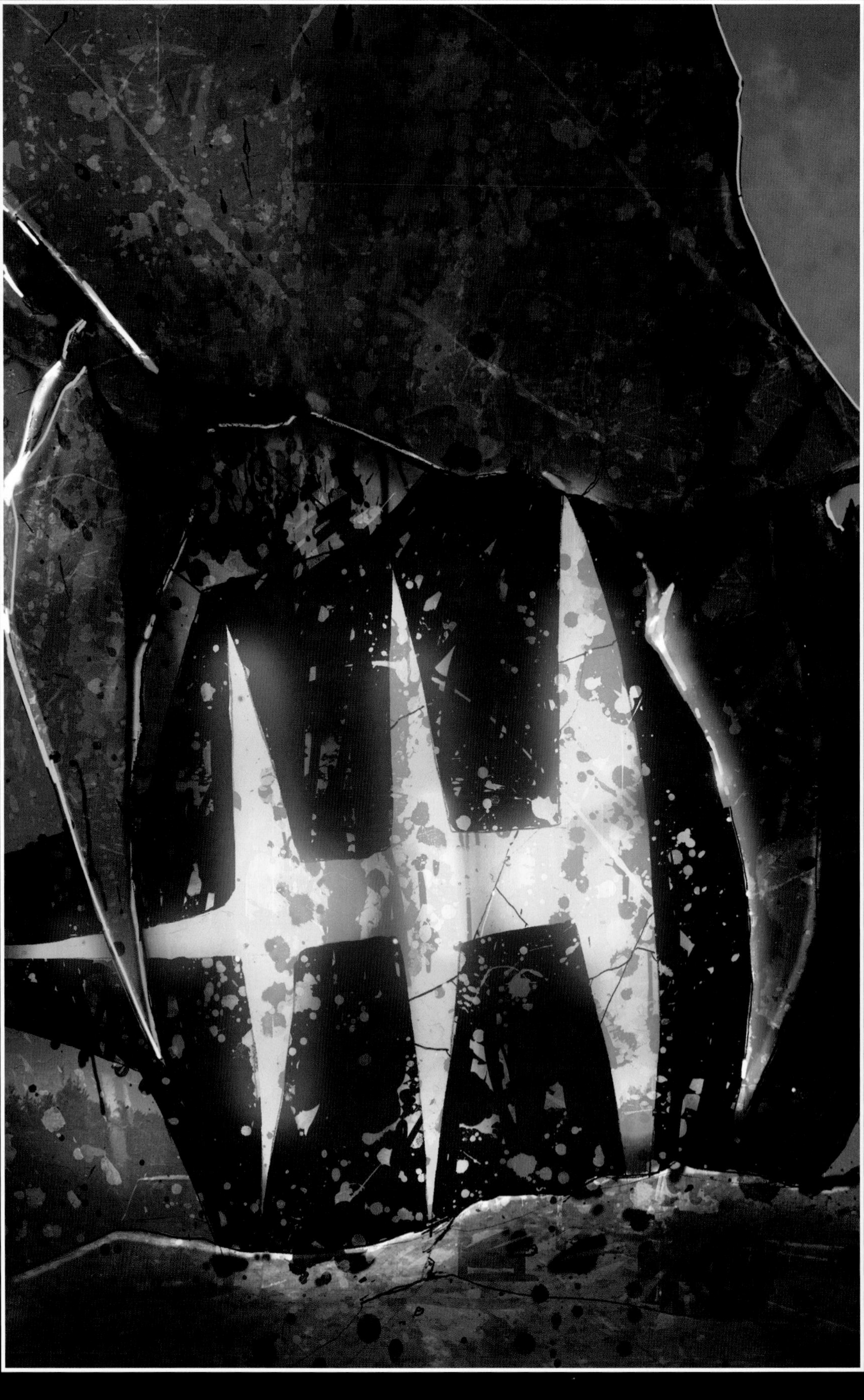

FIVE

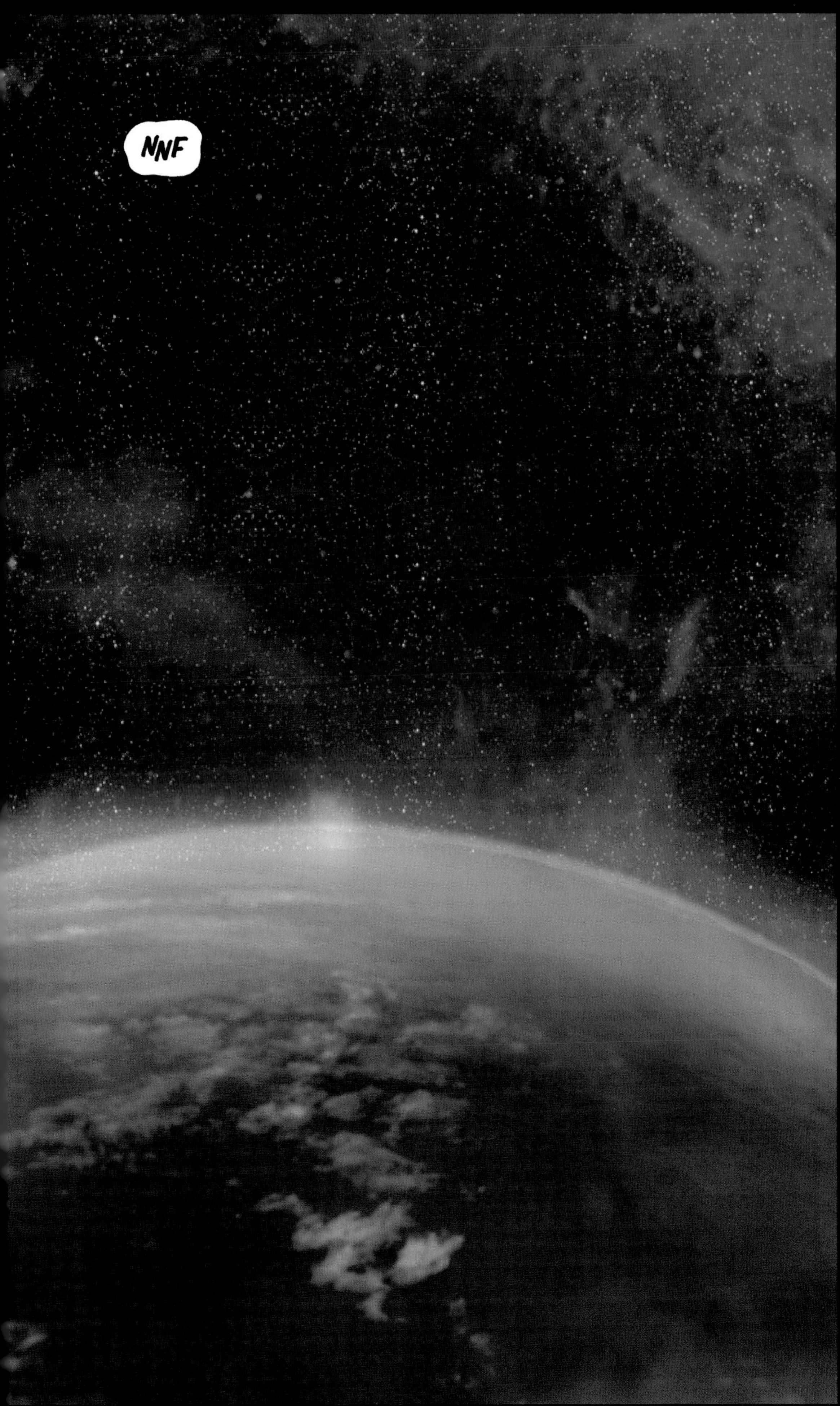
NNF

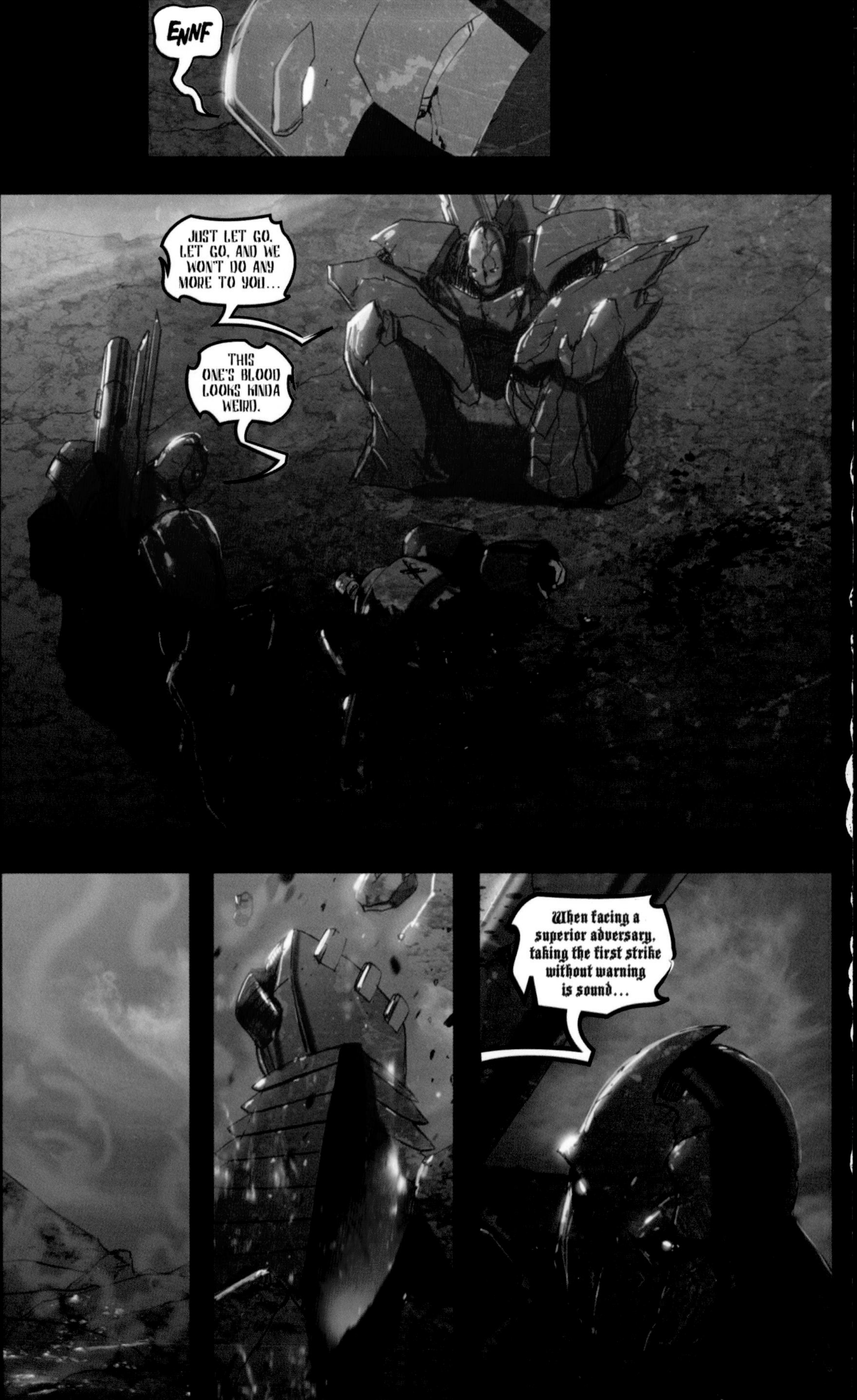
ENNF
JUST LET GO. LET GO, AND WE WON'T DO ANY MORE TO YOU...
THIS ONE'S BLOOD LOOKS KINDA WEIRD.
When facing a superior adversary, taking the first strike without warning is sound...

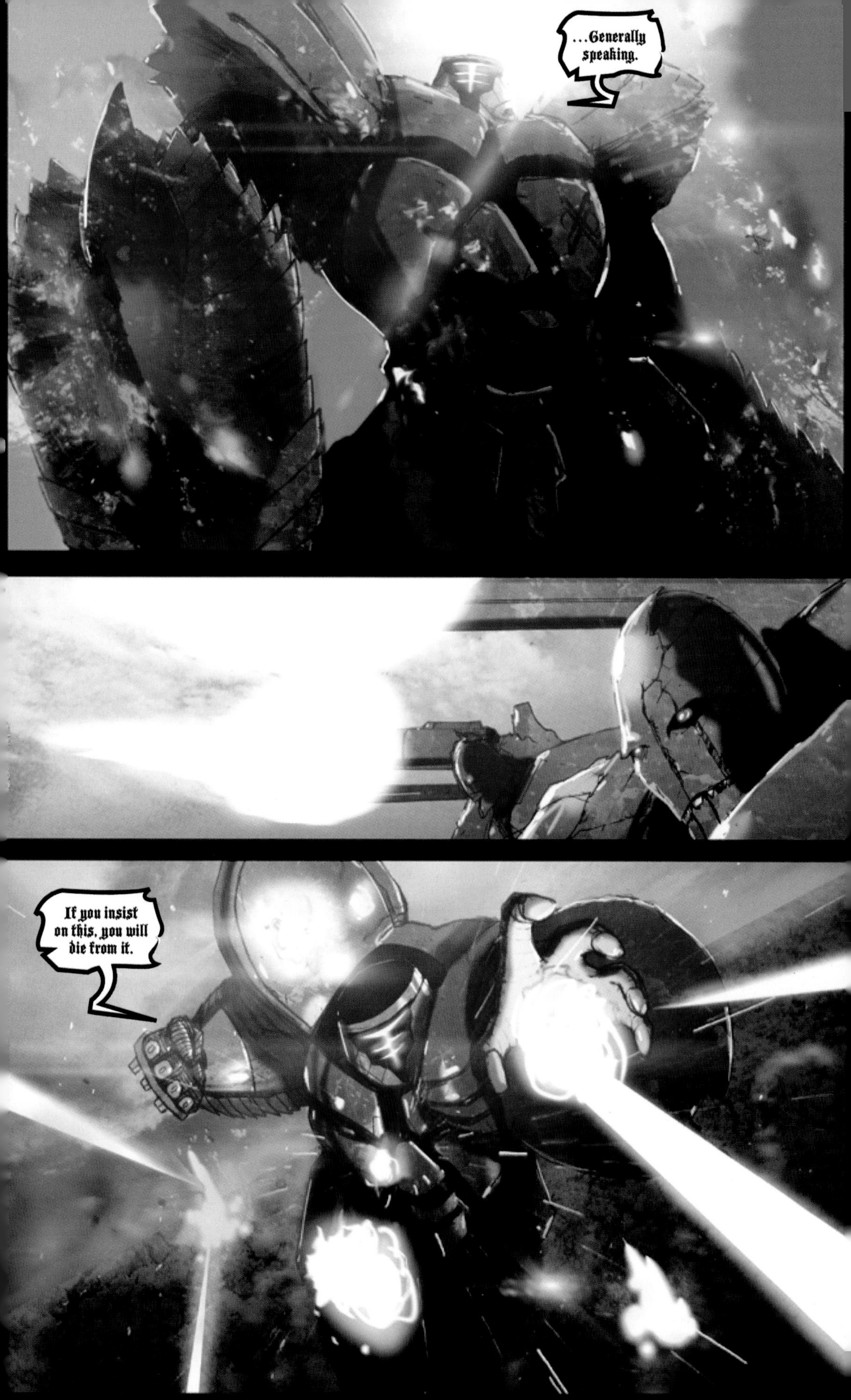
...Generally speaking.
If you insist on this, you will die from it.

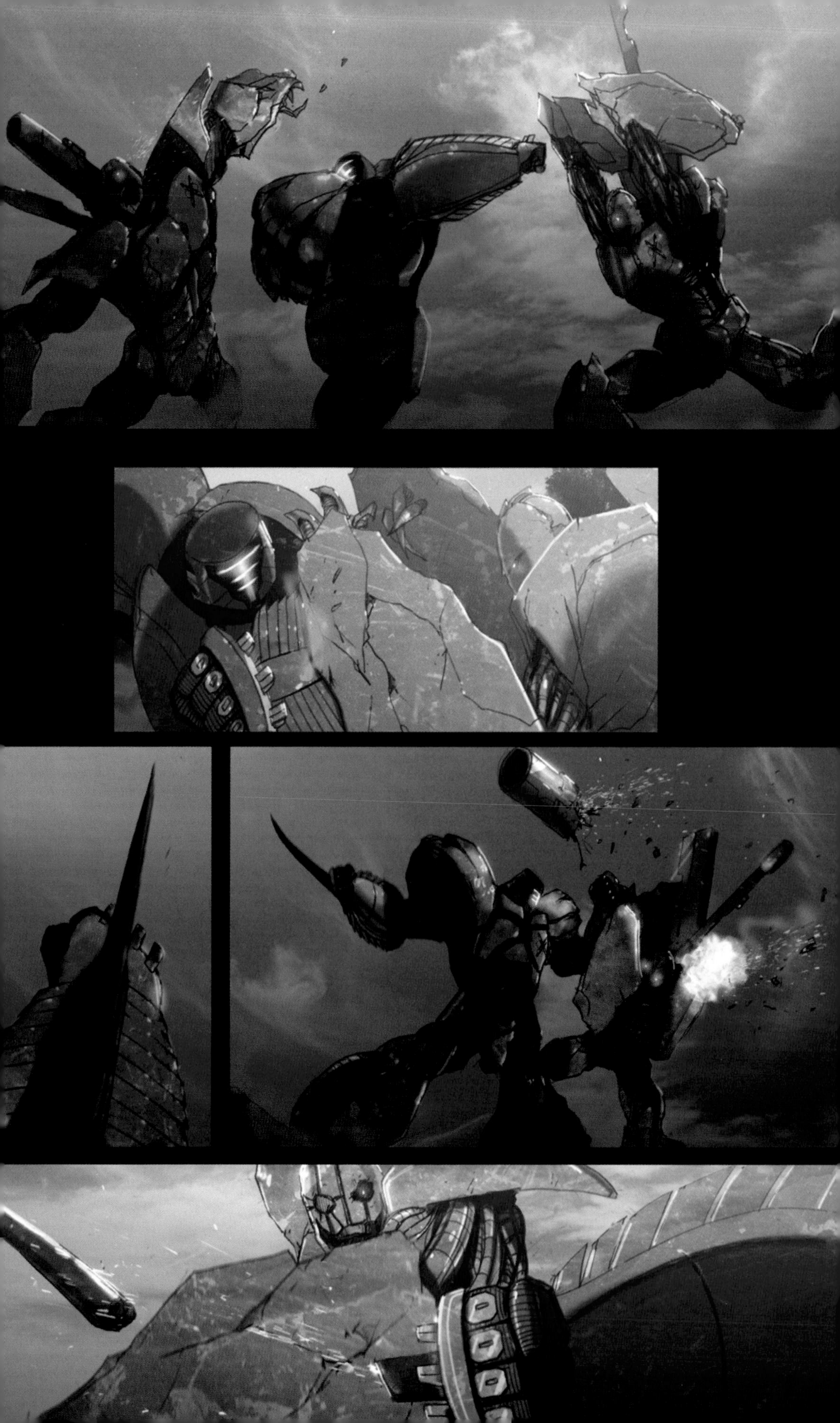

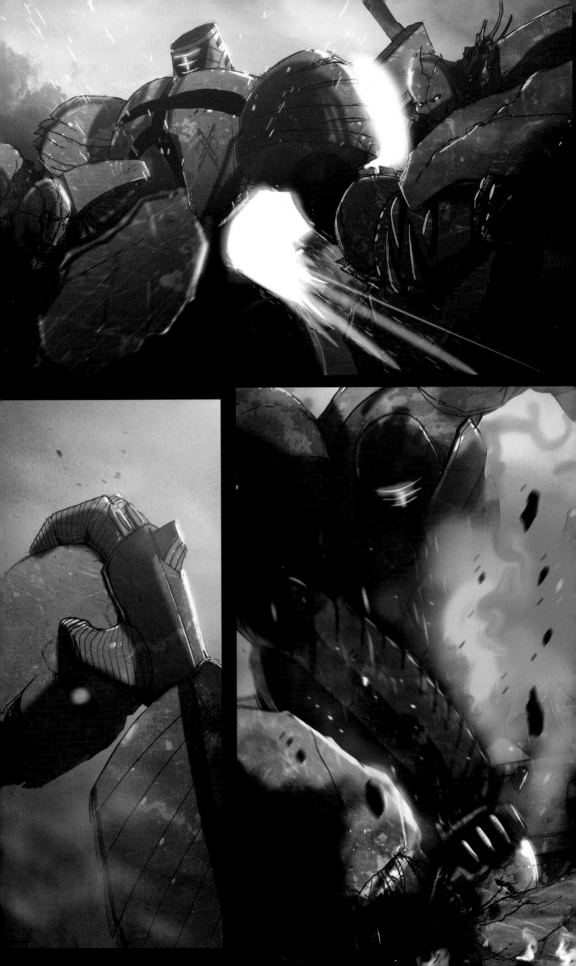

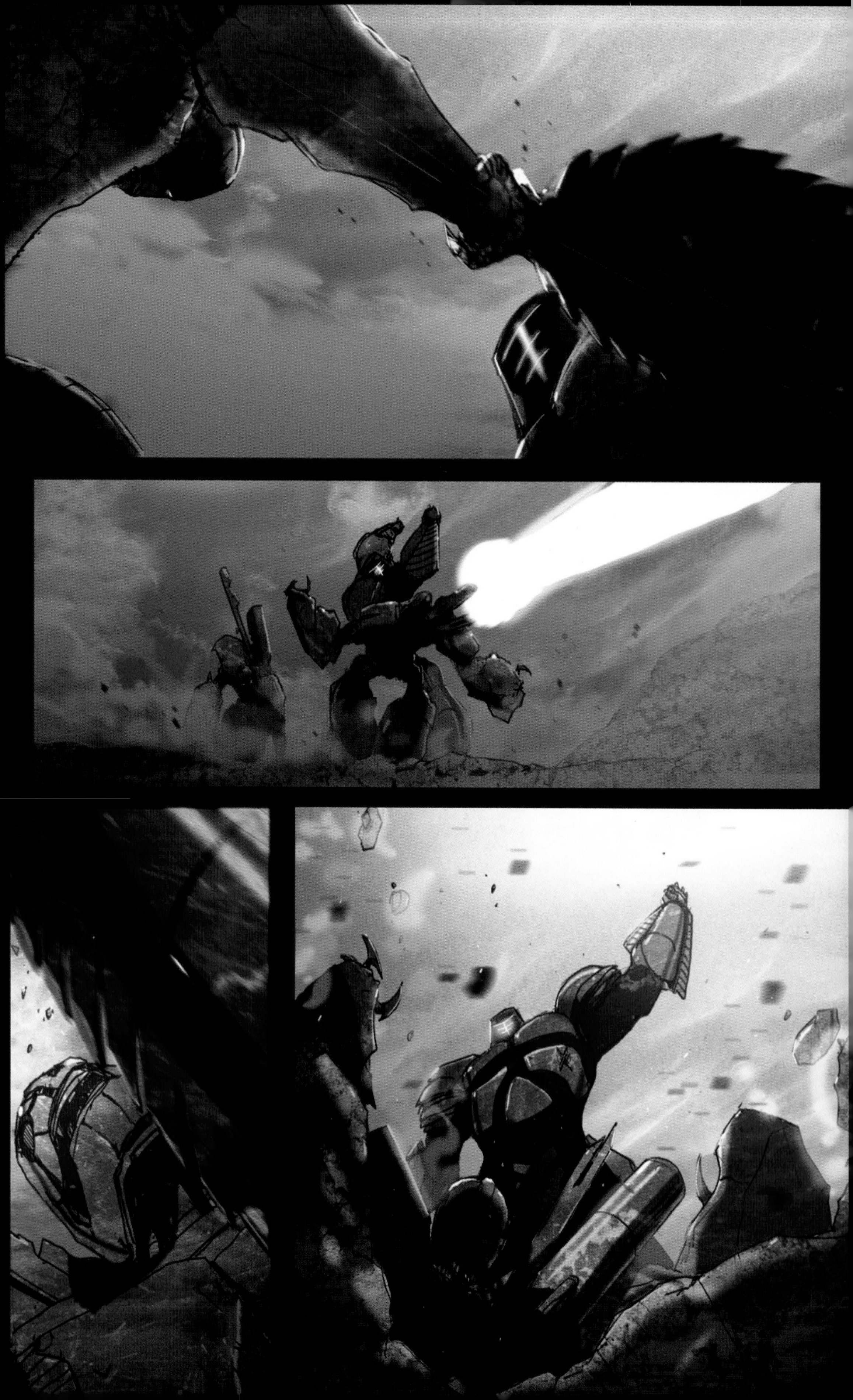

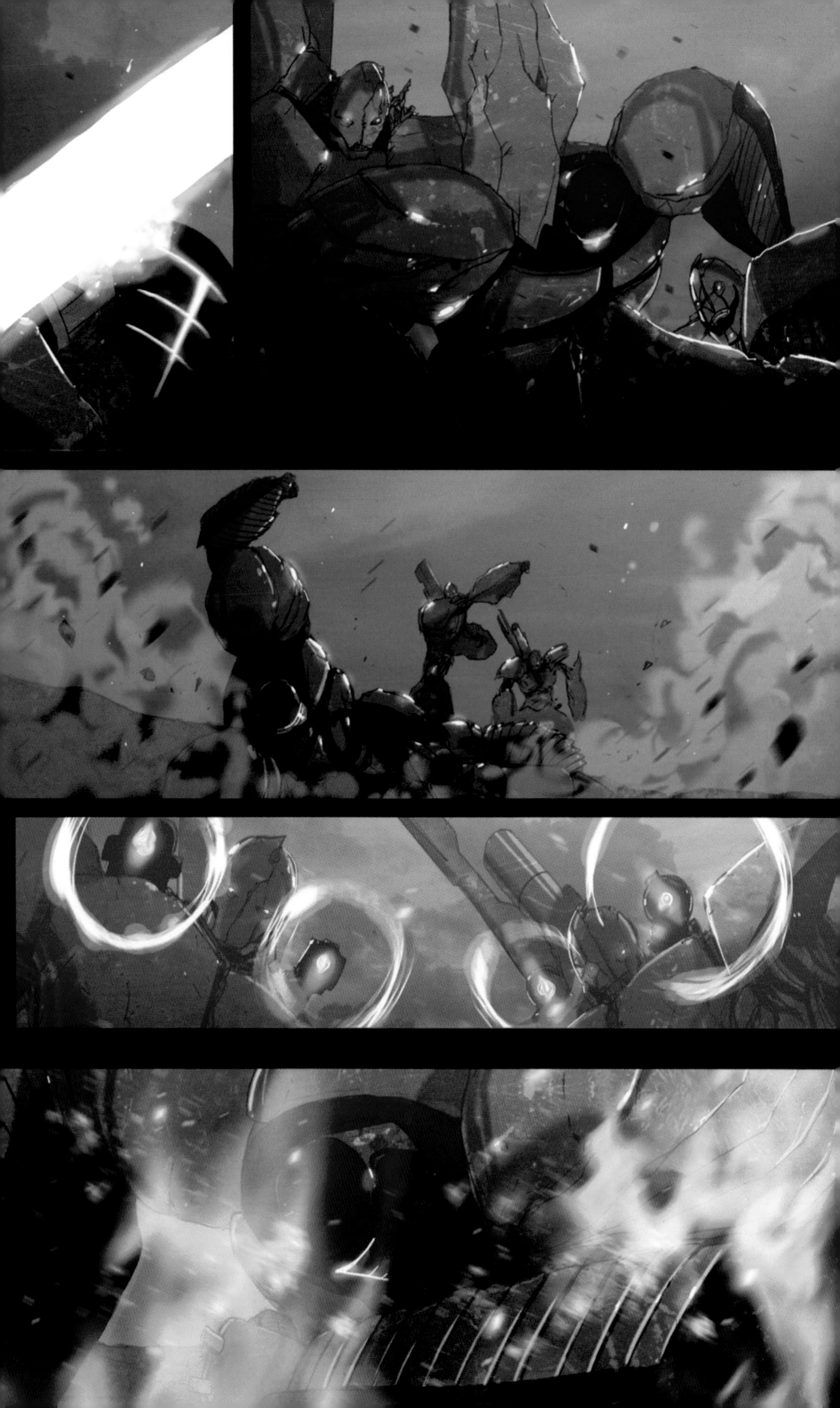

HE LOOKS LIKE YOU.
BUT LIKE A SCARIER ONE.
SHUT UP AND GO SIT IN THAT CORNER AND DON'T SAY A WORD.
THOSE LYING FUCKS.
THEY TOLD ME I WAS THE ONLY ONE OF OUR CLASS EVER EXILED.
YES, I WAS TOLD THE SAME.
BUT THEN, IT BENEFITS THEM TO KEEP IT A SECRET, DOESN'T IT?
WHEELS COMING OFF THEIR SOCIETY AND ALL THAT.
SO I HAVE TO ASK--
--IS THAT OBSIDIAN PAINT DETAILING YOU'RE WEARING?
THAT'S REALLY BEAUTIFULLY DONE.
WHY THANK YOU.
OF ALL THE LITTLE FLIES WE'VE CAUGHT, YOU'RE THE FIRST TO NOTICE IT.
SO, THAT AXIAL. SHE WORKS FOR YOU.
MORE LIKE... WITH.
I'M SURE YOU THINK WE'RE MONSTERS, LURING YOU HERE TO DIE LIKE THIS.
WE'RE NOT. WE'RE YOUR FUTURE. OR, HEH, WE WOULD HAVE BEEN.

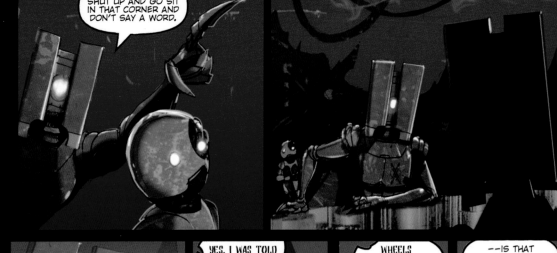

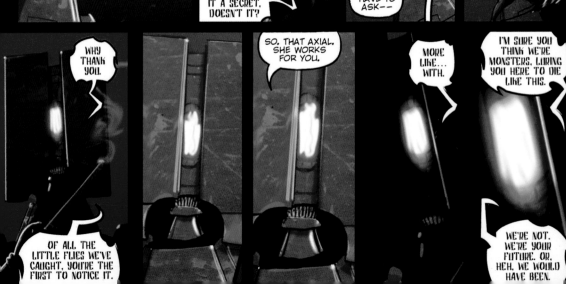

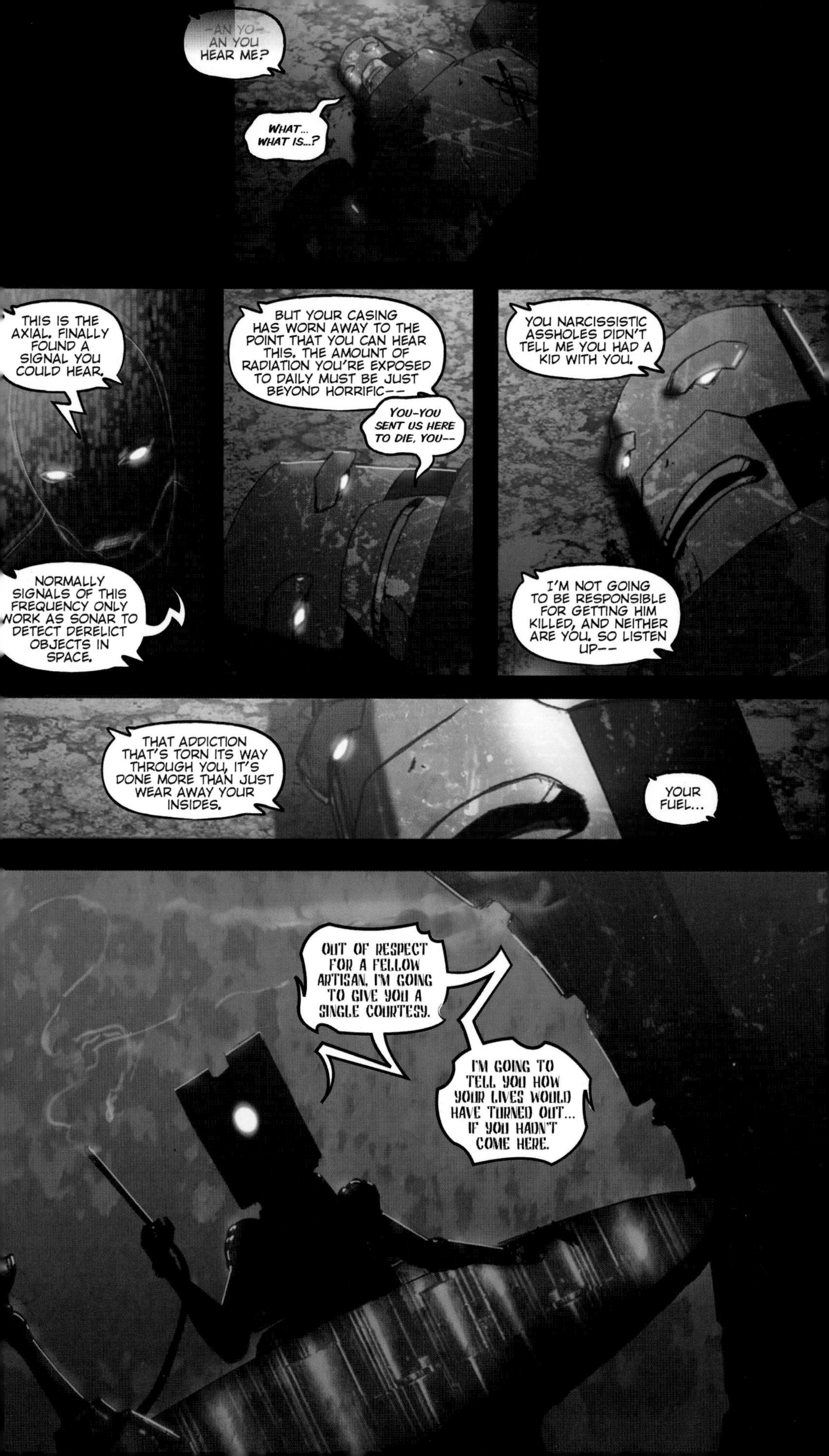
-AN YO-
AN YOU
HEAR ME?
WHAT...
WHAT IS...?
THIS IS THE AXIAL. FINALLY FOUND A SIGNAL YOU COULD HEAR.
NORMALLY SIGNALS OF THIS FREQUENCY ONLY WORK AS SONAR TO DETECT DERELICT OBJECTS IN SPACE.
BUT YOUR CASING HAS WORN AWAY TO THE POINT THAT YOU CAN HEAR THIS. THE AMOUNT OF RADIATION YOU'RE EXPOSED TO DAILY MUST BE JUST BEYOND HORRIFIC--
YOU-YOU SENT US HERE TO DIE, YOU--
YOU NARCISSISTIC ASSHOLES DIDN'T TELL ME YOU HAD A KID WITH YOU.
I'M NOT GOING TO BE RESPONSIBLE FOR GETTING HIM KILLED, AND NEITHER ARE YOU. SO LISTEN UP--
THAT ADDICTION THAT'S TORN ITS WAY THROUGH YOU, IT'S DONE MORE THAN JUST WEAR AWAY YOUR INSIDES.
YOUR FUEL...
OUT OF RESPECT FOR A FELLOW ARTISAN, I'M GOING TO GIVE YOU A SINGLE COURTESY.
I'M GOING TO TELL YOU HOW YOUR LIVES WOULD HAVE TURNED OUT... IF YOU HADN'T COME HERE.

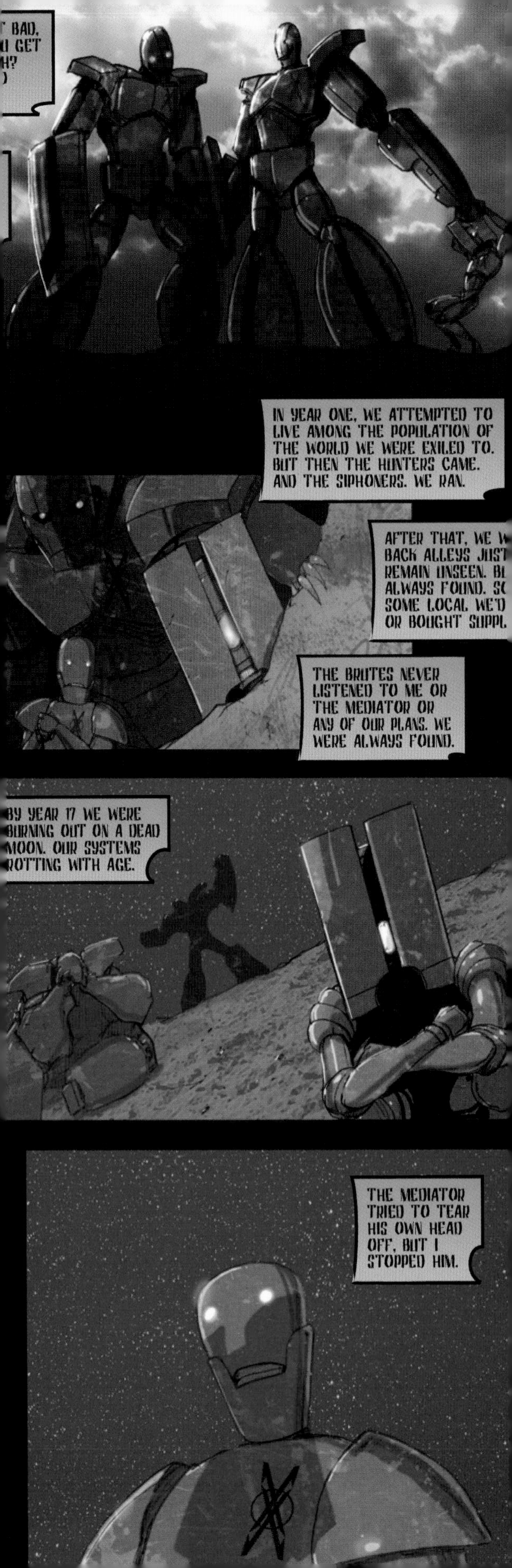
IN YEAR ONE, WE ATTEMPTED TO LIVE AMONG THE POPULATION OF THE WORLD WE WERE EXILED TO. BUT THEN THE HUNTERS CAME. AND THE SIPHONERS. WE RAN.
AFTER THAT, WE W BACK ALLEYS JUST REMAIN UNSEEN. B ALWAYS FOUND. S SOME LOCAL WE'D OR BOUGHT SUPPL
THE BRUTES NEVER LISTENED TO ME OR THE MEDIATOR OR ANY OF OUR PLANS. WE WERE ALWAYS FOUND.
BY YEAR 17 WE WERE BURNING OUT ON A DEAD MOON. OUR SYSTEMS ROTTING WITH AGE.
THE MEDIATOR TRIED TO TEAR HIS OWN HEAD OFF, BUT I STOPPED HIM.

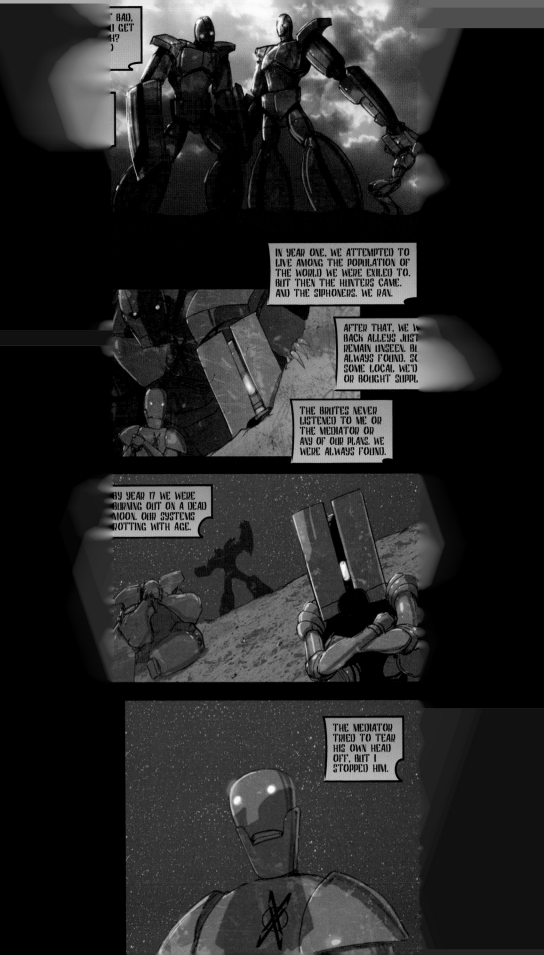

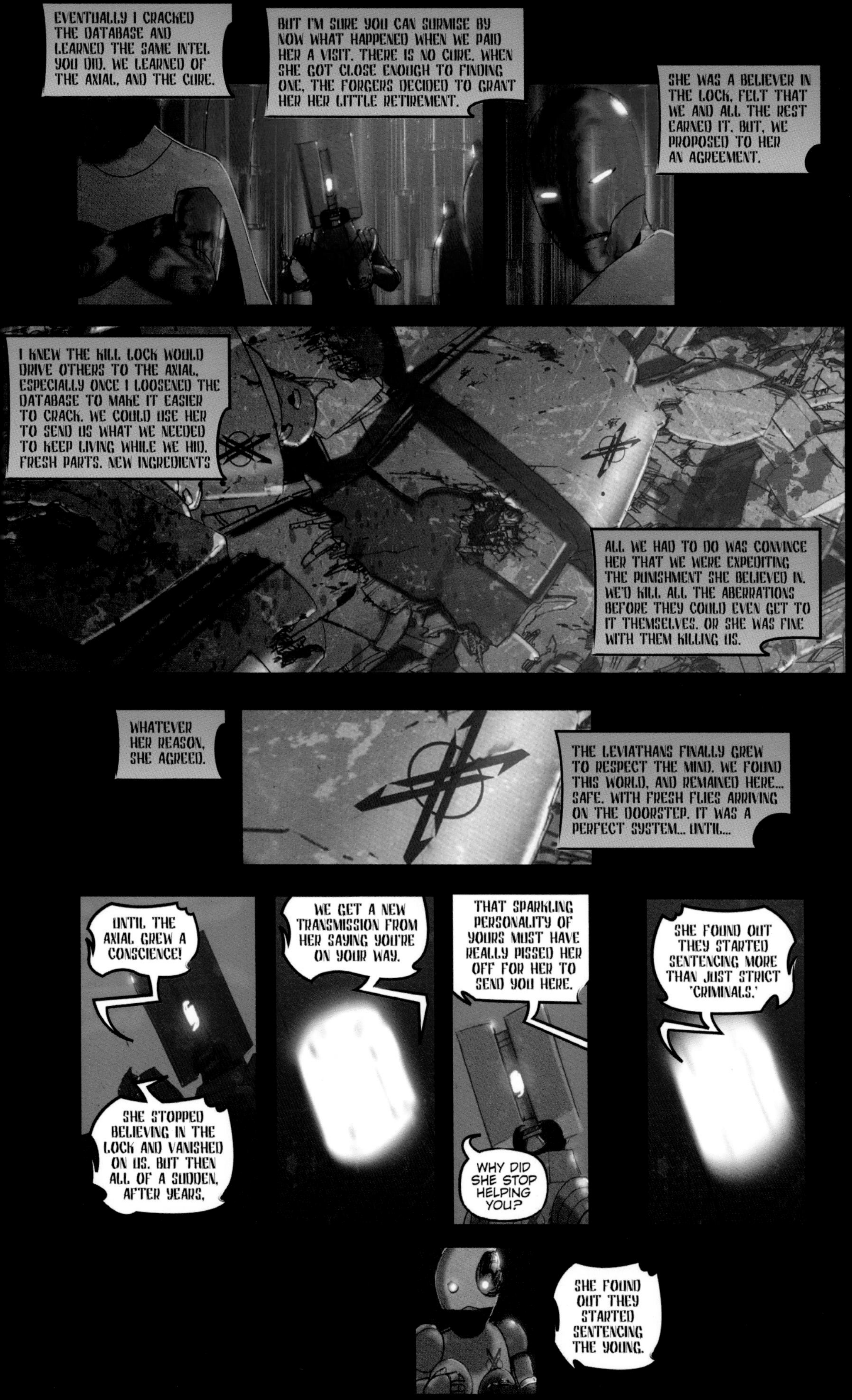
EVENTUALLY I CRACKED THE DATABASE AND LEARNED THE SAME INTEL YOU DID. WE LEARNED OF THE AXIAL, AND THE CURE.
BUT I'M SURE YOU CAN SURMISE BY NOW WHAT HAPPENED WHEN WE PAID HER A VISIT. THERE IS NO CURE. WHEN SHE GOT CLOSE ENOUGH TO FINDING ONE, THE FORGERS DECIDED TO GRANT HER HER LITTLE RETIREMENT.
SHE WAS A BELIEVER IN THE LOCK, FELT THAT WE AND ALL THE REST EARNED IT. BUT, WE PROPOSED TO HER AN AGREEMENT.
I KNEW THE KILL LOCK WOULD DRIVE OTHERS TO THE AXIAL, ESPECIALLY ONCE I LOOSENED THE DATABASE TO MAKE IT EASIER TO CRACK. WE COULD USE HER TO SEND US WHAT WE NEEDED TO KEEP LIVING WHILE WE HID. FRESH PARTS. NEW INGREDIENTS
ALL WE HAD TO DO WAS CONVINCE HER THAT WE WERE EXPEDITING THE PUNISHMENT SHE BELIEVED IN. WE'D KILL ALL THE ABERRATIONS BEFORE THEY COULD EVEN GET TO IT THEMSELVES. OR SHE WAS FINE WITH THEM KILLING US.
WHATEVER HER REASON, SHE AGREED.
THE LEVIATHANS FINALLY GREW TO RESPECT THE MIND. WE FOUND THIS WORLD, AND REMAINED HERE... SAFE. WITH FRESH FLIES ARRIVING ON THE DOORSTEP. IT WAS A PERFECT SYSTEM... UNTIL...
UNTIL THE AXIAL GREW A CONSCIENCE!
SHE STOPPED BELIEVING IN THE LOCK AND VANISHED ON US. BUT THEN ALL OF A SUDDEN, AFTER YEARS,
WE GET A NEW TRANSMISSION FROM HER SAYING YOU'RE ON YOUR WAY.
THAT SPARKLING PERSONALITY OF YOURS MUST HAVE REALLY PISSED HER OFF FOR HER TO SEND YOU HERE.
WHY DID SHE STOP HELPING YOU?
SHE FOUND OUT THEY STARTED SENTENCING MORE THAN JUST STRICT 'CRIMINALS.'
SHE FOUND OUT THEY STARTED SENTENCING THE YOUNG.

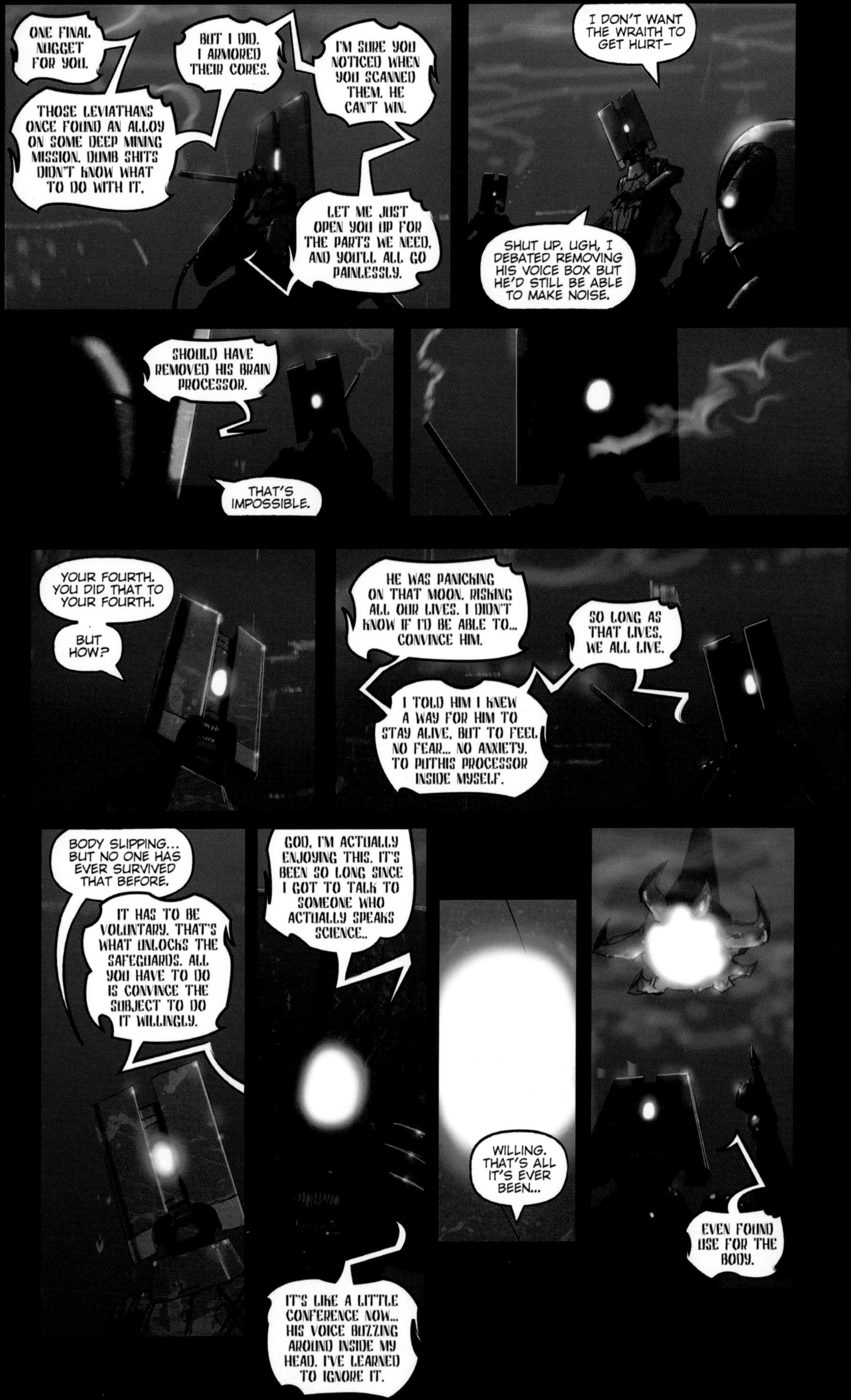

ONE FINAL NUGGET FOR YOU.
THOSE LEVIATHANS ONCE FOUND AN ALLOY ON SOME DEEP MINING MISSION. DUMB SHITS DIDN'T KNOW WHAT TO DO WITH IT.
BUT I DID. I ARMORED THEIR CORES.
I'M SURE YOU NOTICED WHEN YOU SCANNED THEM. HE CAN'T WIN.
LET ME JUST OPEN YOU UP FOR THE PARTS WE NEED, AND YOU'LL ALL GO PAINLESSLY.
I DON'T WANT THE WRAITH TO GET HURT—
SHUT UP. UGH, I DEBATED REMOVING HIS VOICE BOX BUT HE'D STILL BE ABLE TO MAKE NOISE.
SHOULD HAVE REMOVED HIS BRAIN PROCESSOR.
THAT'S IMPOSSIBLE.
YOUR FOURTH. YOU DID THAT TO YOUR FOURTH.
BUT HOW?
HE WAS PANICKING ON THAT MOON. RISKING ALL OUR LIVES. I DIDN'T KNOW IF I'D BE ABLE TO... CONVINCE HIM.
I TOLD HIM I KNEW A WAY FOR HIM TO STAY ALIVE, BUT TO FEEL NO FEAR... NO ANXIETY. TO PUTHIS PROCESSOR INSIDE MYSELF.
SO LONG AS THAT LIVES, WE ALL LIVE.
BODY SLIPPING... BUT NO ONE HAS EVER SURVIVED THAT BEFORE.
IT HAS TO BE VOLUNTARY. THAT'S WHAT UNLOCKS THE SAFEGUARDS. ALL YOU HAVE TO DO IS CONVINCE THE SUBJECT TO DO IT WILLINGLY.
GOD, I'M ACTUALLY ENJOYING THIS. IT'S BEEN SO LONG SINCE I GOT TO TALK TO SOMEONE WHO ACTUALLY SPEAKS SCIENCE..
IT'S LIKE A LITTLE CONFERENCE NOW... HIS VOICE BUZZING AROUND INSIDE MY HEAD. I'VE LEARNED TO IGNORE IT.
WILLING. THAT'S ALL IT'S EVER BEEN...
EVEN FOUND USE FOR THE BODY.

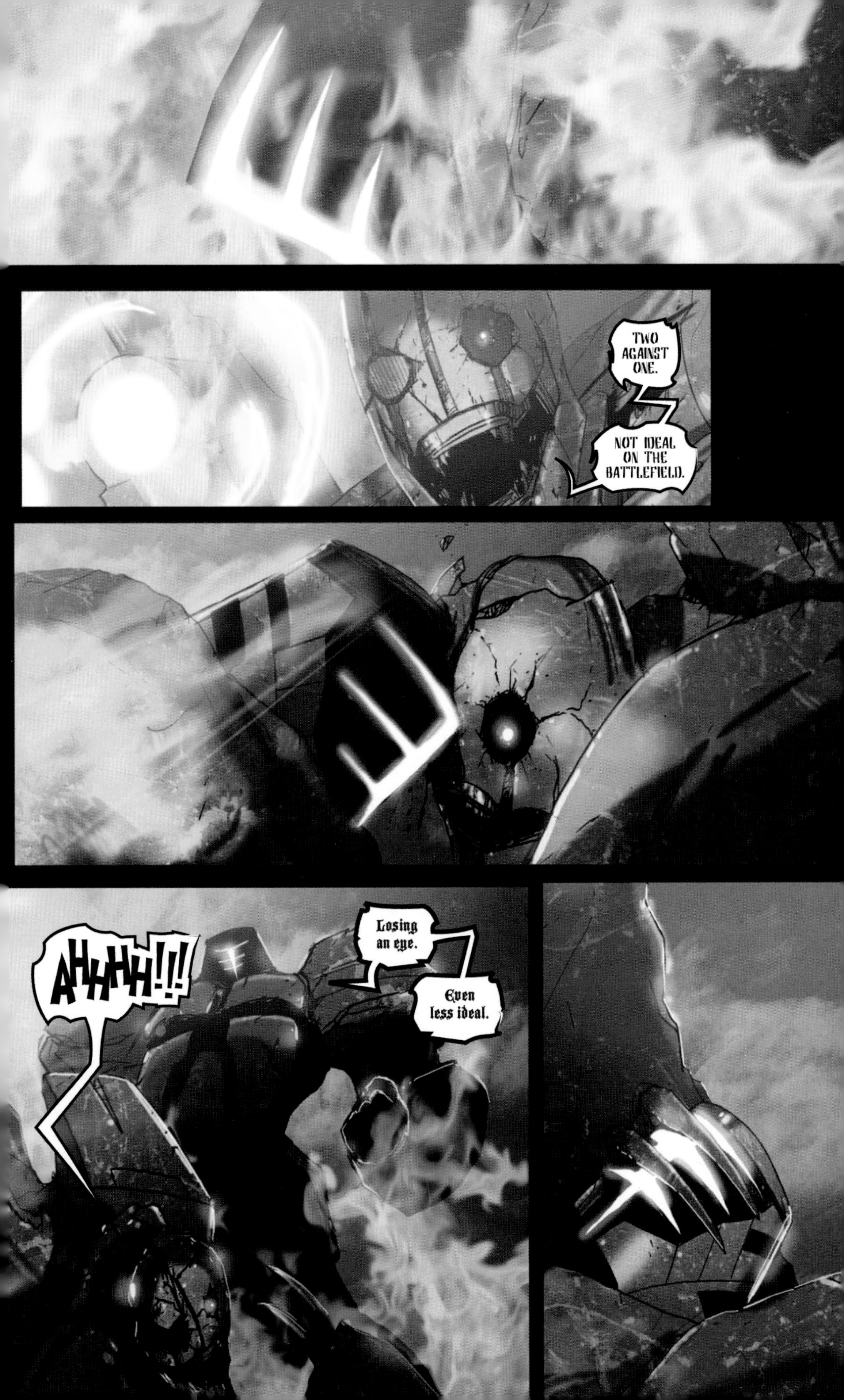
TWO AGAINST ONE.
NOT IDEAL ON THE BATTLEFIELD.
AHHHH!!!
Losing an eye.
Even less ideal.

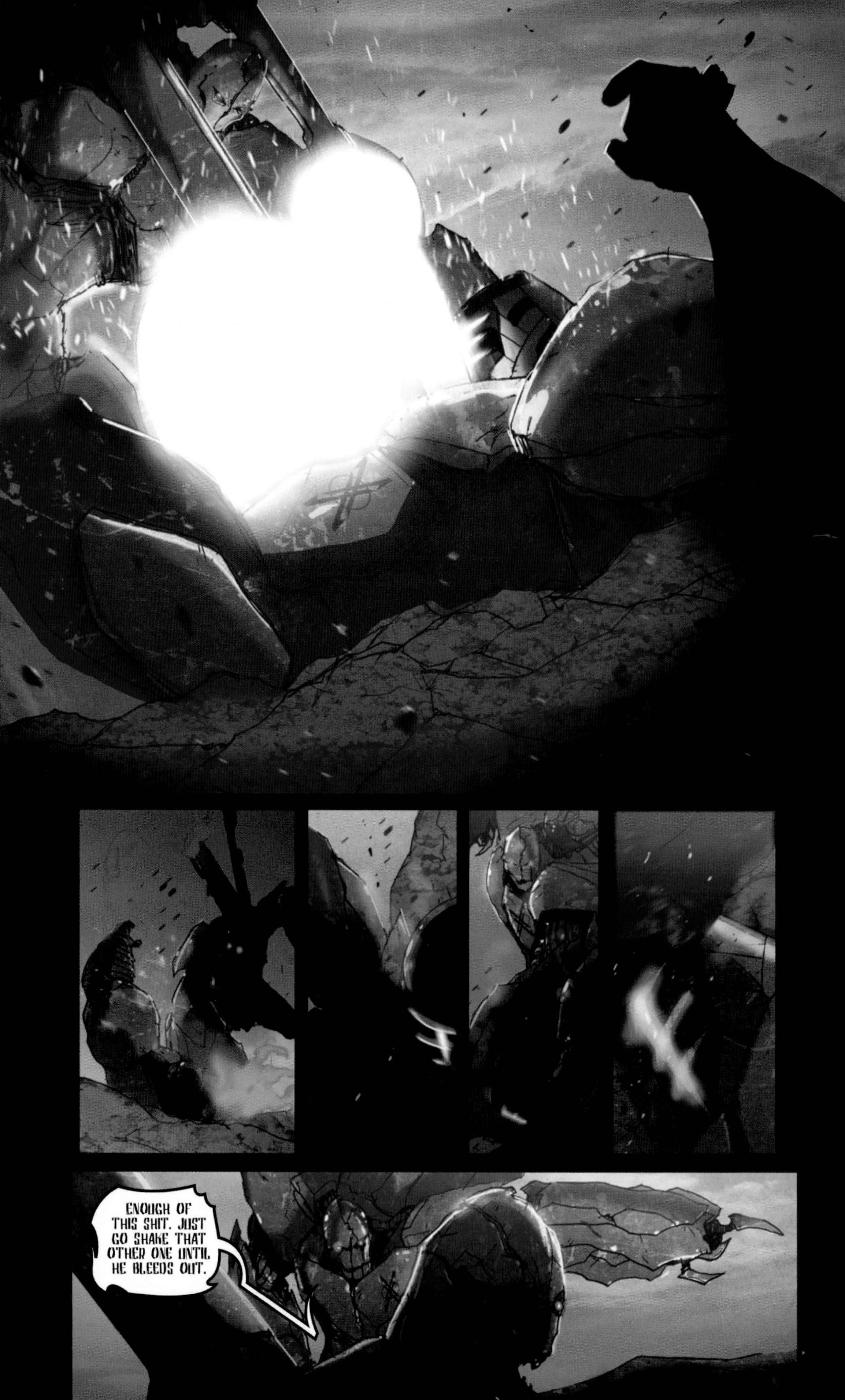
ENOUGH OF THIS SHIT. JUST GO SHAKE THAT OTHER ONE UNTIL HE BLEEDS OUT.

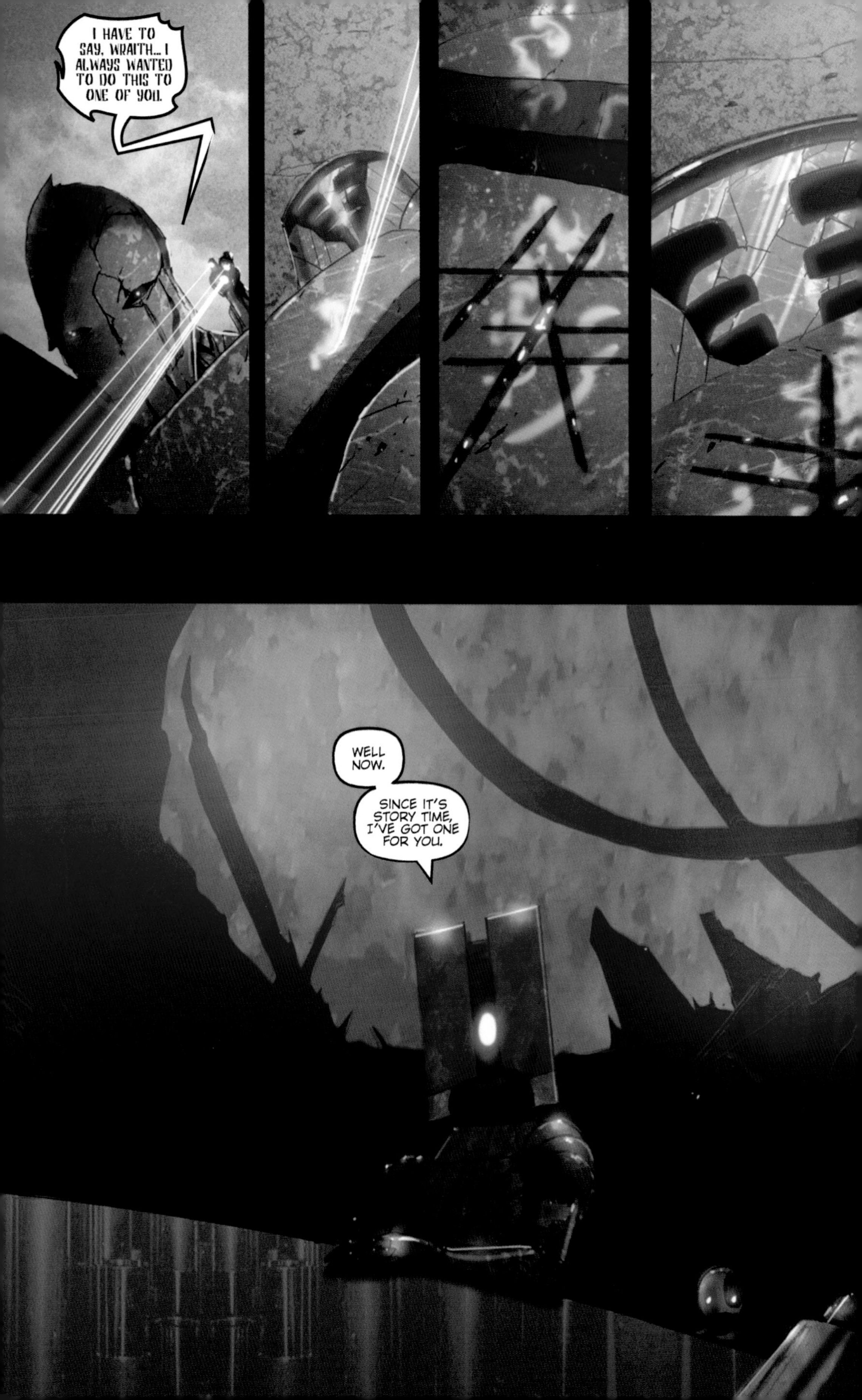
I HAVE TO SAY, WRAITH... I ALWAYS WANTED TO DO THIS TO ONE OF YOU.
WELL NOW.
SINCE IT'S STORY TIME, I'VE GOT ONE FOR YOU.

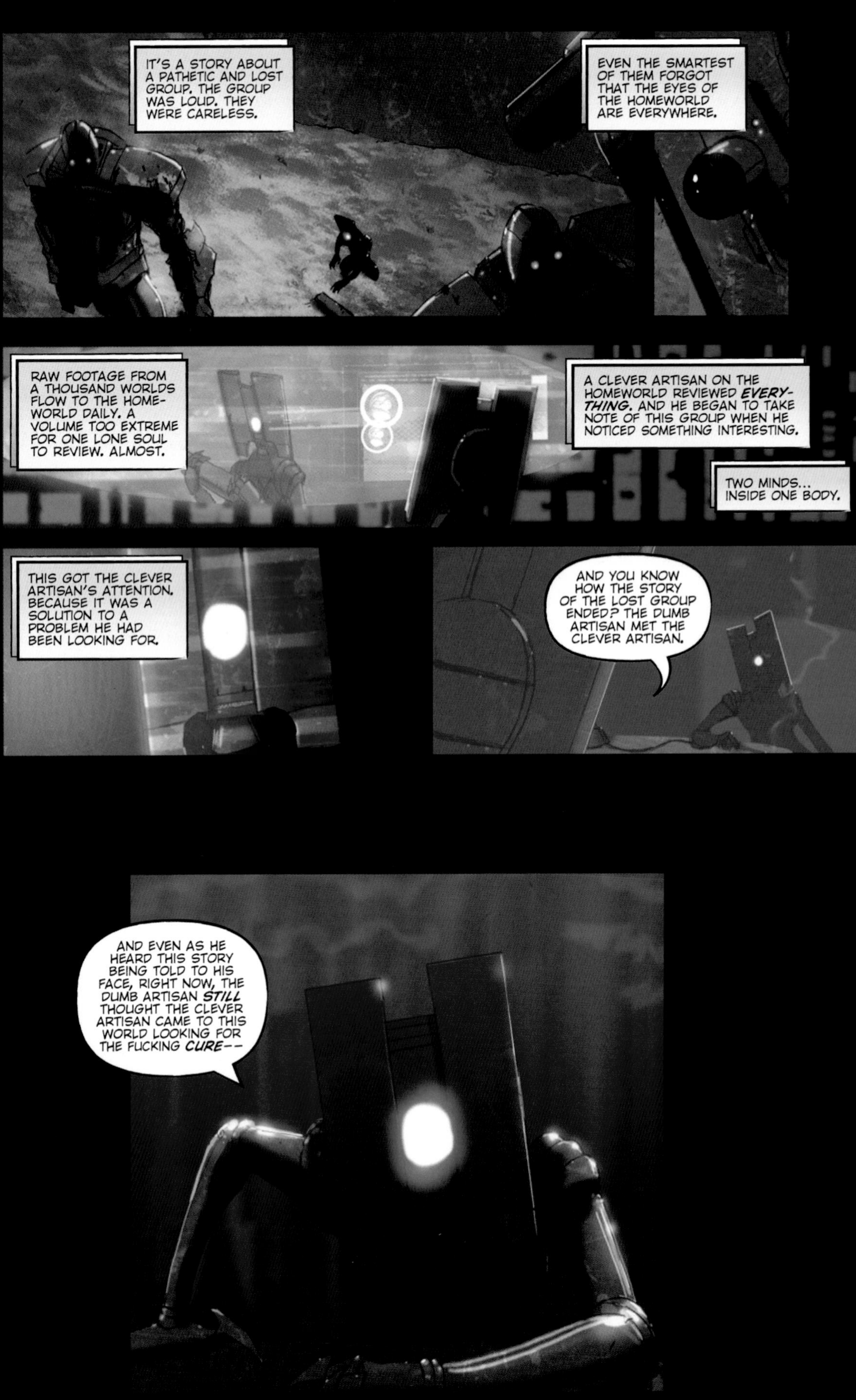
IT'S A STORY ABOUT A PATHETIC AND LOST GROUP. THE GROUP WAS LOUD. THEY WERE CARELESS.
EVEN THE SMARTEST OF THEM FORGOT THAT THE EYES OF THE HOMEWORLD ARE EVERYWHERE.
RAW FOOTAGE FROM A THOUSAND WORLDS FLOW TO THE HOME-WORLD DAILY. A VOLUME TOO EXTREME FOR ONE LONE SOUL TO REVIEW. ALMOST.
A CLEVER ARTISAN ON THE HOMEWORLD REVIEWED EVERY-THING. AND HE BEGAN TO TAKE NOTE OF THIS GROUP WHEN HE NOTICED SOMETHING INTERESTING.
TWO MINDS... INSIDE ONE BODY.
THIS GOT THE CLEVER ARTISAN'S ATTENTION. BECAUSE IT WAS A SOLUTION TO A PROBLEM HE HAD BEEN LOOKING FOR.
AND YOU KNOW HOW THE STORY OF THE LOST GROUP ENDED? THE DUMB ARTISAN MET THE CLEVER ARTISAN.
AND EVEN AS HE HEARD THIS STORY BEING TOLD TO HIS FACE, RIGHT NOW, THE DUMB ARTISAN STILL THOUGHT THE CLEVER ARTISAN CAME TO THIS WORLD LOOKING FOR THE FUCKING CURE--

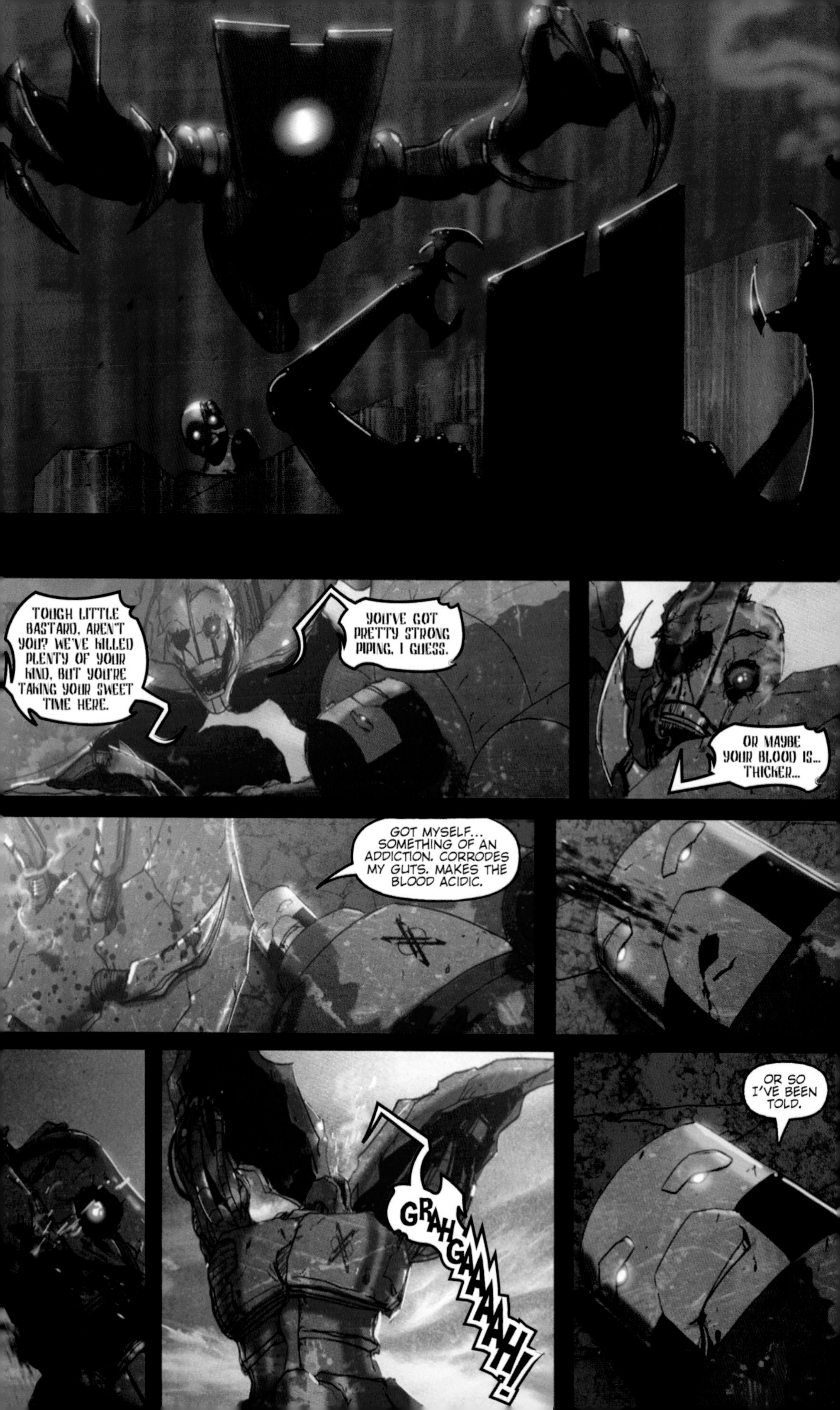
TOUGH LITTLE BASTARD, AREN'T YOU? WE'VE KILLED PLENTY OF YOUR KIND, BUT YOU'RE TAKING YOUR SWEET TIME HERE.
YOU'VE GOT PRETTY STRONG PIPING, I GUESS.
OR MAYBE YOUR BLOOD IS... THICKER...
GOT MYSELF... SOMETHING OF AN ADDICTION. CORRODES MY GUTS. MAKES THE BLOOD ACIDIC.
GRAHGAAAAAH!
OR SO I'VE BEEN TOLD.

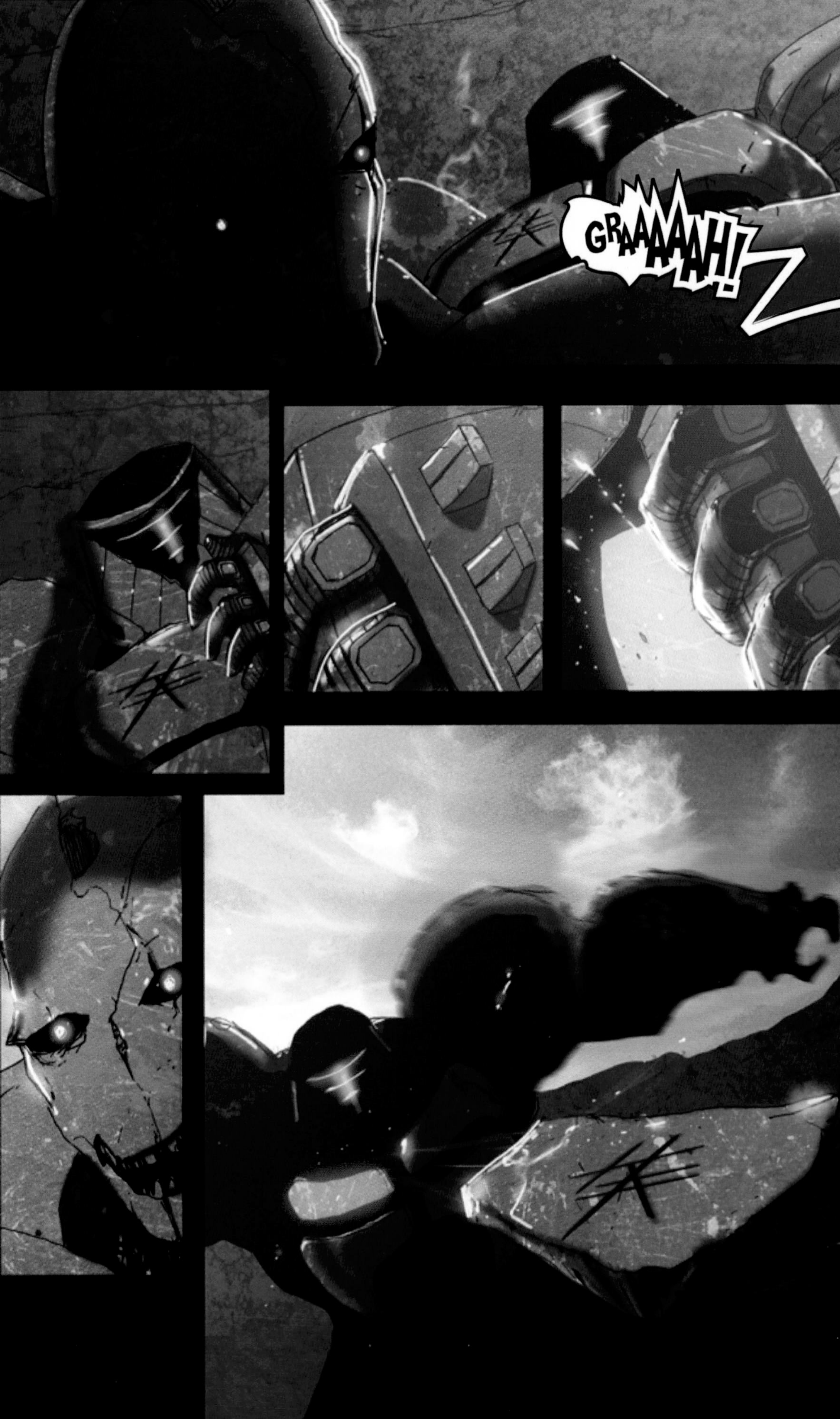
GRAAAAAH!

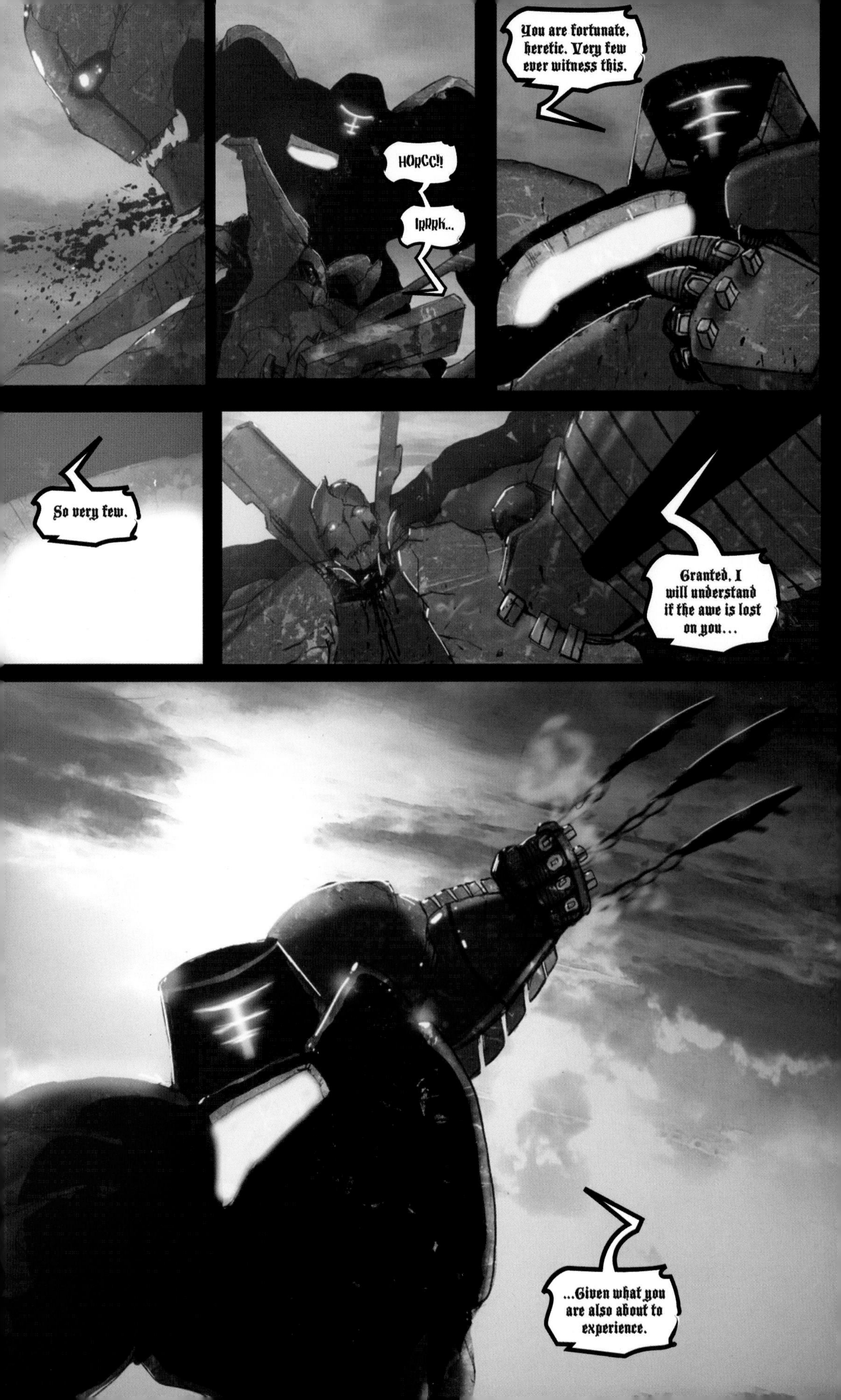
HORCC!!
IRRRK...
You are fortunate, heretic. Very few ever witness this.
So very few.
Granted, I will understand if the awe is lost on you...
...Given what you are also about to experience.

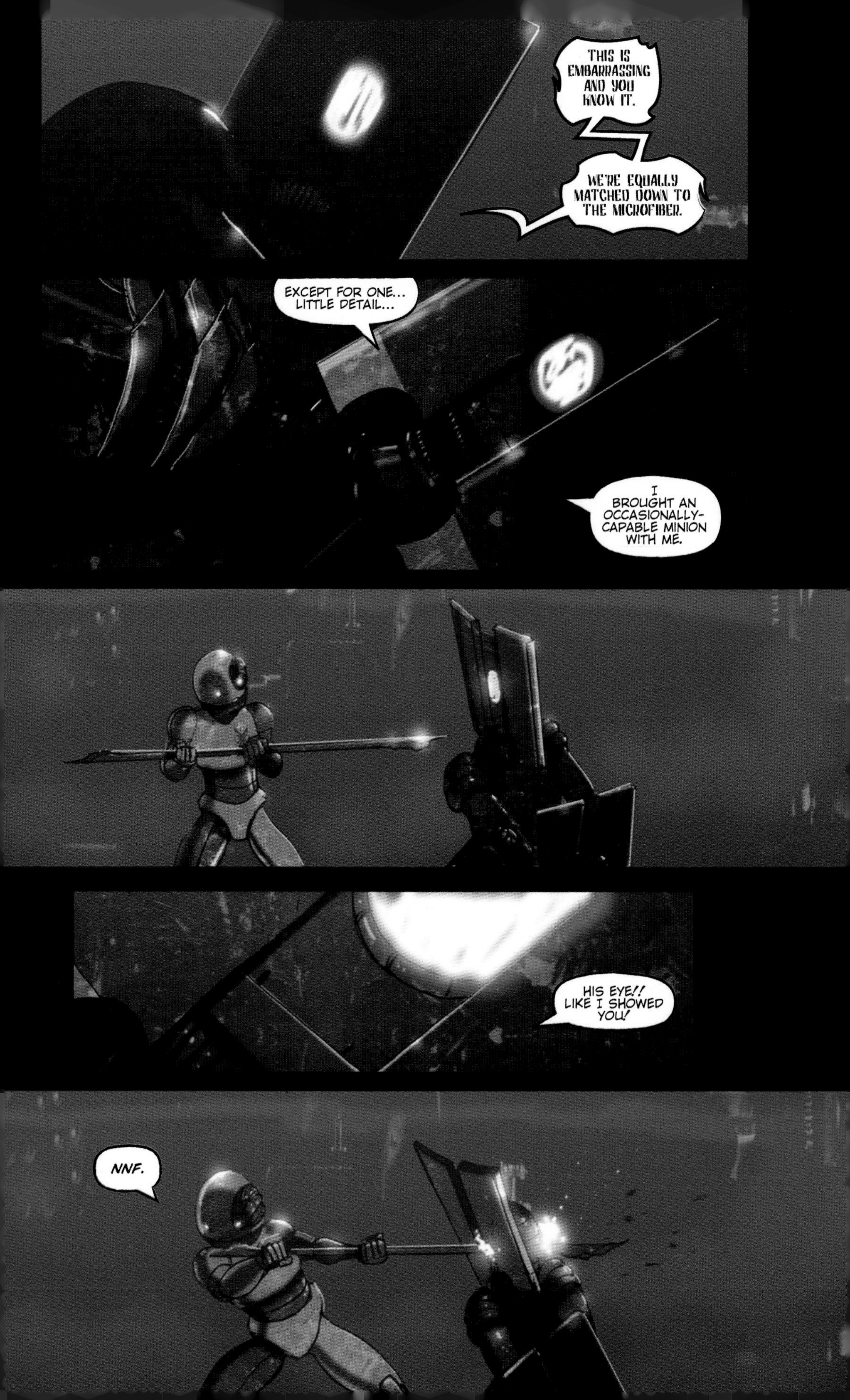
THIS IS EMBARRASSING AND YOU KNOW IT.
WE'RE EQUALLY MATCHED DOWN TO THE MICROFIBER.
EXCEPT FOR ONE... LITTLE DETAIL...
I BROUGHT AN OCCASIONALLY-CAPABLE MINION WITH ME.
HIS EYE!! LIKE I SHOWED YOU!
NNF.

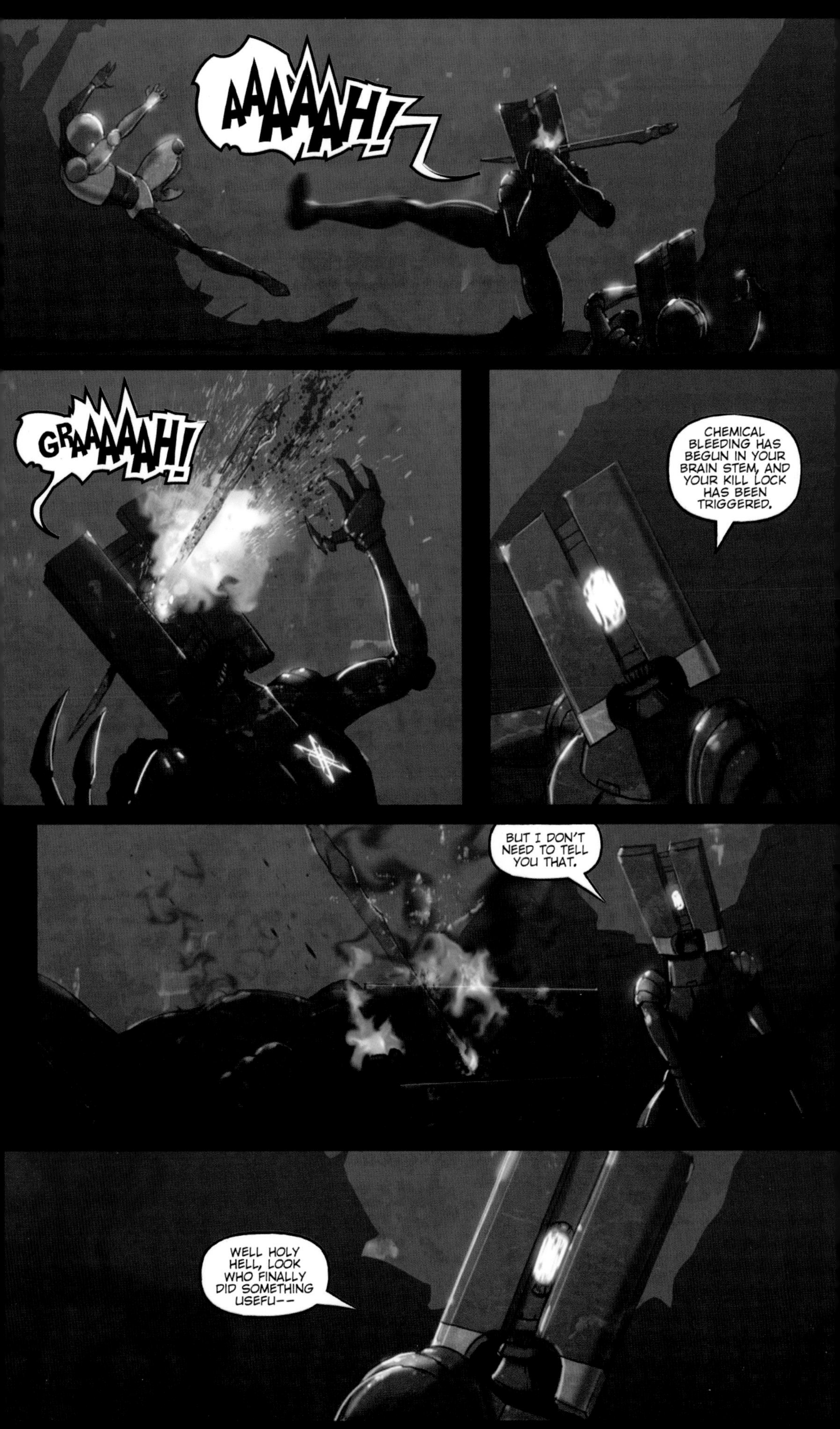
AAAAAH!
GRAAAAAH!
CHEMICAL BLEEDING HAS BEGUN IN YOUR BRAIN STEM, AND YOUR KILL LOCK HAS BEEN TRIGGERED.
BUT I DON'T NEED TO TELL YOU THAT.
WELL HOLY HELL, LOOK WHO FINALLY DID SOMETHING USEFU--

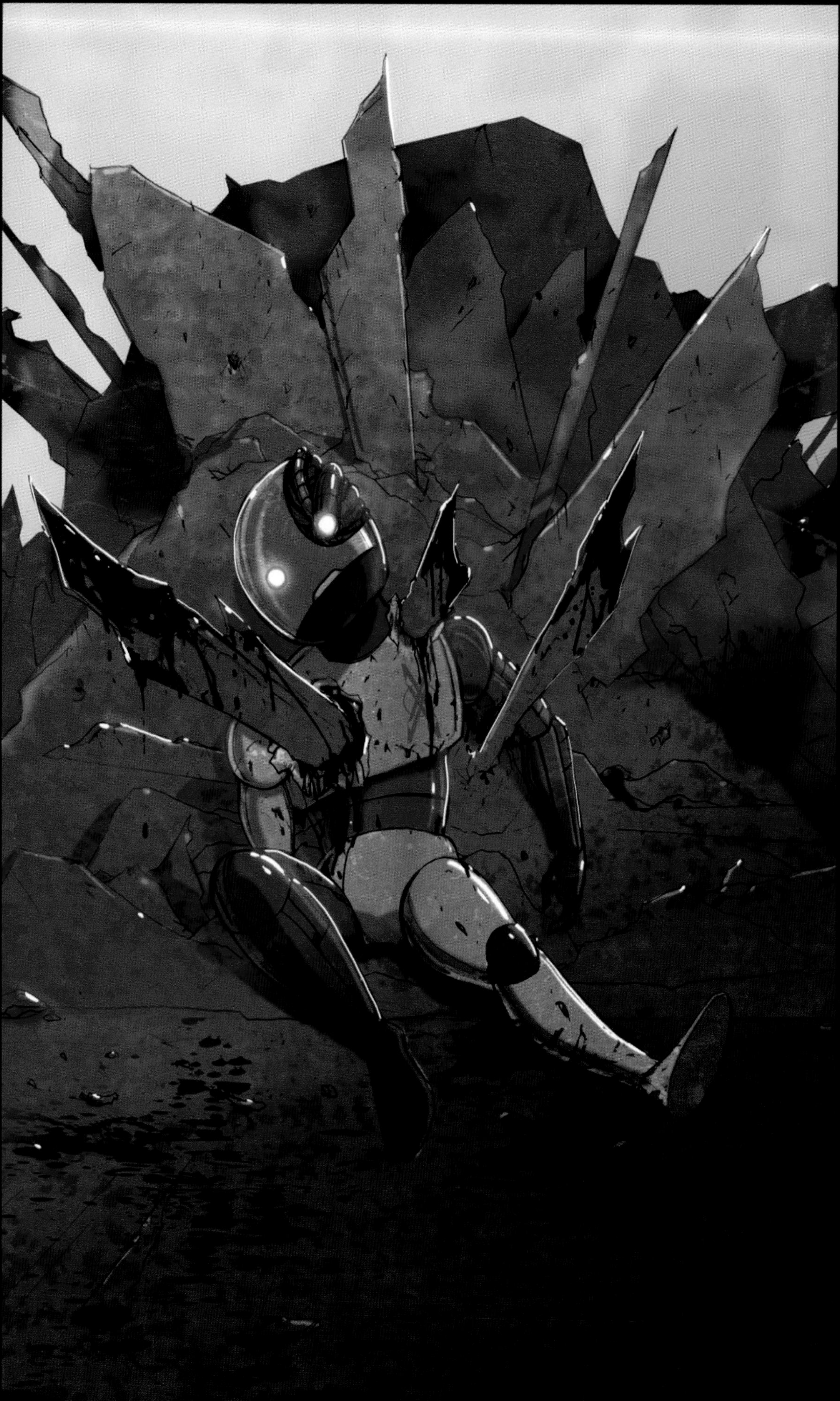

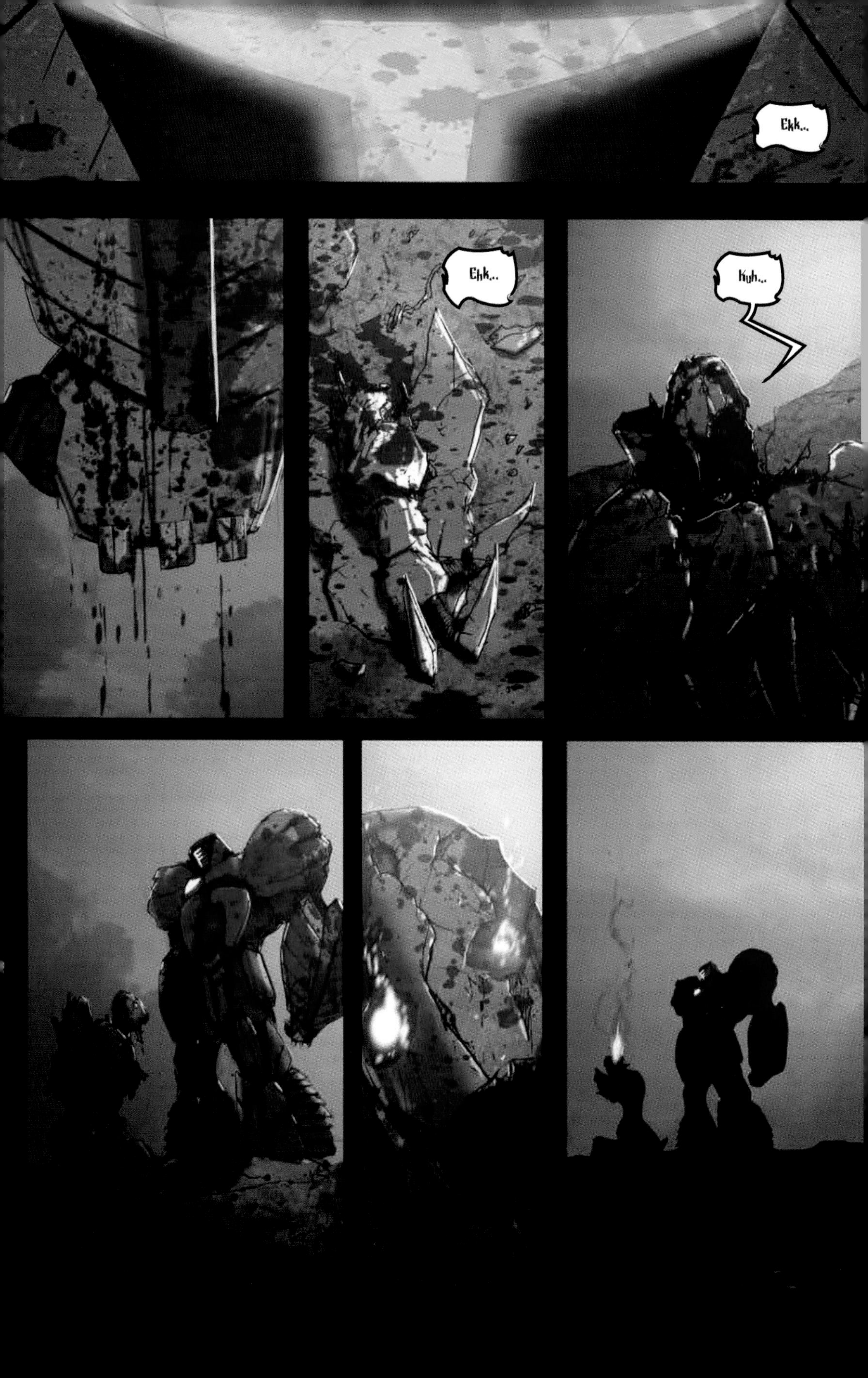
Ekk..
Ehk..
Kuh..

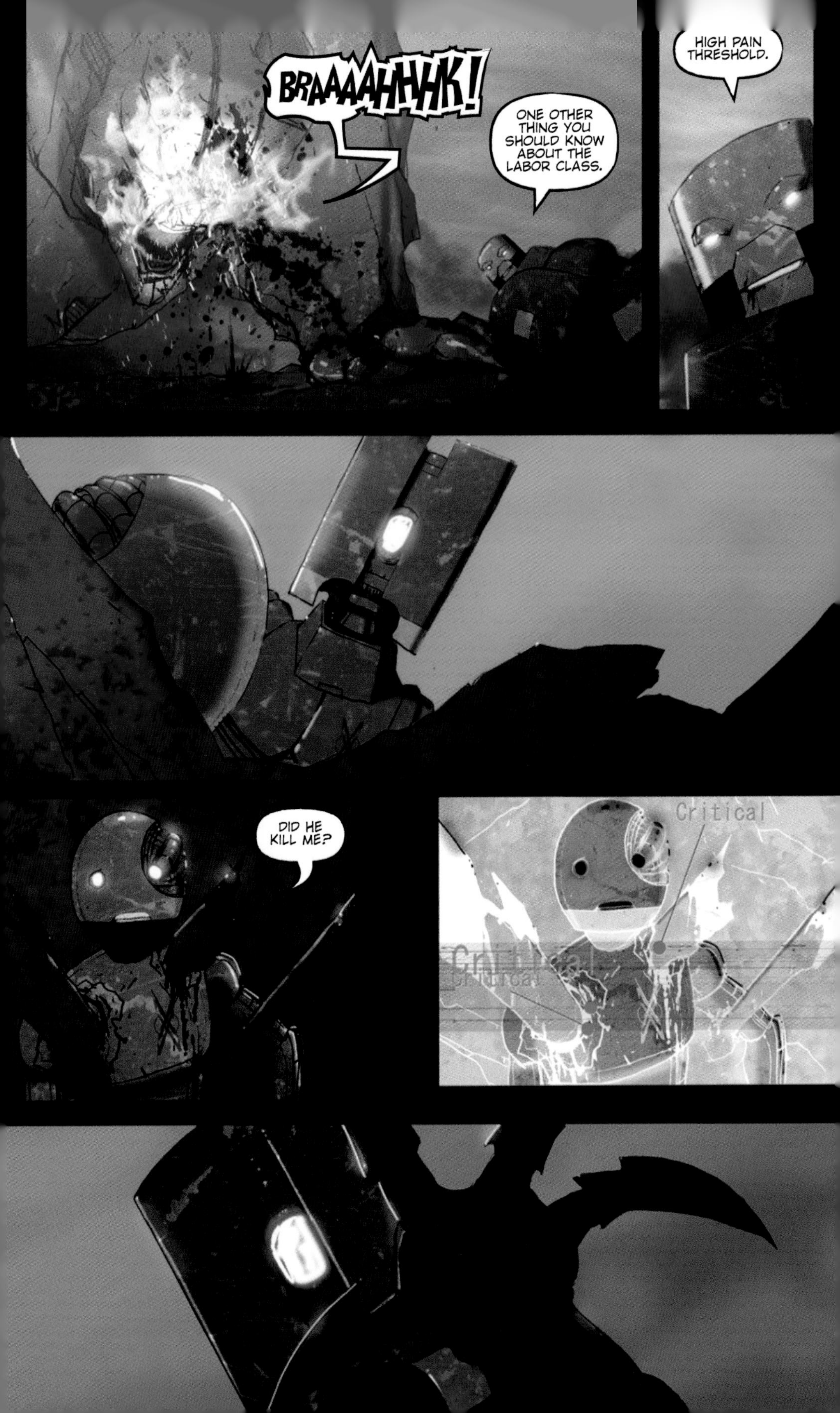
BRAAAAHHHK!
ONE OTHER THING YOU SHOULD KNOW ABOUT THE LABOR CLASS.
HIGH PAIN THRESHOLD.
DID HE KILL ME?
Critical
Critical
Critical

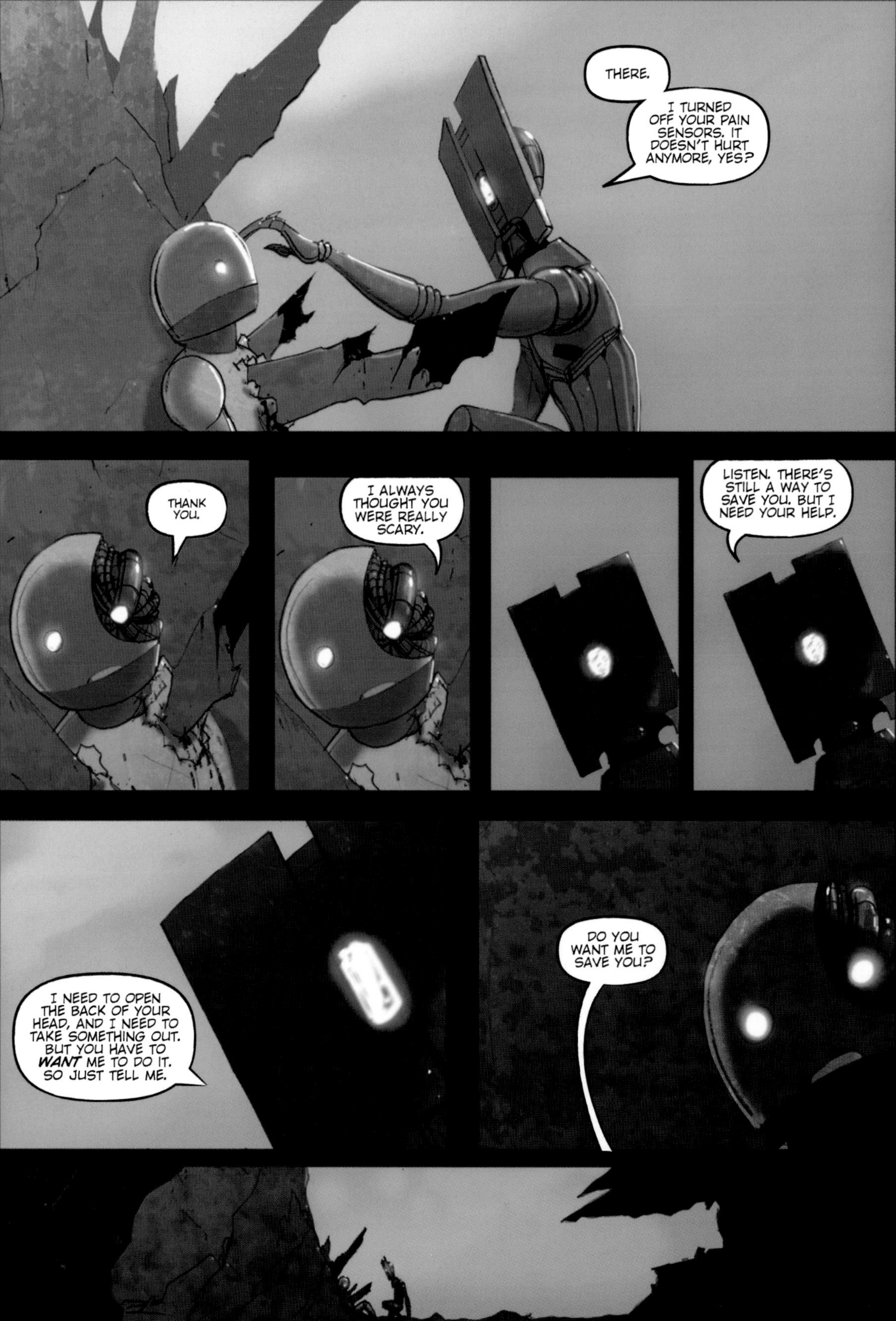
THERE.
I TURNED OFF YOUR PAIN SENSORS. IT DOESN'T HURT ANYMORE, YES?
THANK YOU.
I ALWAYS THOUGHT YOU WERE REALLY SCARY.
LISTEN. THERE'S STILL A WAY TO SAVE YOU. BUT I NEED YOUR HELP.
I NEED TO OPEN THE BACK OF YOUR HEAD, AND I NEED TO TAKE SOMETHING OUT. BUT YOU HAVE TO ***WANT*** ME TO DO IT. SO JUST TELL ME.
DO YOU WANT ME TO SAVE YOU?

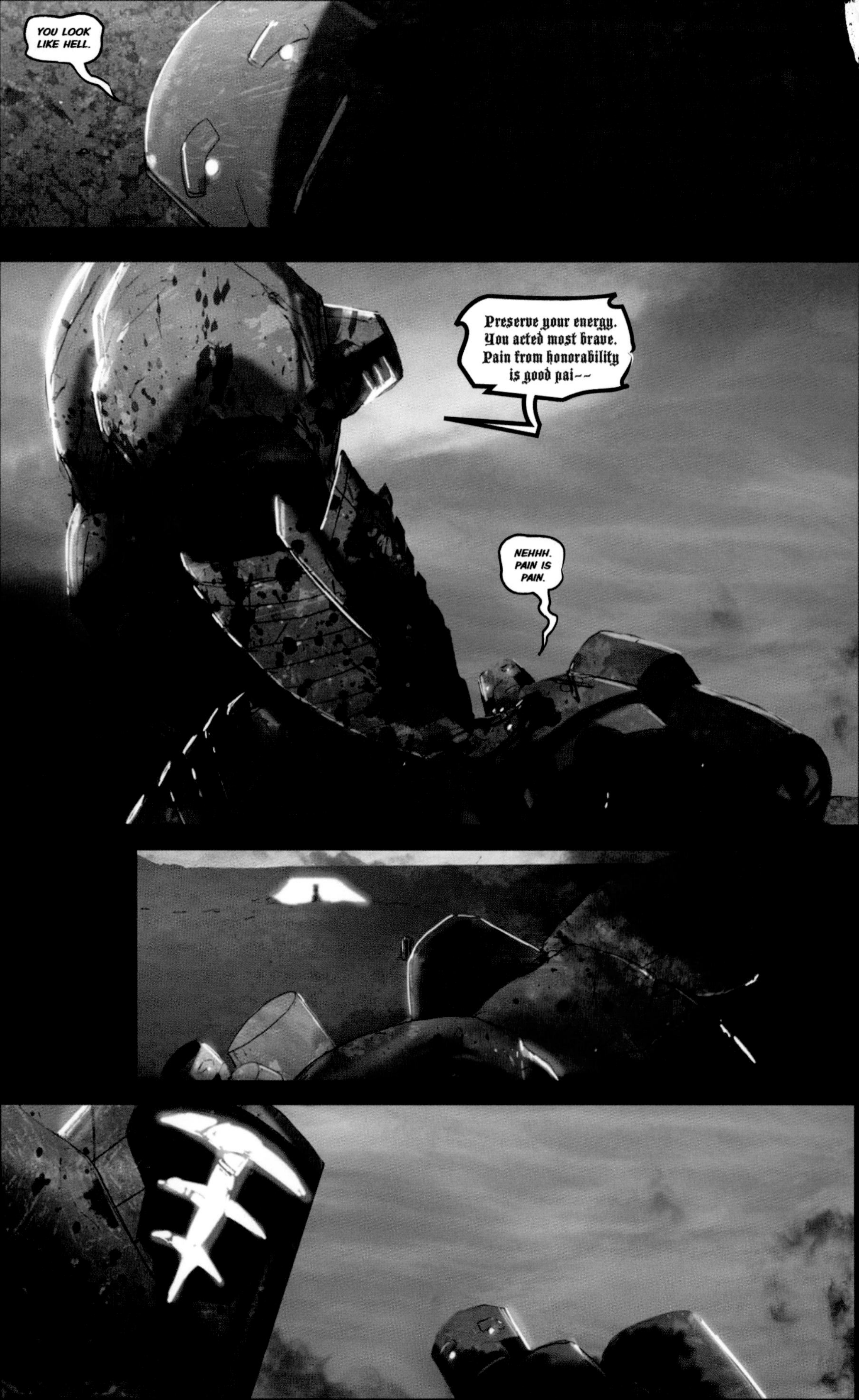
YOU LOOK LIKE HELL.
Preserve your energy. You acted most brave. Pain from honorability is good pai--
NEHHH. PAIN IS PAIN.

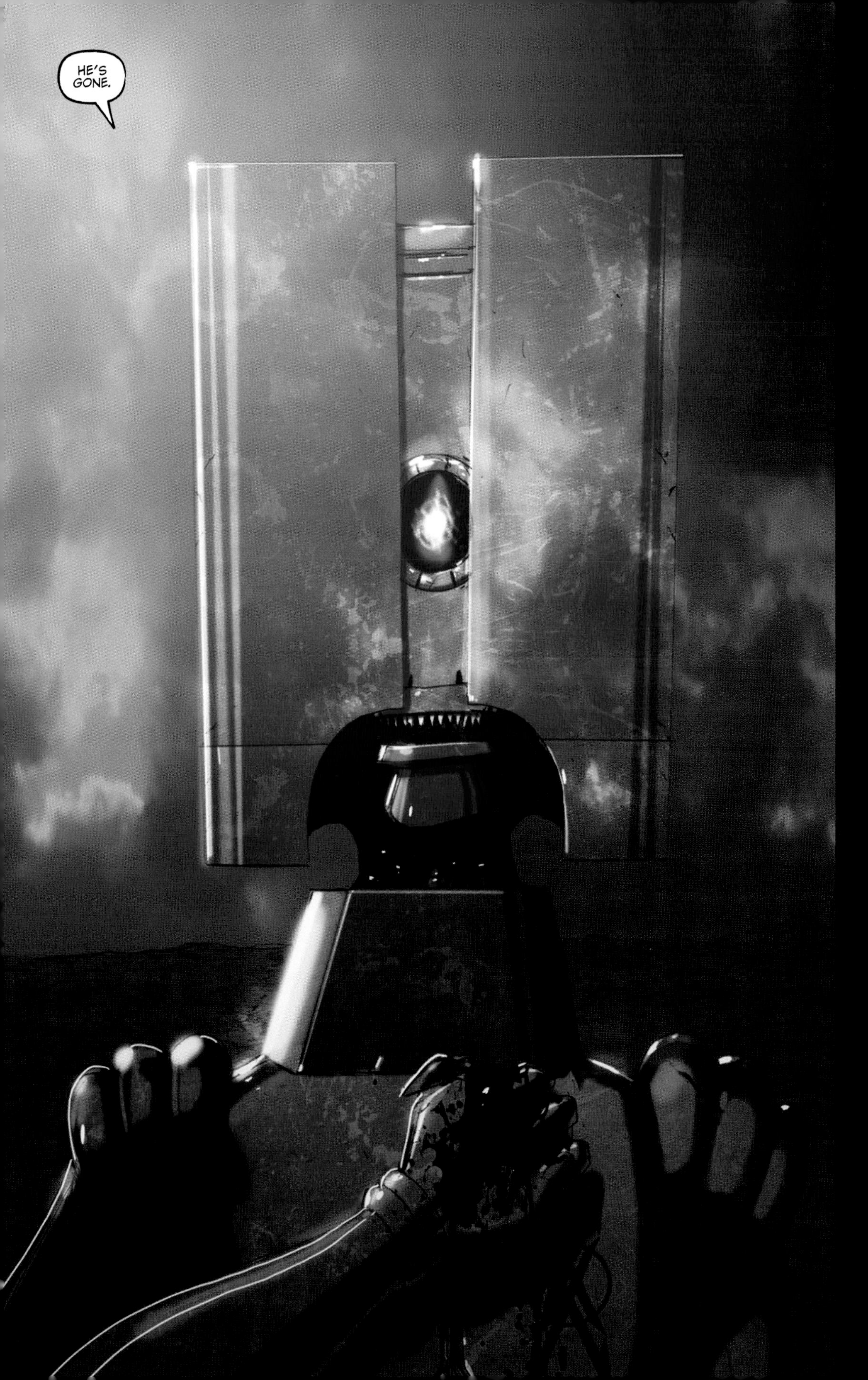
HE'S GONE.

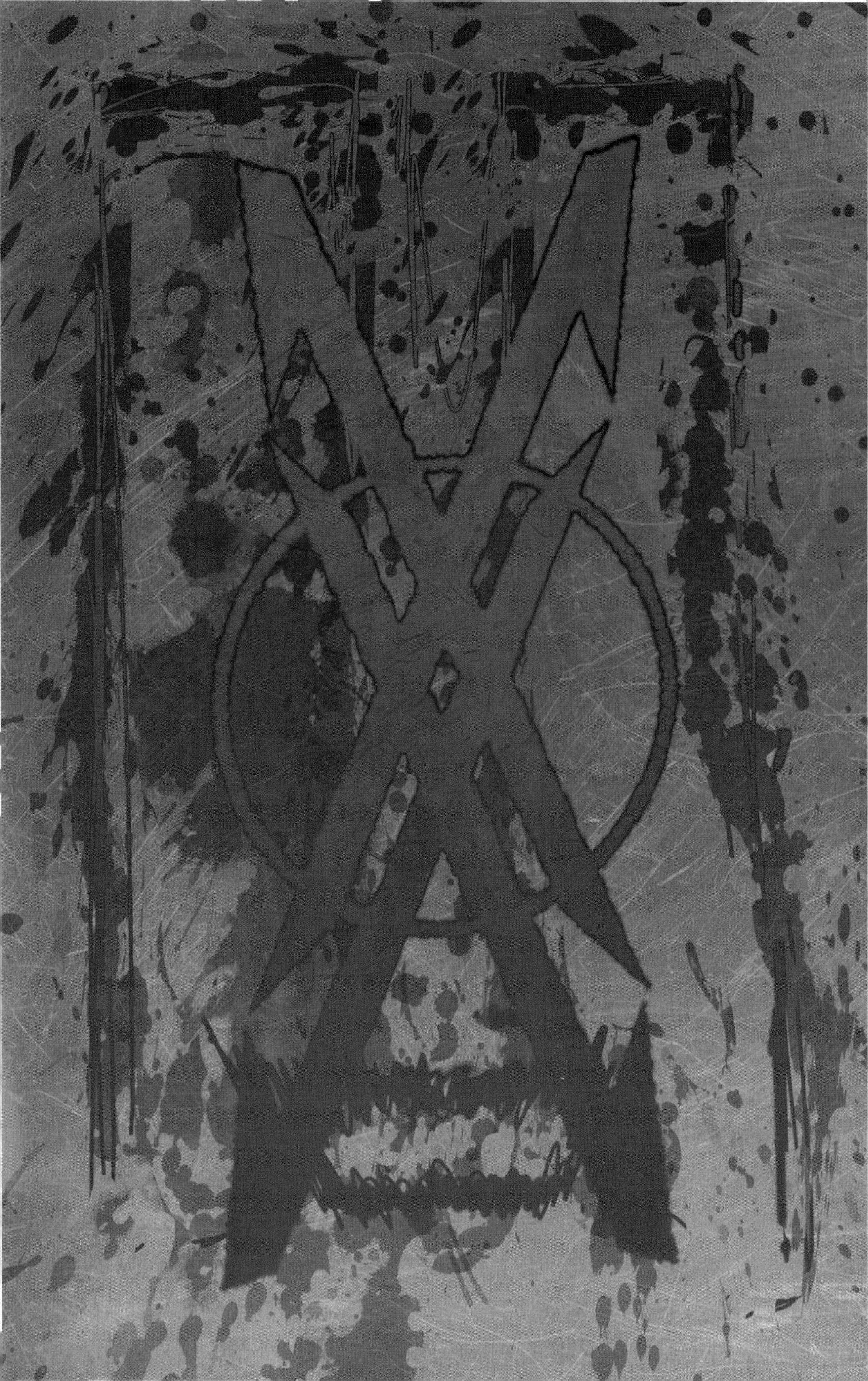

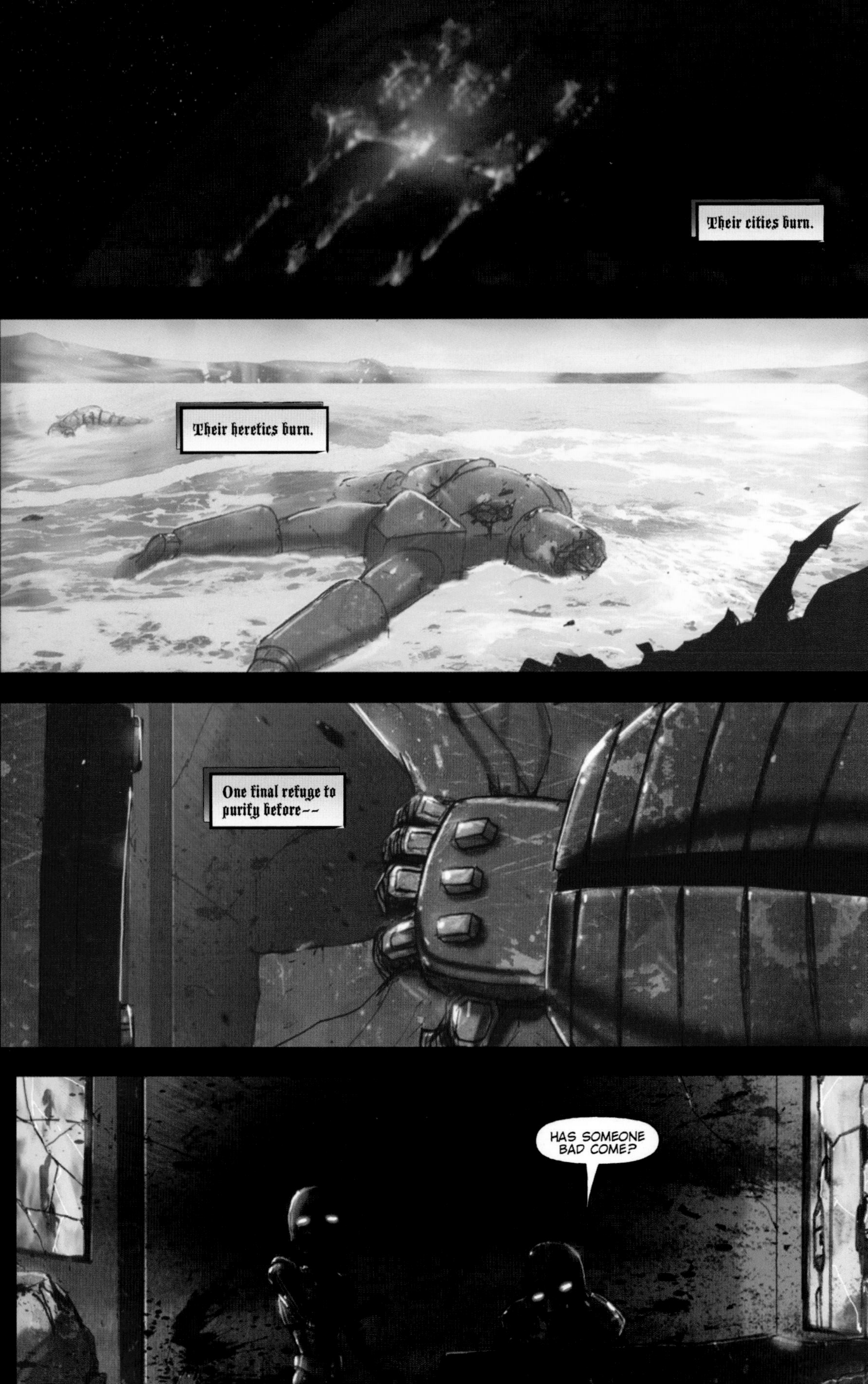
Their cities burn.
Their heretics burn.
One final refuge to purify before--
HAS SOMEONE BAD COME?

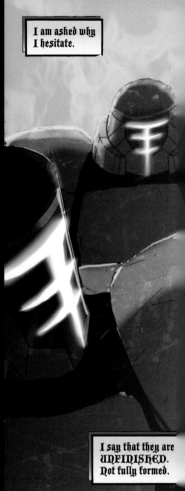

I am asked why I hesitate.

I say that they are **UNFINISHED**. Not fully formed.

I am told that young heretics are still heretics. They have witnessed a colony abandon its duties and live a life of immorality. They have seen this, and will become it themselves.

I say I have never purified Unfinished before. I say that we should visit mercy on these two. Only these two.

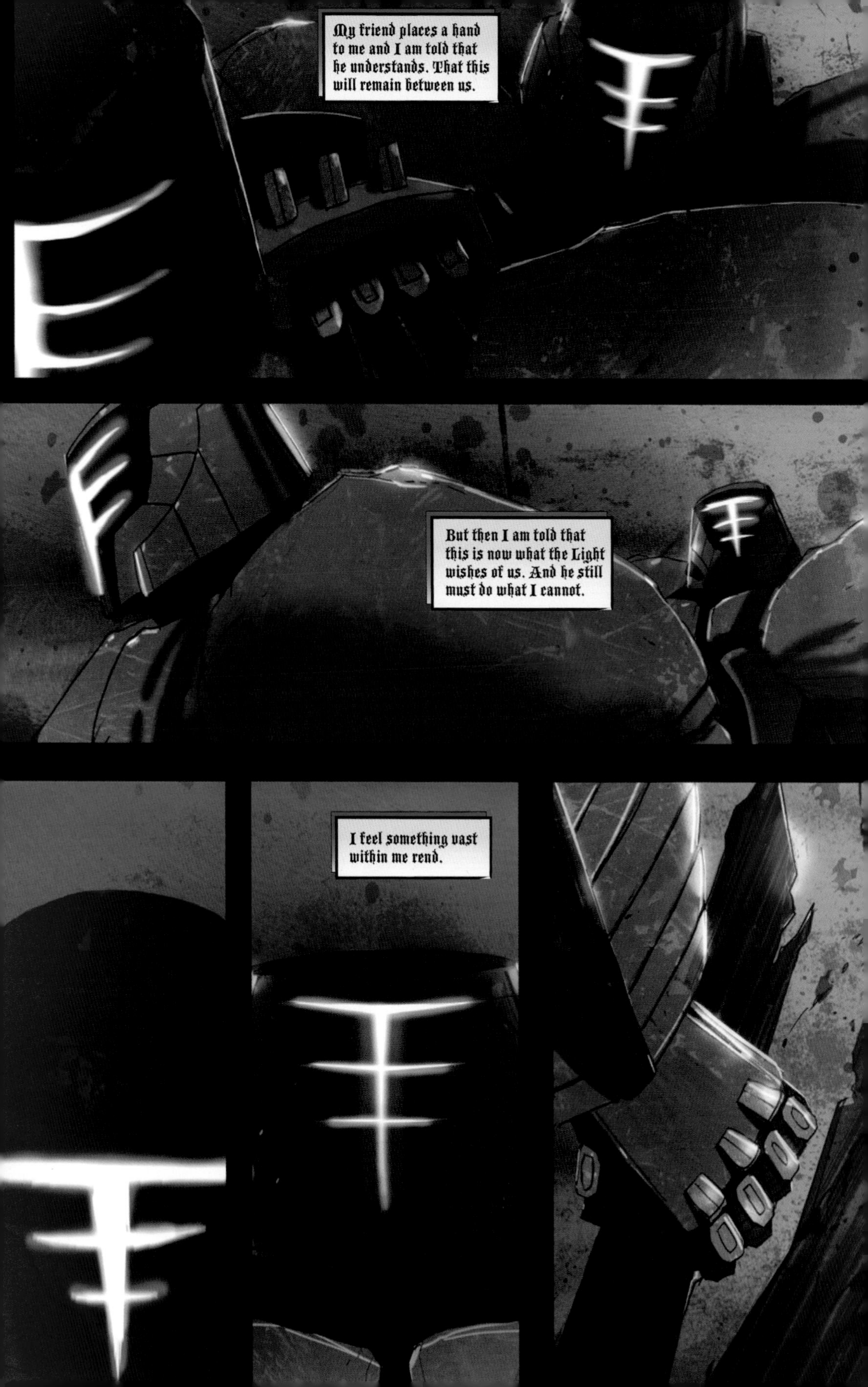
My friend places a hand to me and I am told that he understands. That this will remain between us.
But then I am told that this is now what the Light wishes of us. And he still must do what I cannot.
I feel something vast within me rend.

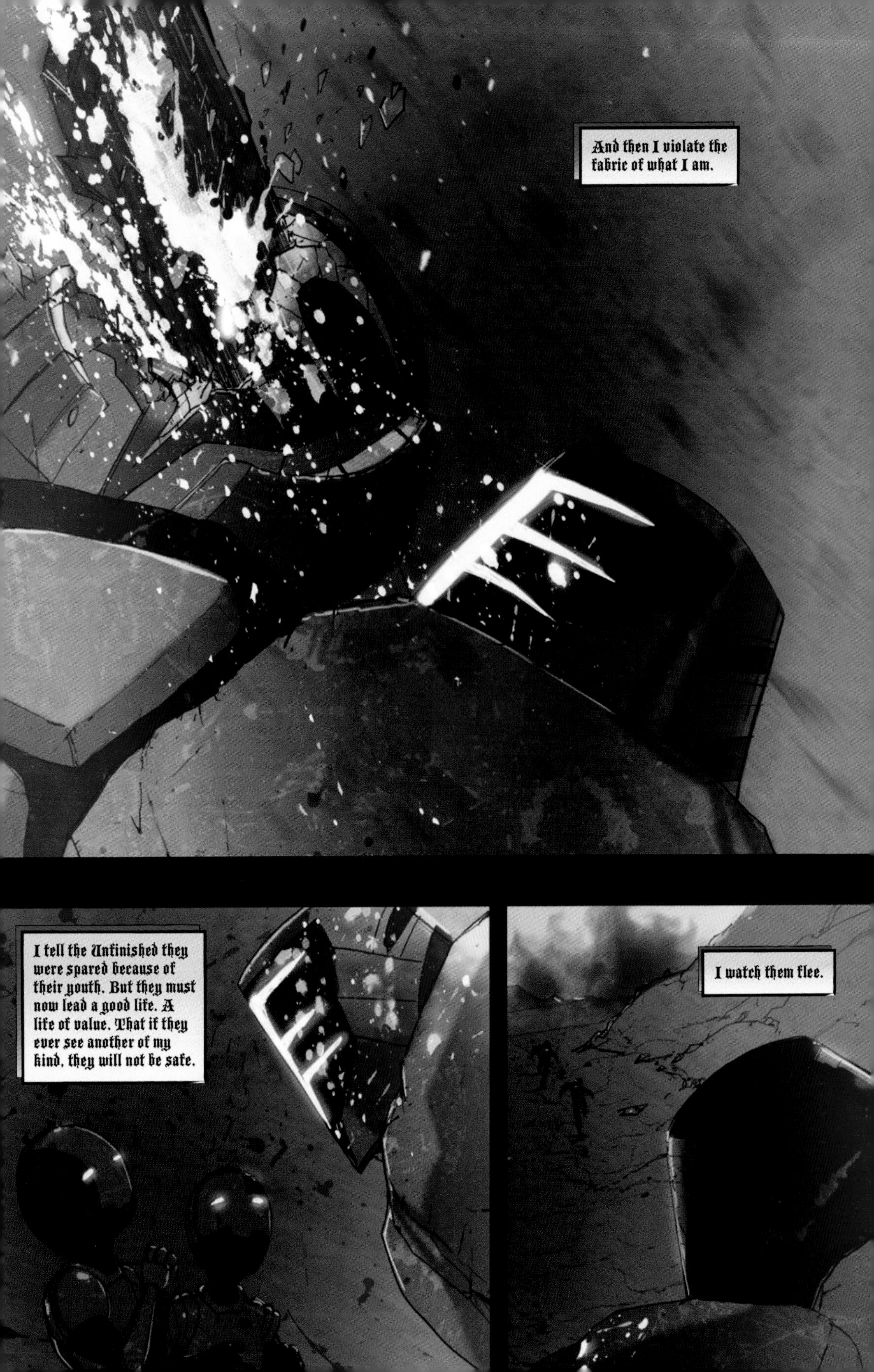
And then I violate the fabric of what I am.
I tell the Unfinished they were spared because of their youth. But they must now lead a good life. A life of value. That if they ever see another of my kind, they will not be safe.
I watch them flee.

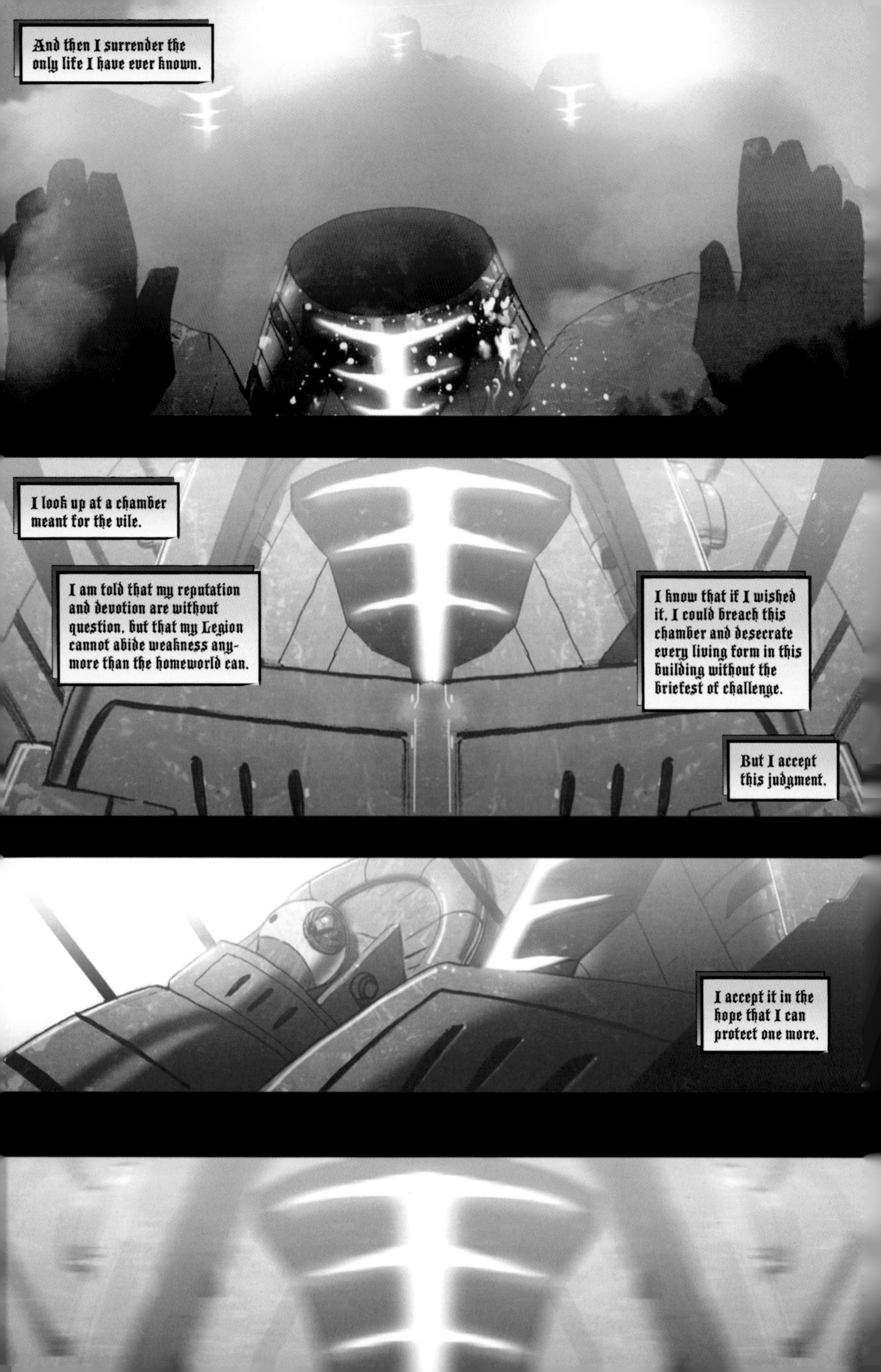
And then I surrender the only life I have ever known.
I look up at a chamber meant for the vile.
I am told that my reputation and devotion are without question, but that my Legion cannot abide weakness any-more than the homeworld can.
I know that if I wished it, I could breach this chamber and desecrate every living form in this building without the briefest of challenge.
But I accept this judgment.
I accept it in the hope that I can protect one more.

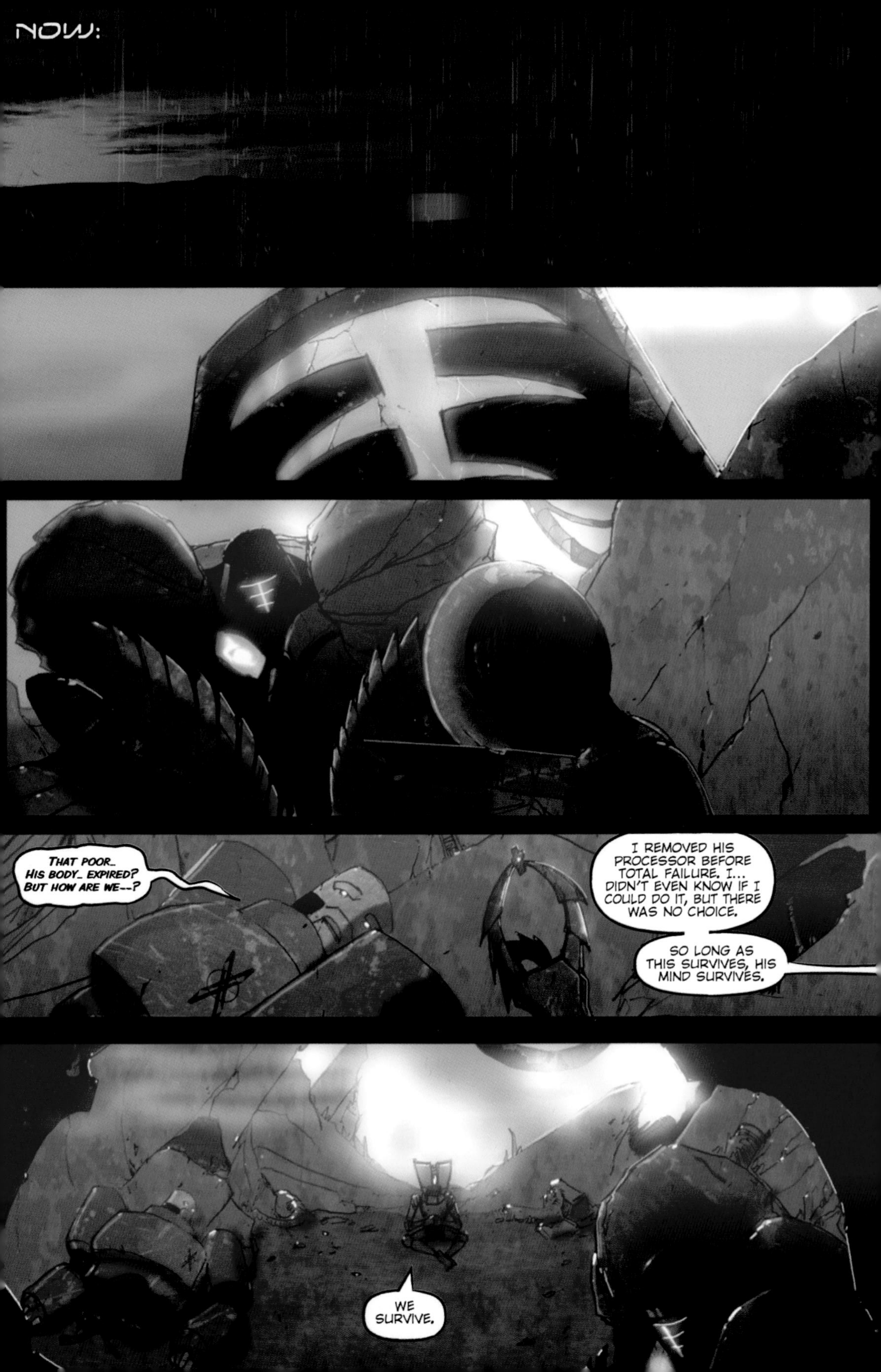
NOW:
THAT POOR... HIS BODY... EXPIRED? BUT HOW ARE WE--?
I REMOVED HIS PROCESSOR BEFORE TOTAL FAILURE. I... DIDN'T EVEN KNOW IF I COULD DO IT, BUT THERE WAS NO CHOICE.
SO LONG AS THIS SURVIVES, HIS MIND SURVIVES.
WE SURVIVE.

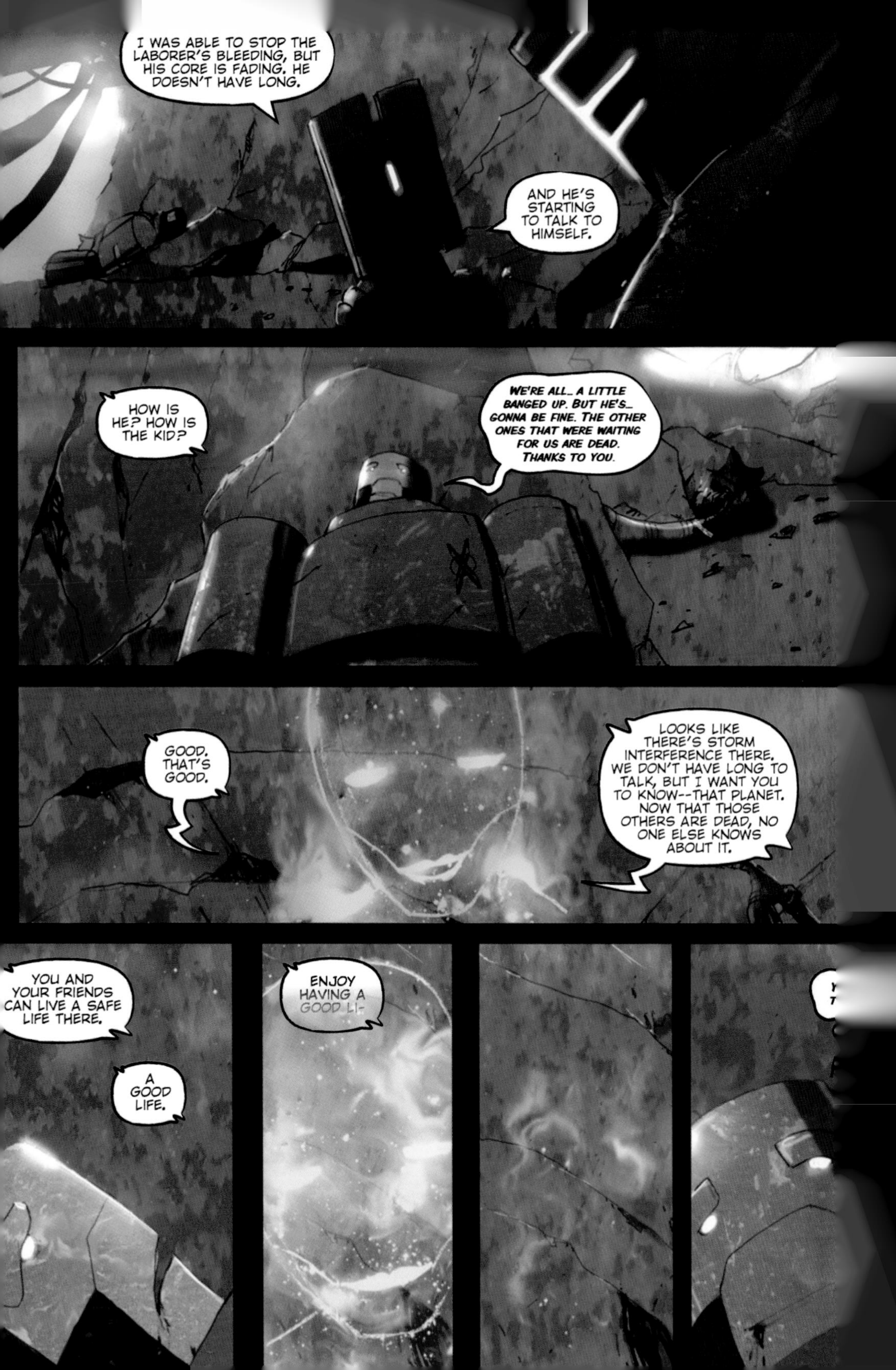
I WAS ABLE TO STOP THE LABORER'S BLEEDING, BUT HIS CORE IS FADING. HE DOESN'T HAVE LONG.
AND HE'S STARTING TO TALK TO HIMSELF.
HOW IS HE? HOW IS THE KID?
WE'RE ALL... A LITTLE BANGED UP. BUT HE'S... GONNA BE FINE. THE OTHER ONES THAT WERE WAITING FOR US ARE DEAD. THANKS TO YOU.
GOOD. THAT'S GOOD.
LOOKS LIKE THERE'S STORM INTERFERENCE THERE. WE DON'T HAVE LONG TO TALK, BUT I WANT YOU TO KNOW--THAT PLANET. NOW THAT THOSE OTHERS ARE DEAD, NO ONE ELSE KNOWS ABOUT IT.
YOU AND YOUR FRIENDS CAN LIVE A SAFE LIFE THERE.
A GOOD LIFE.
ENJOY HAVING A GOOD LI-

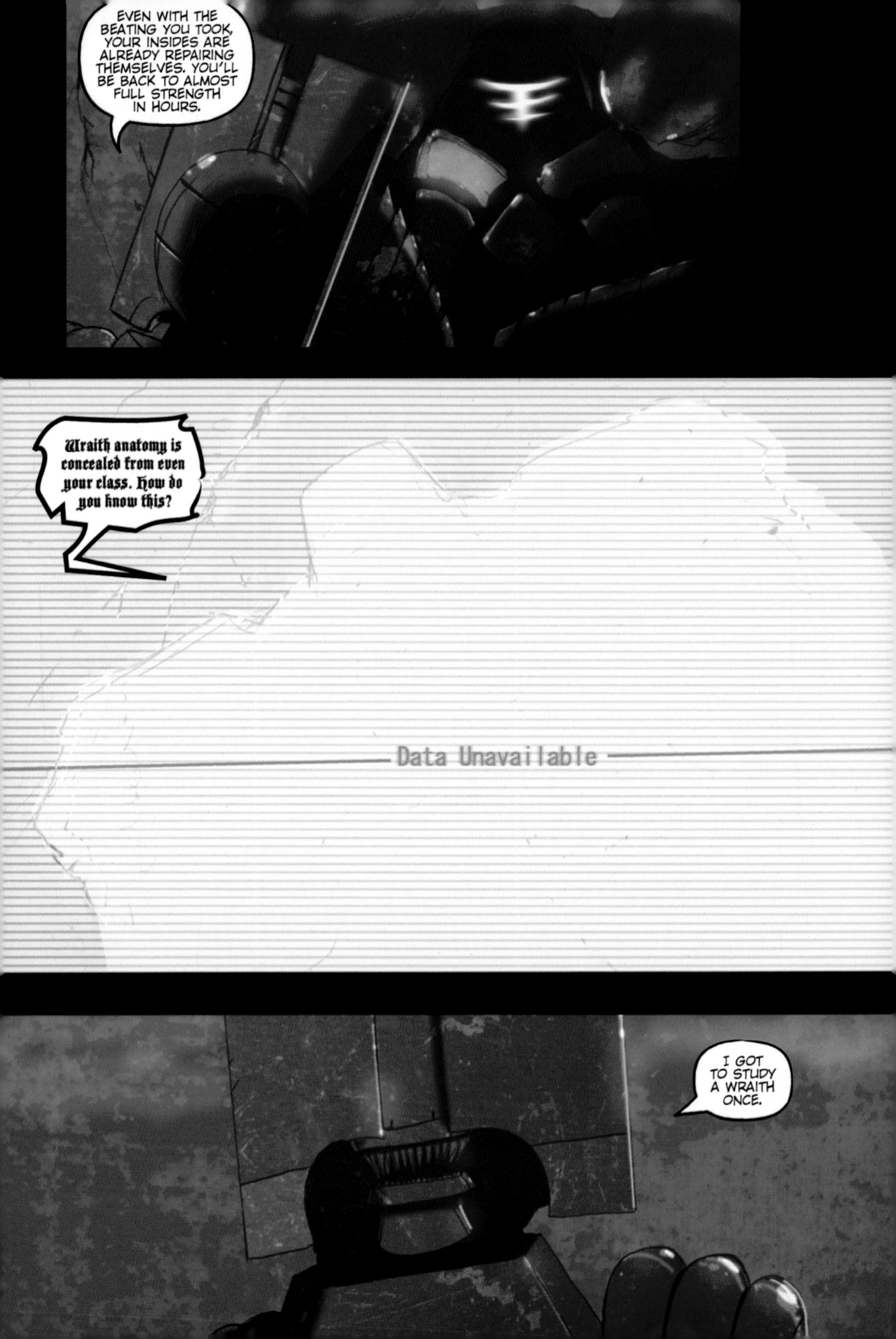
EVEN WITH THE BEATING YOU TOOK, YOUR INSIDES ARE ALREADY REPAIRING THEMSELVES. YOU'LL BE BACK TO ALMOST FULL STRENGTH IN HOURS.
Wraith anatomy is concealed from even your class. How do you know this?
Data Unavailable
I GOT TO STUDY A WRAITH ONCE.

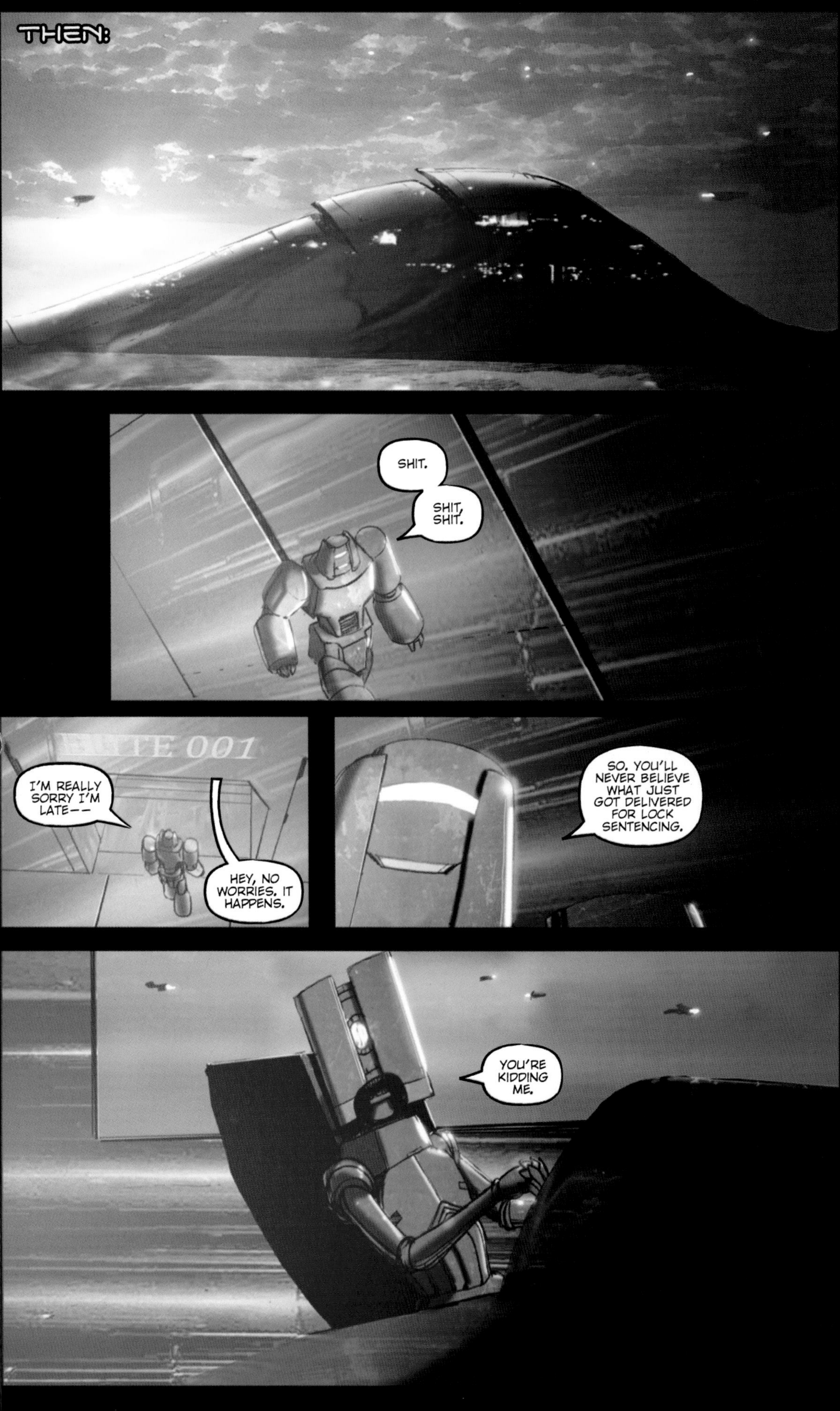
THEN:
SHIT.
SHIT, SHIT.
I'M REALLY SORRY I'M LATE--
HEY, NO WORRIES. IT HAPPENS.
SO. YOU'LL NEVER BELIEVE WHAT JUST GOT DELIVERED FOR LOCK SENTENCING.
YOU'RE KIDDING ME.

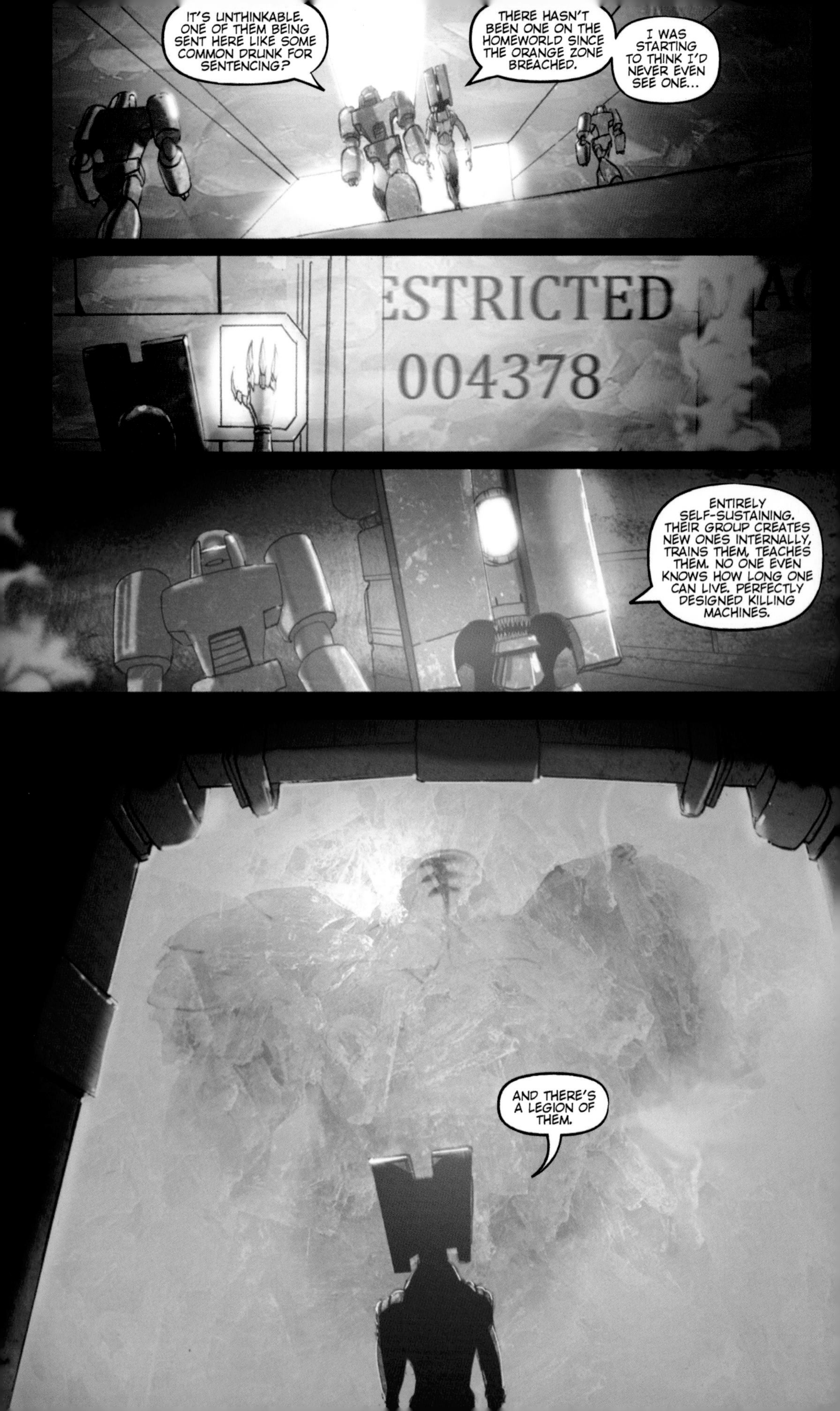
IT'S UNTHINKABLE. ONE OF THEM BEING SENT HERE LIKE SOME COMMON DRUNK FOR SENTENCING?
THERE HASN'T BEEN ONE ON THE HOMEWORLD SINCE THE ORANGE ZONE BREACHED.
I WAS STARTING TO THINK I'D NEVER EVEN SEE ONE...
ESTRICTED
004378
ENTIRELY SELF-SUSTAINING. THEIR GROUP CREATES NEW ONES INTERNALLY, TRAINS THEM, TEACHES THEM. NO ONE EVEN KNOWS HOW LONG ONE CAN LIVE. PERFECTLY DESIGNED KILLING MACHINES.
AND THERE'S A LEGION OF THEM.

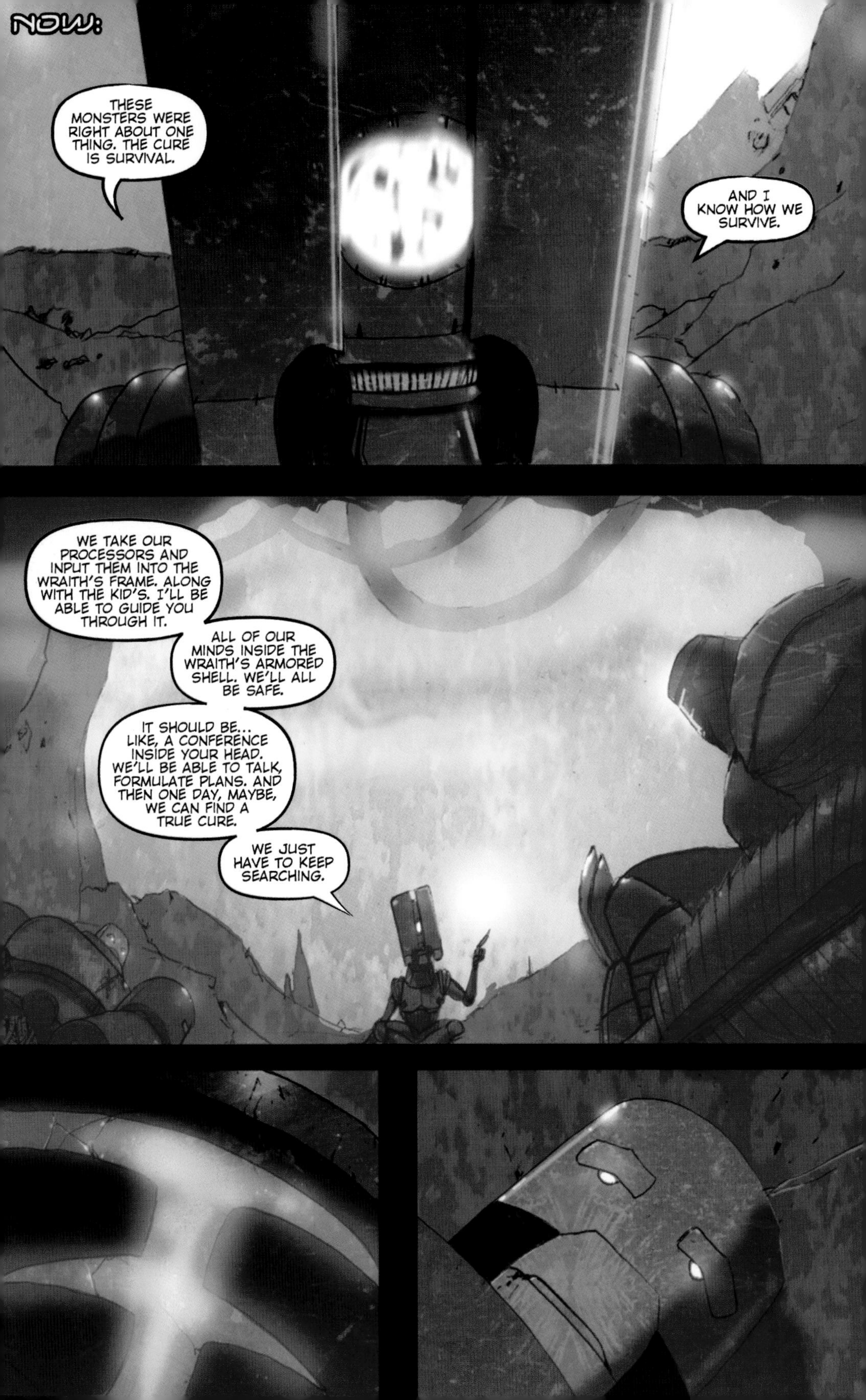
NOW:
THESE MONSTERS WERE RIGHT ABOUT ONE THING. THE CURE IS SURVIVAL.
AND I KNOW HOW WE SURVIVE.
WE TAKE OUR PROCESSORS AND INPUT THEM INTO THE WRAITH'S FRAME. ALONG WITH THE KID'S. I'LL BE ABLE TO GUIDE YOU THROUGH IT.
ALL OF OUR MINDS INSIDE THE WRAITH'S ARMORED SHELL. WE'LL ALL BE SAFE.
IT SHOULD BE... LIKE, A CONFERENCE INSIDE YOUR HEAD. WE'LL BE ABLE TO TALK, FORMULATE PLANS. AND THEN ONE DAY, MAYBE, WE CAN FIND A TRUE CURE.
WE JUST HAVE TO KEEP SEARCHING.

YOU'RE... STILL IN HERE?

YOU KNOW THE DESIGN I HATE THE MOST?

THE SHELL OF THE ARTISAN CLASS. DESIGNED BY THE FORGERS THEMSELVES.

AND THEN THE ARTISAN CLASS DESIGNED EVERY- THING BENEATH US. AND WE DESIGNED IT WELL.

WE TOOK GARBAGE RESOURCES, SCRAPS, AND CREATED AN ENTIRE LABOR CLASS. WE REFINED THE FOUNDATION OF THE ENTIRE CIVILIZATION. AND ALL WITH THE POWER OF THE MIND.

THIS WEAK BOD THE FORGERS NEV WANTED US TO BE POWERFUL... BECA THEY KNEW WHAT WOULD MEAN.

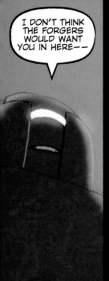

I DON'T THINK THE FORGERS WOULD WANT YOU IN HERE——

I WANT YOU TO KNOW I ALWAYS LIKED YOU. I ACTUALLY CONSIDERED TELLING YOU THE TRUTH ABOUT MYSELF.

BUT I GUESS, YOU FOUND OUT ANYWAY.

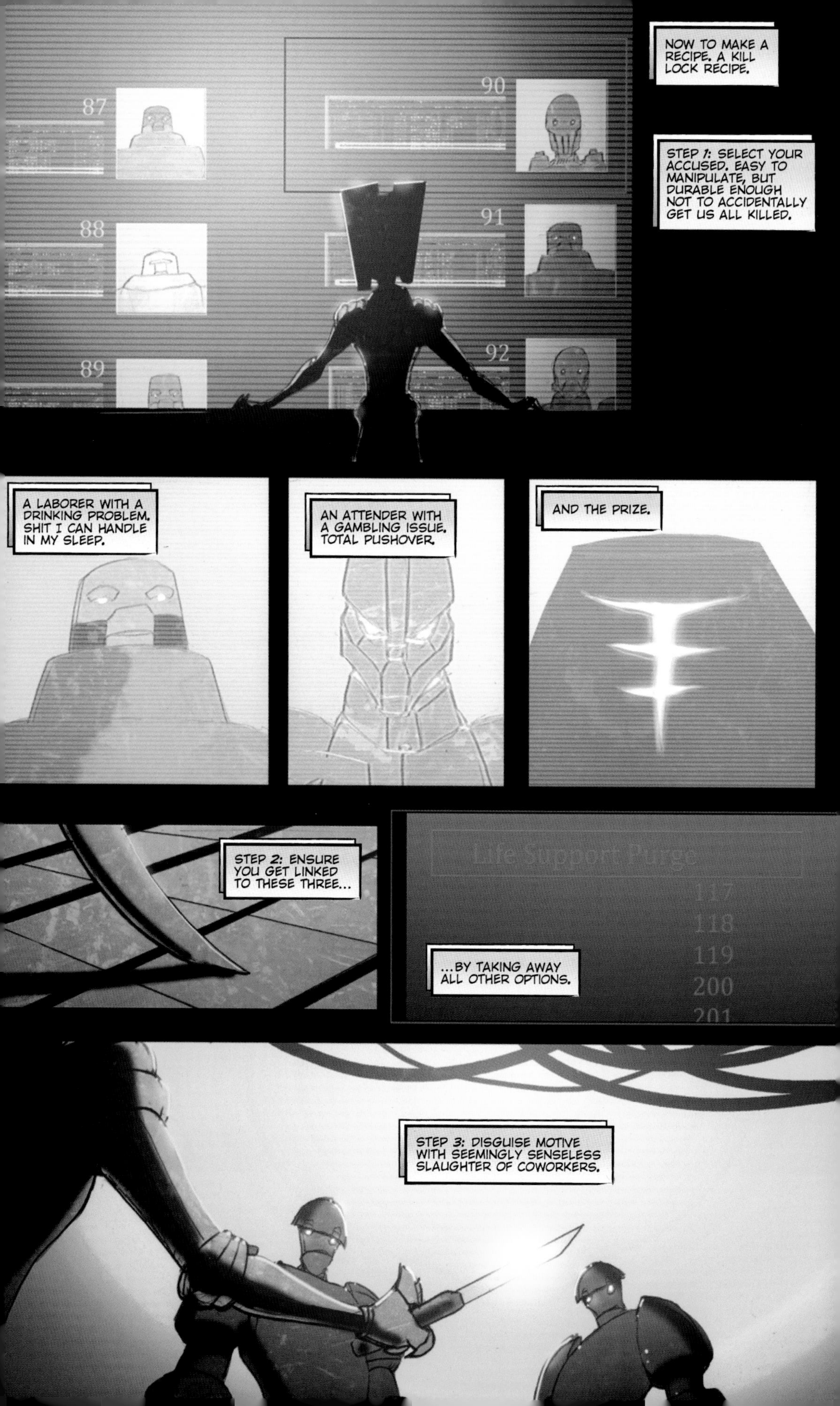
NOW TO MAKE A RECIPE. A KILL LOCK RECIPE.
87
88
89
90
91
92
STEP 1: SELECT YOUR ACCUSED. EASY TO MANIPULATE, BUT DURABLE ENOUGH NOT TO ACCIDENTALLY GET US ALL KILLED.
A LABORER WITH A DRINKING PROBLEM. SHIT I CAN HANDLE IN MY SLEEP.
AN ATTENDER WITH A GAMBLING ISSUE. TOTAL PUSHOVER.
AND THE PRIZE.
STEP 2: ENSURE YOU GET LINKED TO THESE THREE...
Life Support Purge
117
118
119
200
...BY TAKING AWAY ALL OTHER OPTIONS.
STEP 3: DISGUISE MOTIVE WITH SEEMINGLY SENSELESS SLAUGHTER OF COWORKERS.

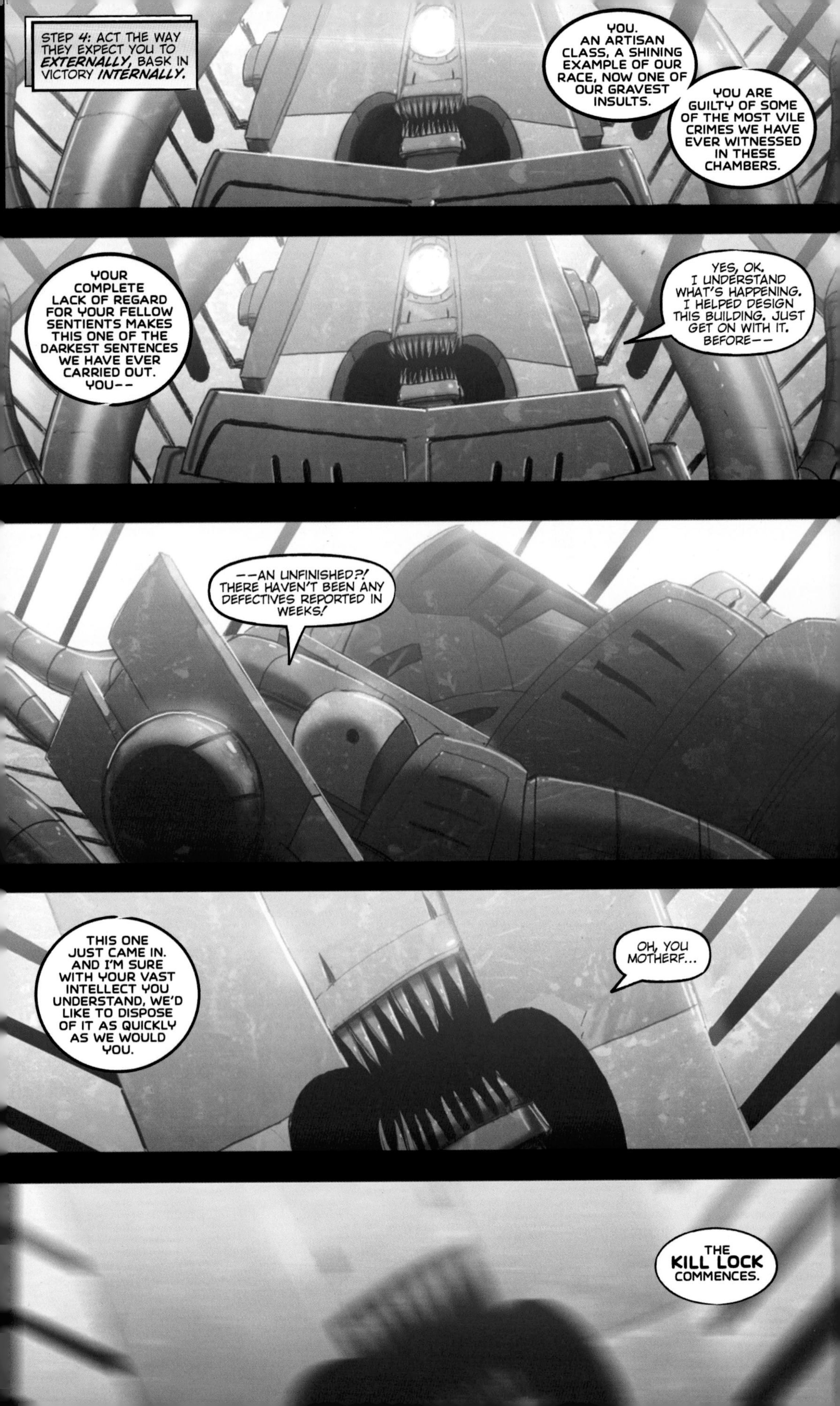
STEP 4: ACT THE WAY THEY EXPECT YOU TO EXTERNALLY, BASK IN VICTORY INTERNALLY.
YOU. AN ARTISAN CLASS, A SHINING EXAMPLE OF OUR RACE, NOW ONE OF OUR GRAVEST INSULTS.
YOU ARE GUILTY OF SOME OF THE MOST VILE CRIMES WE HAVE EVER WITNESSED IN THESE CHAMBERS.
YOUR COMPLETE LACK OF REGARD FOR YOUR FELLOW SENTIENTS MAKES THIS ONE OF THE DARKEST SENTENCES WE HAVE EVER CARRIED OUT. YOU--
YES, OK. I UNDERSTAND WHAT'S HAPPENING. I HELPED DESIGN THIS BUILDING. JUST GET ON WITH IT. BEFORE--
--AN UNFINISHED?! THERE HAVEN'T BEEN ANY DEFECTIVES REPORTED IN WEEKS!
THIS ONE JUST CAME IN. AND I'M SURE WITH YOUR VAST INTELLECT YOU UNDERSTAND, WE'D LIKE TO DISPOSE OF IT AS QUICKLY AS WE WOULD YOU.
OH, YOU MOTHERF...
THE KILL LOCK COMMENCES.

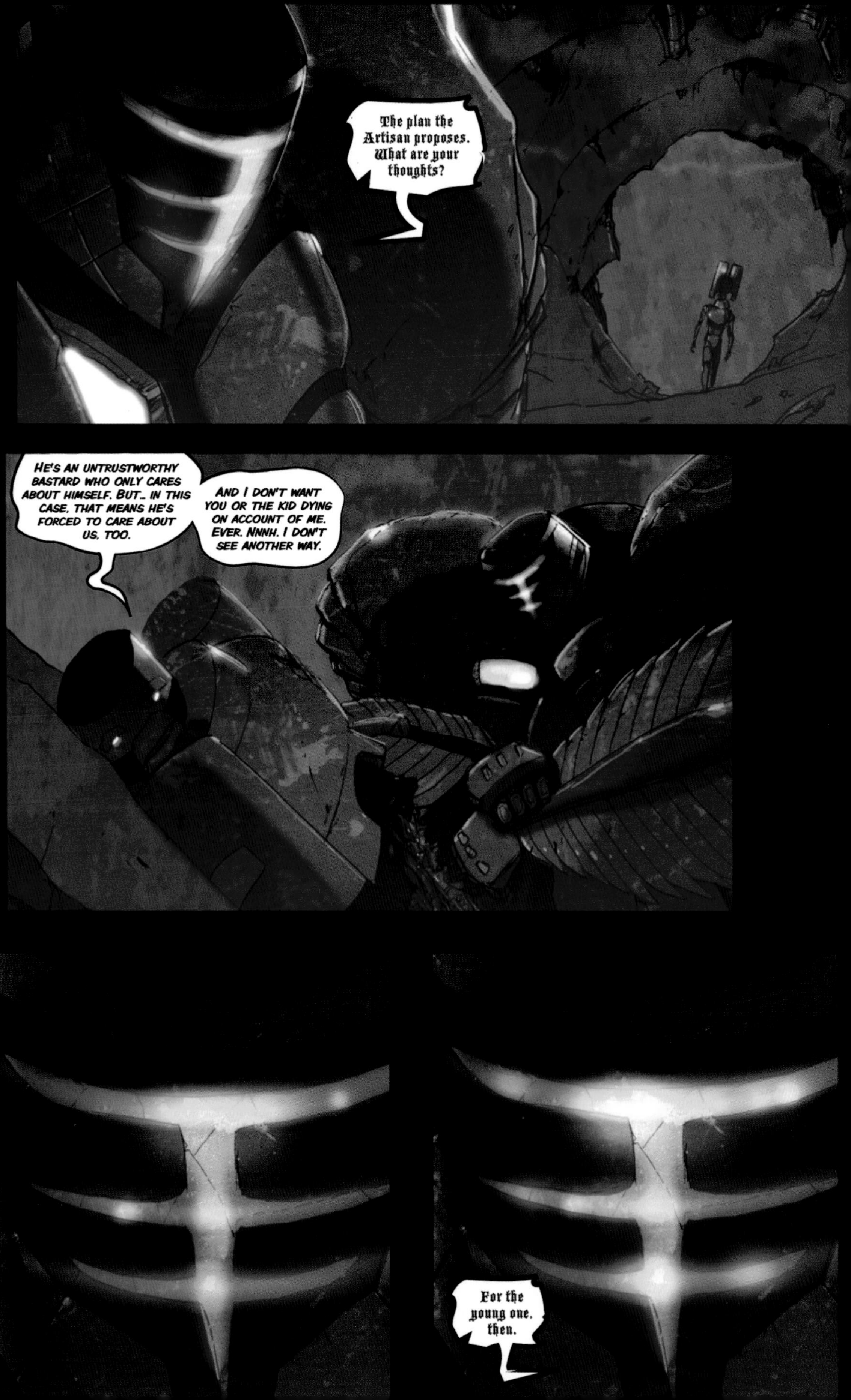
The plan the Artisan proposes. What are your thoughts?
HE'S AN UNTRUSTWORTHY BASTARD WHO ONLY CARES ABOUT HIMSELF. BUT… IN THIS CASE, THAT MEANS HE'S FORCED TO CARE ABOUT US, TOO.
AND I DON'T WANT YOU OR THE KID DYING ON ACCOUNT OF ME. EVER. NNNH. I DON'T SEE ANOTHER WAY.
For the young one, then.

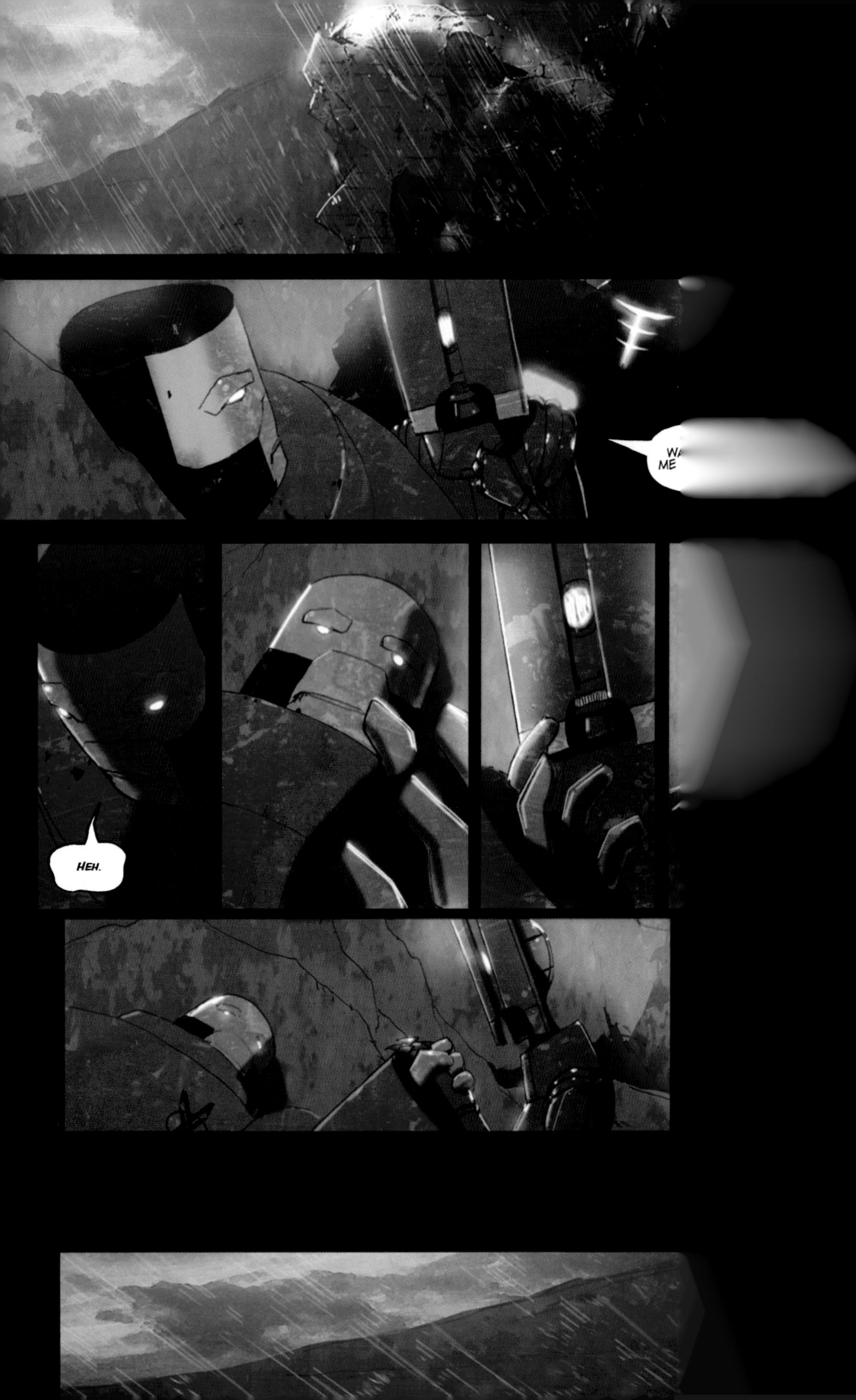
HEH.

JUST FOLLOW WHAT I WROTE HERE. I KEPT IT SIMPLE.

MAKE SURE YOU HANDLE THESE LIKE A SNOWFLAKE, LITERALLY ALL OUR LIVES DEPEND ON IT.

I WILL NOT FAIL US.

I'M TRUSTING YOU.

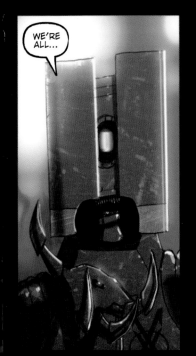

WE'RE ALL...

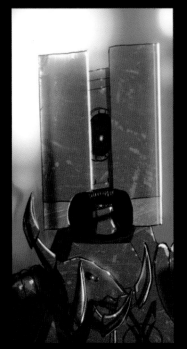

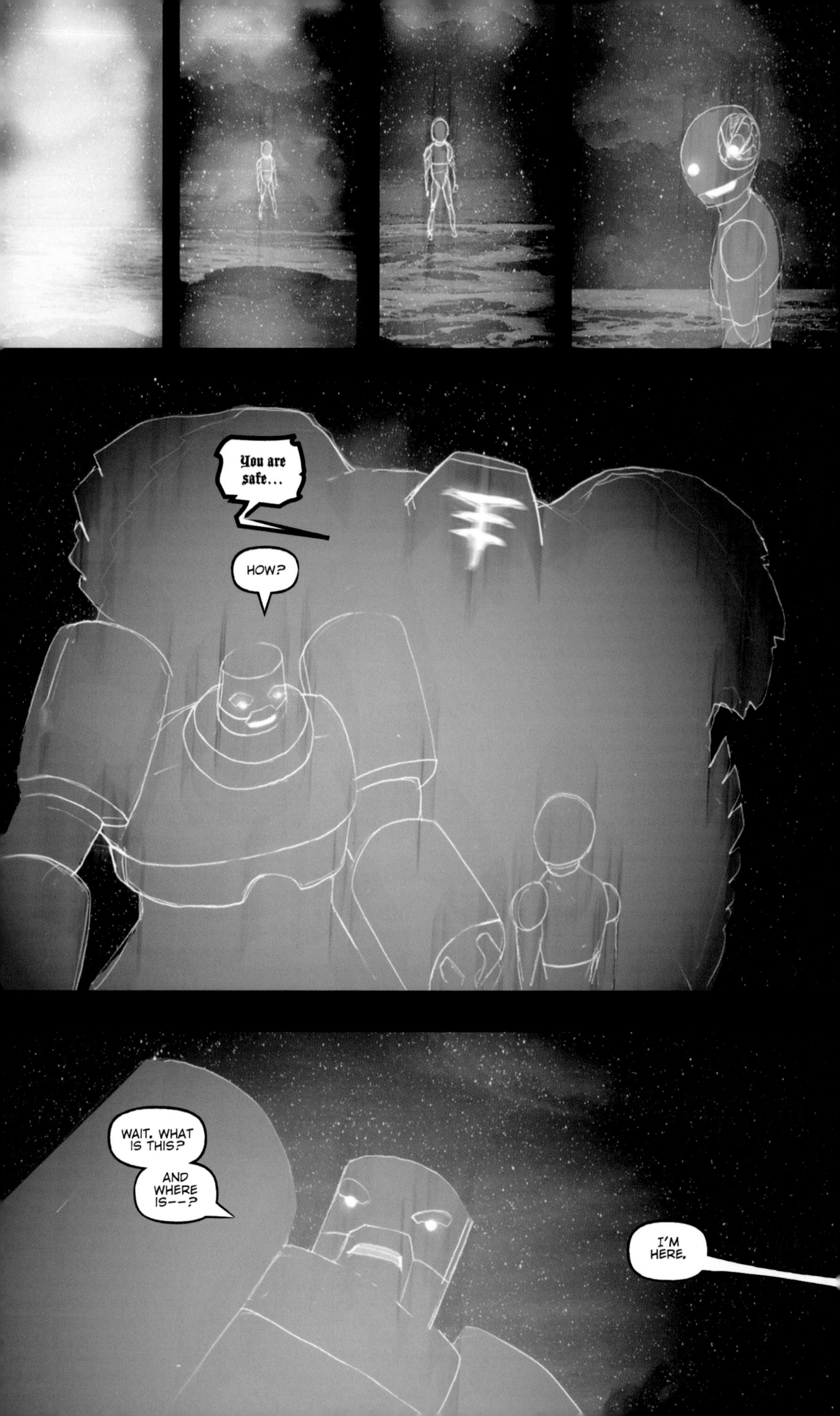
You are safe...
HOW?
WAIT. WHAT IS THIS?
AND WHERE IS--?
I'M HERE.

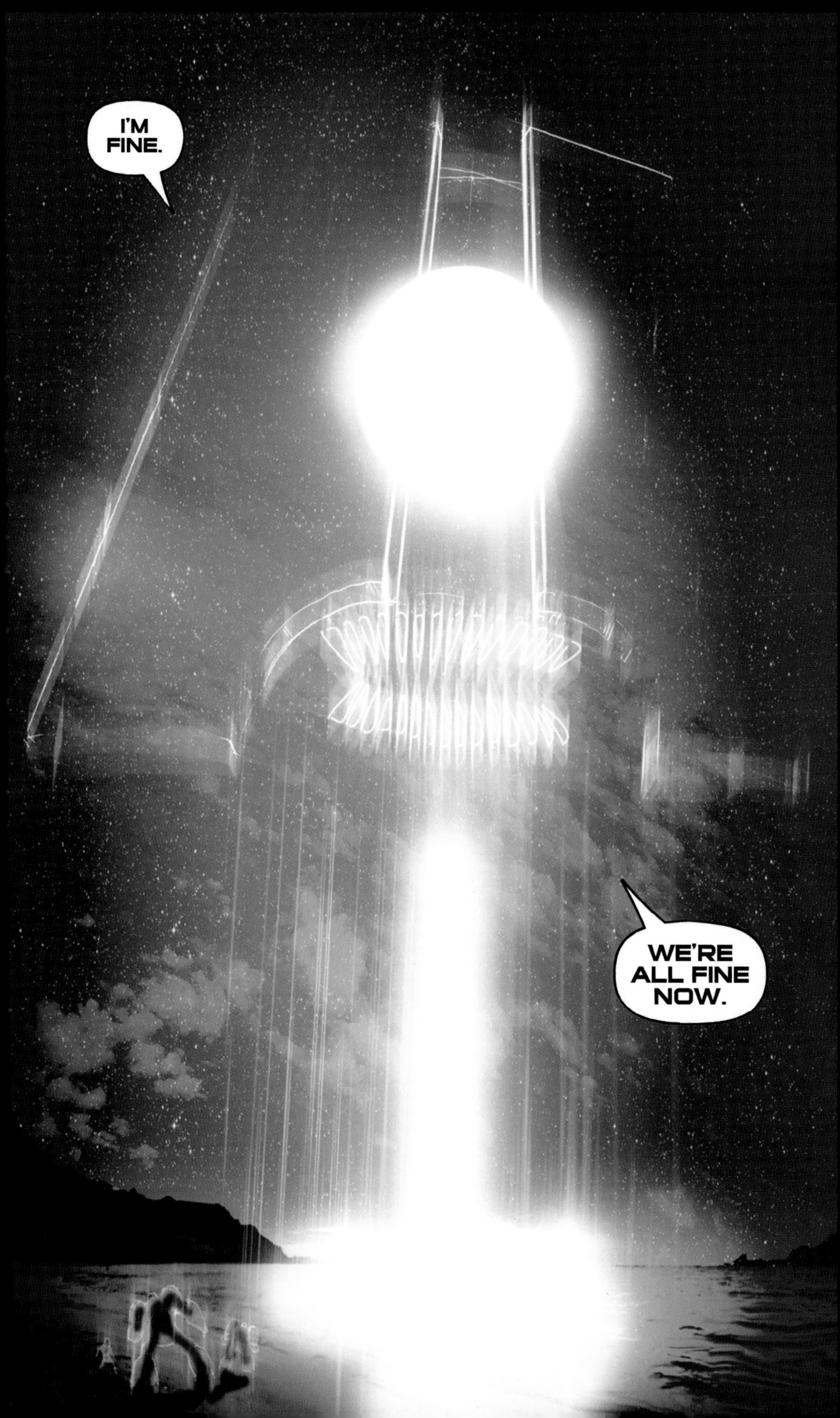
I'M FINE.
WE'RE ALL FINE NOW.

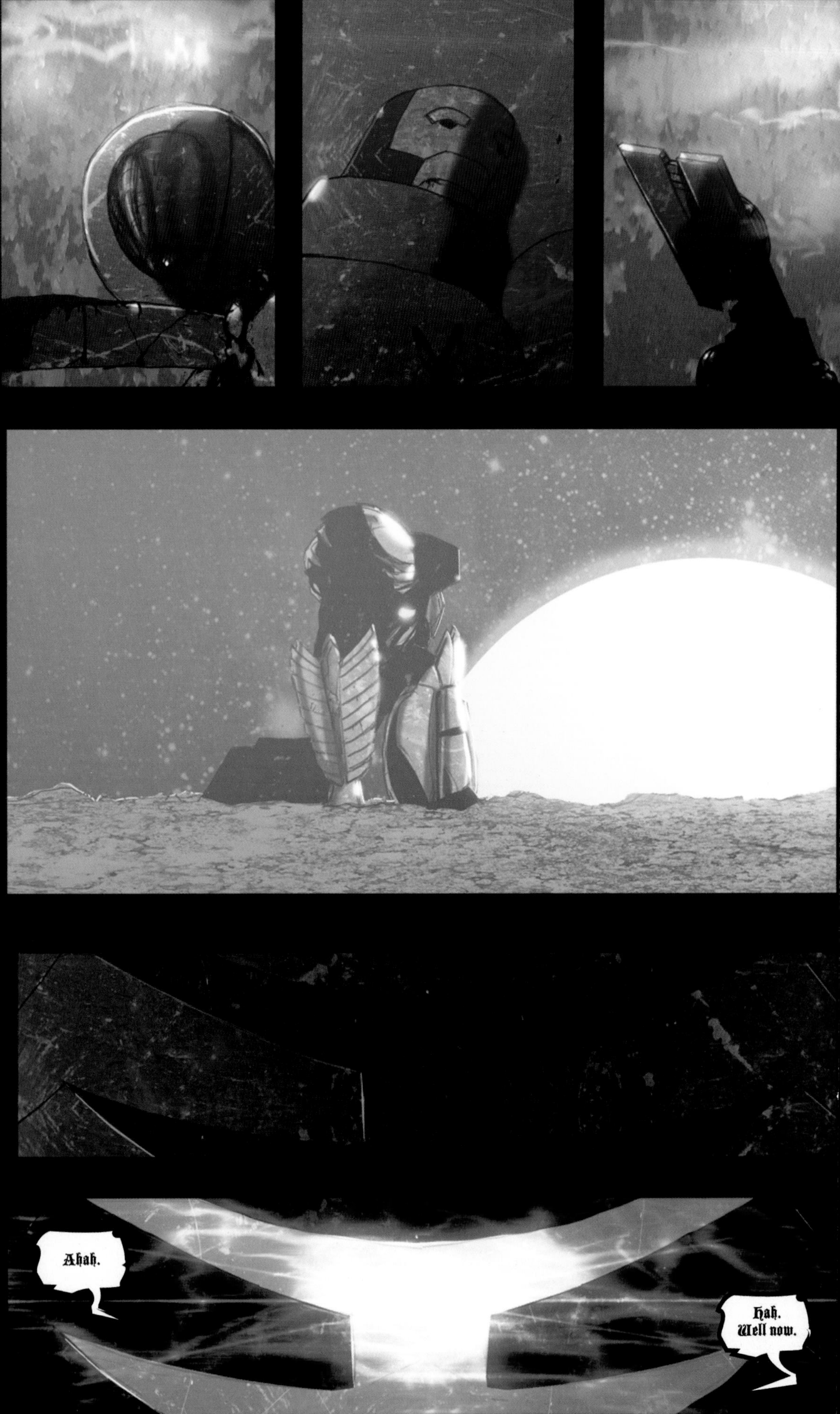
Ahah.
Hah. Well now.

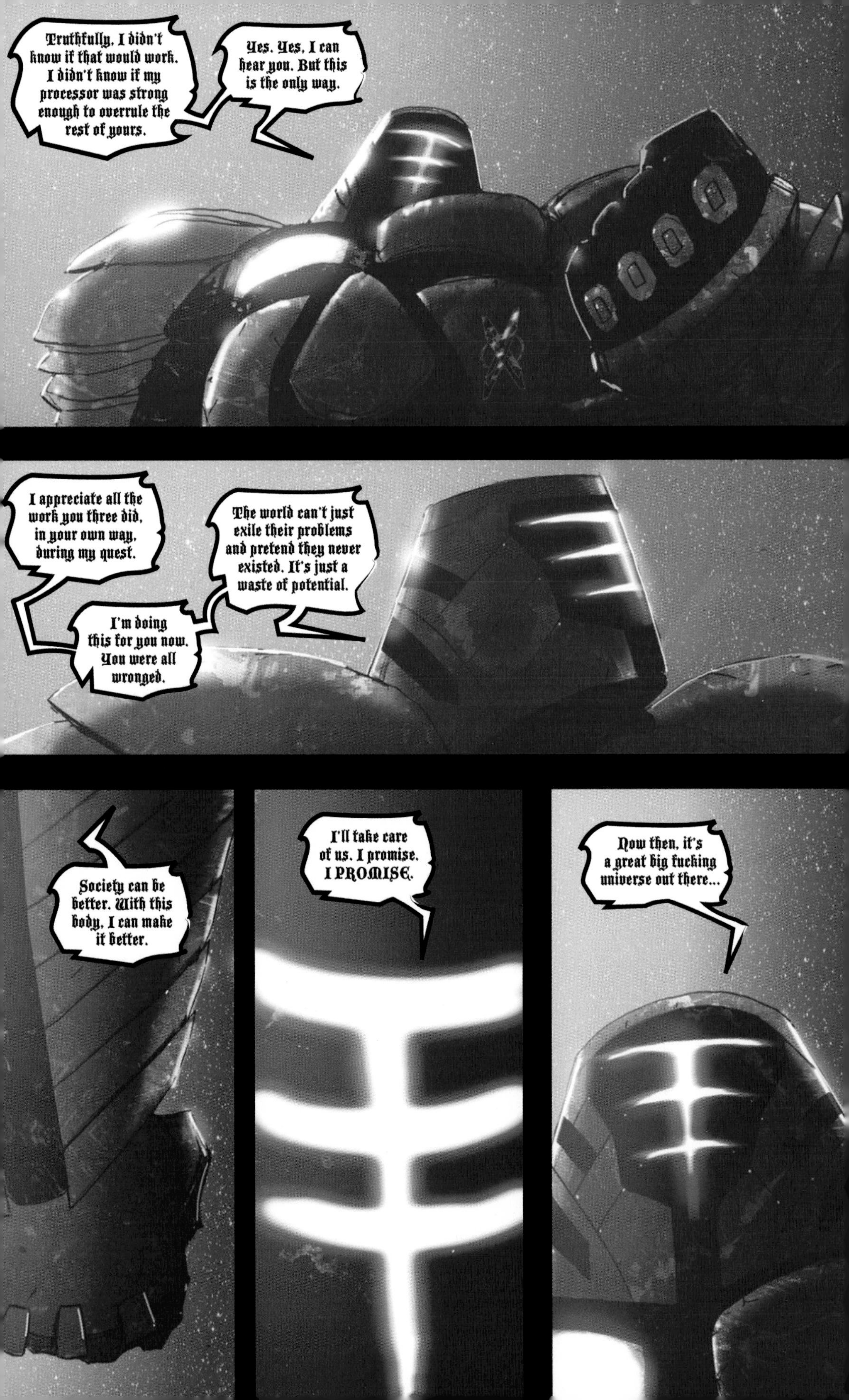
Truthfully, I didn't know if that would work. I didn't know if my processor was strong enough to overrule the rest of yours.
Yes. Yes, I can hear you. But this is the only way.
I appreciate all the work you three did, in your own way, during my quest.
The world can't just exile their problems and pretend they never existed. It's just a waste of potential.
I'm doing this for you now. You were all wronged.
Society can be better. With this body, I can make it better.
I'll take care of us. I promise. I PROMISE.
Now then, it's a great big fucking universe out there...

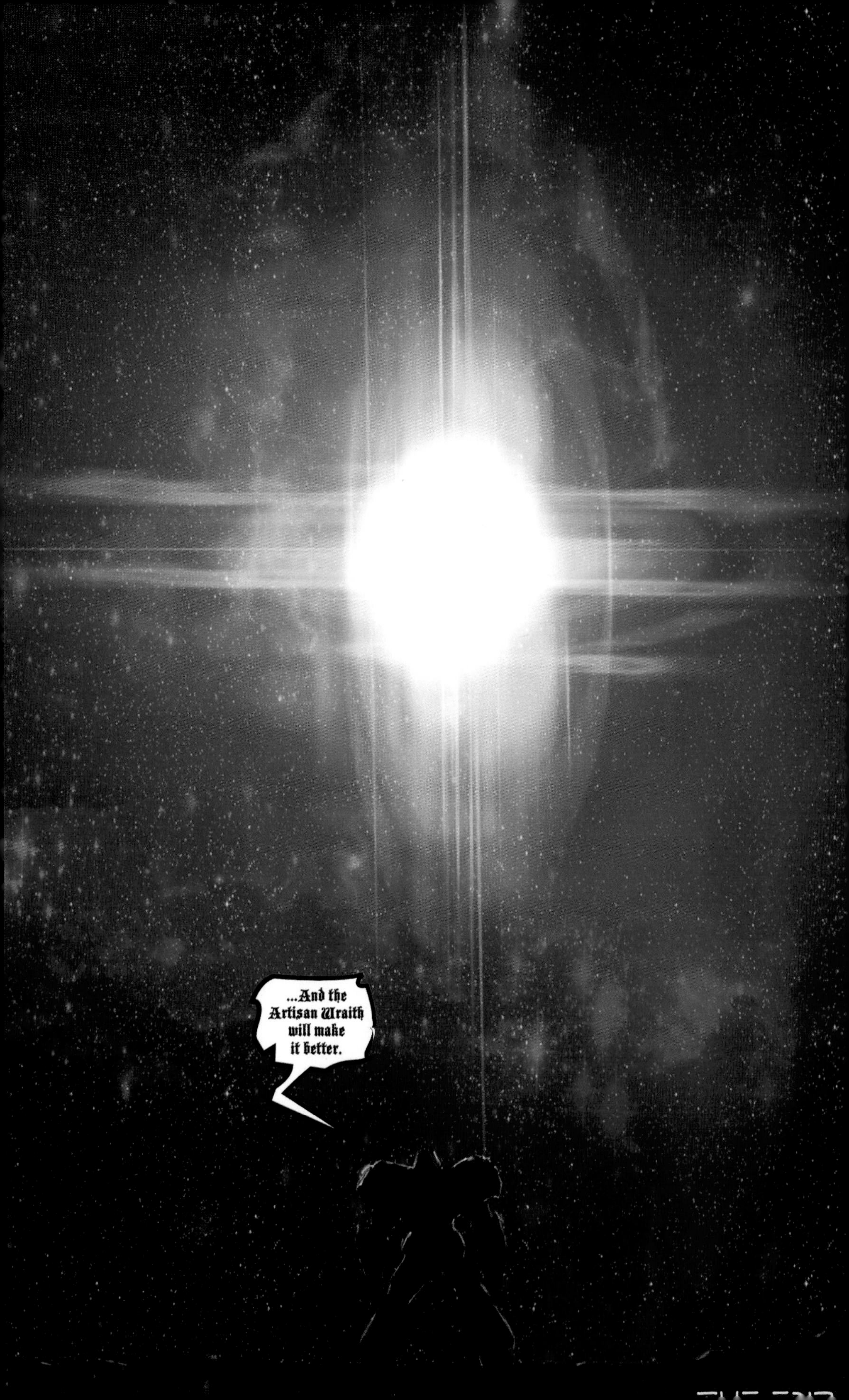
...And the Artisan Wraith will make it better.

THANK YOU SO MUCH for checking out my little sci-fi story here!

The Kill Lock has been a labor of love since I first began working on it a couple of years back—chipping away at writing six issues, around 135 pages, around my other gigs.

There was never a guarantee this thing was going to get published. A non-human cast in a comic book story can be instantly alienating to some people... even, ironically, the same people who would have no trouble investing their emotions in a story about toys, or monsters, or cars, in another medium.

Even with IDW, a company I've loved working with for a decade now, mostly on *Transformers*, there was nothing set in stone that they would be interested in publishing this. I wrote and finished all six issues before even pitching them the concept. I was beyond flattered and very excited that they gave it a green light and that it now has a home there.

I'm eternally grateful to Tom B. Long, who has been quietly lettering and doing logo design on this since the beginning. Also, a big thanks to editors David Mariotte and John Barber for all their invaluable help.

Working on this project has been one of the most rewarding experiences in my career. I've loved watching these characters evolve and, eventually, dictate how they would act to me.

I cannot express how rewarding it's been to see this series embraced. Thanks to every one of you who read an issue, sent me fan art, or emailed me your thoughts on it. It's truly meant the world to me.

I'm beyond indebted to the amazing artists who contributed pinups to this series. Much love to Jeremy, Albert, Kei, Andrew, Megan, Brendan, Eddie, Peter, Chris, Sara, Joel, Beth, Cecil, Casey, Frédéric, and Alex. And also to the great Drea for devoting her time and expertise to the psychological profiles.

I want to thank my brother Yuri for giving me invaluable story feedback early on. To my great friend Robbie for encouraging me early on that this series didn't sound like an insane undertaking. And to my dear friend Brian for all the great late night work sessions.

Just writing all these names out reminds me how lucky I am to know so many great creators. Being surrounded by cool people working on cool projects is one of the things I enjoy most about life.

If there's a dream project you've been chipping away at, finish it. You'll love the feeling.

Livio Ramondelli
Los Ángeles
February 2020

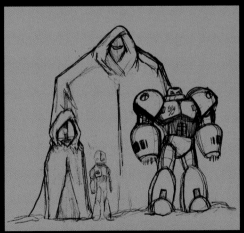

Early group sketch. Circa 2016

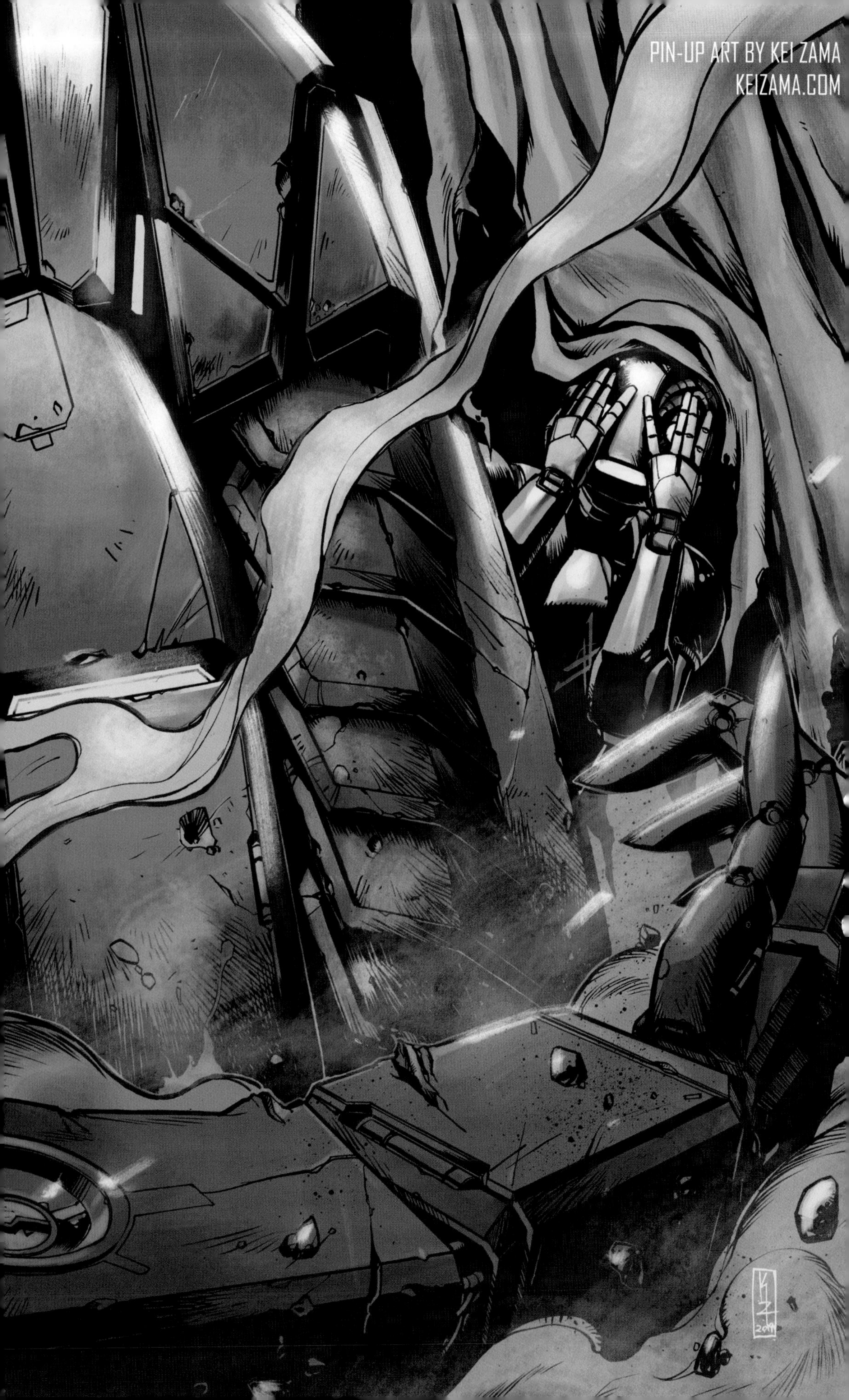
PIN-UP ART BY KEI ZAMA
KEIZAMA.COM

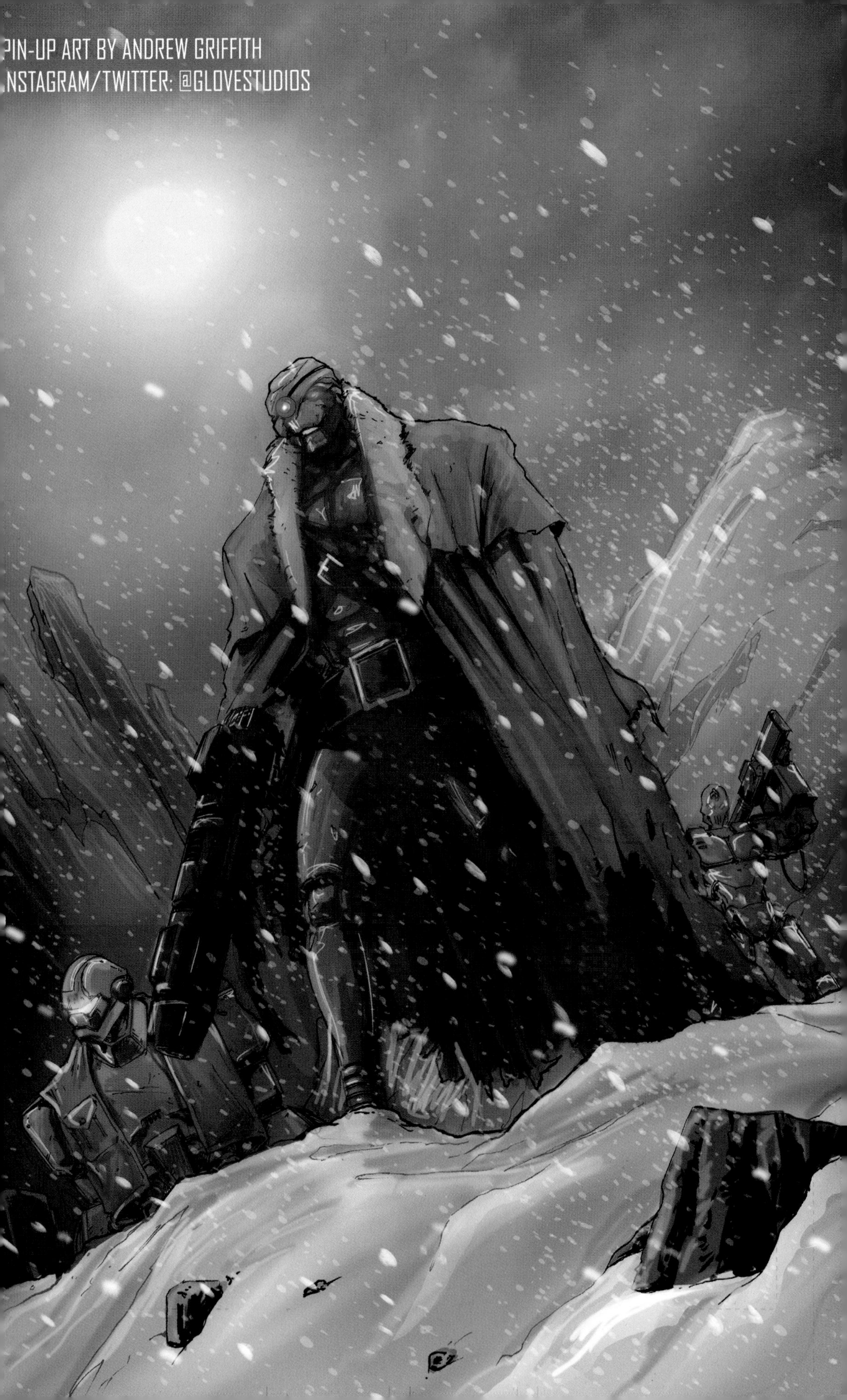
PIN-UP ART BY ANDREW GRIFFITH
NSTAGRAM/TWITTER: @GLOVESTUDIOS

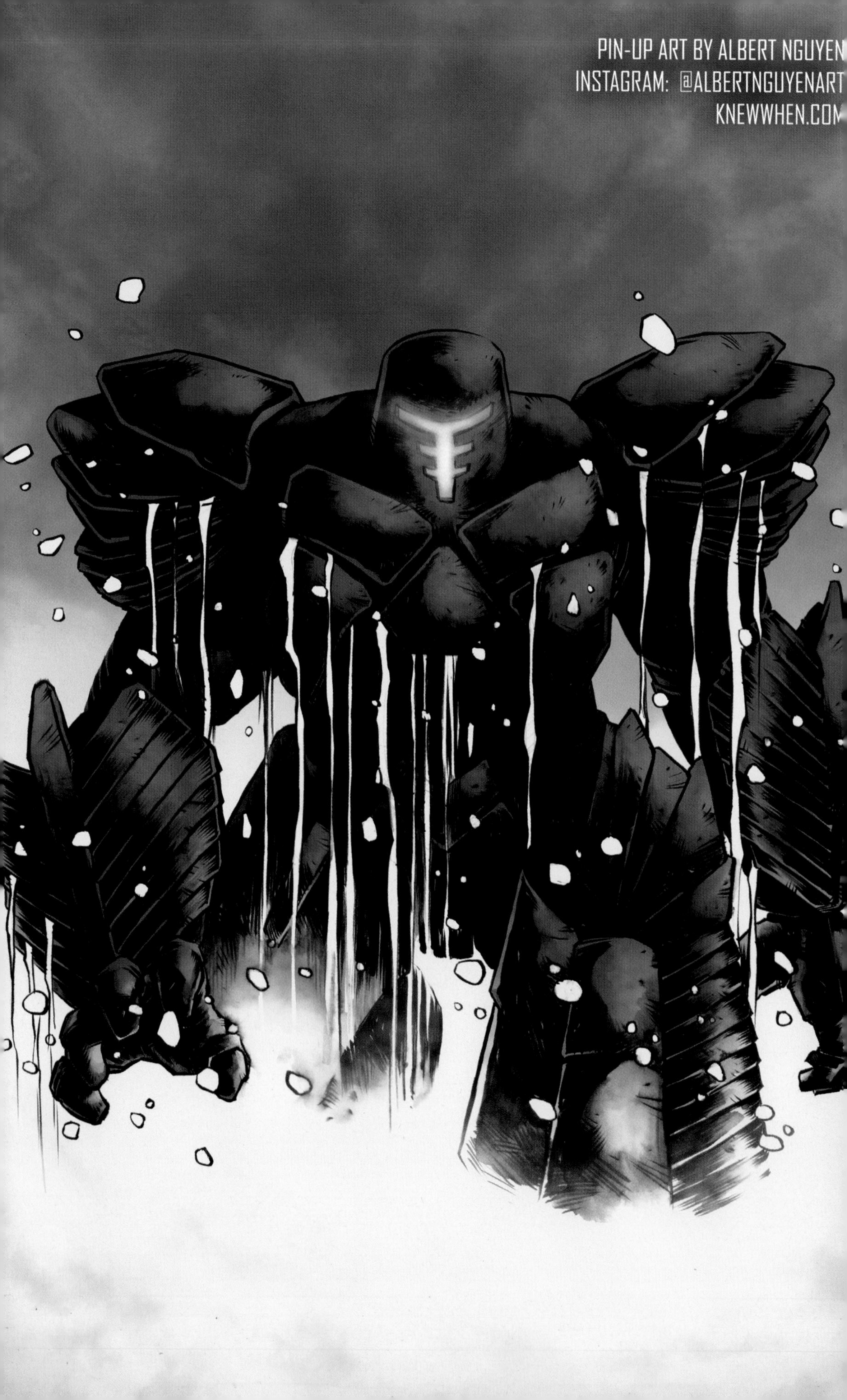

PIN-UP ART BY ALBERT NGUYEN
INSTAGRAM: @ALBERTNGUYENART
KNEWWHEN.COM

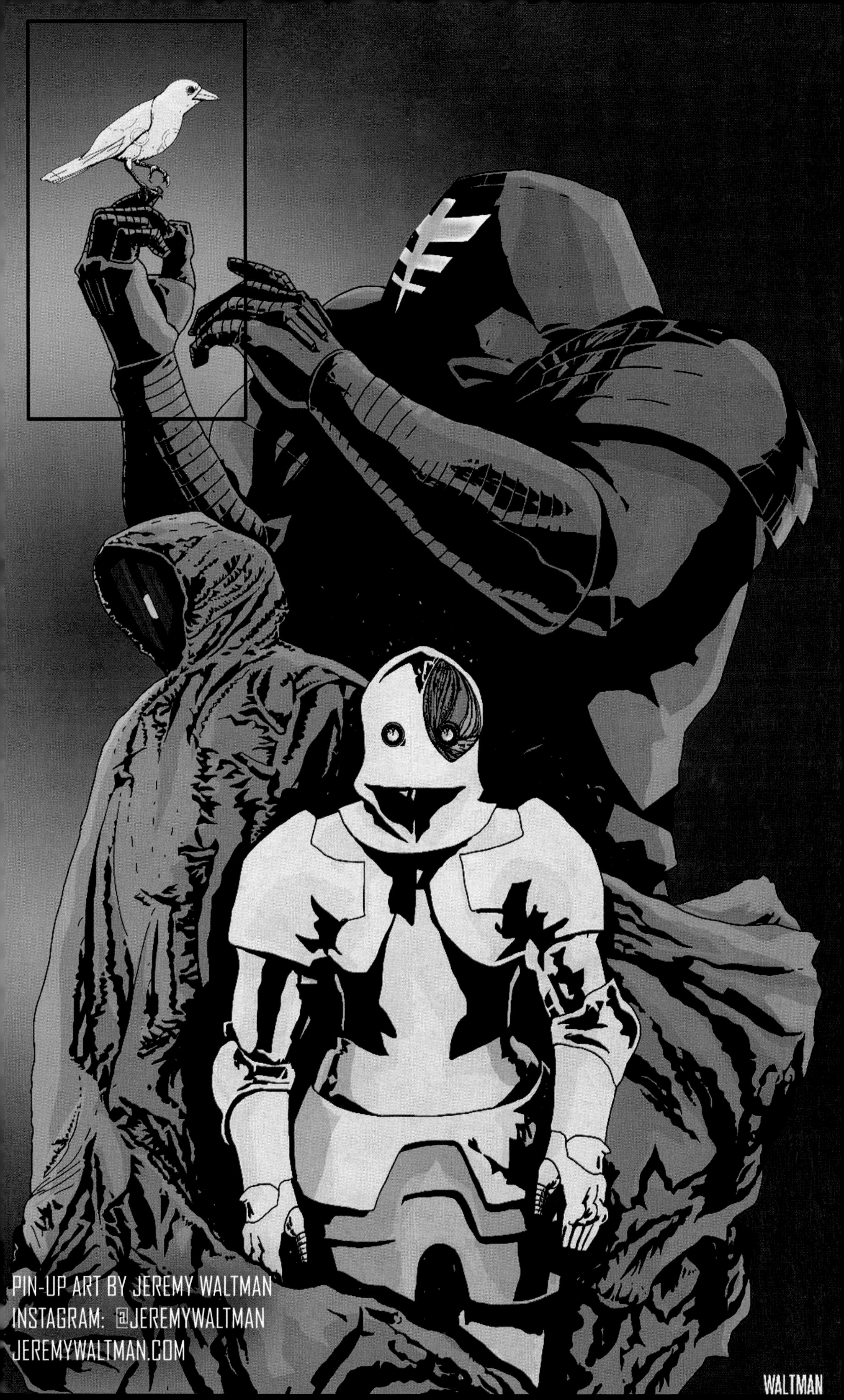
WALTMAN

PIN-UP ART BY JEREMY WALTMAN
INSTAGRAM: @JEREMYWALTMAN
JEREMYWALTMAN.COM

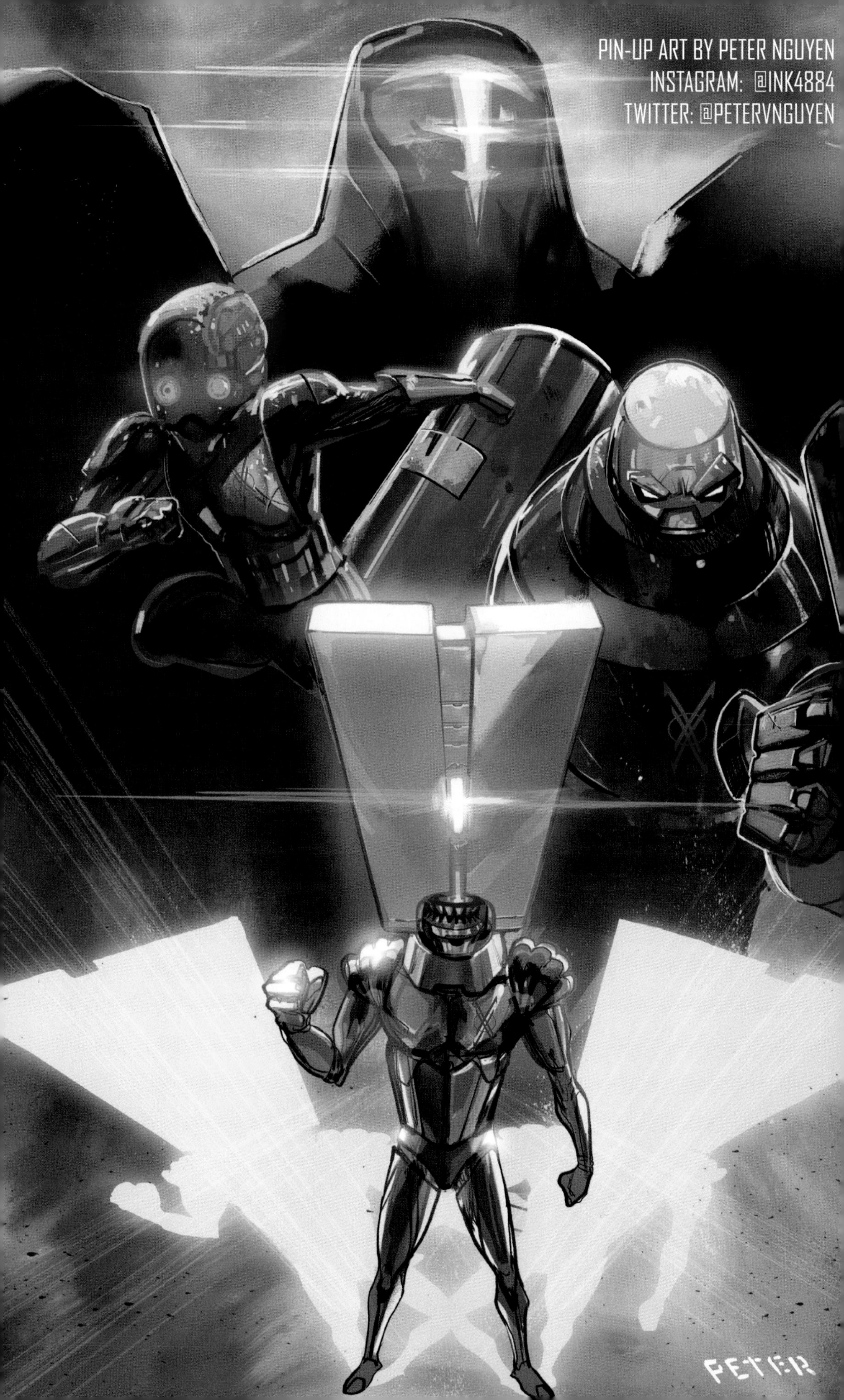
PIN-UP ART BY PETER NGUYEN
INSTAGRAM: @INK4884
TWITTER: @PETERVNGUYEN
PETER

PIN-UP ART BY EDDIE NUNEZ
INSTAGRAM/TWITTER: @EDDIENUNEZART

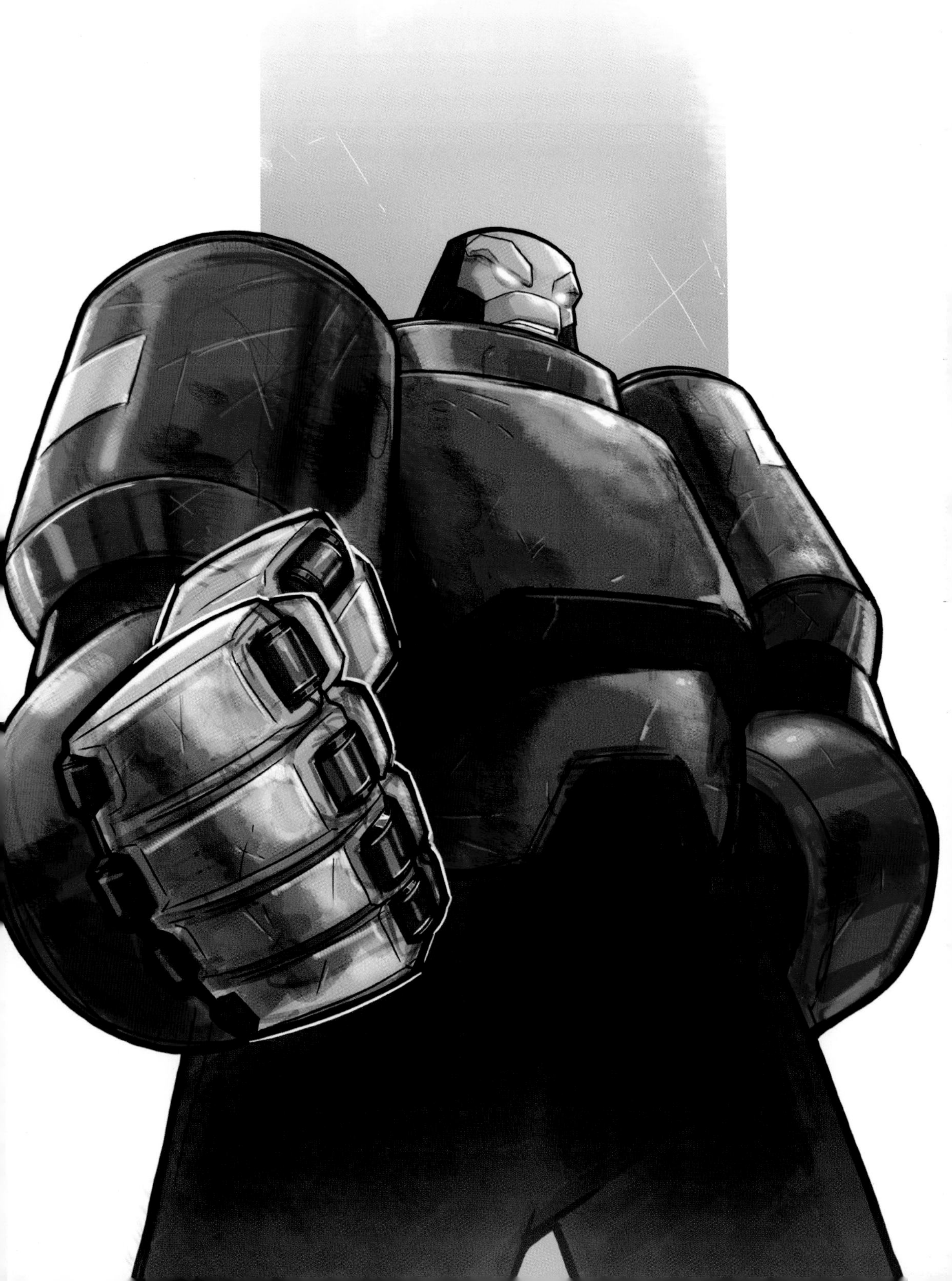

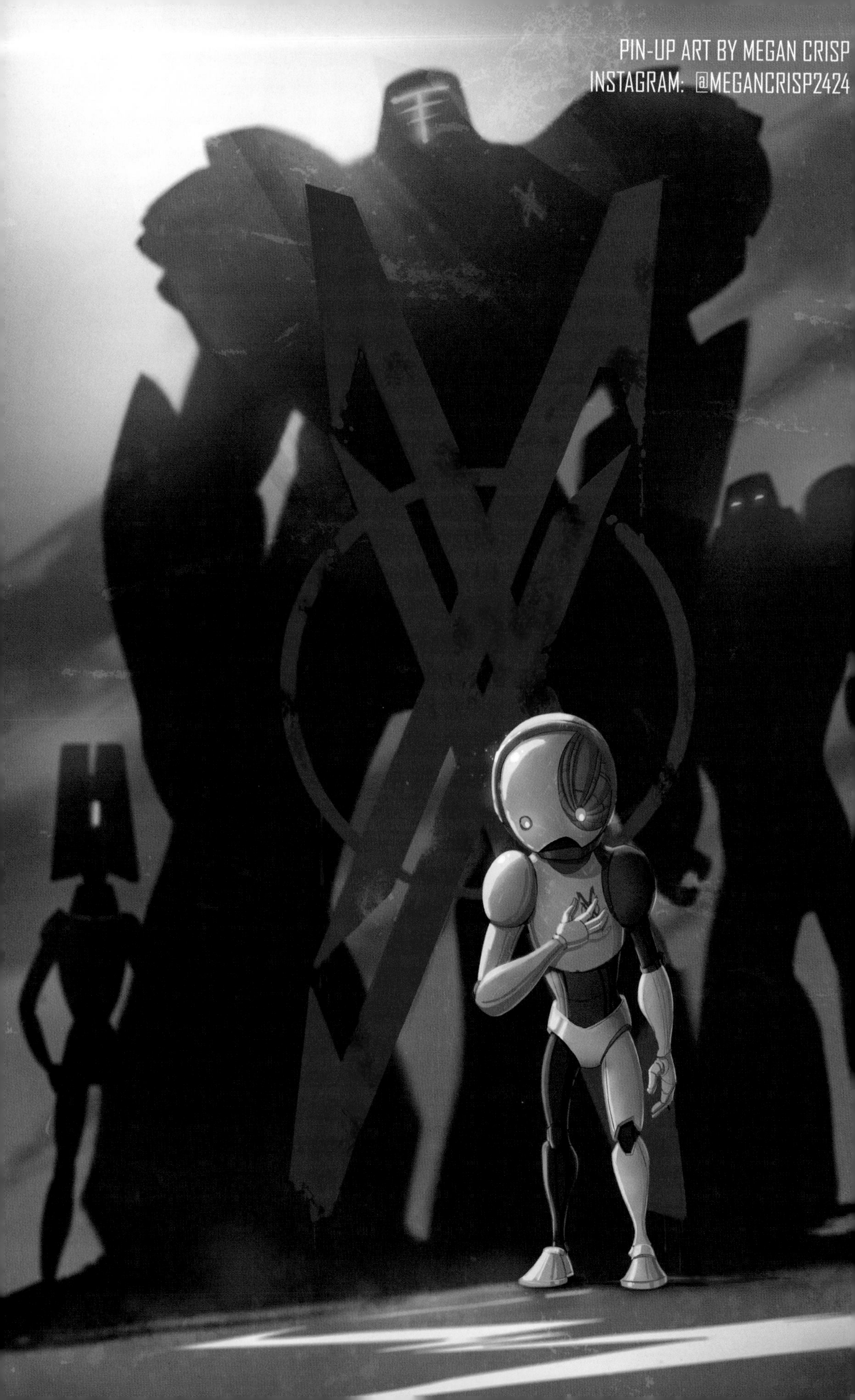
PIN-UP ART BY MEGAN CRISP
INSTAGRAM: @MEGANCRISP2424

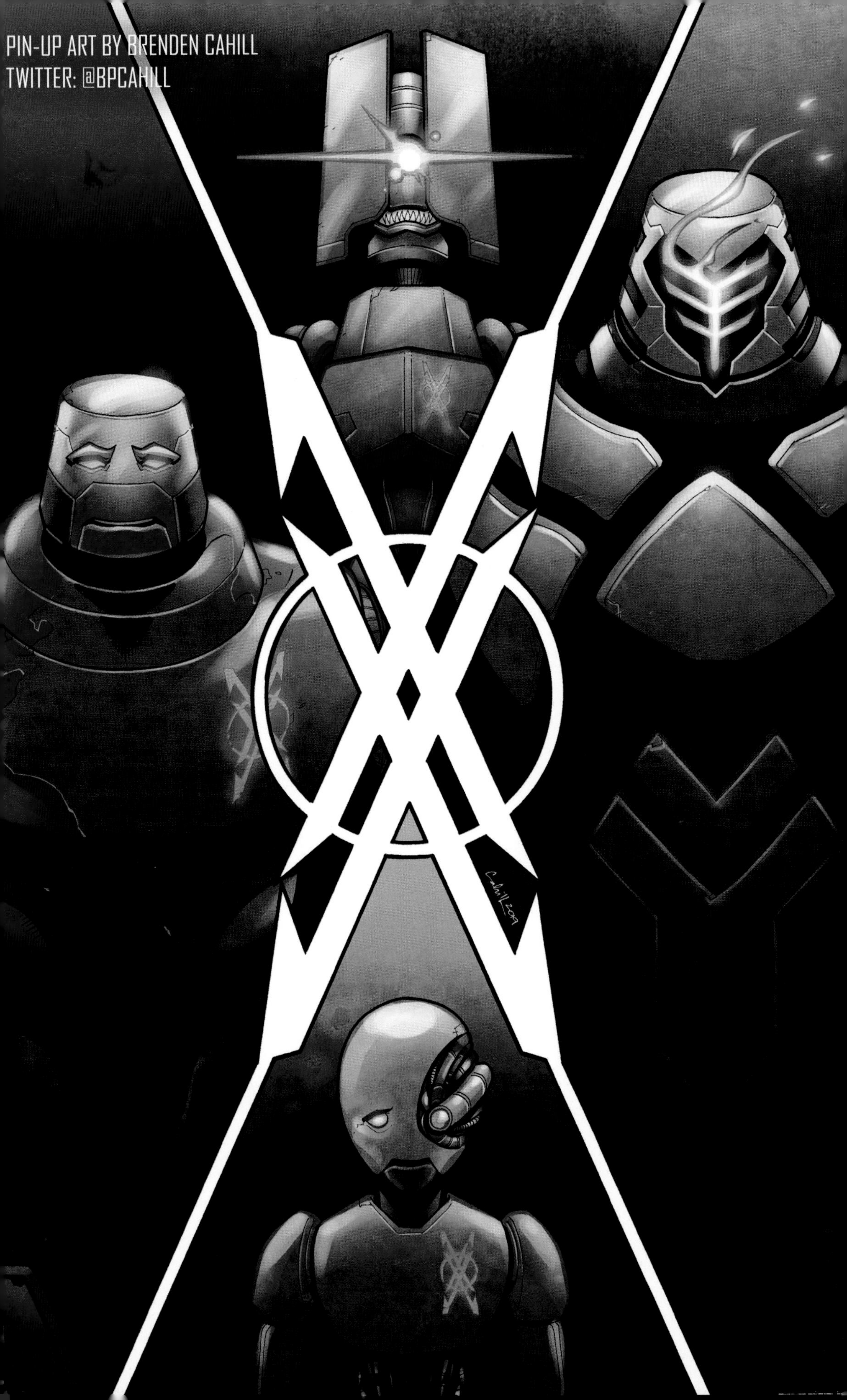
PIN-UP ART BY BRENDEN CAHILL
TWITTER: @BPCAHILL

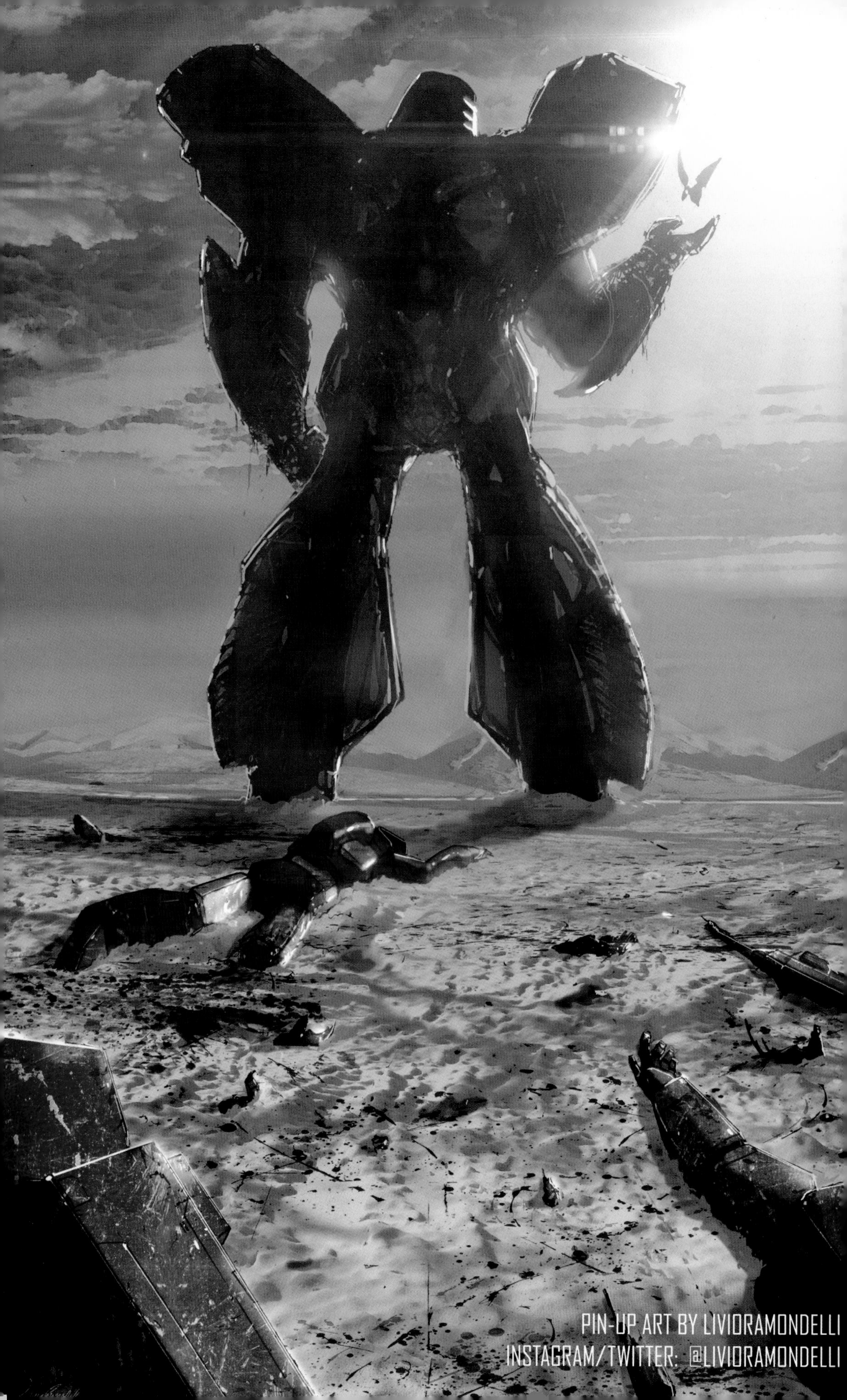

PIN-UP ART BY LIVIORAMONDELLI
INSTAGRAM/TWITTER: @LIVIORAMONDELLI

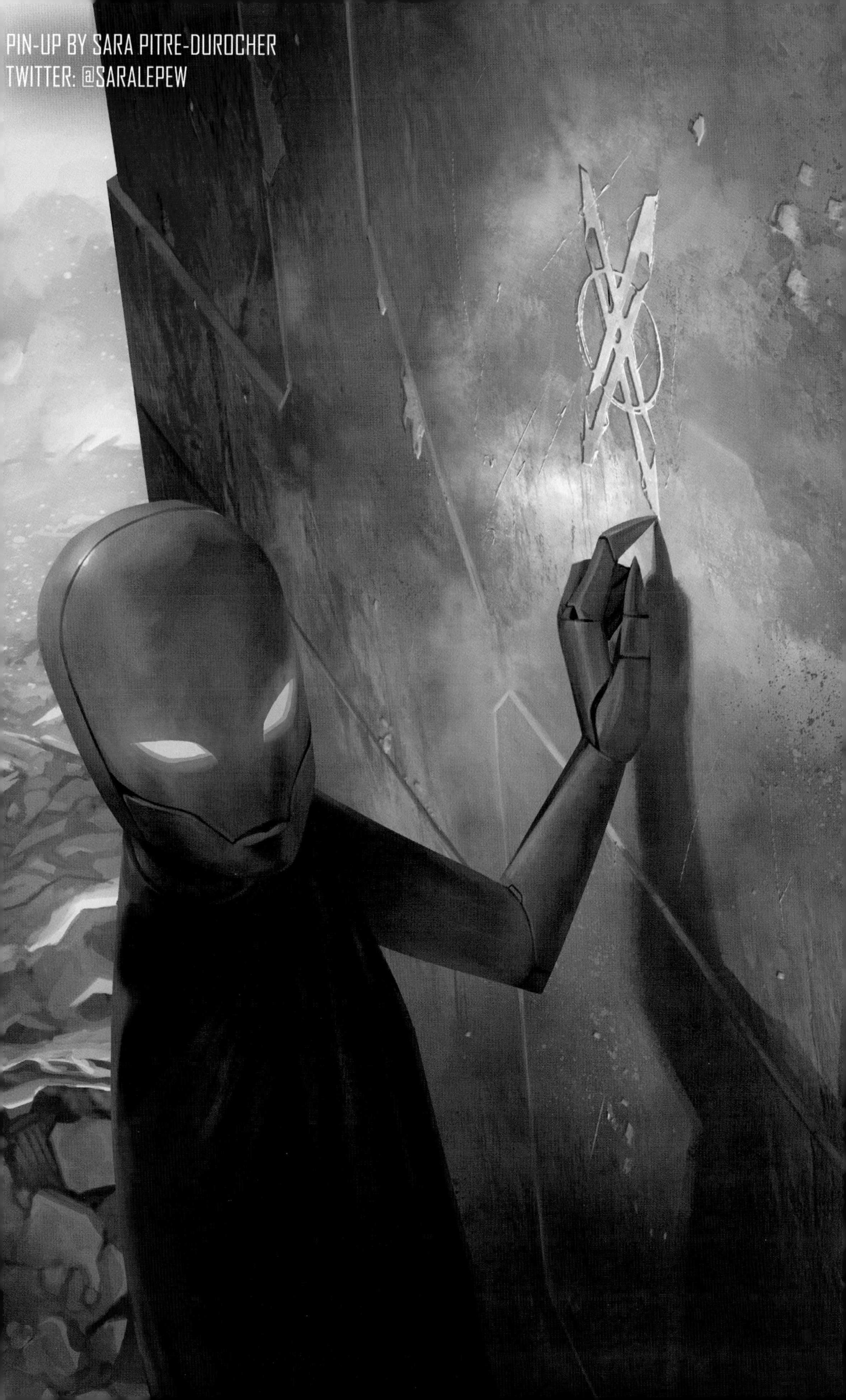
PIN-UP BY SARA PITRE-DUROCHER
TWITTER: @SARALEPEW

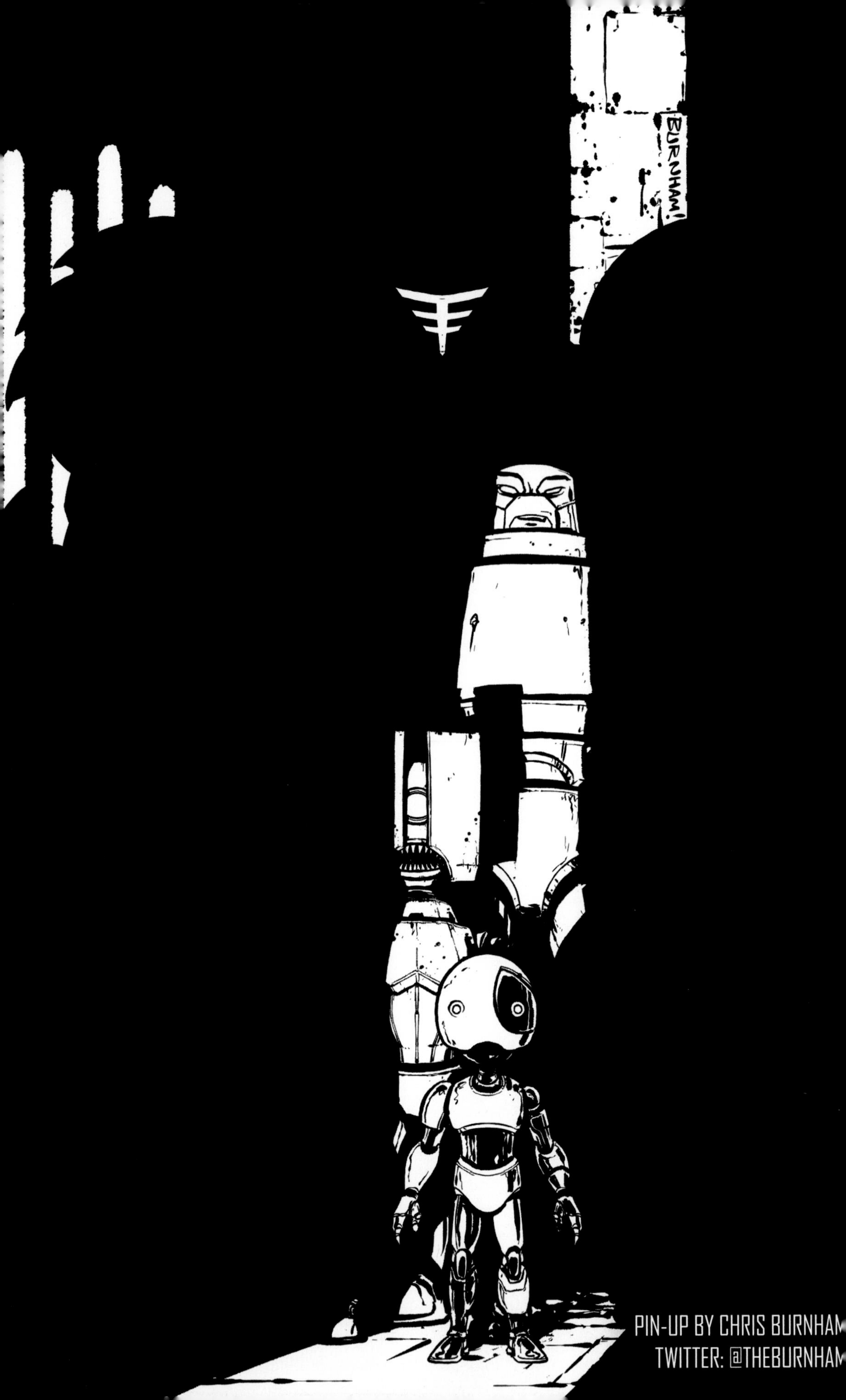
BURNHAM!

PIN-UP BY CHRIS BURNHAM
TWITTER: @THEBURNHAM

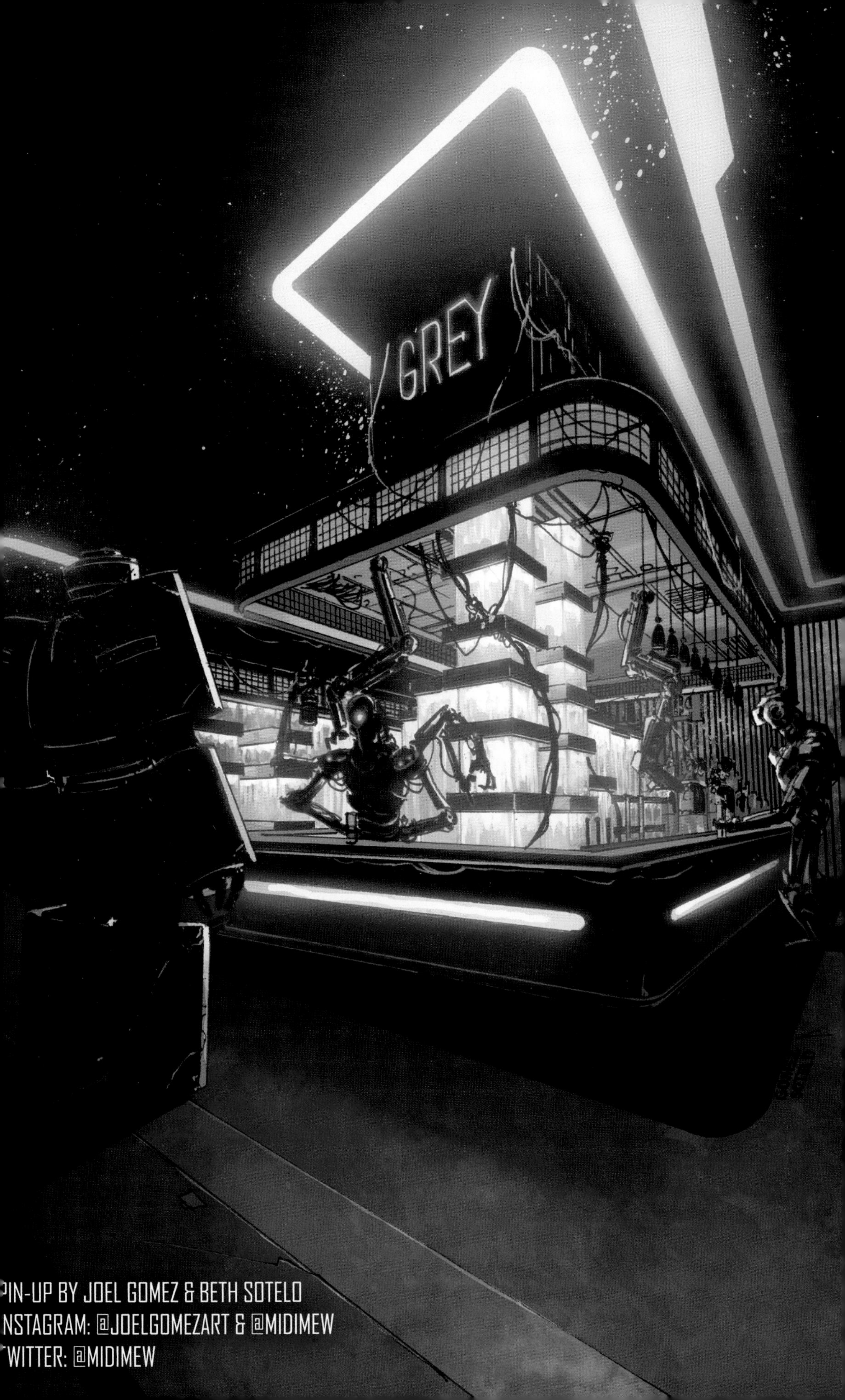
GREY

PIN-UP BY JOEL GOMEZ & BETH SOTELO
NSTAGRAM: @JOELGOMEZART & @MIDIMEW
WITTER: @MIDIMEW

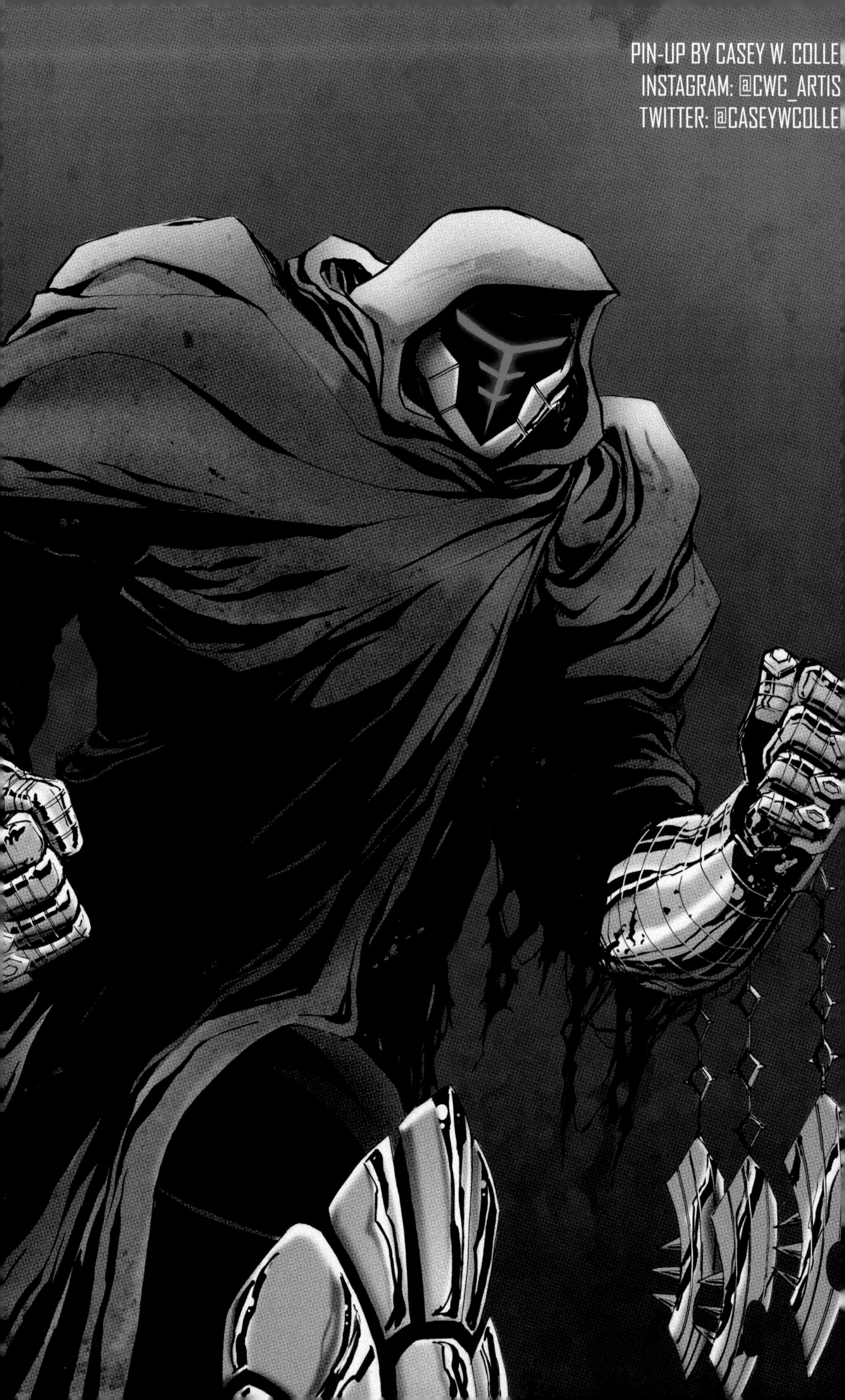
PIN-UP BY CASEY W. COLLE
INSTAGRAM: @CWC_ARTIS
TWITTER: @CASEYWCOLLE

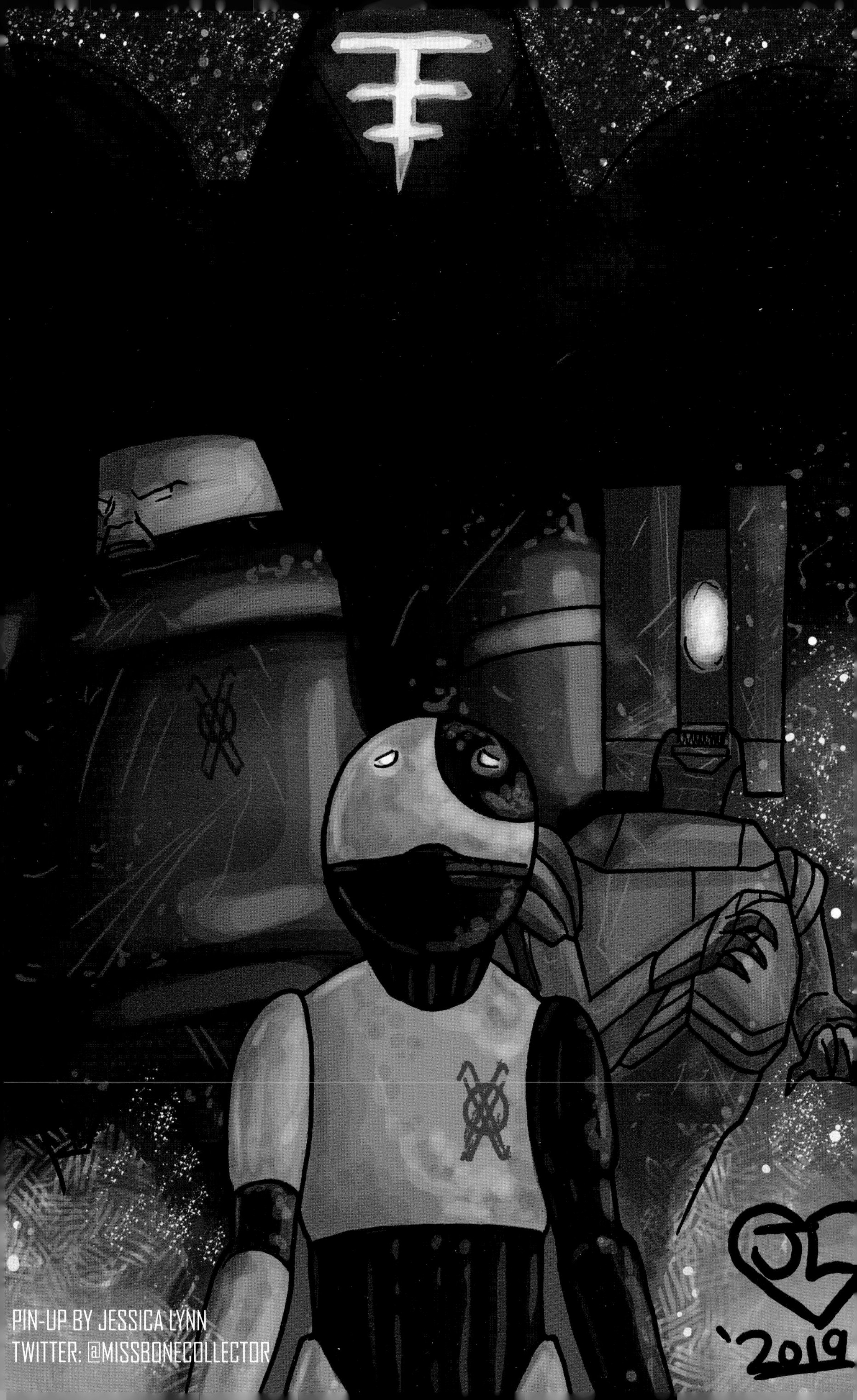
JL
'2019

PIN-UP BY JESSICA LYNN
TWITTER: @MISSBONECOLLECTOR

PIN-UP BY CECIL FISH
INSTAGRAM: @A.CECIL.FISH
CECILFISH.COM

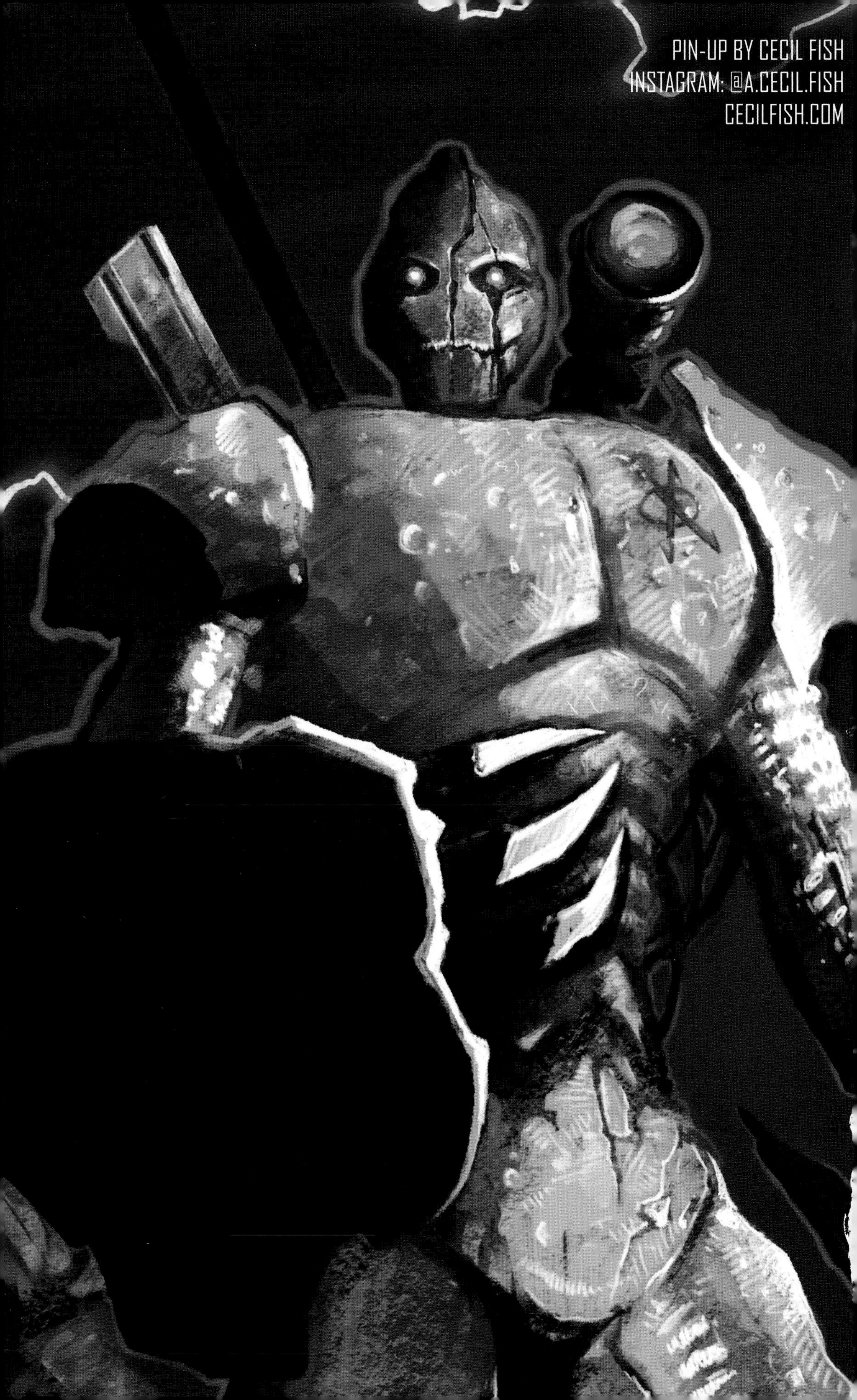

PIN-UP BY FRÉDÉRIC PHAM CHUONG
WWW.FREDPC.FR

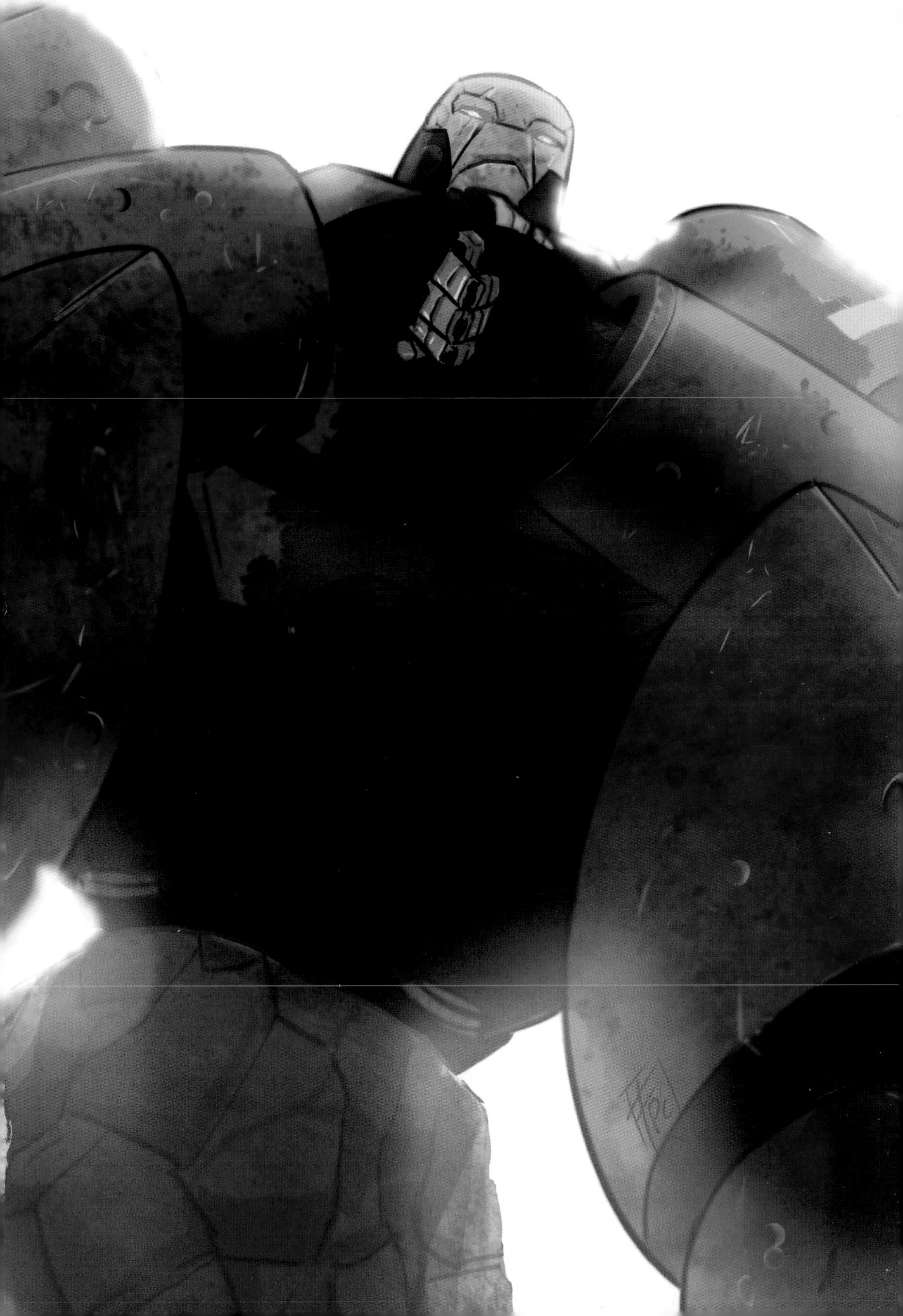

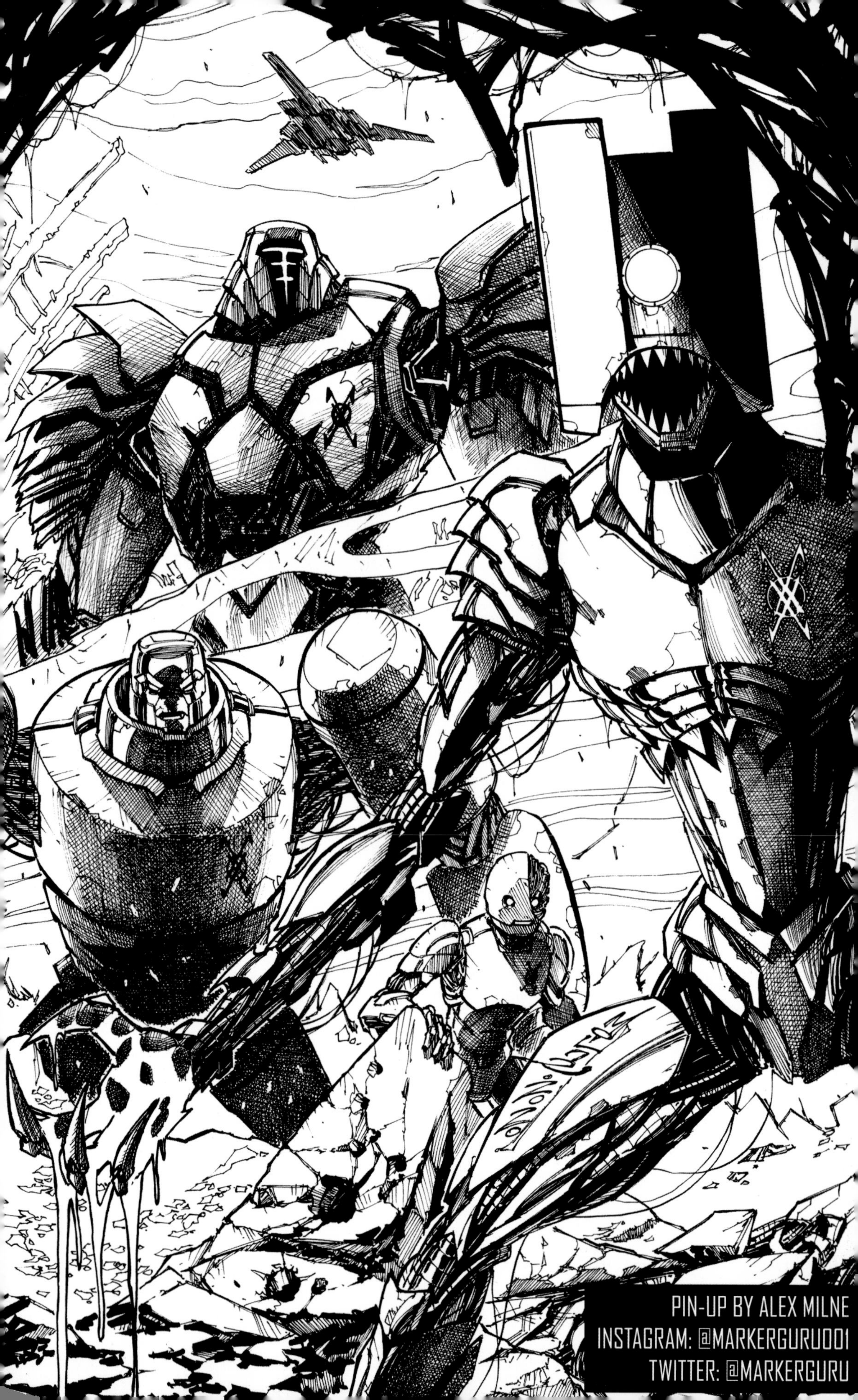

PIN-UP BY ALEX MILNE
INSTAGRAM: @MARKERGURU001
TWITTER: @MARKERGURU

Behind the scenes art and comments by Livio Ramondelli

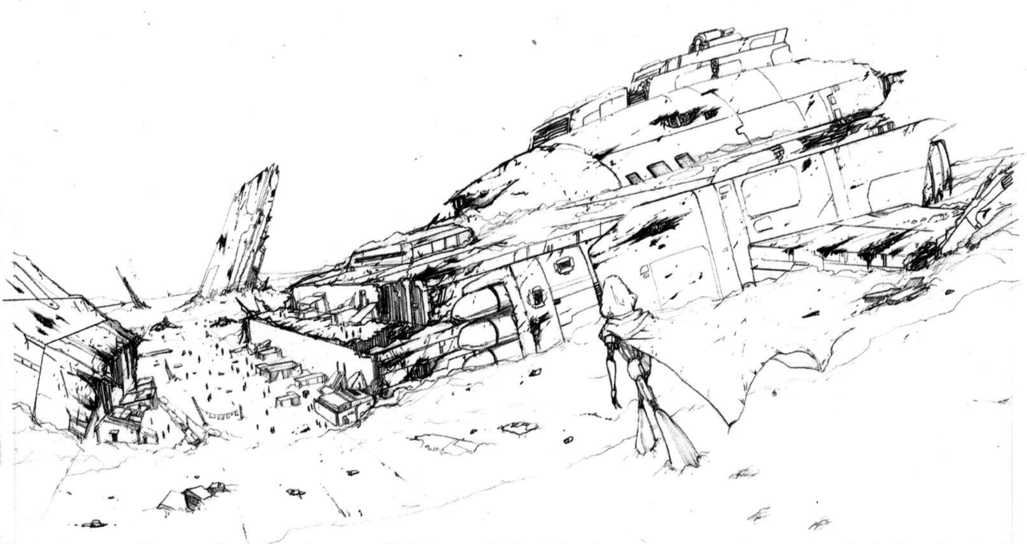

Unused original lineart for issue 1, pages 2-3. I initially had the Artisan approaching a crashed ship that had been converted into a shantytown. But I felt like there was an opportunity to make the planet feel weirder and more interesting, so I changed it to the town now being made out of long-dead bone remains.

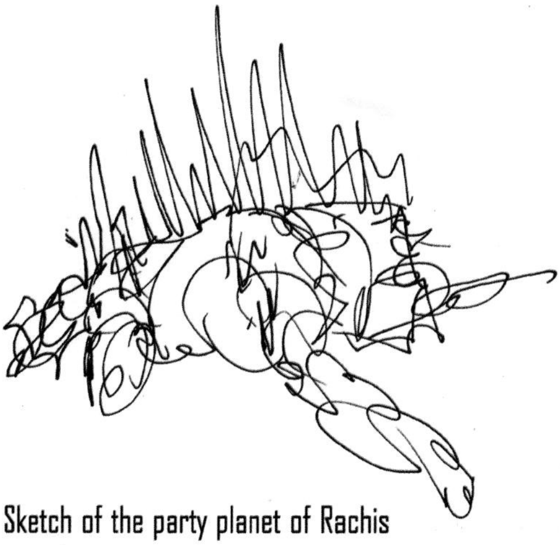

Sketch of the party planet of Rachis

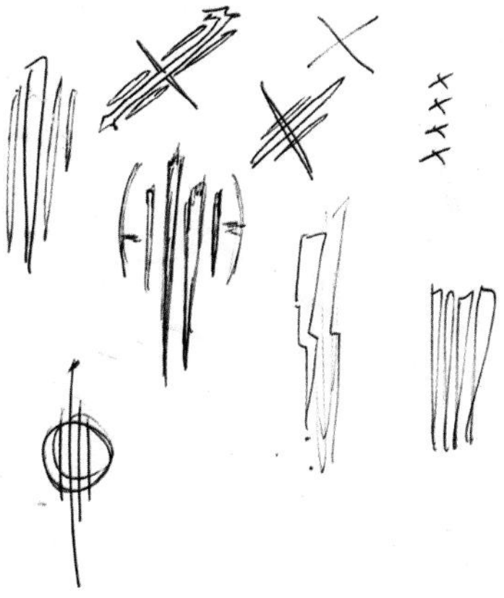

Early Kill Lock symbol concepts

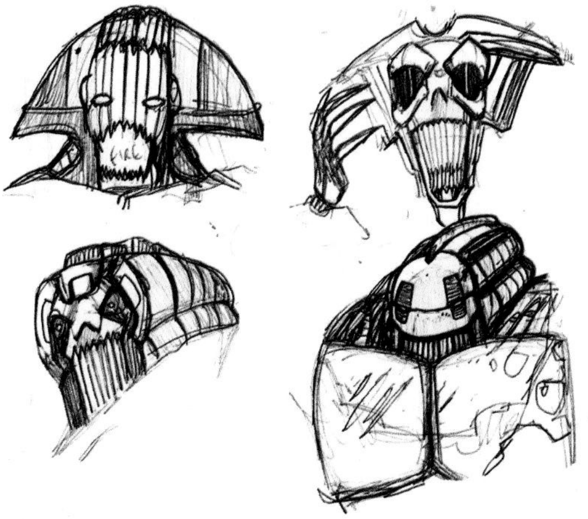

Metal Merchant sketches

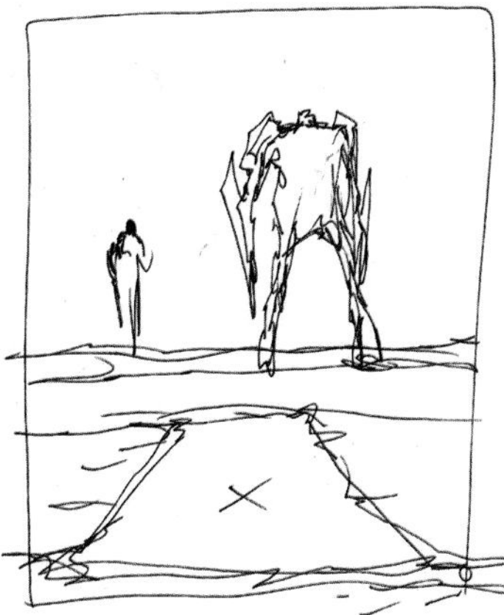

Layout for issue 2, page 22

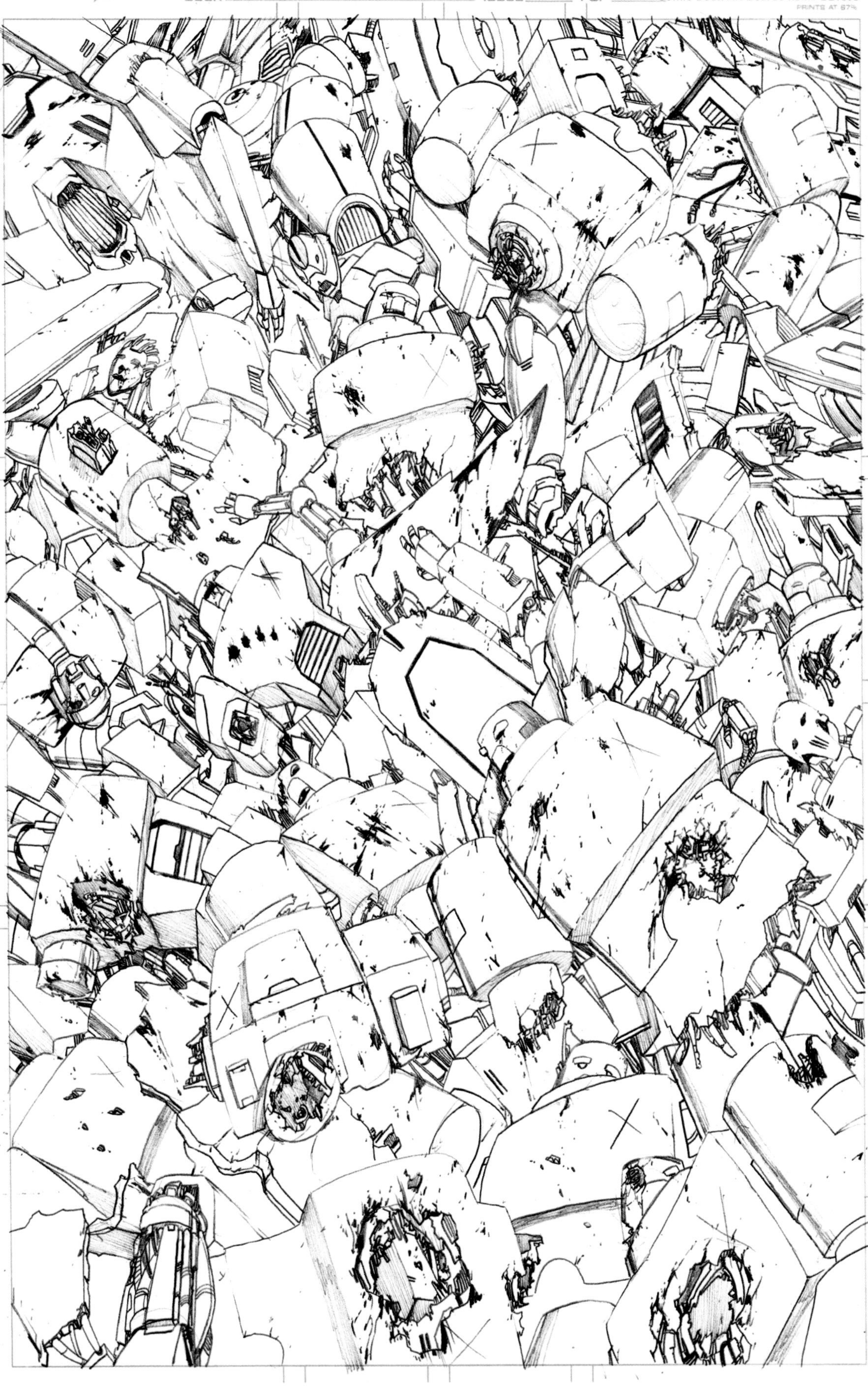

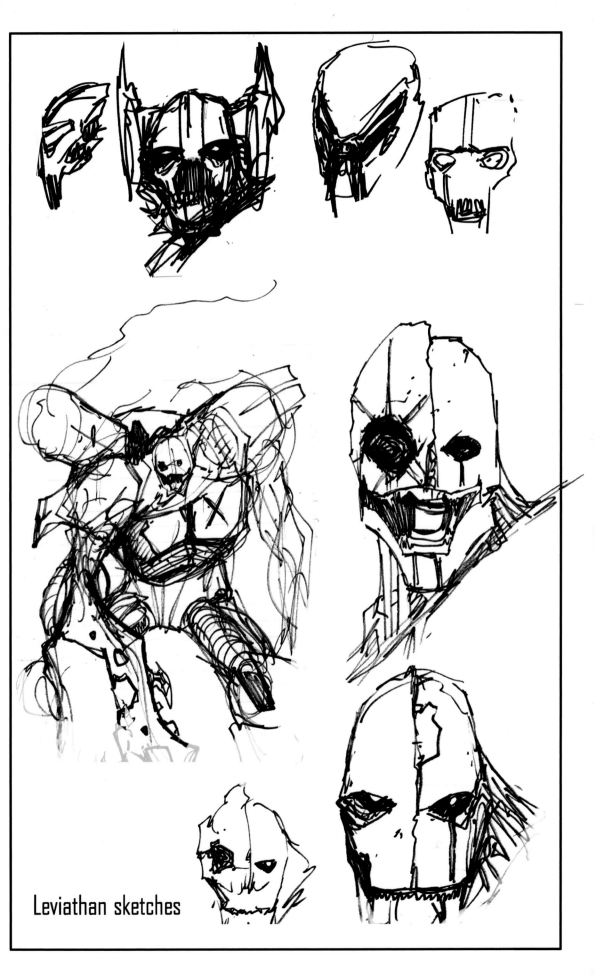

Leviathan sketches

THE KILL LOCK
PSYCHOLOGICAL PROFILES
THE KID

"WHAT AM I? NOBODY WILL TELL ME."

The Kid is unfairly born into an exiled life. He is considered an "Unfinished" model, essentially a perfectly functioning bot, but with a physical defect in his casing due to manufacturing error. The very first words told to him by the insensitive technicians who discard him are that he is the "cause of his own impurity," and as such, his first three brief but indelible memories are characterized as blaming, demoralizing, and punishing. The Kid self-identifies, therefore, as society's waste. During his first days of life, he looks to his new companions to either challenge or confirm that he is, in fact, garbage. Much like Artificial Intelligence, psychological accommodation is a process that occurs in early development when new information or experiences will either modify or confirm existing schemas. Luckily for the Kid, his guardians show a level of protection and benevolence toward him. So, since this new information doesn't fit into his primary schema, the Kid begins to adjust his existing schema in order to accommodate the new data. Perhaps he isn't just spare parts, after all. But what is he?

The Kid is, at first, developmentally unable to comprehend the concept of the Kill Lock. He is only a handful of days old, after all. Not quite sure what death itself means, he clings onto his caregivers innocently. It is only after a brutal lesson in lived experience that he understands his undeserved fate. The Kill Lock means more than just exile; it is mass extermination. Though distraught by the realization of the group's comingled death sentence, the Kid manages to maintain a hopeful outlook. He is told that there is a cure for their situation, but it requires a quest. "Gonna start a life" he mutters to himself with an almost unknowing, fragile sense of determination.

The Kid becomes, in many ways, the most hopeful of the crew despite never having jobs, relationships, or even much joy. Born into bondage, he's not yet had the chance to create an individual sense of self, a solid identity, or sense of purpose. Perhaps due to not yet developing or adopting characteristics of biases and racism, the Kid also has a natural interest in celebrating and prolonging all types of life. He exhibits a significant level of psychological resilience, which is the ability to learn, grow, and even harden following adversity. But as the journey becomes more violent and grim, will the Kid's system be pushed to the edge?

We see the universe through the Kid's eyes. His deep curiosity and pursuit of the truth help us understand the landscape the crew must navigate. Why they are banished, what the Kill Lock does to them, and how they survive are concepts we can examine as they are absorbed through the Kid's processing system. The reality is, they must work together. Four members of society could not, as the Wraith explains, "blend" into a chosen world like a single exile. As the dejected crew pursues the cure for the Kill Lock, the Kid is likely to look to the others to understand the differences between right and wrong, safety and threat, loyalty... and duplicity.

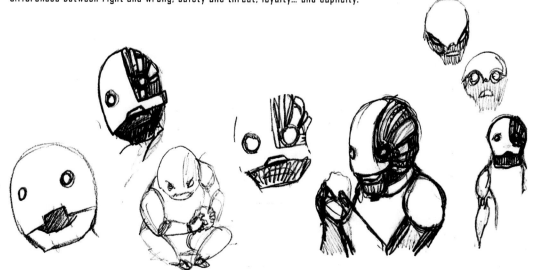

Dr. Andrea Letamendi
Licensed Clinical Psychologist
Co-host, *The Arkham Sessions*

THE KID SKETCHES BY Livio Ramondelli

THE KILL LOCK
PSYCHOLOGICAL PROFILES
THE LABORER

"WE'VE MADE MISTAKES. SOME OF US HAVE DONE TERRIBLE THINGS...
BUT I DON'T THINK WE DESERVE TO DIE BECAUSE OF THEM."

A member of the lower working class, the Laborer dreaded the mundaneness of his manual, monotonous job. Whether due to the degrading treatment from his supervisors or simply the lack of validation, the Laborer began to internalize his life's function. He started to associate what he does with who he is. As such, the Laborer's daily drinking served to numb the horrible feelings of triviality, bleakness, and futility. His addiction is a destructive cycle in which his careless drinking leads to harmful behavior toward himself and others—this then leads to feelings of guilt and shame, which leads to more drinking, and so the vicious cycle continues.

One day, the Laborer's maladaptive pattern of self-numbing irrevocably results in unimaginable consequences. While serving as a landing door operator for incoming ships on an industrial planet, his careless oversight is the cause of a horrific accident—hundreds of lives were lost due to his negligence. Though devastated, he understood that his punishment would fit the crime: The Kill Lock.

The Laborer isn't programmed to have high general intelligence; cleverness isn't "necessary" for moving cement blocks. But this metal heap happens to be equipped with high emotional intelligence (EQ). That is, he has a higher capability to recognize his own emotions and those of others as well as to discern between different, complex feeling states. His EQ explains his addiction—he's programmed himself to believe that drinking is a short-circuit remedy to end the painful feelings of loneliness and insignificance. Most notably, the Laborer is able to use emotional "information" to guide his actions, a trait that helps the banished crew get closer to their goal of finding the cure for the Kill Lock. He appeals to others through connection, understanding, and empathy. He is often the one to volunteer himself for risky tasks during their quest, and he is mindful of protecting the young member of their group, the Kid, from exposure to the threats and terrors they encounter.

As he grows closer to his companions, the Laborer reveals that he holds some pride in his purpose—building statues, towers, and buildings for others to enjoy is something of an achievement. Again, he's able to grasp emotional complexity; he sees his crime as an accident, but is cognizant that he should take some ownership of his participation in the deaths of hundreds. The Kill Lock introduces a new concept for the Laborer: he was content with the concept of killing himself through his addiction, but now grapples with the concept that should he relapse, he is likely to end the lives of three others. He understands the importance of others' success and their opportunity to thrive; the idea that the value of the whole group is greater than the sum of their individual parts. The Laborer's ultimate weakness remains his urge to numb self-hatred and shame... if, along the journey to disable the Kill Lock, the Laborer loses his battle with his internal self, then all are lost.

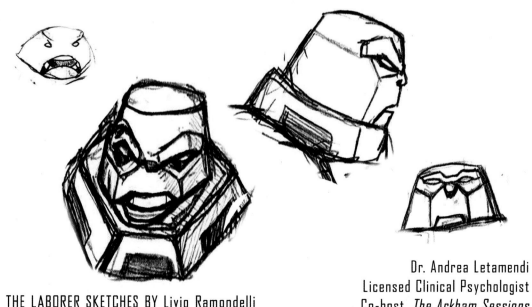

THE LABORER SKETCHES BY Livio Ramondelli

Dr. Andrea Letamendi
Licensed Clinical Psychologist
Co-host, *The Arkham Sessions*

THE KILL LOCK
PSYCHOLOGICAL PROFILES
THE AXIAL

"THE KILL LOCK IS FAR FROM A PERFECT SYSTEM,
BUT IT REMOVES ABERRATIONS BEFORE THEY GET WORSE,
...AND TRUST ME, YOU'LL ALL GET WORSE."

As a gifted technician, the Axial proved her worth by designing the Kill Lock, a punitive program that remotely binds up to four criminals in an irreversible death sentence. Once "locked" together via this sanctioned, multi-transmittal interface, members of a banished chain gang are virtually linked together through their vitals. If one of them dies, they all die.

The Axial is a genius as well as philosopher who holds the conviction that the Kill Lock serves as a reasonable and effective punishment for occupants who committed serious, irredeemable crimes. She genuinely believes in her creation, in theory. Grim as the method is, the Axial's conception is loosely based in her deference for justice, civil obedience, and social advancement. Indeed, the Kill Lock appears barbaric, but it is also progressive. Its outcomes are possible without the high costs of infrastructure, the extraneous labor of direct supervision, or the cruelty of actual chains. No, the Kill Lock is superior in that it operates above wasteful methods such as custodial sentences and inhumane uses of corporal punishment. When applied appropriately, the Kill Lock serves as a deterrent, and thus encourages proper social behavior. In ideal situations, the Kill Lock is corrective. Stabilizing. Cleansing. In truth, the Kill Lock is a product of the Axial's personal concern for deservingness. She believes in bad outcomes for bad people. She is incredibly proud to have originated the system that enforces this belief.

As an untold experiment, the Kill Lock reveals one of the Axial's unexamined curiosities—can goodwill be learned? In fact, the Axial believes her program may offer an opportunity for criminals to develop some form of sympathy, if not true concern, for the other members of their exiled crew. Getting past the devastation of the Lock may have a benefit. Being forced to protect each other, offenders would learn what it is like to consider the rights of others—to co-exist. Eventually, criminals would go on to develop respect, boundaries, and, in some cases, even kindness for the other "residents" of their immaterial prisons.

The Axial was both an outsider and an included member of the established echelon of her home world where she served as a seminal designer for the Kill Lock. She was innovative, on the cutting edge, a pioneer. But her ingenuity came with a price. The Axial did not have control over how her system would be used. The forgers who commissioned her work saw the potential in the Axial, her ability to program a reversal of the Kill Lock. Growing wary not of her virtuosity, but her ability to meddle in the criminal justice system, the forgers granted the Axial retirement on a remote, war-torn planet. Feeling her work was done, the Axial agreed to abandon further engineering of the Kill Lock.

When the Axial first meets the Laborer, she's not surprised to learn that yet another group of offenders are searching for the cure to the Kill Lock. She's even slightly amused by the Artisan's arrogance and familiar threats. The Axial is not opposed to engaging in personal favors, bargains, or agreements, if they can be done diplomatically. If her actions cause harm, the Axial shrugs it off—after all, if the universe works the way it should, victims deserve their fate. Years ago, she settled a deal with a group of banished criminals who explained that they could expedite the Kill Lock if she sent them the parts they needed to survive. (No matter to her that those parts were still in live bodies). But her self-indulgence gets the best of her when the Axial sends the loathsome Artisan and his fellow exiles directly into danger. Upon learning that one of them is a child, the Axial is overcome with immediate regret. The system is... broken. Punishing the innocent was not part of her design.

If the Kill Lock represents the Axial's unconscious efforts to get people to show concern for one another's well-being, what could bring the Axial to tap into her own ability to be merciful and forgiving? After she sees the real aftermath of the Kill Lock, will she develop a change of heart? Does the creator of the Kill Lock believe in second chances?

Dr. Andrea Letamendi
Licensed Clinical Psychologist
Co-host, *The Arkham Sessions*

THE AXIAL SKETCHES BY Livio Ramondelli

THE KILL LOCK
PSYCHOLOGICAL PROFILES
THE WRAITH

"A PATH OF VIOLENCE IS BEHIND ME."

The Wraith is a killing machine. His presence is breathtaking, his unmoving expression devoid of emotion. The Wraith encompasses admirable qualities like nurturance, virtue, and decency, though he hints at a cavernous sadness.

The purging of immoralities—the brutal, violent sacrifice of entire colonies—is seen by the Wraith Legion as an act of profound honor. The Wraith himself has admitted to such offerings of bloodshed, and knows that even when the impure begged him for forgiveness, he did not yield to salvation. Violence and destruction were, paradoxically, seen as humane acts, carried out with dignity and purity of thought. The acts themselves did not matter to the Wraith as much as the symbolism they instilled, the final benefit they presented to the overall system. Thus, to the Wraith, one life—or many lives—matter little in the grand scheme of things. "We are servants of the light," he would vow. This is what it means to be good. He saw no other purpose than this.

The Kill Lock means something entirely different to him. Every fiber, every circuit in his being is dedicated to serve a higher meaning. Now, carrying out his sentence, the Wraith is again examining his purpose. Now, asked only to keep himself and three very different individuals alive, he is quietly pathless, vulnerable, and disconsolate. He must co-exist with very different sets of values and attitudes. He must find a way to live in harmony among differences. Even more, he must be a companion to those who are defiled.

For the others, the Wraith is pure brute force. And despite his capacity for complete devastation, the Wraith is not easily provoked into violence. He is not hot-headed, reckless, or venomous. The Wraith is unlikely a zealot. Rather, he is intentional about his acts, carefully addressing them within his shifting internal moral set.

At times, the Wraith is searching for ways to reconcile his ongoing moral distress stemming from his time with the Legion. Moral distress refers to the unprecedented trauma when a soldier perpetrates, fails to prevent, or participates in actions that transgress his deeply held moral beliefs and expectations. Moral distress is usually experienced pervasively, in the form of multiple incidents or in response to acts encountered as "just part of the job" or in the line of duty. Over time, the psychological disequilibrium caused often leads to feelings of helplessness, powerlessness, guilt, shame, and reduced sense of dignity. Reconciling the pain requires shifts in values and actions, a rebuilding of hope and sense of purpose. The Wraith knew he would be forced to leave the Legion if he attacked his fellow soldier. He has shown that though he can hurt and destroy life, he can also repair life. Can the Wraith be reparative from within and adjust his unraveling wirings?

We see moments where the Wraith reveals his sense of compromised integrity and justice. "I am now merely what remains," he tells himself, knowing he has lost his vigor. He used to live in absolutes, in the good vs. bad. But now, he lives in the gray. As is his nature, he takes on the role of protector quite effortlessly, growing closer to the unfinished member of their crew, the Kid. Here, he searches to validate the psychological accommodations that led him to be Locked in the first place: youth are innocent and, no matter what their moral structure, deserve a chance for redemption. Perhaps his new purpose is to preserve life, not to destroy it.

It is the Wraith's astounding devotion that keeps us drawn to him. With his refined knighthood, his polite paladinism, the Wraith introduces comfort in contrast to a wretched and threatening galaxy. His dutiful and thoughtful mannerisms are almost charming. The Wraith encompasses admirable qualities like nurturance, virtue, and decency, though he hints a cavernous sadness. True, his expression is nearly always steely, but tenderness and safety are not too far from reach.

The Wraith's internal and external integrity, strength, and resolution are the exact reasons he is the most vulnerable member of the group. He becomes the Artisan's target. Now, with his body controlled by the Artisan, will the Wraith even have the moral agency to adjust to his new situation? Will he be emotionally comatose? Perhaps, his sacrifice was worth it in the end. After all, as he has been taught all his life, isn't pain from honorability still good pain?

Dr. Andrea Letamendi
Licensed Clinical Psychologist
Co-host, *The Arkham Sessions*

THE WRAITH SKETCHES BY Livio Ramondelli

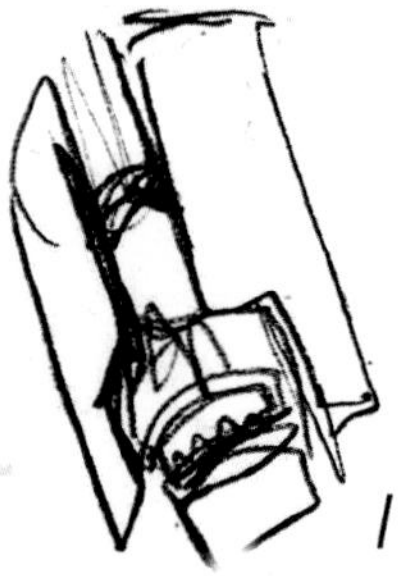

THE KILL LOCK
PSYCHOLOGICAL PROFILES
THE ARTISAN

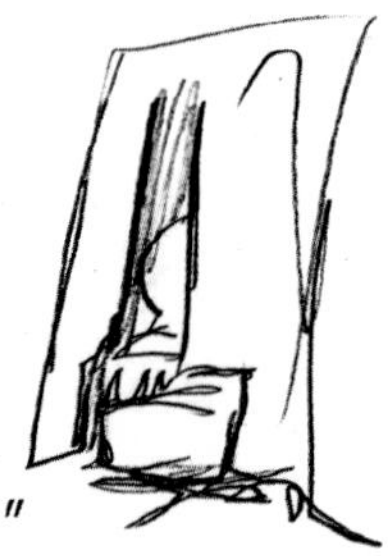

"JUST TRYING TO PROCESS ALL THE WEAKNESSES I SEE IN YOU. DECIDING WHAT TO CHOOSE, YA KNOW?"

Like others in his class, the Artisan is a clever, high-level engineer. Programmed with some of the most sophisticated internal networkings across class types, the Artisan identifies unapologetically, indulgently, and smugly, as an intellectual. He possesses cognitive abilities of the highest order: exceptional memory, critical thinking, problem-solving—and the capacity to plan ahead (wayyy ahead, apparently). The Artisan does not employ the inessential sugar-coatings of decorum and tenderness. Rather, he is direct and straightforward with his intentions, motivated by nothing other than to attain the highest or maximum result, to approximate at whatever cost the one thing he desires: functional perfection.

Though he takes great pride in the designs he builds—the ones that serve in Labor and industry classes—the Artisan harbors a great deal of resentment about his place in the universe. He has the acumen to detect and manipulate the inner-workings of other mechanical beings, even to the degree of objectifying them, but he has little control over his own design. He's inherently skilled in noticing the imperfections of others; it is without doubt that he turns these criticisms inward. The Artisan despises the Forgers who designed him with such technical prowess and yet gave him nothing but a pathetic skeleton in which to exist. It simply does not match. He is nearly delusional from the power he possesses over the functioning and future of other beings, and yet ashamed for how little he can self-improve. He is a textbook narcissist: Outwardly, grandiose and self-righteous; inwardly, self-hating and insignificant.

Feeling justified, the Artisan channels his resentment into actions and atrocities that confirm his superiority on the Homeworld. He manipulates, bullies, abuses, and disempowers others as an exercise in self-preservation. It's not that the Artisan gains pleasure from others' pain—he's not a sadist and was certainly never programmed with a malicious drive. Much like a detached serial killer, he is fascinated with insides. He flagrantly admits to dissecting his coworkers "for the greater good of understanding our race." The depth of his insensitivity, however, makes us wonder. Is something wrong with the Artisan's wiring? His Kill Lock mates, the Laborer, the Kid, and even the Wraith look upon the Artisan with much disdain—and mistrust. They watch the Artisan murder and mutilate with the ease of flipping a switch. Does the Artisan have a condition of sociopathy? Is his consistent pattern of disregarding the rights and feelings of others an exhibition of some kind of mechanical breakdown? Did his wires... snap?

The Kill Lock offers a kind of Rorschach test for the savvy Artisan. True, he rarely chooses to empathize with his victims, but when harnessed to three other individuals, he witnesses suffering and pain more closely than ever. It may seem that the Artisan antagonizes and harms others with little remorse, but he is not impulsive or reckless. He takes calculated risks to achieve an ultimate goal, not to revel in feelings of cruelty. Behind his callous indifference is a scientific, meticulous, and in most cases, purposeful motive. The Artisan is not a ruthless killer. He's not unhinged. One of his strongest traits is his ability to take perspective—after all, only he can understand the layers of systems that create others' experiences. As such, he actually has a great capacity for empathy. On the isolated world of Scoria, the Artisan shows his empathic nature after witnessing the Kid endure a fatal injury. Knowingly, and carefully, the Artisan turns off the Kid's pain sensors to prevent any further trauma. He displays a discernment that rules out psychopathy and even lends us an understanding of his higher goal: to the Artisan, refinement of civilization involves the minimization of suffering.

Early on, the Artisan discovers that the Kill Lock may be the vehicle needed for him to overcome his fundamental shortcomings. Being linked to a Wraith, a literal warrior, offers the Artisan a pathway toward self-advancement. He's found a way to upgrade. But there is something more. After all, the Artisan is a designated engineer skilled for optimizing systems; he sees the corrupt, twisted, sham meritocracy on the Homeworld as a system that sure as hell necessitates rightsizing. If he is the one to dismantle the social hierarchy, he will do what he knows best... he will use the Kill Lock to purge the true defects of the universe. Like he is programmed to do.

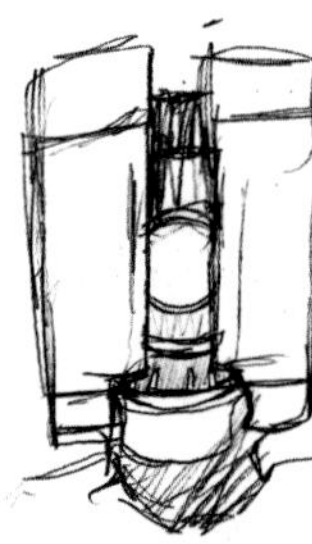

Dr. Andrea Letamendi
Licensed Clinical Psychologist
Co-host, *The Arkham Sessions*

THE ARTISAN SKETCHES BY Livio Ramondelli